D0311739

I2031850

AN ARMY OF SMILES

AN ARMY OF SMILES

Grace Thompson

SANDWELL LIBRARY & INFORMATION SERVICE	
I2031850	
Bertrams	15.02.06
GEN	£18.99

Severn House Large Print
London & New York

This first large print edition published in Great Britain 2004 by
SEVERN HOUSE LARGE PRINT BOOKS LTD of
9-15 High Street, Sutton, Surrey, SM1 1DF.
First world regular print edition published 2003 by
Severn House Publishers, London and New York.
This first large print edition published in the USA 2004 by
SEVERN HOUSE PUBLISHERS INC., of
595 Madison Avenue, New York, NY 10022.

Copyright © 2003 by Grace Thompson.

All rights reserved.
The moral right of the author has been asserted.

British Library Cataloguing in Publication Data

Thompson, Grace
   An army of smiles - Large print ed.
   1. World War, 1939 – 1945 - Social aspects - Great Britain - Fiction
   2. World War, 1939 – 1945 - Women - Great Britain - Fiction
   3. Domestic fiction
   4. Large type books
   I. Title
   823.9'14 [F]

   ISBN 0-7278-7358-X

Except where actual historical events and characters are being
described for the storyline of this novel, all situations in this
publication are fictitious and any resemblance to living persons is
purely coincidental.

Printed and bound in Great Britain by
MPG Books Ltd, Bodmin, Cornwall.

I wish to thank the former Naafi men and women who helped me so generously. There are too many to mention by name but I want them to know that their fascinating letters created the background of this book. They taught me so much, made me laugh a lot and sometimes cry. Many facts gleaned from their memories cannot be found in history books, and I am indebted to them. I hold my hand up to any errors that might have crept in but willingly admit that the best of this story is theirs.

Thanks too to the kindness of the sadly missed Sir Harry Secombe, who read the typescript and wrote a foreword.

My sincere and grateful thanks to you all.

Foreword

Grace Thompson has chosen an unusual subject for her latest novel. It is one which has echoes for me. All those of us who served in the last war are extremely grateful for the ladies of the NAAFI. Many a cup of tea tasted all that much sweeter when it was served with a pretty smile – then there weren't a lot of those in the desert.

The story of three friends, Kate, Rosie and Ethel, it follows their adventures on the home front, in the desert and Italy. Romances, broken promises, the wretchedness of living not knowing whether you'd be alive tomorrow, and snatched moments of warmth during a war that seemed to go on for ever. It's a rattling good story of love and tragedy – I enjoyed it and I'm sure you will too.

Sir Harry Secombe

One

Ethel Twomey was happy. She was so filled with joy that she imagined she might burst into flames as she walked beside her soon-to-be fiancé, Wesley. Her dark eyes had glowed as she'd looked up at him, imagining the fun of telling everyone and also, rather shamefully, the relief of being able to leave her miserable home for ever.

Thought of home dulled her excitement. She had managed to put aside the usual feeling of dread as the time to re-enter her house drew near but now, as the road curved to the left and the hotchpotch building, quaintly called The Dell, came into view, the anxieties flooded back. Whenever she had been out, and had been able for a while to forget, the approach to the house caused an increase in fear. 'One day,' she regularly told Wesley, 'one day, I'll walk in and find my mother knocked out cold and my father still beating her.'

On this special day, when she and Wesley Daniels had agreed on a date for their engagement and their wedding, there was room for nothing else in her mind, just happiness and the thought of leaving home for good. It wasn't until the turn in the road gave her a first sight of The Dell that her mind returned to the dreadful possibility of walking into the house and facing her father in one of his rages, and the sight of her mother, cowed and utterly defeated, listening to his complaints, real and imaginary.

She was returning from the café where she cooked and occasionally served at table. She reflected that she might be the only one among thousands who actually hated it when her day ended and she had to walk away from the busy café and its sometimes difficult customers.

As she walked on alone through the lanes that early spring evening in 1940 she tried to hold on to the happiness for a while longer. It was dark and blackout restrictions were in force, forbidding any light to be shown, so not even the light from one of the isolated cottages and farmhouses she passed shone out to help her find her way, passing fields where she had run to hide from her father's rages, and beyond, the Baileys' farm where she had often worked as a child, helping with the harvest.

She walked over the small footbridge that led to the gate and up the garden path, through the complications of blackout curtaining, and into the house, relieved that at least there was silence, no sound of raised voices. Her father, Dai Twomey, was dozing in his usual chair beside the fire range, dulled with too much food and an excess of drink. His blue eyes, so round and angry, opened and glared at her as he demanded, 'What time d'you call this?' before nodding off again. He slept through most of the evening so the meal was a peaceful one.

One evening a few days later, Ethel and Wesley walked through the town, arm in arm and stopping occasionally to kiss. They had been to the pictures and afterwards had peered with difficulty, owing to the unlit displays, through jewellers' windows to stare again at the engagement ring they planned to buy for her eighteenth birthday a month hence on the eighth of April.

'We'll buy it tomorrow,' Wesley said. 'In case someone buys it first.'

'I'll meet you at three, but I'll have to go straight back to the café,' Ethel told him. 'It's a pity we can't have a day out and celebrate.'

'Tomorrow we're buying it, we'll have our celebration on your birthday when I put it on your finger,' Wesley smiled. 'What a happy day that'll be.'

When they climbed on to the bus in town, Ethel's brother Sid and her sister Glenys called to them from the upper deck, and beckoned for Ethel and Wesley to join them. Sid and Glenys had been to visit friends, young men who had joined the forces and were on leave, determined to enjoy what might be their last visit home for a long time.

'It started with four of us but others joined in, bent on enjoying their last days at home, and it ended with a sing-song,' Sid told them as the conductor handed them their tickets.

The sing-song that had ended the evening was revived and was carried on throughout the journey as Ethel and Wesley joined in. Old music hall songs mostly. 'It's a Long Way to Tipperary', 'Hands, Knees and Bomps-a-Daisy', 'Pack Up Your Troubles', and Ethel's particular favourite, sung to her by Wesley, 'Oh, You Beautiful Doll' – songs that were known to everyone. The other passengers on the bus joined in and even the conductor mouthed a few words.

Ethel was glad they had met up with Sid and Glenys, thankful that she wouldn't have to make that step into the house on her own and grateful too for the cheerful singing to push aside the fears that would accompany it.

Ethel was much younger than both her sister and her brother. Sid had been fifteen and Glenys sixteen when she had been born, a mistake, her mother often told her, quickly adding that it was one she had never regretted. She envied both Sid and Glenys their lovely auburn hair, inherited no doubt from their father's angry red.

'You two make me feel dowdy,' she complained now, looking at her sister's blue eyes and those of her brother, so like their father but without the anger.

'What? You wouldn't really want this colour?' Glenys laughed.

Ethel shook her long black hair free from its restraining ribbon as Wesley said proudly, 'I love your hair, in fact, wouldn't change a single thing about you, Ethel.'

Shouting goodbye to those left on the bus at the copse called Bagley's Bank, laughing for no particular reason apart from being happy, they set off down the dark lane, still singing.

Part of the reason for the announcement of her engagement to Wesley was the imminent conscription. Wesley was talking of joining the Naafi, and her brother Sid, at thirty-three, was already working in a factory recently converted to making machine parts for lorries and armoured cars. So far, both Ethel and Glenys were exempt although there were constant requests for women to do their bit.

As they reached the place where, during daylight hours, the house came into view, she wondered anxiously what her parents' reaction would be when she told them of her and Wesley's plans. Oh how the thought of leaving this house excited her. Marrying Wesley and building a home for him to return to was all she dreamed of, and it was only on rare moments she wondered whether it was love for Wesley or the urgent need to leave her family that was the strongest.

When they passed Wesley's home, a field and a small woodland away from hers, he insisted on walking the rest of the way with her. The singing had stopped, the thin beams of their torches showing the path.

'If you tell your parents we're going to marry, I want to be there, just in case your father – you know – gets a bit wild,' he said.

Flattered by the implied protection he offered, Ethel hugged him and smiled up at him in the darkness.

Sid agreed. 'He's less likely to start a fuss if we're all there,' he said.

'Our dad is more of a worry to us than the war,' Glenys sighed. 'I keep hoping he'll grow too old to pick fights, but there he is, sixty years old and in court again last week for attacking the barman for some unintended insult.'

'Called him a red-headed giant, he did, and for some reason Dad took offence,' Glenys laughed. 'But at six foot three and with thick red hair with hardly a hint of grey, what was insulting about that?'

They reached the bend in the road and Ethel clutched her throat as though already hearing her father's rage. She clung more tightly to Wesley, glad he had decided to see her home.

Inside the back door, the entrance was barricaded with a home-made screen on which black material had been fastened. This prevented the light escaping and presumably, her brother used to joke, would stop a patiently waiting German airman from pin-pointing the area and placing a bomb neatly down their chimney. They all joked about the restrictions after months during which no enemy planes had been seen, but they did as they were instructed for fear of fines.

Dai Twomey was sitting near the fire, wearing corduroys, a torn jumper and in his stockinged feet; his wife in a chair opposite. Molly Twomey stood up and smiled at them but Dai turned his head menacingly and demanded to know why they were so late.

'We've been celebrating, Dad,' Ethel smiled, going to stand near her mother. 'Wesley and I are getting engaged on my birthday, before he goes off to war.'

Ethel's brown eyes looked like dark, secret pools in the light of the oil lamp, her dark hair casting a deep shadow over her face as she waited for her father's reaction. The anxious expression was hidden, but involuntarily Wesley stepped closer and held her arm protectively.

'What d'you want me to do about it?' Dai

demanded.

'Nothing, I suppose. I hoped you might wish us luck.'

'You'll need it,' was the terse reply.

Her mother stood and headed for the kitchen. 'I'll make us some cocoa.'

Deflated, yet thankful the evening hadn't ended in anger and a display of temper, Ethel lay in bed, stared at the old, cracked ceiling and wondered how soon she could get away. The war was a terrible thing, but it did offer the opportunity for freedom where before there had been none. Perhaps she didn't have to wait until she and Wesley married, next year?

She woke early the following morning and went outside, glad as always to escape from the boxed-in atmosphere of the boarded-up house where no single chink of light was allowed to go out or in. Opening the front door she walked down the path to the road. There was a stream running alongside the gravelled road with its grass edging, and the front path led to a footbridge that spanned it. Now, with the melted snow running down from the hills, the water ran fast and furious, close to the rim.

The stream sparkled as it bounced against stones sticking out where the earth had weakened its hold and been worn away. Did she imagine the hint of a rainbow in its spray?

Every year workmen came and dug out the bed of the stream, maintaining its depth so it didn't overflow and flood the garden or the road. Today, with the prospect of going into town to buy her engagement ring, ready for the celebration in a few weeks' time, the stream was beautiful.

As a child she had thought it dull. Too fast for frogs' spawn, too unpredictable for watercress. Now she admired its fringe of wild flowers. Celandines, spreading the banks with shining gold interspersed by the ubiquitous daisies. Later would come the softer yellow of Welsh poppies and the delicate loveliness of enchanter's nightshade. Today, for Ethel Twomey, the war was a long way off and the world was perfect.

She went back inside, revived the fire and slid the kettle over the coals to boil for the first cup of tea. As she waited, she looked around the shabby room noting her mother's attempts to beautify the place with embroidery and a few cheerful cushions. In the silence of the early morning in the sad little room she felt a flood of compassion for both her parents. They worked so hard. Her father worked as a lorry driver, her mother looked after chickens and, during the autumn, also geese and turkeys. Both parents worked in the huge garden, selling their produce to shops and on occasions around the streets, knocking on doors and pushing a handcart laden with their harvest. She suspected that people bought from them out of sympathy for her mother.

Ethel hated working on the land but would sometimes help her mother with some of the tedious jobs outside. At Christmas she kept well out of the way during the killing, and it was her brother Sid who dealt with the preparation of the birds. Her distress was one of the few things that amused her father.

She waited outside the jewellery shop and watched for Wesley's arrival. She had been given an hour off. Time to buy the ring and to go to another café and sit for a few minutes admiring it and talking over their dreams and plans. She saw him coming, footsteps fast, hands in pockets, his thin frame wrapped in a coat several sizes too large. She watched him, noting the serious expression, and waited for him to look up and meet her gaze, see the smile open out and transform his solemn face into something quite beautiful. Life, she decided happily, was good.

Rosie Dreen heard Gran making her slow way down the stairs. As she woke she remembered. Today was her birthday. The day when she had promised herself that everything would change. As she roused herself and rubbed her blue eyes, childlike,

18

with the backs of her hands, she listened to the familiar sounds of her nan busy in the kitchen. Dear Nan. But sentimentality was forbidden from this day on. Today she would do something towards that new life she had promised herself.

She was eighteen and she knew that if she left it much longer she would never get away. Timid, unworldly and lacking in confidence, she was afraid of stepping outside the familiar world of her job at a local farm, and being cared for by Nan. Yet she knew she had to, or spend the most important years of her life in the cocoon she and Nan had built around themselves. She had to get away. And soon, or it would be too late. After a breakfast of porridge she opened the gifts Nan had got for her. Nan stood watching anxiously, afraid her choices would be a disappointment. She had patiently knitted her a pair of gloves and a hat. Hiding her dismay at the unexciting gifts, Rosie hugged her grandmother and told her she considered herself the luckiest of girls. A knitted hat was one of the things she had sworn never again to wear.

She went into town and looked at all the posters asking for women to do something to help the war effort. What could she do? No experience, no skills, nothing to offer. Apart from factory work which she knew she would hate, or the forces, who wouldn't want someone as stupid as she, what was there? She saw her reflection in a shop window, her smallness more apparent because of the ill-fitting coat she wore, guileless blue eyes, her fair hair scragged back and hidden with the brimmed hat that was much too large and made her look even more stupid than usual.

Why hadn't she been born glamorous? she wailed inwardly. Perhaps Mam wouldn't have left me if I'd been born beautiful. Being poor and living with Nan, neither had helped. She continued to stare at her reflection: a coat that had been cut down in an attempt to make it fit, sensible shoes with the addition of heel studs to make them last, and a brown felt hat that had been Nan's! She smiled as she remembered buying lipstick and rouge, trying them out, then being too embarrassed to leave her bedroom before washing it all off.

Best she stayed on the farm where she worked as a part-time housekeeper and occasional farm hand. Yet with the war taking men from the farms, she knew that unless she got out quickly she would never be allowed to leave. What could she do that would take her away from Nan?

She turned to go home when a poster caught her eye. Join the Naafi, she read. Was it possible? She understood that they provided a shop for essentials and prepared cooked meals and snacks for the forces. She'd been cooking simple food for as long as she could remember – perhaps she did have something to offer? Cooking was a skill, of sorts.

She made her way home clutching some leaflets and wondered whether she dare apply. Her love for her grandmother was a part of her reluctance to leave home. Nan would be terribly hurt unless there was a valid reason for her going. Advertisements urging women to do something to help win the war soon became so familiar they faded into unimportance. She doubted if Nan had been aware of them, and knew that even if she had, she would not have considered them relevant.

Rosie wished she dared go into a café alone and order tea, but if she tried, her embarrassment would have her imagining everyone staring at her. 'I am stupid,' she muttered angrily, 'and stupid I'll remain unless I get out and do something soon.'

Rosie had lived with her grandmother since the age of five. It was her nan who had taken her to school on her first day, and Nan who had helped her through her early struggles to learn to read and cope with adding and subtracting. Nan too who went to the school and sorted out a problem with teasing and bullying and persuaded the teacher that Rosie needed extra attention owing to her sad circumstances.

Her father had died when she was two, in

an accident at the flour-mill where he worked. Then her mother had met Geoff, who had given the ultimatum to choose between him and Rosie, as he did not like children. Her mother chose Geoff and a very confused Rosie had been left with Nan. Since then there had been no contact with her mother and Nan had been her only family. It made it very difficult to tell her loving grandmother that she wanted to leave.

Kate Banner was eighteen a few days after Rosie Dreen. An only child, she sat up in bed surrounded by neatly packed parcels, most of which were provided by her parents. The rose-coloured eiderdown and cover were thick, ornately embroidered and obviously expensive. Her elegant pink nightdress was lacy and the bed-cape was crocheted in fine pink wool and fringed with swan's-down. Her fluffed-out hair, a bright blonde which was occasionally assisted by the contents of a bottle, framed her pretty face with its long-lashed, greeny-grey eyes.

She knew she looked a picture and that her parents adored her. How could she tell them she wanted to leave home?

She heard her mother coming up and fluffed her hair a little, rubbed her cheeks to add to their rosiness, and glanced into the dressing-table mirror to satisfy herself that, even without make-up she looked good.

Then she turned her eyes towards the door and smiled.

'Mummy, you shouldn't,' she said as her mother appeared carrying a tray.

'My little baby girl is eighteen, of course I have to give her breakfast in bed,' Mary Banner smiled. 'Happy birthday, darling girl. Daddy will be here in a moment, he's just removing the blackout screens so you can come down to a cheerful room. He's bringing your special present.'

Hopefully, Kate imagined her father struggling up with a bicycle, something for which she had been asking for two years. 'Is it something I really want?' she asked.

'Something you want and need,' her mother replied.

Not working, just staying at home and helping her parents by dealing with the accounts of the grocery business her father ran, she knew she didn't really need a bicycle and also knew that her parents thought riding a bicycle was rather common when they owned a car as well as a van. Prepared for disappointment she managed to show great excitement as she unwrapped a watch.

'Now, Daddy, show our girl her other gift.'

Giving her a kiss, Henry Banner handed her an envelope. Opening it with curiosity creasing her brow, Kate read the note inside which told her she was starting driving lessons that afternoon. Her delight was genuine. The ability to drive would help her decide what she would do when she joined up for some war work. Her thanks, her declaration that she was the luckiest of girls were accompanied by tears, and as she tucked into the breakfast of a fresh boiled egg followed by best butter and home-made marmalade to spread on dainty triangles of toast, her mind was buzzing with plans, which, had her parents known, would have had them in tears of a different kind.

Downstairs there were further surprises. A new dress, in pink, with a hand-knitted jacket to match and a bow for her hair in the same colour.

'Mummy, why didn't you choose a different colour?' she asked with a gentle sigh.

'Nothing suits you as well, and pink is a colour few can wear to such effect, darling girl.'

Unkindly, ungratefully, Kate wondered how her mother would cope with her wearing khaki!

The first driving lesson began in disaster, with the mysteries of double declutching and hand signals seeming to need more hands than she possessed, but by the end of the second, she felt confident that driving was something she would enjoy.

Ethel knew there was trouble brewing. Her father's rage had begun a week ago and had been slowly, terrifyingly building. Next week she would be eighteen and for some reason she couldn't imagine, that fact seemed to be the centre of his fury. He hadn't mentioned it but when she did, she found he was staring at her with a strange look in his round, angry blue eyes.

Not for the first time she blamed herself. It must have been a disappointment for him to have had a child when Glenys and Sid were almost grown up. The extra expense, the lack of freedom when they had been able to come and go more or less as they pleased, her mother giving up the job she had in the wood yard office. Even with Sid and Glenys working, because of her father being in prison several times, twice for long stretches, the family had suffered the lack of her mother's earnings. Her father had been in prison when she was born and hadn't appeared in her life until she was more than one year old. The house was shabby, there was no money for anything beautiful. When something wore out or had been broken, the replacements were never good quality, just sad, utilitarian basics. Her mother's attempts to brighten the place only emphasized its drabness. It must be her fault, her birthday bringing back reminders of how much they had lost because of her unwanted arrival.

She was careful not to cause offence. Anger filled the house, everyone was subdued and as she watched the behaviour of her family she began to realize that her sister was unusually nervous, starting in alarm every time someone spoke. The tension and anticipation of trouble that was almost palpable, was emanating not from her father, but seemed to come from Glenys. Perhaps she was wrong and it was not herself whom her father blamed for whatever was gnawing at him. She wondered what her quiet, inoffensive sister could have done to cause such seething resentment in their father. She gave a sad grimace of a smile as she realized it was April Fool's Day. No possibility of any fun in the Twomey household.

She coaxed her sister to go for a walk. The weather was mild, the April sun weak but adding a cheerfulness to the bare trees and the early flowers. The blossom on the leafless branches of the blackthorn hedges had spread its lacy white beauty around the fields and Ethel's heart lifted with the excitement of burgeoning spring. She glanced at Glenys in the hope of seeing similar joy reflected in her sister's blue eyes, but Glenys's face was sombre, she was clearly worried.

'Glenys? What's wrong?' she asked as they bent low to avoid spiky branches as they went into the wood. At first Glenys forced a smile and denied her melancholy. Some of the sturdy lower branches of ancient ash and sycamore were distorted and made enticing seats though they were damp and covered with mosses. Nevertheless Ethel sat on one and patted encouragement for her sister to join her.

'Have you thought any more about joining up?' Glenys asked before Ethel could repeat her question. 'I think you should. Wesley will be away from home and I ... well, I might be leaving and Sid almost certainly will. I don't want to think of you being here with just Mam and Dad.'

'Dad wouldn't hurt me if that's what you're thinking,' Ethel said bravely, although from the way her father had been with the whole family there, she had wondered whether he might be even more unpredictable with only two people to shout at and bully. She bounced to make the branch swing. 'Where are you going?' she asked. 'You and Sid don't have to join up, your work in the factory is classed as war work.'

'I'll have to go away, I can't stay here,' Glenys spoke sadly. Ethel instinctively hugged her.

They walked on, looking at the ruined barns and other places where they had both played as children. Secret places where they had acted out their adventure games. Years apart, both had enjoyed the freedom. 'Don't go if you'd rather stay. Don't let our dad drive you away. You see,' Ethel admitted, 'I think I might do as you say and join the ATS or something. What would Mam do without either of us?'

'Promise me something, Ethel!' Glenys, with her red hair burnished gold by the early sun and her beautiful alabaster skin, stared at her in such an intense manner that Ethel felt afraid.

'Of course. What is it? You aren't ill, are you? Tell me what's worrying you!'

'I can't tell you. I hope you'll never know. Just promise me that you'll move away as soon as you're able. You'll be eighteen next week, you aren't a child any more. You can be free if you choose to be.'

'How will Mam manage?' Ethel repeated. She was frightened by Glenys's unwillingness to tell her what was wrong and her imagination spiralled into panic. 'You're ill, aren't you? Tell me, Glenys, please tell me?'

Glenys hugged her and said, 'Remember always, that I love you. Very, very much.' Then she ran from the wood across the field towards the distant rooftop that was Wesley Daniels's house but veered off before she reached it and disappeared through the hedge in the direction of town. Ethel didn't see her again that day. The following morning Glenys had gone out before Ethel rose.

It was very early and she walked through the field and into the wood and stood near the tree on which they had both sat the previous day, listening as though the trees could answer the questions her sister had refused to explain. She waved at Wesley as he set off across the field to the hospital where he worked in the kitchens.

The smell of bacon frying enticed her and as she turned to go back inside to eat and get ready for her own day's work, she heard her father shouting. Her mother's voice then, high pitched and fearful. The rumble of her father's complaints was followed by the scraping of a chair, the crash of china and more shouting. She ran in and saw her parents glaring at each other across the room, her mother holding a poker for protection against the huge angry man who was her father. Pointless to intervene. She'd learned that long ago. A number of bruises had taught her to walk away, to leave them to it. Forgetting about breakfast, for which she no longer had an appetite, she grabbed her coat and handbag and ran to the bus stop.

Rosie Dreen stared at the poster and read and reread the words.

Join NAAFI. The Ideal War Job For Women.

Her heart raced with excitement. She had all but made up her mind. Tomorrow – or some day soon – she would make herself walk into what the locals referred to as the call-up office. Telling Nan she was leaving would be easier once she had signed the forms and was committed. Telling Nan first meant there was a strong chance of her being persuaded against it. For a moment she was tempted to do that. Nan would make up her mind for her. She would stay at home and tell herself the alternative was impossible. That her duty was to stay with Nan. She looked again at the poster. *Servitor Servientium* (Service to Those who Serve) – that was the Naafi motto. She knew she had prevaricated too long. Tomorrow she would sign.

She had been shopping, her arms were full of packages. While she had been standing there cogitating about her war effort, it had begun to rain. The moment she moved, the paper carrier fell apart, leaving her holding the cardboard strip and the loops of string. The paper bags gave no protection to the biscuits or silverfoil packet of tea and a bag of sugar would soon be ruined. In her hand she held a white paper bag containing eggs brought from the farm, the paper opaque and useless.

Sheltering in a shop doorway she struggled to get as many packages as possible into her pockets. With the eggs held precariously in her hand she stepped out into the now steady downpour. A girl was running past, wearing a pink dress, and a grey, pink-trimmed coat swinging open. She couldn't see where she was going because of the open umbrella she carried. They bumped together, both sliding on the wet surface of the pavement and slithering to a halt just yards apart and falling to the ground.

'Idiot!' Kate hissed. 'Look what you've done to my stockings. And this is a new dress! Now I'll have to go home and change!'

'Look what you did to my eggs!'

Both girls stared at the growing patch of yellow on the pavement between them and then at the buckled umbrella which Kate still held. Inexplicably they laughed like friends sharing a huge joke.

Rosie picked up the mess of shells and soggy paper, squealed with laughter and threw it into the gutter. When they had picked themselves up, Kate examined her new coat to assess the damage.

'I expect it was my fault, stepping out from the doorway,' Rosie conceded.

'No. I wasn't looking where I was going. I was in a hurry to catch the recruitment office before it closes.'

'You're joining up?' Rosie's wide blue eyes opened in what Kate thought was admiration.

'We have to do our bit, don't we?' Kate replied airily.

'You want to escape from home too?' Rosie queried.

'Well, yes, I admit that's the big temptation.'

'Me too. But we can't go looking like this or they'll kick us out.'

'Come and have a cup of tea in the café around the corner,' Kate invited.

'Nan will wonder where I am,' Rosie said doubtfully, shy of this smartly dressed girl, conscious of her own shabby appearance and surprised at the result of the unexpected encounter.

'If we're going to join up and help fight Hitler you can't start off being afraid of offending your Nan!' Kate announced firmly.

Kate placed her distorted umbrella in a corner and rather haughtily ordered tea and cakes. Rosie rubbed egg from her shoes and tried to hold back nervous laughter. The café was a rather expensive one and a place she had never entered before. Her new friend Kate seemed perfectly at home there.

'I thought I'd join the Naafi,' Rosie told Kate.

'Now that isn't a bad idea. All those hungry men to look after. I hadn't thought of the Naafi.' Her greeny-grey eyes gleamed with mischief as she added, 'I'd better tell Mummy and Daddy I'll be working in the office though, not at the counter! Will your parents cause a fuss?'

'I only have Nan,' Rosie told her. Opening

out to this girl was a new experience for Rosie, who had kept her thoughts, disappointments and dreams locked safely away all her life. She was thankful that Kate Banner accepted the story without excessive sympathy and declared it interesting. 'Interesting', Rosie was soon to learn, was one of Kate's favourite words.

They met the following day and went for an interview at the information centre in the church hall. Rosie went in first on Kate's insistence. She recognized in the unsure Rosie a person who might back out, use some invented excuse and go back home to 'Nan'.

Rosie came out and told Kate that she had agreed to sign up for the Naafi.

Kate went in and was asked if she would consider the army. The thought of marching and the heavy uniform made her shudder. The Wrens didn't appeal either and when she mentioned the Naafi her first question was about the uniform.

'I expect it will make me look like a sack of coal,' she sighed prettily. The officer handed her a photograph of the trim blue counter-overalls and Kate nodded. 'So long as it isn't pink,' she said without explanation. Beaming, she went out to join Rosie and they went to the café again to celebrate.

'Now we only have to tell our families,' Rosie said, making a moue, opening her blue eyes wide.

Kate gave a broad wink. 'Tears. Shed a few tears and they'll be so busy comforting me they'll forget to be angry.'

'If I tried that I'd end up giggling,' Rosie confessed.

Ethel Twomey went home on her birthday not expecting any celebration. The atmosphere at home had made it impossible to even consider a party. She would meet Wesley later and he would give her his ring. It was a Monday just like every other Monday. She approached the house with her usual expectation of trouble. She was not disappointed. Shouts and screams filled the air, punctuated by the sounds of furniture being dragged around. She wanted to run, cover her ears and run, but this was different from the usual argument. She had to make sure her sister and her mother were all right. Then she would run as far and as fast as possible and wait for her father's latest rage to die down.

She heard footsteps behind her and turned to see Wesley running to catch her up.

'I'm coming in with you.'

'No, you might make things worse. You know what Dad's like, it's probably nothing more than a complaint about the fire needing coal or his tea not ready when he wants it.'

'Mam says they've been arguing since dinner time and your sister ran out of the house with a terrified look on her face about an hour ago.'

Ethel's footsteps slowed as she walked over the little footbridge and began to make her way up the front path. 'Perhaps, if Glenys is safely out of the way, I'd better wait until they've calmed down,' she said. Instinct told her that this was something worse than one of her father's usual moods. 'Perhaps we'd better go and find Glenys.'

They went back to Wesley's house where his mother made sandwiches and a pot of tea. Sitting in the front room, a paraffin stove sending out some heat and a lot of smell, Wesley tried to take her mind off the violence going on between her parents.

'I wanted to tell you this in better circumstances, but I'm leaving next week to work for the Naafi.'

'The Naafi?' Ethel frowned, only half her mind on what he was saying. The fact of his leaving so soon didn't register at all.

'I have experience in catering. My first aid certificates will be an advantage too they told me. And, I don't fancy learning to kill. I suppose those are the only real reasons. And the fact the Naafi needs men like me with some ability to feed large numbers of people.'

'I might come with you,' Ethel told him. 'I

can't stand much more of this.' She gestured in the direction of her home. 'Glenys told me she's going away. Sid might too. He might be told he has to do something more than he's doing at present.'

'You'd hate it, love. Stay near, so I can picture you here, waiting for me.'

'I have to get away from Dad's anger.'

'It's rarely directed at you.'

'Not yet. But if there's only me there you don't think he'll suddenly turn into a calm, quiet man, do you? Someone will have to take the stick and I don't want it to be me. I can't think of anything that would be worse than living at home with only Mam and Dad for company. Specially if you're going.'

The following week was worse than anything she remembered. Something had happened and no one would tell her what. Her sister locked herself in her room and refused to come out. Dad looked larger than usual as he stormed around the house, calling Sid evil, her mother spineless and warning Ethel, repeatedly, to stay away from men. He threatened to beat Wesley to a pulp if he saw Ethel anywhere near him.

'You're sure to go bad,' Dai snarled. 'You're as evil as the rest of this tainted family. You mustn't go near a man. Any man, d'you hear me? You have to stay here when you aren't at work and never go out without me or your stupid mother with you, d'you

36

understand? You stay in this house and keep away from men.'

'Why?' she whispered fearfully.

'You'll go to the bad like your ... sister!' He emphasized the word as though it was an insult. What could her inoffensive sister have done to make him so angry? To her horror and disbelief she woke in the morning to find her bedroom door locked, and no amount of knocking brought someone to open it. Bread, milk, boiled eggs and a few apples were on her dressing table.

She climbed out of the bedroom window that night and ran down the road to find Wesley.

Mrs Daniels opened the door in her night-gown and shook her head. 'Sorry, Ethel, dear, but Wesley is forbidden to visit you.'

'Why? What happened?' A movement caught her eye and she looked toward the landing, as Wesley came down the stairs, fully dressed.

'How did you get out? Your father told me you were forbidden to leave the house.'

'I climbed out of the window but I'm not going back that way. I'm going to knock on the door and demand an explanation. I'm not a child!'

'I'll come with you.' Wesley put a coat around her and she was aware for the first time that she was shivering, dressed in only a nightdress, a dressing gown and a pair of slippers – her father having emptied her wardrobe, presumably to ensure she didn't leave.

'Sorry we couldn't celebrate our engagement properly,' she said tearfully. From her dressing-gown pocket she took out the ring and gave it back to him. 'I'll wear it when this trouble has been sorted. I want to wear it proudly, not hide it for fear of sending Dad into a worse rage.'

'I'll walk you back home.' Ignoring his mother's entreaties to be careful, he left to face the furious Dai Twomey with less confidence than he showed.

The house was quiet, no voices could be heard. The door wasn't locked and they went in to see her mother on the floor being kicked by her father. She was making no sound. The hall door opened and Sid staggered in, his face bruised, one eye practically closed, his red hair sticky with blood. As though in a daze he walked past Ethel and Wesley and out into the darkness.

Wesley and Ethel leapt on her father and tried to pull him off her mother. Dai turned and grabbed Wesley, throwing him with ease against the wall. He swung Ethel and released her, forcing her to stumble through the doorway and land at the bottom of the stairs. Every time Wesley stood up, her father hit him until he was dazed. It seemed to go on for ever but it was only a few minutes before Sid had gone, and Wesley was out of the door and staggering away down the path. He stopped at the stream and put his face into the water to cool his head then went back to rescue Ethel. At the door her father waited, smiling. He punched and kicked until the boy gave up and staggered away.

Wesley made his way into town, shamed by his inadequacy, stopping to rest, sometimes crawling, staunching his wounds with handfuls of grass, two miles across the fields, and told the police. Then he sat in a cold damp field and watched dawn break on the rest of his life. A new dawn, new day, and life would never be the same. The shame at being unable to help Ethel and her mother printed on his mind at that moment was destined to stay there for ever.

Her father was arrested, her mother refused to go to hospital and sat in an armchair, propped up with pillows. Ethel was taken to hospital to replace a dislocated shoulder but insisted on returning home to look after her mother. For what was left of the night and through most of the following day she sat near her mother and made her plans. Of Sid and Glenys there was no sign.

Her mother slept quite a lot and every time she roused, Ethel pleaded with her to go to hospital. 'Talk to the doctors and to the police. There'll be evidence now for you to insist on his leaving.'

'I can't go anywhere before Sid and Glenys come back.' She insisted that she would not give evidence. 'I told the police I fell and I won't say different,' she whispered through damaged lips.

In the morning Ethel went out to get some fresh air, wondering how she could prevent her father from returning home. She knew her mother would never be persuaded to give evidence and would also forbid her to do so. Loyalty at any price, even when your very life was at risk, seemed so utterly stupid.

Her mother stood up and shakily made her way to the kitchen and made tea, which she would find difficult to drink. Despairing of talking sense into her, Ethel decided she should concentrate on finding Glenys. Sid had often fled from his father's anger and would come back when he was ready, but Glenys had never run away before. She thought of Glenys's friends; there were surprisingly few. Her sister had led a very quiet life. She would call on them and see if Glenys had stayed with one of them over-night.

It was late afternoon and she looked up and down the road, hoping to see her sister appear. Beyond the field she saw smoke rising from Wesley's house and wondered if he was all right. Realizing with a jolt that she hadn't thought of him as much as someone in love ought to, she walked down and knocked on his door.

Mrs Daniels told her tearfully to go away. After being assured that Wesley was safe but badly bruised and humiliated, she left and began searching for her sister and Sid. Although Sid could look after himself, she needed him and hoped he too would soon return home.

None of Glenys's friends had seen her and, with growing alarm, Ethel walked through the fields towards the wood where she had recently sat with her sister. Glenys had told her she was leaving, but surely not like this, without a word or an explanation?

Without much hope of being heard, she walked through the trees and called her sister's name. There were a few old buildings in the vicinity, the places where they had played childish games. Perhaps Glenys had sheltered there and was still sleeping. Rows like the one her father created were very exhausting.

It was in the barn once used to store grain that she found her, hanging from a beam, swinging slightly in the draught from the open door.

Two

It wasn't a good day for a funeral, Ethel decided. The sun was too bright, the colours of that spring in 1940 too bold and cheerful. Today, with her sister hidden away in the sombre dark coffin, the skies should have cried, the wind should have howled in agony.

She looked around her at the serious faces of relatives and friends, then at the angry expression on the red face of her father. He had always been angry and fast to lash out at some unintended slight. Today was worse. Ever since the days before her sister Gleny's body had been found hanged in the lonely shed out in the fields, his fury had been undiminished. Her mother bore the brunt of it, and she herself still wore a sling to help mend her dislocated shoulder.

Something terrible had happened and Glenys's suicide had been a part of it but no one would tell her the truth. There was just her father's fury and her mother's quiet, almost mesmerized acceptance of his anger. Her sister was dead, yet after the initial disbelief and the crying and her futile search for answers, her parents seemed more concerned with some other disaster. Bemused by it all, her mother silently grieving with no comfort from her father, her father simmering like a boiler about to burst, blaming herself and her mother for everything bad that had ever happened to them all.

Ethel herself hardly coping, constantly crying and trying not to, pleading silently for Sid to come home and help her, dealing with the arrangements and keeping the world turning while everyone else seemed stunned and unable to offer practical help. She couldn't feel for the death of her sister as she knew she should. She was trying desperately to make sense of what had happened.

The reason for her sister's horrific suicide must be in some way connected to her mother's fear and her father's fury. And from the way her father stared at her with such disgust in his angry blue eyes, she had a frightening feeling that she herself was, in some unknown way, to blame. If she could only understand how and why then she might start to grieve properly.

She looked around the room as people were gathering their coats and hats and preparing to leave and it was as though the scene was nothing to do with herself and her sister. She felt sorry for those who tried to offer comforting words. What could they say in such circumstances as these? She heard the women begin sentences that faded away incomplete, and the gruff kindnesses of the men who said even less.

Her mother stood among them looking smaller and older, of her father there was now no sign. He had spent most of the time since his daughter's death digging furiously in the garden making it ready for late spring planting. He worked outside from first light until dusk, clearing the ground and burning the rubbish, and would come in with red-rimmed eyes, his face stained with bonfire smoke and earth. He had hardly spoken a word. The people who had called to pay their respects he ignored completely.

The food was almost gone and people were begining to leave, thankful, no doubt, to escape from the tensions and glowering atmosphere in the house. As they drifted away, some mopping tears for the young life sadly lost, Dai appeared in the doorway.

Ethel glanced nervously at her father as she began to stack the plates on to a tray. He was staring at her mother, then at her, undisguised hatred in his blue eyes, and she knew that the moment everyone had gone, his fury would once more errupt. She knew also, that she had to get herself and her mother away from this place before her father killed one of them.

She packed the left-over cakes into a tin and was pained to see the remains of the birthday cake her mother had made. What a birthday it had been. Instead of a happy party to celebrate her engagement to Wesley Daniels, there had been this eruption of unexplained anger followed by the death of her sister. Tears flooded her eyes and she wiped them away angrily. Now was not the time for tears. Now was the time for action, but what form that should take, she didn't quite know.

Wesley wasn't there. She hadn't seen him since finding Glenys's body, and his mother had told her he was away from home. He would have helped her to cope, and would have taken her away until her father had calmed down – if he ever did. His furious temper had never lasted this long before. It usually exploded suddenly and briefly, then sent him to sleep for a couple of hours.

'Where's Wesley?' she asked her mother and the only reply was an urgent demand to be quiet.

'But he should be here.'

'He won't be coming here again,' her mother whispered, keeping her eyes on her husband, afraid he would hear. 'Your father has forbidden him to see you again.'

'What? But why, Mam? We're getting married!'

'Hush,' her mother begged again. 'Your father only wants to protect you.'

'From what?' Ethel hissed.

The heavy hand on her shoulder made her

legs weaken. She leaned against the table, dropping the plates she had been holding, as her father said, 'You aren't to speak to Wesley again. In fact, if I see you with any boy, you'll have the worst beating you've ever known.'

'Why?' she dared to ask.

'Because I don't want you going bad, that's why. You come from wicked, evil stock and I won't have you going bad and bringing disgrace to this house!'

Disgrace to this house? Ethel thought cynically. Bring disgrace to this house that was noted for violence? Where her brother had run away without a word and her quiet, inoffensive sister had killed herself rather than go on living there? What disgrace could be worse than that?

She pleaded with her mother to go away with her, find themselves a room, anywhere away from her father and his barely controlled violence.

'We could both get work in a factory. They pay good money, we'd manage well enough. Please, Mam, before something else happens. I don't know why Glenys died but I know whatever it was isn't finished.'

'I can't go. I don't deserve better. You get what you deserve in this life.'

'What on earth did Glenys do?'

'Oh,' her mother cried softly, 'that was my punishment, losing her like that.'

46

No matter how Ethel pleaded, there were no explanations.

From then on life was utter misery. Whatever Ethel did she was punished, her shoulders where Dai constantly grabbed her and shook her, were never free of bruises. No one would explain why, or tell her the reason behind her sister's suicide. She worked at her job in the café in town, and was given food as part of her wages. For this she was grateful as it meant she didn't have to sit at the table with her parents in silence and fear, swallowing her food in indigestible lumps. Instead she sat and dreamed of escaping to freedom.

Several times she tried to find shelter while she made plans to run away. She had few friends, as the house was two miles out of town and most of the girls she had known at school lived far away. Few people visited her at The Dell. It was all right in the summer but in the winter with its long dark nights few ventured there.

Whenever Dai Twomey's work as a lorry driver allowed, he would be waiting outside the café to escort her home. 'You're unclean,' he would constantly tell her. 'Not fit to mix with decent people.' When she dared to ask for an explanation, he cuffed her around the head and told her not to question his authority. He had to look after her and do what was right.

Kate had told her parents that she had decided to join up and do her bit for the war effort and they had stared at her in disbelief.

'But Kate, dear,' said her mother, 'there's no need. We have to have you here, we can't manage the business without you! They'll understand. Food retail is war work and equally as important as other occupations.' She nudged Kate's father and added, 'Tell her, Daddy, explain that she mustn't go.'

Kate told them it was too late, that she had signed and would be leaving within the month. She dried her mother's tears and hid the excitement behind tears of her own. As she comforted her mother, said soothing words, she wondered how Rosie was getting on with her explanations to her Nan.

'I'm going away, Nan,' Rosie said. 'I've joined the Naafi and I'll be leaving in a few weeks.'

'Oh Rosie, love, do you have to go? I thought with you working on the farm you wouldn't feel the need to do anything else.'

'I don't really want to leave you, Nan, but I want to do something and the Naafi seems a suitable job for someone like me.' She laughed, coaxing her grandmother to do the same. 'Scrubbing and cleaning and a bit of cooking, that's all I know. Besides, I can't imagine me marching and saluting and all that stuff, can you?'

She felt distressed when she saw how upset her grandmother was during the rest of that day, and went around to see Kate knowing that her new friend would cheer her up. They bought fish and chips and sat eating them on the wall of the park while they discussed their anxieties. Neither had been away from home before and Kate wondered whether she would be able to sleep in a room with other people.

'My biggest worry is not having enough to eat,' Rosie admitted, helping herself from Kate's paper package as her own had all gone.

'Are you going to make changes?' Kate asked.

'How d'you mean?'

'Well, for one thing, are you going to wear make-up now Nan won't be there to stop you?'

'I did try once,' Rosie giggled. 'I put rouge and lipstick on and then washed it off before going out, I felt so stupid.'

'You've got lovely eyes. I think you should wear eye-shadow and mascara.'

'What?' Rosie couldn't have been more shocked if Kate had suggested she became a prostitute. Kate smiled. She would persuade her, in time.

'I wonder if we'll stay together. Perhaps if we make a formal request they might arrange it?' Kate mused.

'I hadn't thought of that. It'll be awful if we can't. Imagine sharing with someone we didn't like.' They went home each more gloomy than before they had met.

Ethel didn't see or hear from Wesley and was distressed by his absence and lack of explanation. What had been so terrible that he had left so suddenly? Was that her fault too? She couldn't understand how. If she had been wicked surely she would remember? Besides losing her future, losing Wesley meant she had lost her childhood as well. He was her friend with whom she had spent so many happy hours, the recipient of all her innermost thoughts and dreams and he had let her down so badly she couldn't imagine ever being free from the pain of it.

When her father was out of the house she sometimes dared to call at the Daniels' home but each time she was sent hurriedly away. She and her mother were not the only ones with cause to be afraid of her father's anger. She wrote to Wesley, care of his parents, but if he replied, her mother never let her see the envelopes with his familiar spidery writing on them.

She continued to plead with her mother to leave, but Molly only shook her head dully. 'I'm needed here to look after your father and see to the chickens and the garden.'

Ethel became more and more depressed,

imagining that her present life would continue until she died. Then one day, Wesley's mother came into the café, ordered a cup of tea and a scone and confided that when Wesley had left, he had joined the Navy Canteen Service, a branch of the Naafi, to serve on ships, providing food and shopping services for the seamen.

Accepting that her mother would never abandon her father and regretfully leaving her to face his wrath, she made her decision. With Mrs Daniels' reluctant co-operation, Ethel began to make preparations to leave. A letter of application, forms to fill, and the replies were sent to Mrs Daniels' house and were passed on in the café.

Summer in The Dell passed in a long procession of monotonous days, she and her mother creeping around trying not to anger her father. Few people called. With Glenys dead, the grieving distorted by lack of understanding, the house was unable to lift its shroud of mourning. As well as the tragedy of Glenys's suicide, Ethel's brother Sid hadn't been seen nor heard of since the dreadful day she had found her sister's body.

When they were alone together, Ethel still implored her mother to leave, but Molly refused. 'I married him and I have to stay,' she insisted in the whispering voice they both now assumed, even when Dai was out of the house.

As the time came for her to leave she told no one except the Baileys where she was going. She had taken a chance and trusted the family on the farm across the fields from where she lived, with her confidences. She felt the need to tell someone but only after she had made them promise not to reveal her whereabouts to her parents. Mr and Mrs Bailey, their son Colin and their daughter Barbara had known her all her life and would understand as no one else could how much she had suffered from her father's temper. She had helped on the farm during busy times from a small child and had loved the busy, friendly house with its ever welcoming family.

Early one autumn morning, with dawn nothing more than a glimmer on the horizon, and while the household still slept, Ethel took a small bag filled with essentials, including her post office savings book taken from her mother's locked box, and left. She called at the Daniels' cottage and threw gravel up at the window of Wesley's room. She foolishly hoped Wesley would be home and she would be able to talk to him, make sense of it all, but when the window opened, it was his mother's face she saw in the semi-darkness of the early morning.

'I don't suppose Wesley's there?'

'He's long gone, love. I'm so sorry.'

'Please give me an address, I need to write

to him, tell him where I am,' she pleaded. Mrs Daniels shook her head slowly, her face a pale oval in the early dawn. 'I daren't, Ethel. Your father beat Wesley so badly the last time he tried to interfere, I daren't risk him finding my son again. I've helped you as much as I dare.' The woman wished her luck as she closed the window and pulled the curtains across, leaving Ethel alone in the silence of the morning.

Pulling her coat more tightly around her and hitching her bag high on her shoulder, Ethel turned and headed towards the town. Walking across the fields, soggy with the October rains, she passed places where she and Wesley had hidden to enjoy their first shy, sweet kisses and mourned for the loss of him.

Somehow she would find him. There might be a war on, separating people and making things difficult, but she and Wesley had vowed to marry and nothing could keep them apart, not the war, not her father and certainly not apathy. No longer would she be cowardly Ethel Twomey, scared of her bully of a father. From today she was Ethel Twomey, a woman who would go all out for what she wanted. And now, what she wanted was as much distance as possible between herself and her miserable home. She was leaving it behind and the shadowy figure that was her former cowardly self would stay there too.

She had no idea how to set about finding someone serving on some unnamed ship in some unknown port somewhere in the wide world, but she knew that they would meet again and they would start a new life, far away from here, where her father would never find them.

The atmosphere at the railway station was emotional as Kate Banner and Rosie Dreen waited for their train to arrive. Mothers, sisters, girlfriends and wives were there to say goodbye to their loved ones, seeing them off to fight in a war they didn't understand, fearing that the anxious faces at the carriage windows would be their last sight of them, ever.

The two girls were oblivious of the tension on the faces around them. They were going on an adventure and the realities of war had not yet risen to create anxiety for them. For Kate Banner, being away from home for the first time was intoxicating. She was unable to hide her smile at the thought of the freedom promised. A pretty girl, fair with unusual greeny-grey eyes, she wore her long hair loosely around her shoulders, curled laboriously each night, with a bright ribbon bow to enhance its loveliness. The smile on her full lips attracted a few wolf-whistles, to which she replied with a sideways glance and a provocative wink. Beside her, Rosie Dreen blushed in embarrassment.

'Stop it, Kate,' she whispered, 'everyone is looking at us.'

'Stop what? I was only being kind to these boys, and we'll never see them again so what's the worry? Going off to war they are, the least we can do is smile at them.'

'There's a lot more in your smile than in the others I see around here,' Rosie giggled. 'Promise them heaven you do, with your smile, Kate Banner.'

Rosie was dressed in a brown tweed skirt and jacket over which she had a raincoat. Sensible shoes were laced firmly around her trim ankles, washed-out beige lisle stockings disguised the shapeliness of her legs, and she wore a wide-brimmed felt hat which cast a shadow over her face.

'For heaven's sake get rid of that stupid hat, Rosie,' Kate sighed as the shy Rosie caught the eye of a young sailor and tried to disappear further into its protection.

'I can't go without a hat,' Rosie exclaimed. 'Not in October.'

'Not in October,' Kate mocked. 'Heaven forbid you tried to look nice!'

The train was approaching the platform and the crowd began to shuffle towards the edge, all determined to get in first and make sure of a seat. The engine puffed slowly and importantly towards them and, as it drew near, Kate grabbed Rosie's hat and threw it on to the line.

'Kate, that's my best hat!'

'I'd hate to see the worst one! Come on, push in after that man with the bowler. He's not in the army, I bet you. Soft job he'll have and I'll make sure he doesn't have a seat if we're standing. On our way to do our bit we are and I'll tell him that if necessary, see if I don't! Go on, get in and stop apologizing. Those days are over for you, Rosie. Different girl you are since your hat got squashed.'

The compartment was already crowded and the few seats were quickly taken. Kate and Rosie moved back along the train, squeezing past those standing, including the man in the bowler, and near the end managed to find two seats.

The train didn't move immediately and a man sitting opposite took out a newspaper and opened it in front of Rosie's face. In their excited mood, they chattered loudly about their destination and the other occupants stared at them with disapproval, subduing Rosie but encouraging Kate to talk even louder.

Embarrassed by Kate's uninhibited excitement and the accompanying sour looks, Rosie dug into her pocket and drew out a couple of toffees wrapped untidily in greaseproof paper. 'Here, this should keep you quiet for a bit. Nan made them and they're stubborn-hard,' she grinned.

'You don't shut me up that easily, Rosie Dreen. We're going to have fun now we're off the leash, see if we don't!'

The guard blew his whistle and waved his green flag and just as the huge engine began to pull away, their carriage door opened and a girl struggled to get in. Kate grabbed her suitcase and dragged it in, then reached out a hand to help the girl aboard. The girl, who was about their own age, had been running, her face was dotted with perspiration and her cheeks were flushed. She had a mass of strong black hair and her brown eyes, as she looked around the carriage, were twin beacons of suspicion. She cautiously looked out of the window as the train picked up speed, and, apparently satisfied, gave an almost inaudible sigh of relief.

'Thanks,' the newcomer said as she picked up her small case and threw it neatly up on to the luggage rack above the newspaper owner. She stood hesitantly, looking around the compartment assessing the passengers, judging whether she would be able to find a seat.

'Interesting,' Kate muttered behind fingers which covered her mouth. 'Running away from something I bet you.'

On the platform a man burst through the entrance holding a platform ticket in his thick fingers. He was heavily built and more than six feet tall. His hair was long and wild, standing out from his head and making him appear even taller. Like the late arrival on the train, his face was drenched with sweat. His eyebrows were bushy, his blue eyes bright with anger. The few people near moved away, his aggression clearly apparent.

He questioned the station staff, demanding to know it they had seen his daughter, grabbing the shoulder of the guard and describing her as the man began to return to the office. A picture of frustration, he glared at the tail of the train and hit a hand with the fist of the other before walking back to where he had left his powerful motorbike.

Kate Banner and Rosie Dreen watched as the late arrival nudged a man in civvies and asked, 'Any chance of a seat?'

Without a word the young man stood and smiled before limping slowly to the sliding door and going to stand in the corridor.

'He was wounded,' Rosie whispered in frowning disapproval of the dark-eyed girl.

Ethel was ashamed but defiantly refused to show it. She stared down at Rosie, a haughty expression on her face. Others looked up, staring at the newcomer and then at Rosie, who looked away, embarrassed by the encounter. She really hated to be noticed and wondered at that moment whether she would be able to cope with being away from Nan, living among strangers and having to meet girls as confident as this one appeared to be.

'Want a sandwich?' she whispered to Kate.

'Don't tell me you're hungry already, Rosie Dreen!' Kate laughed.

'Starving,' Rosie admitted.

The man with the widely spread newspaper moved slightly to take more of the space offered. The girl, who hadn't yet sat down, snatched the paper, folded it none too neatly and said, 'Now, if you'll move back up a bit there'll be room for me. Thank you.'

Without waiting for him to comply she wriggled in between the man and a rather plump woman and handed him his bedraggled paper, slapping it on to his lap.

She looked at the two girls, who stared in admiration. 'What are you two staring at, never seen a woman with black hair before?'

They lowered their gaze for a moment, then when they looked at her again, she was smiling, her teeth even in the full, generous mouth.

'We're off to Bedlington,' Kate said. 'Joining the Naafi we are.'

'That's where I'm going! I'm Ethel Twomey, cook, heaven help 'em. Who are you?'

'I might have guessed you'd be a boss,' Kate whispered, gesturing to the man sitting beside her, who stared ahead having abandoned his attempt to read his crumpled paper in the limited space.

Introductions completed, they exchanged

information on what they had learnt about the job ahead of them. Their knowledge of what was expected of them was pitifully limited. Others in the carriage joined in with a discussion of the war, and the conversation was loud and clearly irritating to the offended man with the newspaper, which only goaded Kate and Ethel to livelier debate. Any qualms she suffered made Ethel remind herself silently of her new persona. She was never going to be afraid of anyone, ever again.

Rosie said the least. She was so shy she hesitated too long to add a comment and the subject had changed before she could speak. Sometimes she did say a few words but her voice was so low the others didn't hear. It was only Kate who sometimes deferred to her and asked for an opinion. On most of these occasions Rosie's reply was, 'I don't know.'

'I'd hoped your inhibitions were in your hat,' Kate whispered at one point. 'We'll have to get rid of those damned awful shoes as well!'

Rosie blushed and smiled. The future promised to be exciting and she knew there would be many changes in her attitude to life. She *would* become braver, less easily embarrassed. She *would*! Away from her loving but stifling grandmother she'd be able to step out and find herself. She was lucky to have Kate as a friend. And this new girl Ethel Twomey promised to be fun, once she was used to her!

Rosie opened her parcel of food twice before they changed trains. The other girls were told that beside the food for the train journey, Rosie's Nan had given her a box of emergency supplies, in case she didn't have enough to eat at camp. Ethel was amused to see that the small, shy little girl with the huge blue eyes ate more than she did. Kate only smiled, being used to Rosie's appetite.

It was a long journey. They went on two more trains and at every change during their journey, Ethel Twomey held back and only moved from the train after looking cautiously around her. She didn't explain and Kate and Rosie hadn't known her long enough to ask, but they accommodated her and waited until the platform had cleared before beckoning her forward.

A bus took them on the last stage of their journey from the town of Bedlington to their destination. It was an RAF station from where Spitfires flew. At the guard room they were told to wait and a man came to collect them and take them to their quarters. The accommodation was their first shock.

'A tent? I can't sleep in a tent, it's October!' Kate exclaimed in horror.

'It's quite big,' Rosie said encouragingly.

'Big, draughty and perishing cold!' Ethel

said. 'We aren't sleeping in that so you can find us somewhere else straight away.'

'Somewhere bomb-proof too,' Kate added, a shudder of anxiety clouding her pretty face.

'Where do we wash and – you know – all that sort of thing?' Rosie wanted to know.

'Ablutions in the small hut with the gravel path around it. Now, come on, I have to show you the kitchen before I go off duty.'

'Who are you? And where do we find the supervisor? I'm not having this,' Ethel said loudly.

'I'm Walter Phillips and I am the supervisor, so will you please hurry up and put your cases in the tent and come with me. I haven't got all day.'

'Come on, you must have somewhere better than this,' Kate pleaded.

Walter leaned towards her and smiled as he replied. 'I'll look after you girls if you're nice to me, I can't say fairer than that. I do have others to look after you know, but I've been known to have my favourites.'

Ethel and Kate exchanged glances as he went a few paces ahead of them to allow them to enter the tent. His swaggering walk, and the way he stood tossing a bunch of keys from hand to hand in what he imagined was a nonchalant manner, made Rosie begin to giggle in spite of the anxiety his words created. That tent wasn't lockable. Thank goodness she and Kate had met the formidable Ethel Twomey. She'd be a better guard than a bulldog!

It was getting dark and the gloomy interior was reluctant to give up its secrets. With the aid of Walter's torch they could just make out four small camp beds in the tent and a rickety table and two chairs. They didn't have time to explore further as Walter hurried them across a field through a hedge weakened by the constant passage of people, across a second field, where he stopped and pointed to a wooden building looming out of the darkness.

'That's your canteen, ladies, and your first customers will be arriving for their break at eleven hundred hours tomorrow so get cracking.'

'What d'you mean, "get cracking"? We want to get settled in first. It's too late to do anything tonight!'

As he disappeared into the darkness he called back the usual excuse for anything unpleasant: 'Don't you know there's a war on?'

'We do now! And we know where Hitler's brother is, masquerading as a bloke called Walter!' Kate called after him.

The room that greeted them when they had stumbled around and finally found a light switch was filthy. Spider webs adorned the corners and mouse-droppings littered the floor. There was a counter, which they had been told to call a bar, with glass-covered sections for displaying food. Behind a partition there was a cooker of sorts, a large sink and draining board, and, over the sink, a water heater on the wall that was powered by gas. Against an outside wall was a filthy oven range that still contained the ashes of a previous fire. Tables and chairs in the main area indicated that it had been used as a canteen in the past, but there was a lot to be done before it could be used to serve and eat food in again.

In the partitioned-off area beside the huge sink they found a couple of new buckets, a mop, some brushes, dusters and cleaning materials. Vim, carbolic soap, large containers of disinfectant and boxes of soap powder stood beside the buckets, and wearily Rosie took off her coat and began to fill one of the buckets.

'Surely they don't expect us to do this now?' Kate frowned.

'We might as well,' Rosie said. 'I don't think we'll find our way back to the tent, do you?'

'Let's try and make a cup of tea,' Ethel suggested.

'Good idea, and I've got some chocolate in my bag,' Rosie added, pointing to the large shoulder bag her nan had packed with treats for the journey.

'Interesting,' said Kate.

While Ethel experimented with kettle and stove, Rosie flicked water over the floor to dampen the dust and began to sweep up the litter. After examining her fingernails with some apprehension, Kate picked up a scrubbing brush and cloth and went in search of hot water to the gas heater. It was scattered with rust like confetti and obviously there was a blockage somewhere in the flue because as she lit it, the flame flared and the boiler blew back with a resounding blast that terrified them.

Walter poked his head around the door and demanded that they made less noise. He disappeared again before an outraged Kate or Ethel could take a breath to respond. Rosie was convulsed with laughter.

They started off in an orderly manner but after half an hour of sweeping, and an hour of washing counters, they began filling buckets, using cold water and disinfectant, then throwing the contents up the walls and over the floor and, using the sweeping brushes, managed to clean the place reasonably well. With the lights turned off, and using a torch, their last job was to pull aside the dusty wooden blackout screens covering the windows and chase away the last of the spiders.

It was two a.m. when they gave in to tiredness and began to make their way back to the tent. Ethel's sense of direction was good, having been brought up in a country village with fields and woods for her playground, and they crept inside intending to flop into bed fully dressed, and sleep. One of the beds was occupied and an extremely pompous voice told them to, 'Please, do be quiet!'

Searching for their belongings with only dim torches to help them in their overtired state was difficult; trying to be quiet as well was their undoing. Rosie choked back stifled laughter but she was unable to suppress her giggles. The others quickly joined in, their exhaustion and the newcomer's reaction causing it to increase in volume as the occupant of the fourth bed became more and more angry. When she told them to stop acting like children, Rosie squealed and threw a pillow and soon a pillow fight ensued which succeeded in weakening the guy ropes of the tent. The walls lurched inward and, leaving the irate newcomer to sort out the problem, they grabbed what blankets they could, returned to the canteen, and slept on the floor.

Still longing for a cup of tea, which neither Kate nor Ethel had managed to produce, they had finally dropped off to sleep on their uncomfortable bed when the siren warned of enemy aircraft approaching. Half asleep, they held a blanket around themselves and scuttled to the dubious protection of the

66

counter, pushing pans and boxes of supplies out of the way to get as far underneath as possible.

'Fat lot of use this is as protection against bombs,' Ethel muttered.

'We should have kept your hat, Rosie,' Kate chuckled.

'Better than a tent,' Rosie spoke with such seriousness the overtired girls laughed, until the first ear-numbing blast of the guns took away the humour and they clung to each other in fear. A wailing, moaning roar filled their ears and was eventually identified as low-flying planes. They had never been so close to one before and the sound seemed to fill their heads, confusing them and terrifying them with its volume. They squeezed their eyes tightly shut and clung to each other.

When the guns finally ceased they crept to the doorway and peered out. As their eyes became accustomed to the poor light, they saw figures emerging from buildings, running around in what appeared to be a haphazard manner. There were men and women on bicycles wobbling their way along the roads, and voices were heard shouting orders. Heavy doors rumbled open and shut, other doors slammed. Buckets clanked. In the distance, vehicles were heard driving around the airfield, their headlights barely visible.

As they continued to watch, planes began to land. Seeing them flying low over their canteen made sense of the noise and no longer frightened them. An irate man ran past them, stopped, and shouted, 'What the 'ell you doing in there? I've been looking for you.'

'You didn't expect us to stay in a tent, did you!' retorted Ethel.

'Where's your tin hats?'

'Tin hats?' they queried in unison.

'Probably in the tent,' Rosie whispered.

'We haven't been given any!' Ethel said loudly. 'Fine protection we're getting from Hitler's bombs: a flimsy tent to sleep in and not even a tin hat. What sort of an outfit is this!'

'A bunch of amateurs,' Kate added.

As the man turned away, Ethel grinned, her teeth bright in the early morning haze. 'Best form of defence is attack, eh girls?'

They opened Rosie's large shoulder bag again and finished a packet of biscuits on the instructions of Rosie who insisted that Nan said carbohydrate was good for shock. 'A feed of cake or biscuits and a good pee,' she added knowledgeably. 'Takes away the shock better than anything.'

Two young RAF boys woke them at six thirty and stayed to help them scrub the store cupboards which were then filled with supplies delivered during the few hours they

68

had slept. They were on 'jankers', punishment for some undisclosed misdemeanour. They also lit the fire in the ancient oven range which the girls had fervently hoped had nothing to do with them.

'You mean we have to light that every morning before we can have a cup of tea?' Kate groaned, as other men in airforce uniform wandered in to look at the new arrivals. 'And cook cakes in it?' shrieked Ethel.

'It isn't difficult.'

'It took you long enough!' Kate complained.

'It'll draw better tomorrow now the chimney's warmed up.' The man who spoke wore the unmistakable uniform of a pilot. He offered a hand to Ethel and then the others. 'I'm Duggie. Don't worry, there'll be plenty offering help to three beauties like you. There's nothing this lot likes more than damsels in distress. The lads will make sure you have plenty of dry wood. The men who were here before managed all right.'

They were told to expect supplies from the temporary canteen which was now closed and they left the kitchen girls to finish cleaning cupboards, and concentrated on the seemingly impossible task of cooking cakes and making sandwiches in time for the first break.

Walter came with instructions for their first morning, with recipes and prices, and warnings about how much money he was expecting from each batch of ingredients.

The bad-tempered geyser blew out gases on two occasions, making them run for cover, but apart from that the next two hours went reasonably well. The net bar, displaying small necessities like soap, toothpaste, combs, writing paper and all the usual needs of men away from home, was open for business. Two lots of rock cakes and several kinds of sandwiches were ready by eleven o'clock when they opened the doors for their first customers.

Kate unlocked the door and was pushed back as a crowd of uniformed customers flooded in.

'Blimey, we've got the whole of the airforce in here,' she said, flicking her hair with her fingers, pulling her hat to the back of her head at a saucy angle and smiling at the eager face in front of her.

'Char and a wad, please, miss.'

'What the 'ell's that?' Ethel asked, to much amusement.

Rosie, who had been busy behind the scenes finishing off the cooking, was given the job of clearing tables, but when she walked in and saw the sea of faces smiling at her, and heard the welcoming remarks flying about, she backed out and hid herself in the kitchen. 'I'll wash every dish you can find me and never complain, so long as I don't have to face that lot,' she gasped, shyness colouring her cheeks and spreading up into the roots of her hair.

It was Rosie who soon learnt the knack of dealing with the oven and, ignoring the instructions of Walter, when the three of them were on duty she did most of the cooking. Ethel and Kate served at the counter in their blue uniforms, and they all shared the preparation and the cleaning. So different in personality, but they made a good team.

Three

The hours of duty for the three girls were seven a.m. until eleven p.m. with a few hours off during the afternoon. For those whose turn it was to light the boiler, the morning began before six. Their first task was to deliver tea and snacks to the hangars for the men on early shift. The trolley was not easy to push with its small wheels and the occasional expanse of grass, and behind it, Rosie's small figure was almost horizontal as she struggled to manoeuvre it over the uneven surface. From some directions the cart with its urn, boxes of snacks and cups and saucers seemed to be moving unaided. Men usually saw her coming and ran to help, her shyness making her dread as well as welcome their assistance with its accompanying teasing.

There was a great deal of cleaning to do: besides the piles of dishes to be washed and dried and stacked in their places, there were tables, cupboards and floors to be scrubbed. They were so tired that on their afternoons off they slept. The occupant of the fourth bed in their tent had not returned. Walter had been persuaded by the flirting of the glamorous Kate to find them some extra blankets and they had dragged the beds together for added warmth and slept in reasonable comfort. By the end of their first week they were rested and able to consider going out during their hours of freedom.

Walter came in daily to inspect the books and deal with the money. He attempted mild flirtation with both Kate and Ethel, who played up to him in the hope he might deal kindly with any requests. He often asked for tea and cake and they all insisted that he paid for them as he constantly reminded them that they were on ration the same as the rest of the population and shouldn't take more than their entitlement.

'There are perks of the job,' he said smiling at Kate, 'if you know the right way about it.'

'Interesting...' said Kate.

Ethel refused to go into town. 'I don't

mind a walk through the fields and into one of the villages, but I don't fancy town.'

They pleaded, but to no avail. Ethel was adamant. Her worst nightmare was walking along a road and coming face to face with her father. She didn't know how helpful the service would be if her parents asked to be told her whereabouts. She had lied about her next of kin, giving a completely false name and address, telling the board she had been brought up by an aunt who was now dead. Perhaps they would check, but she depended on there being so many people arriving and departing that checks would be minimal.

Remembering Ethel's hasty, last minute arrival into their railway carriage, and the way she had held back at each station, Kate and Rosie guessed she was avoiding someone. They had all spoken a little about their families, but Ethel had not been very forthcoming. She was running away from someone or something, rather than joining the Naafi out of a need to support the war effort. But who or what they couldn't guess.

They got on well but they hadn't known her long and weren't sure enough of her friendship to question her. 'Let's give it a few more weeks,' Kate suggested when she and Rosie discussed it. 'Then, if she hasn't mentioned it, we'll be bold and ask.'

'I agree. We might be able to help at some time, if we know.'

They had been on the camp for a couple of weeks, and when Ethel refused an invitation to go to the pictures with two of the RAF boys it seemed a good opportunity to bring up the subject of her wariness. Kate waited until she and Ethel were alone and asked quietly, 'Who are you running away from, Ethel?'

'Running away? Don't be soft.'

'Boyfriend? Someone you've upset?' Kate persisted. 'Come on, we're stuck here together and we have to be friends and trust each other. And Rosie and I might be able to help if we know the facts. Run away from a boyfriend, have you?'

'Hardly. In fact my boyfriend ran away from me,' she said bitterly. She was standing looking out of the canteen window, a duster in her hand. 'Rosie's coming.' She pointed through the window at the hurrying figure of Rosie, pushing the trolley she had taken to the hangars with the mid-morning drinks and snacks. Kate looked through the now clean, shiny windows and waited. Perhaps Ethel didn't want to discuss the problem in front of Rosie. But when Rosie came she talked to them both.

'My father is a foul-tempered bully. He's always fighting, threatening, getting his own way because he's known as a hard man,' she began.

'You mean he hits you?'

'Not badly, until earlier this year.' She paused, her mouth working nervously, obviously having difficulty relating the next sentence. 'My sister Glenys was sixteen years older than me. My brother Sid was fifteen years older. I was a mistake!'

'Your father took it out on you as if it was your fault?' Rosie coaxed.

'No, he seemed protective, but nothing more. I was pushed around a bit when he was drunk, but no, I had a good childhood really. Dad was gruff but never unkind. In fact he ignored me most of the time. Being so much younger than my brother and sister I was protected and loved. It was like having two sets of parents looking after me. Dad was away a lot, long hours driving the lorry, and he was in prison on occasions, for unruly behaviour of one sort or another, mostly fighting. They usually managed to keep me well out of the way when Dad was home and in one of his rages.

'When he was away there was only Mam, Glenys, Sid and me. No other family and few friends called. In fact, even when he was home he was rarely in the house. There was the garden where Mam and he worked for hours every day. When he wasn't driving or working outside, he was at the pub. That was my life and I never thought about the different lives other people led.' She paused and her two friends waited in silence for her to continue. 'Then ... then something made him really angry, he went wild, forbade me to see Wesley and drove him away. I didn't believe it at first but Wesley was so frightened by his violence on that awful day that he never came back. He left and joined the Naafi without a word. And soon after,' she paused again before saying the words that still seemed impossible to believe, 'my sister killed herself. From then on everything got much worse.'

The two friends muttered conventional words of sympathy and waited.

'It was the week of my birthday when it started. Something had happened that made Glenys kill herself rather than face it, and no one will tell me what it was. My father came home in a drunken state and attacked Mam and my brother and called me horrible names. Mam wouldn't go to hospital and refused to say who was responsible, although many guessed. Sid left without telling us where he was going and we haven't heard from him since. Dad was really out of his mind with rage. He dislocated my shoulder, throwing me against the wall, knocked Wesley almost senseless and beat my mother so I thought she was dead. Then I found my sister in that barn.'

'You found her?' Rosie gasped. 'Oh Ethel, you poor thing.'

'My father started watching every move I

made. I wasn't allowed to see Wesley Daniels any more though he and I were more or less engaged to be married. If I was seen talking to a boy, the boy was threatened and told to stay away from me. Thank goodness we needed the money and I was allowed to work. Apart from the café I wasn't allowed out except when Mam went with me, and Mam didn't want to leave the house. Dad met me from work whenever he could. I didn't know when, so I was too afraid to do anything except go straight home as fast as I could.'

'Your mother didn't stop him?' Disbelief showed in Rosie's wide blue eyes.

'I think she was afraid of upsetting my father even more.'

'Didn't you have any friends who would help you?'

'I thought I had Wesley. I was convinced that once he recovered from the beating my father gave him he'd be back to take me away, put everything right. He and I have been friends since we were about seven years old. I thought I could always rely on Wesley. But after that hiding from Dad he went away too. His mother relented and told me he had joined the Naafi and was serving on a ship but I don't know any more than that. He probably can't face me after running away like he did.'

'So you ran away and joined up and you're

still scared of being found by your father and taken home?'

'I'm never going back. I'd kill myself first, like Glenys. I want to know what went wrong, what turned our home into such a battlefield, but I'm not curious enough to ever go back. I don't know where I'll go on my weekends off, but it won't be anywhere near my family.'

'My Nan'll have you, don't worry about that,' Rosie told her fervently.

'Don't stay in hiding, Ethel. Come to the pictures. You can't let him ruin your life. If we see your father we'll protect you,' Kate said.

Ethel laughed. 'You'd run if he said boo! He's over six feet tall and his red hair denotes his temper. Red hair and temper don't always go together but in my father's case they do, believe me.'

'Oliver Hardy and Stan Laurel are on at the pictures,' Kate coaxed.

'Nan sent me some home-made coconut ice...' Rosie added enticingly. Food was always the deciding factor, and they went.

There was a lorry departing when they left the guard house, having declared their intentions; it waited for them around the corner of the lane and gave them a lift.

It was the first of many such outings as Ethel's confidence grew. They began to know the young airmen, accepted dates, and

78

watched as the planes took off, then with beating hearts counted those returning, dreading the homecomers being fewer than those who had left.

The evenings in the canteen were enjoyable. There was a piano and always someone who could play. Duggie came when he was free and would help a still-shy Rosie to clear the tables and stack the dishes near the sink.

Ethel sometimes stood and watched the young men and wondered how they could appear so carefree when at any moment they could be called to climb into their aircraft and set out to take part in a battle, fight for their lives.

For all three girls the worst time of their day was the early morning. Dressing in the tent, where the heater had gone cold during the night and with not enough time to justify relighting it, washing in cold water and having to wait for that first cup of tea. They took it in turns to get up earlier to walk through the darkness and open the canteen to get the fire lit and the heaters on.

It was an unpleasant start to the day, that solitary walk across two fields, pushing their way through dripping hedges and across grass that was white, stiff and crackling with frost. The camouflaged building offered no light, no reminder that there were people near. The wait for the wood, then the coal, to slowly catch light, warming stiff, painful hands, and the long wait for the kettle to boil for that first cuppa were a constant nightmare. The girls used water from the bad-tempered boiler even though they were not supposed to. Its occasional blow-back, rattling the cups on the shelves, had Walter or one or two light sleepers coming in to complain, with a cup of tea offered to them as consolation.

Another tedious job was filling the boiler and the tea-urn, ladling it in and out with a heavy saucepan. Rosie, being smaller than the others, found it very difficult and had to climb a chair. She was always grateful when one of the lads came to help her. Duggie hadn't been around for a few days and she wondered if he had been transferred to another airfield.

One morning when it was her turn to light up, it was frighteningly dark, not a glimmer of light from anywhere, no moon, the horizon not yet showing. It was unnervingly still, mist draping the hedges like curtains that refused to open, and Rosie had a creepy sensation that she was being followed.

She looked around her but her eyes were unable to pierce the gloom, and the torch she carried, with its thin beam, simply emphasized the darkness. Then near the hedge, a few feet away, she was alarmed to see a white shape moving slowly as she went into the second field. It was the size of a football and was floating about five feet from the ground. Trying not to be afraid, she continued walking. The whiteness was remarkable and she couldn't think what it could be.

Pushing through the second hedge, she looked around but it had disappeared. She ran the last few yards and locked herself inside the canteen building with a sigh of relief. She saw Walter later that morning and told him about her experience. If she expected sympathy and a promise to investigate she was disappointed. He laughed and told her to take more water with it and stop wasting his time.

Later that day a young man came in for the lunchtime break. Removing a balaclava from his head to reveal a white bandage, he said, 'Sorry if I frightened you, Rosie. I often go out early and watch the day break.' It was Duggie.

'What have you done?' Rosie asked, at once concerned.

Duggie refused to explain, insisting he had been bitten by a dog.

'A dog, on your head?'

'A very tall dog!' he laughed.

'Why didn't you call me, say something?' Rosie asked.

'I wanted to but I thought it might frighten you even more.' He gave a twisted grin and added, 'I could see by the way you were bent forward and taking great scuttling strides that I'd frightened you.'

'Nonsense,' Rosie grinned. 'I just couldn't wait to get started on yesterday's cold ashes!'

She was blushing furiously as he smiled at her and wondered why she had been able to answer to him so freely. She usually avoided conversations. 'It must have been because he's very kind,' she told Kate and Ethel later.

'Interesting,' said Kate with one of her broad winks at Ethel.

Duggie appeared twice more on her early mornings, and on each occasion he walked with her and followed her into the canteen, lit the fire for her and dealt with the cantankerous water heater. Once he gave her a bar of chocolate and, starving as she always was, she kept it all day before sharing it with her friends. She had never received a gift from a man before and she marvelled at it, kept the fact that Duggie had given it to her as a secret to enjoy. They chatted easily as they worked, and she learned that he was the youngest in his family, with three older sisters.

As the time for the bandage to be removed drew nearer she knew that it would also mean he would have to return to his place in the cockpit of one of the ferocious little Spitfires and have to get up there and protect the airfield against enemy bombers. That thought frightened her as no other had. Reading about the war in newspapers and even seeing it on newsreels at the pictures was frightening. But the real thing, involving people you knew, liked and cared for, was quite different.

There were air raids on most nights but so far the airfield hadn't been bombed. The planes were on their way to other targets. Each time the fighter planes took off as the enemy bombers headed towards them, to defend the airfield and also to avoid the bombers catching them on the ground – an easy target.

The area around the town had suffered casualties though, and during their time off they were upset to witness the scenes as people carried what they could from damaged houses, and areas were fenced off and notices were placed warning of buildings in imminent danger of collapse. There was an air raid once as they were heading for their bus and they had to go down a shelter with the rest of the shoppers.

When they emerged they were distressed to see stretchers being carried across rubble-strewn areas that had once been neat and orderly streets. Men were using anything they could find, and in many cases their bare hands, to search the rubble for survivors. A dog wandered around barking occasionally, searching for his home and family. A cat sat on a wall washing itself, as though to say life goes on and we mustn't let things slide.

Having overcome their tiredness and settled into the routine of their work, the three girls enjoyed their trips into town. It wasn't a daily treat as their wages were too low for such extravagance. Rosie and Kate sometimes received postal orders from home, and Rosie's Nan kept them supplied with food parcels on a regular basis. Kate occasionally treated them to afternoon tea when she had extra cash. She liked dressing up and sitting in a café, looking at the airmen, soldiers and sailors passing by. She enjoyed flirting, but during their visits to town never left them to go out with one of her conquests. They always went back to camp together. Ethel and the shy Rosie considered her a good, reliable friend. She frequently complained abut her lack of money but was generous with her friends when her purse was full.

When their first weekend leave came, Ethel went home with Rosie. Mrs Dreen welcomed her and enjoyed spoiling the two girls with breakfast in bed and silly luxuries, like Christmas crackers she had saved for a special occasion and 'lucky dip' parcels containing small gifts of a hand-made handkerchief and a knitted scarf each.

A letter came while they were there. Rosie picked it up off the mat and handed it to her nan after looking curiously at the handwriting. Mrs Dreen hastily pushed it out of sight. 'Someone I was at school with,' she explained vaguely.

Ethel imagined having a letter and tried not to think of her own home with its air of fear and anxiety. She enjoyed her days with Rosie but a part of her grieved for the place she called home. In spite of all the problems, she wanted to see her family. She had no news of her brother and there was no way she could receive any.

They went back to camp with a basket of goodies to share with Kate. And when they shared their news of their first weekend home, Ethel was enthusiastic in her descriptions of Mrs Dreen's kindness.

Money was far from plentiful for any of the girls. Their wages, which were little more than a pound with a few shillings more for Ethel as cook, had to provide for their entertainment and travel during their days off as well as items of clothing. The uniform supplied only included two blouses, a skirt and a jacket, plus the blue overalls they wore while at work. Everything else they had to find for themselves. Ethel had no generous parents to help and for her money was difficult to manage.

She never complained about being hard-up. She didn't smoke but bought her allocation of cigarettes and gave them one at a time to airmen who were without any. She never wrote letters and she went out only when persuaded by Kate or Rosie to go into town to see a film or have tea in a café; she was still nervous of being found.

Rosie spent money on postage stamps, writing home to Nan and to many of her friends. She went to the town whenever Kate went, and one afternoon was persuaded to buy a lipstick which she put on amid much hilarity by pursing her lips, while Kate was demonstrating the better way. By the time she had blotted it and rubbed it in there was little to be seen.

Regarding money, Kate was different. She was always broke. She wrote several letters each week to her parents and friends, one each Monday pleaded for her parents to give her a ten bob note for the weekend, which they often did. Whenever there was news of a shop receiving supplies of make-up or other toiletries, she dashed into town, usually scrounging a lift from the willing airmen, and bought all she could. Make-up, soap, perfume, curling lotion, plus a secret formula of bleach for her hair, which she did herself. No matter how late they were getting into bed, she never failed to remove her make-up, cream her face and hands and roll up her hair in curlers ready for the following day.

Her looks were her absolute priority and from the pleasure given to the men by her cheerful, saucy attitude towards them, the dedication and expense were justified. Her cheerful face was a tonic to the men on the camp, her flirting a relief from the tragedies unfolding all around them.

Ethel neither received nor wrote letters. She considered writing to Wesley at his home address but the risk of her parents learning of her whereabouts stayed her hand. Whenever new personnel arrived at the camp she questioned them, asking if any of them had met Wesley Daniels, but so far she had not been lucky. Nor was there a simple way for him to find her.

It was easy to get to know some of the young men on the station. Coming in for snacks and for the small items such as combs, hair cream, shaving soap, pens, ink, writing paper and all the other necessities, or just sitting to chat to others during the evenings, their faces became familiar. Some flirted, others just wanted to talk about their families, and the three girls became adept at saying the right thing as they admired photographs of loved ones. Very few grumbled or related their fears, although there were a few who had received 'Dear John' letters from girls they had hoped to return to one day. These the girls comforted, listening to their grieved stories and helping them to accept what they couldn't change.

Duggie, still wearing his white bandage, came often to talk to Rosie, who still blushed when she saw him, sometimes hiding when her embarrassment became acute. He soon learnt the routine and when it was Rosie's turn to light the dreaded boiler and fill the urn he was often there to give a hand.

Kate had many dates, but with only one evening off each week, it was difficult to fit them all in, so most were refused. She didn't want to 'get serious' she told Ethel. 'I just want to have a bit of fun and make sure the boys do too. When I marry it'll be for love but he'll have to be rich too!'

Rosie refused dates to the few who invited her. She was too inexperienced, and avoided situations she felt unable to manage. The only man she spent time talking to was Duggie and it was some time before she realized he asked more questions about Ethel than herself. She felt a slight disappointment but soon shrugged it aside. Who wouldn't prefer the confident, outgoing Ethel to someone like herself?

Ethel had plenty of invitations too but she refused them all, although she was getting braver as days passed without a sign of her father. Perhaps she would be safe here after all. She began going out more. Sometimes with one of the girls, occasionally with an airman but only as part of a group, never as a couple.

One day she left the camp alone after the lunchtime shift and walked to the bus stop.

It was the first time she had done this and she felt vulnerable. A lorry slowed as the driver recognized her and offered her a lift. She hesitated, then, as she saw the bus approaching she thanked them and said she was meeting a friend on the bus.

'Why did I do that?' she asked Rosie when she got back to camp. 'They were only being friendly.'

'You're still thinking about your family, I expect,' Rosie surmised. 'Until you find out the reason for their behaviour you won't be free of fear.'

'It isn't that I presume every man is going to be violent like my father.'

'Not violent, necessarily. It could be because your father forbade you to talk to any male, clearly suspicious of their ... non-violent intentions?' she grinned cheekily, her blue eyes wide.

'I can't be that stupid, can I?' Ethel frowned.

'Only one way to find out. Next time accept and thank them with a smile,' Rosie advised.

When she next went into town, determined to take Rosie's advice, her resolve was wasted. The bus came before there was any sign of a vehicle leaving the camp. It was on the way home that she was offered a lift. Losing her nerve in a way she couldn't explain, and which made her angry with herself, she thanked them and shook her head.

There had been an air raid which she guessed might have delayed the bus, and as she watched the lorry disappear she wished she hadn't been so foolish. She tapped her cold feet impatiently, hugged her shoulders for warmth. Where was the bus? After ten minutes she knew it wasn't coming and, aware she would be late for her shift, she began to walk. Rain began, slowly at first, then in an increasing downpour that threatened to soak her to her skin. The lorry had stopped somewhere and it overtook her again just outside the town. The driver slowed and repeated his offer of a lift. Without thinking she shook her head and waved them on. There was a corner not far off and as the lorry slowed to take it a man jumped off the back and waited for her.

'I know a short cut,' he said after introducing himself as Dave. 'You'll be late on shift if you take the road.'

He led her along the road then cut through a hedge and began to walk at the side of a ploughed field. Once out of sight of the road, he put an arm around her and tried to kiss her. His face was rough and his breath was tainted. She pushed him away and he pleaded, then grew angry.

'Ice maiden they called you. Did you know that, Miss Frosty Ethel Twomey? There's bets on for who'll melt you, but I don't think

I'll bother to try,' he shouted as she hurried away from him, across the field in the direction of the camp.

What is the matter with me? she asked herself as she walked across fields of soggy, beaten-down grass. Her feet were so cold she couldn't feel them. Her uniform skirt was already soaked and sticking to her thighs at every step. Kate managed to stay friends with the boys who tried to go further than she wanted. She had the skill to deal with these incidents in a friendly way. Even Rosie managed to keep her dignity and smile her way out of embarrassing teasing and the occasional stolen kiss. Why did she have to lose her temper and make a fool of herself? It would probably have been nothing more than a kiss, a hand to hold, a moment's fun. Now she had added to her reputation as an ice maiden. She thought of her father and blamed him for her inadequacy with men. Blaming him wouldn't help her now. She had to deal with it, face it and overcome her stupid attitude or she was in for a miserable war.

The walk was longer than she had imagined, as twice her progress was restricted by barbed wire and she had to make a detour. Her legs and feet were painful and stiff with the cold, her forehead was hurting with the icy wind that blew the rain against her face, tormented her and tangled her hair. Discomfort and anger at her stupidity made her brown eyes look heavy against the paleness of her skin.

Without waiting for explanations, Rosie ran a bath, the maximum five inches. It was not enough to thoroughly warm her, the water was tepid, the bottom of the bath never really warming up. Walter heard the geyser roaring and the water running as he passed the window and shouted in complaint. 'This isn't the time for bathing. Don't you know—'

'—there's a war on,' the others finished for him.

They were still sleeping in the tent, which they had made more comfortable by the addition of a second heater and more blankets, when December came. By this time they were well in control of the job and each girl had settled to do the jobs they did best. So it was a surprise when Walter Phillips came in one day to warn them not to be sloppy and to make sure everything was in good order.

'What d'you mean?' Ethel demanded. 'What's wrong with the way we do things?'

'It's good but it's got to be better because the Area Manager's on his way.'

The three girls looked at each other and groaned.

'No afternoon off then,' Kate said.

'At least we can ask about getting out of

that damned tent,' Ethel added. 'It's winter and soon we'll have snow and the tent will be like an igloo. Can you imagine tunnelling out through six feet of snow one morning?'

'We'd better ask Walter for a compass!' Rosie joked.

The arrival of Albert Pugh was an anti-climax. Instead of the dragon roaring complaints, he walked in unannounced and didn't introduce himself, just called them outside to see the arrival of their new accommodation. A small building built of arched corrugated iron was being lowered from the back of a lorry to be placed on the ground. It was in sections and, before the afternoon was over, the team of engineers had it erected and complete with beds, lockers and a stove.

No one seemed to be in charge, the group of men all worked together, each doing what was necessary to get the job done. Albert Pugh was simply one of the gang, serious and hardworking.

'Blimey, all this done and no foreman with a whistle!' Kate teased. 'There must be a war on!'

'I bet all this is getting done in a rush so the visiting Area Manager doesn't come here and find us poor helpless girls sleeping in a tent,' Ethel said loudly.

'I am the Area Manager,' the serious-looking individual who had been working all afternoon told them. 'And I have been trying since before you arrived to get this hut delivered.'

'Thanks,' the girls muttered.

'Is it bomb-proof?' asked Ethel with a grin.

'You'll go into the slit trench wearing your tin helmets as before,' he replied.

'No sense of humour,' whispered Kate sadly.

Albert Pugh surprised them even more the following morning by being at the canteen before them, having the fire in the range blazing merrily and a kettle boiling for their cups of tea. When Ethel filled the trolley and set off for the hangars with tea for the engineers and ground staff, he went with her.

'Is there anything you want to report?' he asked.

'Not now we have somewhere warm to sleep and to spread our possessions.'

'I'm really sorry about the tent. These buildings are slow to come and they're allocated according to need.'

'That puts us in our place then, doesn't it?' she retorted.

'You should have been allotted extra pay, hard-living allowance. I'll see if I can claim back pay for you.'

She glanced at him, his face shadowed in the gloom of the early morning. He looked sad and she at once apologized.

'Sorry, I'm sure you're doing your best.'

'He was in Norway,' one of the men told her later.

'During the evacuation?'

'They were trying to repulse the Germans but were attacked while they were still unprepared.'

'They were overrun?'

The man nodded his dark head. 'Several of the Naafi staff including his two best friends were injured. Naafi men stood beside the soldiers and helped fight their way through as they got away in front of the German invasion. He saw much of the fighting, some terrible deaths, and he's finding it hard to forget.'

Ethel saw Albert later and mentioned the tragedy of Norway, believing that it was better to talk about things rather than keep them burning away inside.

'Don't forget,' she said. 'Why should you forget? Just make sure you remember the good times as well as the tragedy at the end.'

He told her that one of the men had been blown up as he ran in search of bread, only yards from where he himself had been standing. Ethel listened, saying very little, just trying to make him believe she understood.

'It should have been me,' he said more than once.

She spent several hours talking to the sad, subdued man who seemed to carry such a heavy burden. She even told him about Wesley and the death of her sister, managing to extract from him the fact that he had no girlfriend. She wondered afterwards why it had been important. He was comforting, telling her to let go of the past, think positively about the future. 'That's especially important now,' he reminded her. 'To look back just distorts everything. We have to go on, accepting what happens and believing that the future will be good. Forget who you used to be, and the problems that person had to face. Think of the woman you are now, not the same, I'm sure. You'd deal with those problems differently now, wouldn't you?'

She had to agree about that. She was stronger, better able to cope. Although thoughts of her father in one of his rages still made her quiver.

After a week Albert left and Ethel was sorry. She was beginning to think that if anyone could make her forget the misery of her home life, he was the one to do it. As well as sadness there was kindness in his face and his thoughtfulness had already been revealed to them. He had made sure their supply of dry kindling was topped up and had helped move the heavy tables when they were giving the place their weekly extra clean, tackling the corners and getting into awkward places with scrubbing brushes.

Talking to Albert had helped her to open

up to others and she began to accept more invitations to go to the weekly concerts and dances with Kate and Rosie. The weekly dances were popular – even those who couldn't dance enjoyed the cheerful atmosphere. On duty or not, they all helped set up the counter ready for when the men came back. They would be selling snacks and tea and coffee, and, with everything ready, they felt able to spend an hour or two at the concert or dance. Until one day when they had arranged to go to the concert with Duggie – now minus the head bandage – and a couple of his friends. Walter arrived and told them firmly that the concerts were not for them.

'You have to get the canteen ready for when it's over,' he said emphatically.

'We've done all that, you miserable worm,' Ethel protested.

'There's always cleaning to do. The cupboards could do with a scrub. I noticed spilt sugar – that will encourage mice. Cleanliness is our priority.' The girls looked at the spotlessly clean shelves, the shining glasses and china and the well-scrubbed tables and floors, then each with one hand on a hip they looked at him with tightened lips.

'And while I'm here,' he went on, avoiding their eyes, 'I might remind you that you aren't getting the right number of cakes for the ingredients you're given. There's too much margarine going on the sandwiches too. We are rationed, remember! And we have to make a profit. It goes back into the fund for more facilities for the armed forces. You aren't here for fun!'

'I'm surprised he knows the word,' muttered Kate.

While laughter echoed across the field from the Friday night concert, Walter gave instructions.

'Flat baking tins lined with pastry, mixed fruit soaked overnight and spread over it evenly. You'll cut it into thirty-two pieces and sell it at twopence a slice. Right?'

'Right, Walter, we'll do that first thing tomorrow.'

'You'll do it now. The fruit has to soak overnight, you aren't deaf as well as lazy, are you?'

'What?' Ethel said with a look of gormless innocence.

'I'm going into town and I want the pastry made and the fruit in soak when I get back at ten thirty, right?'

'There's no way it'll take three of us to do that,' Rosie said. 'I'll do it. Go and enjoy the rest of the concert and tell me all about it later.'

It was that evening Ethel began to get to know Duggie. He had kept seats for the three girls but as the time approached for the curtains to open, he'd had to give them up. He stood against the wall still hoping that the girls would appear. As the curtains opened jerkily on the first singing group, he sat near the end of a row and settled to watch the performance.

There were still a few seats available and Kate and Ethel split up, promising to meet afterwards to walk back to their new hut together. Ethel found herself sitting next to Duggie. In her determination to live down her nickname of ice maiden, knowing he was a friend of Rosie, she talked to him as though he were a friend. They commented on the acts and she offered him one of the cigarettes she habitually carried.

He took one and offered to light hers. She explained that she didn't smoke, but kept some for when the airmen were broke and in need of one.

At the end of the evening, he asked her to meet him the following week at the dance.

'I don't think I can.' Excuses were buzzing around in her head. What would Rosie think?

'Please. I don't know a soul here, and,' he teased, 'I miss my sisters something chronic.'

'What about Rosie?' she asked. 'I thought you and she were friends.'

'We are. I help her when I can. But I don't feel anything more than friendship, whereas with you that could easily change...'

She thought of Wesley and hesitated, shook her head, but then changed her mind. A dance – learning the steps so familiar to the other girls – would be fun, and her life had certainly lacked fun.

Wesley had left her, abandoned her to a violent father who had almost pulled her arm out of its socket, and a mother who was too weak to help her. Without an explanation he had walked away, leaving her with a father whose heart was inexplicably filled with hatred.

Then the momentary resentment faded. She told herself she loved Wesley and he loved her. There were so many unexplained things connected with her sister's death. Wesley's disappearance was only one of them. She hadn't heard from Sid up to the time she had left home. There was so much she didn't understand. Albert had advised her to put aside the past but how could she until she knew all that had happened? There would be a good reason for Wesley leaving her without a word. She had to trust him. He would explain when they met. There was no harm in meeting Duggie and she would tell Wesley all about him.

'Please come,' Duggie pleaded. 'It's only a dance.'

'I can't dance.'

'I'll teach you.'

'As long as Walter Phillips isn't around I'll try,' she promised, knowing it was unlikely. 'But I'll have to be like Cinderella and run away before the end. We have to be ready for customers who come for late-night snacks. Hungry lot, you airmen.'

Over the following days she worried about the dance. She didn't want to go. Her enforced new courage was leaving her. She couldn't dance and no amount of confidence would make that sorry fact go away. She would be unsure of herself, and make a fool of herself, embarrass Duggie. Going to the dance with Rosie and Kate was one thing. Watching others, enjoying the atmosphere and the music. It was different altogether to go with Duggie. It was a proper date and Wesley wouldn't like it. And there was the need to tell Rosie, and that was something she didn't want to do. She couldn't go, she wouldn't go, but what excuse could she invent?

During an afternoon off when the weather was dry and pleasantly sunny, the three girls went into the fields and gathered holly and ivy and decorated the canteen as well as they could in preparation for Christmas. On another day, they went into town and bought Christmas cards. For Ethel the occasions were melancholy. Apart from Kate's parents and Rosie's Nan, she had no one to whom she could send a card.

Christmas had never been fun in the Twomey household and the only happy memories were of visits to the Baileys' farm to see

101

the cheerful, overheated room with its great log fire and the decorative displays taken from the hedges. And to admire the tree, under which there were always gifts for herself and Glenys and Sid.

New arrivals came fairly frequently as the losses of both men and machines meant the need for replacements. One of the first things the new recruits suffered was a medical examination and batch of injections, and sometimes they reacted badly. The girls had their first experience of this the night before the dance. That evening, a line of young men stood in front of the bar, flirting and making jokes, when without warning, as Ethel began to hand them their food, one disappeared. Then another. She jumped up and looked over the bar and saw they had fallen to the floor in a faint. Before Ethel could get around to see what was wrong, another had keeled over. Some of the 'veterans', who were all of twenty-two years old, explained to them that the injections they had all been given were beginning to take effect.

The stricken airmen were helped to chairs, heads on folded arms resting on tables, hushing their apologies, trying to make them less embarrassed. Duggie stayed for a while and, in a lull, Ethel said, 'Better forget the dance tomorrow night, you'll need to look after this lot.' She was relieved. There was now no need to explain to Rosie she was going on a date with her friend Duggie.

'Nonsense, I've been looking forward to it for days,' he said, rubbing a finger slowly down her cheek and staring into her eyes in a way that made her body respond in an alarming manner.

She told Rosie about her date but not who she was going to meet.

Albert came on a brief visit to check the stock and inspect the books. She was about to climb a ladder to replace a bulb and he took it from her and did the job for her. Then he relieved one of the girls of the job of moving heavy tables to wash the floor, promising to return to put them back in their places.

'Decent bloke,' she overheard one of the other assistants remark. 'Always willing to muck in, do more than he's paid for.'

The dance was held in a rather primitive hall that was in serious need of repair. There was no band that night, only a young pianist who played without music, competently dealing with all requests, sometimes singing as well. The hall was hot and crowded, the people more than the heaters contributing to the heat, and the smiles on the young faces reflecting their usual determination to have fun.

Air raids were always a regular part of their nights. It was unusual not to be woken two or three times and have to leave their beds and make their way outside, where the planes had already taken off and were going into the attack. They donned their heavy coats and tin helmets and dropped down into a slit trench and watched the air battles taking place. It was late December, as German bombers set fire to London with parachute mines followed by hundreds of incendiaries, that the first bombs fell on the airfield.

The screaming of engines, the rattle of anti-aircraft guns and the occasional crunch of bombs exploding filled the night, and searchlights lit the scene to help the gunners. Outside, with no escape from the noise and the terrifying battle taking place above them, the girls crouched in the slit trench but were unable to resist looking up into the dark skies. A voice frequently told them to 'Keep yer heads down unless you want shrapnel ruining yer lovely faces, girls.' When the raiders were overhead and earth erupted in huge moving mountains around them, they didn't need telling. They felt as vulnerable as the men in the planes once incendiaries had fallen to light the field like day. The raid was more alarming now they knew many of the pilots in the air.

A stick of bombs fell, straddling the buildings, landing either side of the terrified girls. The sound of engines filled their ears, and they covered them in a futile attempt to deaden the sounds. The flames of several fires lit the airfield, and the madness went on and on, then seemed to die down a little. They cautiously removed their hands from their ears and heard footsteps running towards them. There was a lull as planes moved away from their vicinity. Then, as they heard the guttural sound of a plane increasing its speed, coming down and down, filling their heads with terrifying noise, to which was added the unmistakable squeal of a falling bomb, a flying figure landed on top of them just as the second of another stick of bombs fell.

'What's that?' Rosie's quivering voice asked. 'Ethel, help me, I think there's a body landed on top of us.'

'Hello, ladies, what a wonderful place for an unscheduled landing. I'm George Morgan. Who are you?'

Slowly things became quiet as the flames flickered and died and the planes disappeared from the skies. Stiffly, Rosie, Ethel and a tearful Kate emerged from the filth of the earth and rubble with which they had been half buried. The young man who had arrived so unexpectedly and who Rosie had first thought to be a dead body, stood up and helped them out of the trench. Not waiting for explanations, the three girls hurried to the canteen and began making a brew. The trolley was quickly stocked, and the canteen filled up while the newly arrived George Morgan helped Rosie manoeuvre the trolley between bombed buildings and piles of rubble as she went around the airfield providing food and drink to the men sorting out the chaos of the raid.

Teams of men, each man knowing exactly what was expected of him, swung into action. Rosie and George Morgan went from group to group with reviving cups of tea and snacks. No money changed hands, this was an emergency – 'and if that Walter Phillips complains, I'll chuck him down one of the craters,' Rosie said.

Rosie had never seen a dead person, and the sights and sounds from the wounded, and the unnerving stillness of the bodies from which life had gone, terrified her at first. The cries of the trapped and the wounded, and the low groans of the badly injured were something she knew she would never forget.

Bundles of what at first looked like carelessly abandoned clothing revealed themselves to be people, their positions, the angle of head and limbs, leaving her in no doubt that they were dead. She was afraid to pass the first victim they met, lying in a place where they had to step over him, manoeuvring the trolley around his inert form. It was as though turning her back on him and walking away was disrespectful as well as bringing inexplicable fear. She was shaking. Her legs threatened to let her down. When she spoke her voice was unrecognizable. Her thoughts were in turmoil. She should be helping these people but didn't know what to do.

What was she doing here? She had never wanted so much to wake up and find it had all been a nightmare and to see Nan waiting to soothe away her fears.

It was George Morgan who reminded her firmly but with kindness that the sad victims were friends and were no more to be feared than they had been the hour before.

'We should be helping them,' she sobbed.

'We are. We're doing what we do best. Let the medics help them and we'll help the medics.'

Jokes and encouraging remarks from George Morgan helped as the large number of injured and dead became apparent, as did his strength when the trolley got stuck. He wasn't tall but surprisingly strong, and Rosie was grateful for his assistance. He would stop sometimes to help a group of men to move an obstacle, and return to the trolley to deliver more food and drinks. They were kept so busy there wasn't time for her to feel shy.

They ran back and forward to the canteen replenishing the urn and the food, while others made sandwiches and even baked a few scones to help the dwindling supplies.

George Morgan introduced himself properly as morning broke after the disasters of the night.

'George Morgan, ground crew,' he said offering a hand.

'George, welcome. You're a hero.'

George shook his head. 'I'm no hero,' he said, his Welsh accent strong. 'It's them boys have that title.' They all looked up into the skies and wondered fearfully how many of their boys would fail to return.

Four

While the girls served the men, the clearing up after the bombing raid went on – the priority as always was the landing strips. As dawn broke on a cold, clear morning, fires still burned, showing the devastation of the night. The Spitfires had landed at other airfields and it was late evening before they were able to return. Ethel found herself wondering about Duggie, who had now returned to his duties and had been one of the pilots attacking the German aircraft throughout the raid.

She stood beside Rosie as the planes landed and saw with relief that she pretended was for Rosie, that Duggie's plane was among those safely returned. There had been losses, but already they had learnt not to comment on the numbers. In a Spitfire station as on all the others, grieving was a brief and very personal affair, there was no looking back, no time to share regrets or even dwell on the loss of good friends. Too much thinking about the dead could result in a lack of concentration and that could lead to more tragedy. The men had to push grief aside as firmly as they dealt with their fear; the fight went on.

Walter tried to comfort Ethel and Kate as they silently grieved for those who were missing, putting an arm around each of them and allowing his hands to wander. Ethel pushed him away angrily and Kate shouted loudly so that anyone near was aware of what was happening. Furiously, Walter left them, pushing Rosie out of his way as he went.

'Why won't he take no for an answer!' Kate shouted.

'I think we've made an enemy there,' Rosie said. 'I hope he doesn't make things difficult for us.'

'How can he? He isn't that important!' Ethel replied.

Replacement crews came with alarming regularity, taking the places of men who had lost their lives in the battles overhead or on the ground. Whenever there was a group of new faces, Ethel asked them if they had seen Wesley Daniels. She knew it was useless. The last she had heard of him she had been told he was serving on a ship not an airfield. She asked anyway.

At the end of January 1941, Ethel and Duggie were in the canteen after the others had gone. She spoke to Duggie about Wesley. 'I sometimes feel closer to him,' she told him. 'Like now, I imagine him sitting somewhere unfamiliar and thinking about me.'

Duggie smiled and told her she could be right. 'Thoughts travel without the use of trains and buses,' he smiled. 'Specially when there's strong affection holding people together. Affection or love,' he added, leaning over and kissing her, staying close, staring into her eyes. 'I take thoughts of you with me every time I take off, Ethel. I imagine you sitting beside me, my good luck charm, keeping me safe.' His voice was low, his lips so close and so tempting. Just inches between them. She leaned towards him and they kissed, this time a slow loving kiss, reminding her of her need to belong somewhere, to someone, a need to drive away the loneliness, at least for a while.

They were alone in the canteen. Outside it was cold with a few small, hard flakes of snow falling on to the frost-bound earth. There was only one light, a small lamp over the part of the bar that, after closing, Ethel used as a desk. Duggie moved closer and held her and she needed the warmth of another human being so badly she didn't resist as his kisses grew more urgent. She felt herself succumbing to the desire that filled her body and her mind, she wanted so much to belong, to be loved. Then a vision of her father startled her and she pulled away. This was what he had warned her about.

'It'll be all right, nothing will happen,' Duggie urged, kissing her, touching her secret places. 'I know what to do, you'll be safe with me. Trust me.'

Then she was overwhelmed with love for him, but feelings she had never imagined slowly subsided, joy and guilt battling within her. This was what her father had meant when he was convinced she would 'go bad'. Had he recognized something in her that told him she would be weak? She knew that next time it would be harder to refuse.

She stayed outside for another hour before she dared to go back to join Kate and Rosie in case, like her father, they would know how weak she was. Surely it would show in her eyes? She couldn't possibly look the same after such a wonderful awakening.

'Where's she been?' Kate whispered as Ethel greeted them very hurriedly before scuttling into the bathroom. 'Looks interesting.'

'Only cashing up,' the innocent Rosie frowned.

Kate shook her head. 'From the look on her face it was something far more than that. I wonder if she'll tell us?'

Ethel said nothing, just hid herself behind a book until the lights went out. When she slept she dreamed not of Wesley, whose image was fading from her mind, but of Duggie. Sweet dreams without a thought of an angry face, or a moment of guilt.

Wesley Daniels was fighting his own war, far from home and with only a lone photograph of Ethel for consolation. He heaved himself out of his hammock, folded it neatly away and stood on the deck, feeling through his feet the vibrations of the engines below him as they idled in preparation for departure. It was three a.m. on that cold miserable January morning and as he reached the small room where food and drinks were prepared for the ship's company he saw that once again he was the first of the unpopular four o'clock shift to arrive.

There was only a slight uneasiness in his stomach as the ship slipped her moorings and moved slowly out of the harbour. Once outside the protecting arms of the harbour walls a stiff breeze hit her and she shook slightly. Wesley took the stance that would hold him steady and began to prepare tea and food for the watch who would leave their positions at four a.m.

As always he worked in silence, ignoring the chatter of the other men with their stories about girls they had met and pretended to love while on shore leave. His love was Ethel Twomey and he had let her down. He had walked away and left her to her father's anger, beaten and bruised by the man who had lashed out at his daughter and wife, and who had punched and kicked him until he was hardly conscious when he had tried to intervene. He should have stayed, made Ethel and her mother come away from the man, but to his eternal shame and humiliation, he had made his escape and left them. He had called the police, but hadn't gone back. He told himself the reason had been fear of worse reprisals on Ethel and her mother. But, if he were honest, hadn't he really been afraid for himself?

Dai Twomey was notorious and had regular appearances in court for causing an affray and for fighting. He had served two prison sentences, one for grievous bodily harm which had run close to being attempted murder. He was a gigantic and dangerous bully and Wesley was no match for him at eighteen years old and weighing little more than nine stone. How could he have stopped him? He only knew that he would never forgive himself for not trying.

The ship steamed through the darkness of the early morning, making its way to the convoy with which it would travel for the next few days. Wesley tried not to think of the U-boats waiting for them below, and the German airforce above, both determined to send every British ship to the bottom of the sea. He was a coward and his strongest fear was failing the other members of the ship's company when they met trouble, as they certainly would. Sooner rather than later.

When the men had eaten their fill and settled in the mess room for an hour of relaxation before sleep, Wesley told the other men on duty with him that they could go for a smoke. Alone with his melancholy thoughts he began the cleaning and restacking that was more important on a ship than on a shore base. A storm or an attack could mean untensils flying about and causing unnecessary injuries if they weren't firmly fixed in their places. He worked fast but efficiently, taking no short cuts, doing as thorough a job as was possible, in fact far more than was necessary, treating himself harshly, punishing himself for his failures. Always these days he played two roles, accuser and accused, victim and villain.

George Morgan who had landed so unceremoniously on Rosie in the trench, was a Welshman. Small, dark, fast moving and efficient. His brown hair was always falling across his deep brown eyes, half disguising their merriment. Always cheerful, he soon became popular with the men and the Naafi girls as he was so full of energy and always willing to help. He was not tall, at five foot five, and, looking about four years younger than his nineteen years, he quickly earned the name of 'Baba' Morgan, reduced to Baba. He didn't mind, believing that openly used nicknames were given only to the most popular people.

As soon as things had calmed down after the raid, he was deeply apologetic for his dangerous arrival, and explained that he'd thought the slit trench was empty. To make up for his gaffe, he helped them with some of their heavy work during his free time. From the moment they untangled themselves and introductions were made, Kate and Rosie could see he was attracted to Ethel.

Kate could also see that shy little Rosie had been bowled over by him. She clearly thought him the most wonderful person she had ever met. It was painful for the confident Kate to see the way Rosie blushed, stuttered and, whenever possible, avoided Baba when he came into the canteen.

She knew Rosie wanted to talk to him very much, but her shyness prevented her from trying. She understood Rosie's conviction that she would look and feel unworldly and innocent. Innocent is not how a young woman wishes to appear to a man like Baba. Better to do as she, Kate, did, and convey a confidence that was not, in fact, backed up by experience, something the guileless Rosie could never do.

Concert parties came to the camp sometimes to entertain them. Many, including well-known entertainers, gave their time to help entertain the forces. The group would arrive with their van or a lorry which contained all they needed to put on a show. Lights, curtains and costumes plus a few pieces of scenery which would be painted and repainted to suit whatever they planned to perform.

On other occasions an impromptu concert was presented, with men and women on the station doing whatever they could to add variety to the evening. Unrehearsed, depending on one or two people able to play the piano or, failing that, accompany the acts with a mouth organ – usually the only other instrument available – they sang the popular songs of the day. Some even ventured into comedy or magic acts, laughter at their failures kindly meant, amicably received, and adding to the fun.

Hearing Kate and Ethel singing one evening as they finished cleaning the canteen and putting everything ready for the following day, Duggie tried to persuade Kate to take part.

The day of the camp concert arrived and Kate, flattered by Duggie's praise, agreed, persuading Ethel to sing with her.

'And Rosie,' Ethel insisted firmly.

Rosie refused, promising to scrub floors for ever if they let her off, but with their promise to sing loud enough for her as well, and not expect her to make a sound, they persuaded her to go with them. What had finally convinced her to give it a try was the promise of make-up that would disguise her completely.

'I'll only be there to make up the number, mind, you promise me?' she said nervously.

They hid behind the temporary stage knocked up by the camp's chippies. A few drapes were found, left behind by earlier concert parties. If they were daunted by the high standard of some of the earlier acts, they said nothing, each gathering strength from the apparent sang-froid of the rest.

Some of the performers had been semi-professionals before the war had interrupted their careers, and even those who hadn't been on a stage before volunteering for the concert party included many who, now they had tried it, were considering making it a career once the war finally ended. Ethel, Kate and Rosie were nothing more than im-pertinent amateurs.

Hands crossed behind their backs, wearing

a large quantity of Kate's treasured make-up, the three friends had dressed themselves like Tyrolean dolls. Hiding behind the disguise helped them all but particularly Rosie, who surprised them by singing a chorus with her unexpectedly sweet voice, rather than miming. Sadly her voice was not powerful enough to reach even the front row.

Most of the audience failed to recognize them at first, with eyelashes drawn halfway up their foreheads and down their cheeks on faces dotted with the most unlikely-looking freckles. There were precise circles of rouge on their cheeks and lips drawn in bright red lipstick to almost cover them from chin to nose.

When they left the makeshift stage they dashed back to their hut to remove their make-up before returning to find Baba and Duggie and to modestly accept their praise. Baba kissed them all, which made Rosie run out into the cold night to cool her flaming cheeks.

Rosie was so excited by her achievement and Baba's kiss, she couldn't sleep. She opened her nan's latest food parcel and they had a midnight feast as in all the best schoolgirl stories they remembered reading. Understanding how much the evening had meant to her, Ethel and Kate talked until exhaustion finally silenced her.

'By the time this damned war ends, our

118

Rosie will be a different person. I wonder what her family will think of her then?' Ethel whispered.

'What family?' Kate replied. 'There's only a grandmother. Her father is dead, remember, and her mother left when her new boyfriend told her to choose between Rosie and him.'

'Poor lonely little kid.'

'Not any more she isn't. She's got us.'

'I hope we can stay together if we move from here,' Kate sighed.

'So do I, but it might not be possible. Nothing stays the same for long. Don't you know there's a war on?' she joked.

'I do think they could give us a posting together if they tried. That won't help Hitler, will it, you and Rosie and me staying together?'

'Perhaps we could flatter the stupid Walter and persuade him to help?' Ethel murmured sleepily.

'What's it worth?' Kate chuckled.

'Not a thing! He'd get his reward in heaven.'

'Fool that he is, it might work. Will you do the persuading or shall I?'

There was no reply and Kate smiled and settled to sleep for the few hours left before reveille.

As punishment, the men were sometimes sent to help the girls with some of the heavy cleaning. Washing walls and cleaning windows were unpleasant tasks in the cold of the winter. So was giving the cold fire ovens a thorough cleaning before lighting them. The men agreed that 'jankers' was not so bad when Ethel, Kate and Rosie were there. They were generous and the men on punishment duties always managed to hide from Walter the fact that they were given food and extra cups of tea as well as the opportunity for a quick fag.

Baba Morgan was one of the ground staff involved with the servicing and maintenance of the vehicles used around the airfield. Whenever possible, he was the first to arrive in the morning to help whichever of the girls was responsible for opening up and lighting the fire. When it was Rosie's turn, she rose early and already had the kettle humming ready to make him a cup of tea. He came in, humming or whistling, wearing a smile that warmed her for the rest of the day. He checked on the supply of sticks, cut any that were needed into the correct size and stacked them to dry beside the cooker. Between Duggie, Baba and the rest, the coal bins were constantly refilled and the water carried from tap to heater and tap to tea-urn.

For Baba the best mornings were when Ethel arrived first.

'How did we manage without you, Baba?' Ethel sighed one morning as he handed her a bar of chocolate and her first cup of tea.

'If you want to thank me,' he grinned, 'how about the dance on Saturday, my treat if you'll come? I'm a good dancer, small but neat, that's Baba Morgan!'

'I don't know. I think Kate and I are going into town. It's our weekend off.'

'And you aren't going home?'

'I don't want to, there's nothing there for me, and Kate isn't going because she can't afford the fare. She doesn't want to keep asking her mam and dad for money. Ever so generous they are, but they've only got a small grocer's shop and they aren't wealthy, specially now with food rationing limiting what they can sell.'

'What about Rosie, isn't she going with you?'

Ethel shook her head.

'You aren't leaving her here on her own, are you? Can't have that.'

'Why don't you ask her to the dance?' Ethel suggested with fingers crossed. She'd seen the look in Rosie's eyes when Baba Morgan appeared. 'She might like to go with you,' she said trying to sound offhand.

'I don't think she'd enjoy dancing, she strikes me as a quiet type.'

'Right. Yes. You couldn't imagine her singing on stage, could you,' she said pointedly. 'There's more to our Rosie than people think!'

121

'I couldn't believe you three singing and dancing and all dressed up. How did Duggie persuade you?'

'He asked us nicely, that's all. Now, about Saturday. Kate and I want to go into town together and we'd appreciate it if you'd take her off our hands,' Ethel lied.

'Why? You two got a heavy date then?'

'No, just the pictures, but it's one Rosie doesn't want to see.'

Walter overheard their discussion and offered to drive Kate and Ethel into town.

'I have to go in to pick up some stores,' he explained.

Forgetting any idea of flattering him into helping with any future posting, Ethel told him with an exaggerated smile that they'd rather walk in bare feet.

Rosie was hesitant about accepting when Kate told her of the possible invitation from Baba. She'd make a fool of herself, say all the wrong things, forget the dance steps and make him run a mile every time he saw her from then on. 'I don't fancy it,' she said. 'I planned a quiet evening listening to the wireless.'

'Rot!' Ethel said. 'You're going and that's that! Anyone who can stand on a stage dressed daft and sing to this lot can't be afraid of a thing! Kate and I won't leave for town until we see you meeting Baba all dressed up and ready to knock him senseless with lust.'

Reddening profusely, Rosie laughed. 'Now you've made me feel even worse,' she said. 'I won't be able to look him in the face!'

Thinking of it as a favour to Ethel, Baba did invite Rosie and, walking as though floating on a cloud in a romantic dream, she told the others about the invitation. At once Kate took out her cache of make-up and began discussing the best colours for Rosie to wear. Ignoring Rosie's protests, she and Ethel set her hair and made up her face, softly, in pale colours that added to her charming look of innocence.

As Baba and Rosie were passing through the guard room on their way to the dance, they heard a burly, aggressive-sounding man asking about Ethel Twomey. Baba, ever anxious to help, called across and asked, 'Did I hear you say you were looking for Ethel Twomey?'

'No, don't tell him,' urged Rosie, pulling on his arm in panic. 'Please, Baba!'

Quickly reacting to her alarm, he added, 'Ethel Tovey, did you say? Tall, leggy, Scottish girl, is she, with blonde hair and a lisp? Sings well? Would that be her?'

The man lumbered across and thrust a photograph towards him. It was Ethel, there was no doubt about it. 'No, sorry. That's nothing like the Ethel Tovey we got here,' he said, handing the photograph back. 'Nothing like her, is it, Rosie?'

123

Without a thank you, the man walked angrily away to where a motorbike stood on the roadside. Rosie stood beside Baba, her hand still on his arm as the motorbike roared away. 'Thank you,' she said. 'Wrong description and wrong name. That was quite a performance.'

'What's the trouble? A family row, is it?' Baba asked. 'God 'elp, don't tell me that ferocious-looking animal is her father.'

'Well, yes, I think he is, but I can't explain. You'll have to ask Ethel.'

'I won't bother to ask. If she wants to tell me she will,' he replied without curiosity. 'Now are we going to the dance or shall we have a dance of our own here on the field?' He took her in his arms and they did a crazy waltz in time to his singing as they waited with others for the bus.

A mile up the road the motorbike stopped and the man walked slowly back to the nearest point to the camp entrance. His information was that his daughter had two friends and one of them was called Rosie.

He sat near the turning, his collar turned up, a cap pulled down on his head. It was bitterly cold and the air had a feel of imminent snow. It was too dark to see the time on his watch and he was afraid to shine a torch. The camp was well guarded. Guns were carried and were only the movement of a finger away from being fired.

Rosie didn't think she could ever be happier than now, dancing in the arms of the very athletic and accomplished Baba. She knew from shy glances around the packed room that she was the envy of many. Yet she had to leave before the end. Unwilling to give up the precious time in Baba's arms, she delayed as long as she dared.

'Sorry, Baba, I'm having a wonderful time but I want to leave early. I need to find Ethel and warn her about the appearance of her father.'

'How can we find her?' he asked, slowing their steps and guiding her to the edge of the dance-floor. 'She and Kate are at the pictures.'

'Would you mind if we leave early and make sure we're there when they get back?'

' 'Course I don't mind if that's what you want. I've enjoyed it though. Perhaps we'll do it again, is it?'

'Please,' she smiled. 'I'd love to.'

'How d'you plan to get back before her?' he frowned, looking at the big wall clock. 'We'll be on the same bus. They aren't that frequent and I don't think there's one now until the last one to pass the camp.'

'Isn't there a way to get there first? You can surely think of a way.' She looked at him in complete confidence.

'Only if we walk. Or ... come on, Baba has a wicked plan.'

Dai Twomey knew the men and women had to be back in camp before eleven and the hours dragged slowly past as he waited. The cold air seeped into his clothes and deadened all feeling in his feet but he didn't move. His blue eyes stared into the darkness broken only by the occasional passing of a bicycle, the hooded lights barely visible. It was with relief that he heard the low rumble of a bus and the sound of voices as people began returning from their various nights out.

He had to get Ethel back home before further harm was done. His family was already twice cursed with a birth and a death. There had to be no more.

Rosie and Baba waited near the entrance to the camp after making themselves known to the guards on duty. He put an arm around Rosie to help stop her shivering. The night was excruciatingly cold with the stillness that accompanies a deep frost. In the short time they had stood there it had eaten into their bones. They had spent only two hours at the dance, Baba surprised and pleased with the nimble-footedness of Rosie. Ethel was right, Rosie had a few surprises for anyone willing to look for them. They had arrived ten minutes before, having stolen a couple of bicycles to get them home before the last bus. They propped the bikes against the fence near the entrance where they would be found the next day. They weren't the first to take a bike and use it in this way. It was such a regular occurrence that any person finding theirs missing would look first around the periphery of the camp before bothering to tell the police.

It was sheer good fortune on Ethel's part that her father didn't see her. Moving forward to see more clearly, he suddenly felt an arm on his shoulder and turned to see two military police, one aiming a gun towards his heart. A signal was given and two more men appeared silently out of the darkness. With one on either side of him and one behind and in front he was marched towards the gate.

As Rosie and Baba found her, Ethel heard his protests and recognized his voice as he was marched towards them under arrest. She began to shake with fright.

Kate put an arm around her. 'What is it? What's happened, are you ill?' she asked in concern.

'It's my father. He's found me. Now I'll have to apply for a transfer.'

Walter was on the bus, having intended to travel home with Ethel and try to talk to her. He hadn't succeeded. He quickly realized what was going on and stared at the big angry man, marvelling that this could be Ethel's father. He took careful note of the licence plate of the powerful motorbike now being pushed in through the gate by one of the guards. You never know when that sort of information would come in handy. And a chat with the men in the guard room wouldn't be a bad idea either.

Ethel didn't sleep much that night and Kate and Rosie sat up for most of the hours of darkness to keep her company and re-assure her that they would take care of her.

With some trepidation the three of them went to open the canteen the following morning and as soon as they unlocked the door, Baba appeared. Duggie was with him.

'He's my father and he's violent,' Ethel said succinctly as the two men waited for an explanation.

'Enough said,' Baba told her.

'You don't have to tell us any more.' Duggie turned and disappeared across the still-dark field towards the Nissen hut where he slept. Twenty minutes later, a warrant officer came to talk to Ethel. He assured her that the man had been escorted from the area with a warning and having received no infor-mation about personnel. He also told her that the police had been made aware in case of any threatening behaviour in the future.

'I still don't feel safe,' Ethel said when the officer had left. 'I'll be too scared to step outside the camp.'

'That's great,' the ever-optimistic Baba smiled. 'There's a talent competition on

Saturday and you three are entered again.'

Among protests and jeers of derision, he persuaded them that he would sing with them, be their coach and also boasted that he was a 'dab hand' at dancing. It was not Ethel's intention to take part but she was glad of the diversion from her wildly fearful thoughts.

'Like Duggie, I've got three sisters, see,' Baba explained, 'and we're always singing and larking about. You'll have to take their place. Miss 'em I do. You can be my deputy sisters, Baba's girls. Lucky Baba Morgan.'

'Hush up, Baba, or they'll be expecting the Andrews Sisters and we'll be a disappointment!'

'You could never disappoint anyone.' His eyes travelled from one to the other but lingered longest on Ethel.

Walter offered to take Kate into town to buy the few oddments they needed for their act. 'I have to go in to collect fresh stock,' he explained. 'Take it or leave it, I don't care either way.'

Kate accepted, feeling mean for the way they used him between firing insults at him. They planned to dress as gypsies, this being an easy dress to make from second-hand clothes, the cheapest way of making costumes.

'Going shopping for yourself?' he asked as they went through the gate.

'I wish I were. But I don't have any money,' Kate sighed.

'I can help any time you're short,' Walter promised. 'Just between you and me, any time, just ask.'

Rosie's Nan placed the last bar of chocolate into the box which she was sending to her granddaughter. With a cake made with the butter she had saved from two weeks' rations and a small bag of home-made toffee, and some gloves she had just finished knitting, she couldn't fit anything else in. Her letter she placed on the top before tying the string around the box and writing the address on the top.

She had replied to Rosie's most recent letter and added news of the people she knew. The other letter stood on the mantelpiece sending out waves of guilt. How could she tell Rosie about that one? She finished wrapping the parcel, then picked up the letter and put it in the drawer with all the rest.

Ethel and Duggie rarely had a chance to meet in private. He was a pilot and most of the time either in flight or waiting for the call to scramble, sitting in the smoke-filled room where men sat and tried to read or write letters home while expecting every moment to hear the siren that meant they were needed. Then would come the rush to their plane, grabbing what they needed, fastening their clothes as they ran, and the frantic activity as the planes took off.

Eyes would follow them until the planes were no more than dots in the sky and the hours would be counted until they returned.

Albert Pugh came at intervals to check on the canteen but had no cause to complain. When he was there, Ethel usually managed to find an excuse to spend some time with him and she began to look forward to his visits. At the same time she still thought of Wesley and wondered where he was. 'Dad was right,' she told the other girls jokingly. 'I'm a tart and I love them all.' She hadn't mentioned just how much she loved Duggie.

Nicknames abounded in the camp, but Walter never became anything other than Walter. He pretended it made him superior. 'They wouldn't dare use anything but my proper name and title,' he boasted, but he knew he was not popular. Keeping a very tight hold of the provisions and insisting on a certain amount of money coming in for every allocation he provided, had given him a reputation for meanness that was not un-deserved. He also annoyed many of the girls by touching them more than was necessary, leaning against them as he passed, bending over them when he had cause to speak to them, hands under their arms as he moved them aside. He had hinted repeatedly that he was prepared to offer favours if there was something for him in return. He was blissfully unaware that for Ethel, Kate and Rosie his nickname was The Creep.

He had a plan for the lovely Kate. Twice she had come to him to borrow money, and in his experience anyone who couldn't manage money was vulnerable. He needed someone to help him make a little extra. He had heard it said that this war would make some people very rich. He intended to be one of them

It was early April 1941 when Ethel's birthday was near that Kate went to Walter again to borrow money. 'Just five shillings until pay day,' she said. 'I want to buy her something nice, like a scarf she saw in town last week. She really liked it and I know she can't afford it.'

'Neither can you,' he teased.

'No, but Mam promised to send me five shillings next week and I'll gladly spent it on Ethel. A scarf and tea in town, she'll love that.'

'You're too generous, Kate. If you were less kind to your friends you wouldn't need to keep borrowing money. You could do with an extra income if you can't change your ways.'

'I don't want to change my ways,' she told him seriously. 'What I have I like to share. I could do with a second income though, the wages are awful.'

'Put a box of margarine outside when you lock up tonight, in another box next to the rubbish,' he said, staring at her quizzically. 'A shilling or two for you at the end of the week if you can do a few favours like that.'

'What? Steal, you mean? I couldn't!'

'You never know how much you have in stock, I see to that. Who would miss it? I can easily revise the books.' He could see she wasn't convinced. With butter, margarine and cooking fat rationed, as well as sugar, tea and bacon, he knew he would have no difficulty finding customers for whatever he could get out of the camp. He could also see she was tempted. He took out a ten shilling note. 'Take this ten bob, double what you asked me for. Let's say you needn't pay it back, shall we?'

With ten shillings, plus the money her parents had promised, she would be rich! More than enough to treat Ethel to the pictures and buy the scarf. Uneasily, she nodded.

It wasn't easy to be the last one out at night. There was always so much cleaning to be done that the three girls always stopped to share the work no matter who had been given the task. During that evening, Kate somehow managed to hide the margarine in a second carton and put it with the rubbish which was ready to be placed outside before

133

they left. She insisted on putting the rubbish outside, dealing with the job herself, and placed the box of margarine beside it. She walked away imagining guilt written across her face and on her back, her shame visible from every direction.

The ten shillings seemed to burn her through the pocket in which she had hidden it.

Ethel's birthday arrived and Kate's mother's money didn't. A bomb had damaged the sorting office and if it survived at all, it was unlikely to turn up for a while. Walter's ten shilling note burned against her fingers as she touched it. She swallowed her guilt and invited Ethel and Rosie into town for tea and cakes to celebrate the birthday. The café she had in mind was an expensive one and perhaps the scarf would have to wait.

'Just tea and cakes?' Baba said. 'Is that the best you can do for Ethel's birthday, then?'

'I wanted to buy her a scarf that she liked, but it's two shillings and sixpence and if I buy it I might not have the money for bus fare and tea. I couldn't bear the embarrassment if I couldn't pay the bill.'

Baba put a hand in his pocket. 'Here, take this half-crown, get the scarf and tell her it's from you and Rosie, she'll be pleased about that.' He went off whistling. He had nothing now until pay day, but it wasn't long, he'd manage without his visits to the Naafi for a

134

few days.

Ethel and Duggie managed to meet quite often, although it was difficult to keep their affair a secret from Kate and Rosie. She regretted not telling them about their first date. Now the secret was stretching into weeks and it was becoming more impossible to explain her secrecy. It was Duggie who told them. One night he had told Kate and Rosie that he wanted to take Ethel home to meet his family. 'It's her birthday soon and I want her to celebrate it with my family.'

'Interesting,' whispered Kate.

'The trouble is, I don't think she'll come. I want you two to persuade her.'

Excited at their inclusion in his secret plans, they set about reminding Ethel that to live for today was important. She agreed wholeheartedly but refused to go home with Duggie.

She loved him, she had never been surer of anything than that, but she was afraid for him. He was a pilot and everyone whispered that their days were numbered when they had flown so many times. Every day he went up in his small plane with eighty and more gallons of fuel practically on his lap. Life was too precarious to give in to love and start dreaming about that golden future.

Kate went out with a young man occasionally and she and Rosie sometimes made up numbers when a group of men and women went into town, but Rosie always refused an invitation to go out with one of the airmen alone. She hadn't looked at a man with even the slightest interest since the dance with Baba. She held on to the hope that he would ask her to go with him again.

Since the visit from her father it was difficult to persuade Ethel to go into town, and she refused to go any further than the café near the bus stop so she didn't have to walk along the streets. At every turn she expected to see her father, even though nothing had been heard since his arrest and subsequent removal from the camp.

With food rationing in force, the availability of decent cakes was seriously reduced. So they were delighted to find that the café Ethel had chosen promised luxuries like warm freshly-made doughnuts, and pancakes spread with lemon curd. Fresh lemons hadn't been available for months. They were in uniform so the manageress of the café made sure they had extra helpings. In celebratory mood, they set off to make sure Ethel had some fun.

Ethel loved the scarf, and Kate told her it had been a present from Baba, aware of Rosie's forced smile. She hid her dismay philosophically, telling herself it was no surprise that Baba found Ethel more interesting than herself, but she knew her feelings for the lively fun-loving Baba would never change.

Walter was waiting for them when they got back in time to open for the evening session at five o'clock.

'Enjoy the birthday party?' he asked Ethel. To Kate, he whispered, 'Ten pounds of sugar, Saturday night, usual place.'

Kate was first out of the canteen the following night and if Ethel and Rosie wondered why she didn't stop to help, they said nothing. Going back to the hut at eleven thirty, they expected her to be asleep. She was in bed, but not asleep; she was crying.

It wasn't long before they persuaded her to tell them the reason for her behaviour. What Walter was doing horrified them. Taking money from the Naafi was something they couldn't tolerate.

'We have to report him,' Ethel said firmly.

'But if I do, I'll have to admit giving him margarine and being paid ten shillings,' wailed the terrified Kate.

'Not if we go about this properly.' Ethel opened her purse and poured the contents on to her bed. She encouraged the others to do the same and they found ten shillings and fourpence. Exchanging the money for a ten shilling note was easy and with the money to pay back, and Walter caught, Kate would almost certainly be in the clear.

'Albert is coming tomorrow, I overheard the others talking about it. Report it to him and tell snake-in-the-grass Walter that what he asked for will be put out the following night.'

'He'll kill me!'

'After this I don't think he'll be around long enough to cause us any trouble, do you?'

Albert Pugh was still rather difficult to approach. A quiet, solemn man, he never spoke to anyone other than the minimum necessary for the business of running the canteen and net bar. Supplies for the net bar were sometimes difficult to restock. It was Walter who arranged for their stock to be replenished from the bulk stores and one of his responsibilities to make sure they didn't run out, but now Ethel discussed the intended theft with Albert.

Ethel had sometimes used this side of the job as an excuse to talk to him but it was never easy. Since their first conversation, attempts to discuss more personal things resulted in failure. He had the habit of walking off whenever anyone tried to intercept him, refusing to even slow down as he listened to their comments or complaints, at the same time promising to deal with them.

She didn't know why she tried, it certainly wasn't sexual attraction, specially now when Duggie was so much a part of her life. But there was something about him that intrigued her. 'He seems so beaten down with

138

unhappiness,' she tried to explain to the others. 'I can't tell you why, but I want to help him. I don't want to pry exactly,'

'Oh yes you do,' Kate laughed. 'Stop pretending your attraction for him is innocent and pure. You like him, he attracts you, what's wrong with that? You're not serious about Duggie, so you're fancy free. Dreams of Wesley are long forgotten, aren't they?'

'I suppose it's sympathy I feel.'

She had often talked to Kate and Rosie about Wesley, but had scarcely mentioned him recently. Thoughts of home didn't seem relevant to her life any more, her father's violence had ended a stage of her life and it would be pointless to drag it with her into the next. Now there was Duggie and an intriguing attraction for the taciturn Albert Pugh.

Ethel was coming out of the canteen on her way to check the post room for Kate, who as usual was waiting for money to arrive and help her survive until pay day. She saw Albert walking across the field in the direction of one of the hangars, where Kate was apparently struggling with a trolley, taking the mid-morning snacks, her blonde hair shining like gold in the sun. She smiled to see that the trolley was immediately surrounded by willing helpers.

She called across to Albert, who waved a sheaf of papers and walked on.

This time Ethel refused to be brushed aside. Time was running out for their trap to be sprung. She ran after him, touched his arm and insisted he stopped to listen. He looked at her quizzically but stopped, folded the papers he was carrying and pushed them into a briefcase and stood waiting to hear what she had to tell him. Even though he had stopped, there was still a look of impatience about him, a desire to be off.

'There's been some pilfering,' she began.

'Stealing,' he corrected firmly. 'It's stealing and calling it something else does not make it any better.'

'All right, stealing. We know who it is and we've set him up so you can catch him.'

'How kind of you to do my job for me,' he said, sarcasm in his tone, disapproval on his face.

'All right, so you don't want to know. That's fine by me. Just don't ask for our help when you find out we're telling the truth.' She turned to go and it was his turn to touch an arm. He gripped her elbow firmly, walked with her and slowed her angry footsteps to a halt.

'Sorry,' he said.

'You should really lighten up a bit, Albert. We're all on the same side, aren't we? Or are you fighting this war with your own private army of one?'

To her relief he smiled and led her slowly

back to the canteen.

Afraid of being overheard, she lowered her voice and began telling him about the intention to rob the stores. Then someone called and he moved away, telling her to put the complaint through the usual channels. 'But Albert...' she called after him. She was late for duty but this was important.

Back in camp, Ethel explained their dilemma to Duggie.

'I'll have a quiet word with some of the lads,' he said.

That night, Kate put the sugar outside as she had promised Walter, and hid herself with Ethel, Rosie and a willing Duggie inside the canteen building.

They grew colder as they waited in the now unheated hut. At half past midnight Ethel was beginning to think their plan would fail when the almost inaudible sound of feet walking through the longer grass around the edge of the field met her ears. She touched the shoulders of the others to alert them and tensed for action.

It wasn't Walter. Much to their disappointment, it was a young airman with one of the other canteen assistants and they had sought the shadows for a loving interlude. Afraid to step out and move them on, Duggie gave a slight cough. The shadowy figures stiffened, murmured softly, then moved away.

'Thank Gawd for that,' Duggie whispered.

141

'Voyeur I am not. Prefer the real thing I do,' he added, his fingers stroking Ethel's cheek in the darkness.

'Hush,' Kate murmured.

It was an hour later when Walter appeared, a mere shadow moving towards them, bending to search through the rubbish before picking up the box containing the sugar and moving off. Silently, cautiously, they followed, using the buildings for cover. He made his way to the perimeter fence, waited for the guard to pass, then dropped the box where it could be collected with comparative ease through a weakened stretch of wire.

Whistles pierced the night's silence, Walter froze, then looked around him in disbelief as four men appeared, their teeth visible in the darkness as they smiled in satisfaction. Other men ran up to the intended recipient, approaching the spot on the outside of the fence. Walter's customer had arrived on a carrier bike which was in the hedge, covered by a piece of sacking.

Walter at once began to bluff his way out of the situation.

'It's young Kate you have to blame for this, setting her up I was, she's the one you need to question, I was only doing my duty!'

The morning was taken up with interviews during which Kate was accused. The cold hard expressions on the faces of the Military

Police terrified her. Knowing she had been guilty, however briefly, didn't help, but she stuck to the story she and the others had rehearsed, not deviating by an iota, and eventually they let her go.

The others supported her and explained that she had taken money from Walter in the past but had always paid it back. The most recent ten shilling note was in Duggie's possession and his words more than any others convinced them that the girls were doing what they considered their duty.

They were heroes for a few days when the news got out. Baba was so pleased he kissed Kate, then Ethel and then a flustered Rosie.

They were called into the supervisor's office a few days later, after being told that Walter had been sent to another station and given a more menial job. They half expected more praise but in this they were disappointed. In harsh words they were warned that never again should they deal with such a matter on their own. 'What d'you think you have people like Albert Pugh for? It's his job to deal with things like this and I want you to remember that. Any problems, you put them in the hands of your superiors, do you understand?'

'Lucky we didn't deal with our superior this time, sir, or Walter would have been very pleased, wouldn't he, sir?' said Ethel with a sickly smile.

'I'll ignore that this time, Miss Twomey, but please remember your position,' the man growled.

'And you remember that we depend on you to give the right people the right job,' she retaliated. 'Accused we were, treated like criminals, just like you're doing now! And all because you gave a job of trust to a man not to be trusted. Sir.'

'That's right,' Kate said in support. Rosie nodded vigorously, wide-eyed with conviction, unable to open her mouth, her jaws locked with nerves.

The following day, at eleven a.m., as they had finished with the trolleys and were opening the canteen, Ethel, Rosie and Kate were told to be packed and ready to leave at six that evening. They were being transferred to another station.

They dealt with lunch and spent the afternoon giving the place a thorough clean. They were saddened to go, but did not regret the complaint that had caused them to be moved on.

Duggie was away from the station and Ethel left him a note, unable to tell him where to find her as they wouldn't know themselves until they arrived. As they stood near the guard room with their small suitcases beside them, Baba came across the field. 'Rumour is, there's been a crash just outside the town,' he told them. 'Your replacements have been injured. I don't think you'll be going after all.' He winked, gave the thumbs up sign and hurried on to disappear inside one of the hangars to talk to one of the fitters about repairs to his radio mike.

Sure enough, after standing there for another hour, the solemn-faced Albert came to tell them to return to their billet and resume duties. 'I have to tell you that you're still down for transfer,' he told them. 'You can't get away with saying what you think. Your behaviour will remain on your records.'

'Pity for us,' Ethel snapped. 'I don't know how I'll sleep, do you, girls?'

'Ruined my life that has,' Kate sighed prettily.

Rosie just nodded, rapidly and repeatedly, to show her support.

When they were unpacking their cases and hastily preparing to open up for the evening session, Kate said thoughtfully, 'I think I might apply for an overseas placing, how do you two feel about that?'

Thinking about Duggie but not admitting it, Ethel shook her head. 'No, let's stay and annoy this lot for a while longer. Perhaps later, if we get transferred to somewhere really unpleasant.' She wondered what could be more unpleasant than being transferred away from Duggie.

Five

The ship steamed steadily through the night. Two days out and without a sign of enemy action. Heading away from North Africa they had expected to receive unwelcome attention before this. Wesley put the finishing touches to the men's late-night food and stood back waiting for the first arrivals.

In this small ship the food was prepared by a few men who cooked and delivered the plates of food to the seamen, the mess hands running up and down the alleyways with the hot meals. In a space smaller than the average understair cupboard, the Naafi provided snacks and hot drinks throughout the twenty-four hours to the men coming into the mess for brief relaxation.

There was also the usual net bar where they could purchase small necessities. Keeping the men satisfied and making sure the stock was sufficient was a full-time job and all the staff worked longer than the hours for which they were paid. For all of them it was a question of pride to be at their counter providing for the men's needs throughout the day and night, time-watching was something they never bothered to do. When in port they went shopping to find fresh food and whatever luxuries they could buy to add variety to what they offered in their canteen.

At this time of the night most of those not on duty were in their bunks, fully aware that the peaceable voyage could not be expected to continue, that any moment the klaxon would sound the alarm and they would have to get to battle stations immediately.

The murmur of several conversations reached Wesley, the other assistants chatting to the few customers drinking cocoa before going to their quarters. No one bothered to speak to him. Attempts to involve him in conversations, talk about their families and their hopes and dreams had failed and now most left him alone. In a fighting ship how could he tell them of his disgrace? Heading for home through a route that took them through dangerous waters, where bravery counted, a place where you had to be able to trust your colleagues, how could he admit to his cowardice? How could he be sure he wouldn't let them down and run, as he had from Ethel's father?

As he began stacking away the last of the newly washed enamel dishes, he wondered where Ethel was. All his mother had been able to tell him was that she had been seen getting on the London train, but with so many stations in between, she could be anywhere. He just hoped she was safe and didn't think too badly of him.

The ship gave a sudden lurch. He reached out to stop the last of the plates falling and then hung on as the explosion made everything shudder and heave to starboard. Leaving the galley he ran along the juddering passageway, being thrown first one way then another as the ship floundered and tried to right herself. Up to the deck he ran, joined by others heading for their battle stations, a highly organized team doing what was expected of them, slotting into place with machine-like precision, dealing with the emergency in a well-practised way.

Voices were calling, men running, dressing as they went, stopping to hop into boots, grabbing what they needed as they passed fire extinguishers and choppers and hurrying on, each one knowing where to go and what to do when they got there. Wesley knew they had been hit but there seemed no immediate prospect of them sinking or the order would have been given to abandon ship. He needed to know the site and extent of the damage and from that deduce where his services would be best used.

The ship had slowed and, as the rest of the Naafi team arrived, he guessed from the voices heard shouting orders that the damage was in the after end. There was a terrifyingly loud whoosh, as a fire began.

'That's all we need,' he muttered, aware that fire would make them visible for miles, a perfect target for roaming aircraft. To his mild surprise, he wasn't afraid, his brain working out how best to help. The rest of his team had arrived and leaving some men to organize drinks and sandwiches, which would certainly be needed later, he made his way to where the ship's crew was dealing with fires.

The ship was slowly turning, one of the engines damaged, and below, men were making rapid calculations while others assessed the damage.

The fire had taken hold. Wesley joined the fire-fighting team, following the instructions of the fire duty officer, and they worked through the night as the flames were slowly quenched only to revive again and be tackled again, and then again.

When the fire was finally defeated the men were exhausted but their troubles weren't over. Their position had been radioed to planes nearby and out of the slowly lightening sky three planes zoomed down on them, firing on the men still on deck. The guns on the starboard side were mostly useless but on the port side they were quickly trained on to the diving planes.

There was a second torpedo which sped through the water and missed the bows by a few feet. Below decks, torpedoes were checked but the damage had rendered them useless. A depth charge was aimed on a point where it was judged the U-boat's position to have been when the damage occurred. The ship was listing heavily to starboard and on the port side it was difficult to lower the sights sufficiently for precise targeting, but they fired anyway. The noise was deafening, it was impossible to see through the billowing smoke, and the smell of burning and the acrid fumes from the gunfire made the men choke and splutter. Through it all the men followed their training instructions and the firing went on as though they were unaware of the continuing attack on their ship.

Above the chaotic row, a muffled roar was heard and those close enough to look in the direction of the fresh assault on their ears saw a bubbling cauldron in the sea close by, as air escaped from the stricken submarine. The weary men passed the news and a ragged cheer was heard. Scramble nets were lowered over the side in case any of the submariners managed to escape.

With the fires under control, Wesley helped take the wounded below as men were manning the guns and a few were positioned to look for survivors in the darkness that was distorted by the dying flames. Filthy faces, weary limbs, the men stood momentarily in small groups and drank the tea supplied by

Wesley's men, and the work went on.

A second torpedo raced towards the ship like a relentless fish but missed, rushing harmlessly past. There were other U-boats down there bent on revenge. The depth charge fired in an arc of death, as the men concentrated on the danger below, leaving it to others to watch for danger from above.

It was when he came up on deck for the third time that Wesley heard, then saw the planes, three abreast screaming towards them, guns aimed at the deck where men from the damaged areas worked. He was deafened by the sound of the anti-aircraft gun on deck close to where he stood. The gun ceased firing and for a second he was relieved. Then realization came and he ran to where the gunner had fallen sideways, the sight of him leaving Wesley in no doubt that the man was dead.

There were extra Naafi personnel on board on their way home. Many of them went to the first aid post to assist, others helped maintain the supply of ammunition to the gunners. All Naafi staff serving overseas were trained in the use of guns, but not the powerful anti-aircraft weapons used on the ship. Their knowledge and training was simply sufficient to enable them to stand beside the fighting men and take part in any action. Wesley looked at the huge monster on deck and in those few seconds thought it was beyond him. With everyone employed clearing the damage, dealing with the wounded or in the fight against the U-boat attack, he knew he had to try.

Lifting the young boy from the metal seat, lying him as respectfully as he could against the deck rail, he took his place. He was not a complete stranger to the workings of the gun, they had spent some time with most weapons and, quickly understanding the method, after a few false starts he began to fire towards the wave of enemy aircraft some distance away, heading towards them, increasing speed. Beside him a man stood ready to help with the ammunition.

The planes circled once and it was those precious moments that gave Wesley time to prepare. Hatred was in his heart. Seeing the boy no older than himself lying there brought such cold determination to him he wanted to kill in retaliation. Once he had a plane in his sights he fired, followed it and fired again, long before there was a feasible chance of hitting it.

When the plane was close enough he hit it and it changed direction, the engine spluttered and died. He watched as it glided gently down at an oblique angle and went into the water with hardly a splash.

There was no thought in his head for the young pilot. There was only a machine heading for the ship with deadly intent, no image of flesh and blood, or a youngster similar to the one he had just placed on the heaving deck. Moving the heavy gun around, he prepared to deal with the next.

Men who weren't involved with fighting or with the wounded were busy clearing the debris from the decks preparatory to getting the ship back to order. Others searched the seas for survivors of the U-boat. In all the mêlée, they miraculously heard a call and threw scramble nets over the side, leaning over ready to help the seaman aboard.

He was obviously injured and couldn't scramble up unaided. One of the Naafi staff went over the side with a seaman and together they helped the man aboard. To their surprise he spoke English. 'Blimey mates, I ain't 'alf glad ta see yer. Me arm's broke and I couldn't climb that net for all the tea in China.'

There was no time for explanations as to where he had come from, and if they thought about it at all, their curiosity was brief. There was no time to think about anything but fighting off the attackers and saving the ship.

Throughout the fierce battle the Naafi staff did what was demanded of them. Several ran around providing cocoa and corned beef sandwiches to the usual grumbles: 'Where's the horseradish relish then, son?' Or, 'Are you sure you put sugar in this tea?' Or the favourite, 'Cocoa you say? Smells like tea and tastes like coffee, it *must* be cocoa.'

Some handed out food, some were involved in the fighting, others worked in the sick bay; several Naafi personnel were injured, some seriously, but fortunately there were none on the list of those who died.

The man who had been rescued from the sea was covered in oil and members of the crew were helped by Naafi staff as they washed him down and provided him with fresh clothes. He was weak with shock and said nothing after his initial bravado as they cleaned him up and prepared him to see the doctor. His watch, on the broken arm, was bent, the glass shattered, and it was doubtful whether it would ever work again.

'What were you doing out there? Going in after them, now?' One of the rescuers teased as he wrapped a towel around the man's shoulders to support the injured arm.

'Hoping for some fish, I was. The Naafi's a bit short of something for tomorrow's dinner,' the exhausted man retorted. To their amazement he was one of the ship's crew. He had been blown over the side with the first explosion and had narrowly missed being killed with the direct hit on the U-boat.

The double escape made him famous and from then on he swore he would considered himself immortal: 'At least till I get home to the missus. She'll kill me for ruining her father's wrist watch,' he joked as he headed for the sick bay.

There were only three survivors from the submarine. Covered thickly in oil from the surface of the sea, their eyes were red and painful and they were exhausted, trembling, believing they were going to die. As they were helped on to the ship and washed down, they were given a hot drink by one of Wesley's staff. '*Gott sei dank*,' was all they said.

Once the remaining two planes had disappeared, and in an attempt to avoid being finished off by the enemy below the waves, the ship closed down and silence was the order. Nothing moved, even the slightest sound would help the listening U-boats to work out their position. U-boats hunted in packs, there would be others seeking revenge for the one they had destroyed.

When the captain decided they were safe to move, the ship began to make way on one engine, still with an ungainly list to starboard, and the Naafi reopened for business. The men had been awake and on duty for twenty-four hours.

Wesley was praised for his part in the battle, and as they limped into port, he lay, unable to sleep, and wondered if Ethel would think more kindly of him.

Duggie tried not to think about averages.

Everyone mentioned them, the average life of a pilot, the average number of flights before 'curtains'. He had done more sorties than many of the men on the field. People were beginning to look at him with admiration and with that certain superstitious anxiety. He looked around him at the fresh young faces of the new arrivals. They weren't much younger than himself, but they had not yet had time to become weary or battle worn. To the young men, some only months his junior, Duggie was one of the old ones whose days were numbered. Believing him to be only days away from death, they were unnervingly polite.

He tried to talk to Ethel about how he felt, telling it as a joke, laughing at the gullibility of the fresh young sprogs, at the tricks the 'old' ones played on them, afraid of sounding scared. Counting the flights, remembering the averages, his dreams were filled with crashes, with the faces of the German pilots laughing at him as he spiralled down to the pitiless earth. He saw the faces of men who had gone; those who had died and others who had been injured and sent home. He saw too, expressions of sadness on the face of Ethel and wondered whether her grieving for him would be more or less than for the others who had failed to return. She showed love for him, but was it more than her being away from home, estranged from

156

her family, and lonely for affection?

They met whenever they were both free, usually in the canteen after closing, where the warmth of the dying fire gave an illusion of comfort. Their loving was so intense that had their whereabouts been a luxurious bedroom or a barn, it wouldn't have made it more perfect. There were occasions when they just talked, comforting each other by their shared warmth and forgetting for a while the horrors awaiting them, that could fall upon them at any moment. They both wondered if it was love on the part of the other, or the need for pretence.

It was near the end of June when Ethel realized she was several days late. There was no way of finding out whether a baby was the reason. She couldn't go to the Medical Officer, she might be asked to leave and she had no idea where she would go. The thought frightened her very much and after two more weeks had passed, she confided her fears to Rosie.

'I don't know what to do,' she said, wringing her hands together nervously. 'I don't know how Duggie really feels about me. He could be moved away tomorrow and I might never see him again. What will I do?'

'Do nothing and tell no one until you've thought it through,' Rosie said. 'You do have somewhere to go – my Nan'll have you. Our house is big and there's plenty of room.'

'Oh, Rosie,' she smiled sadly. 'You can't expect her to take in a stranger with a baby and no husband.'

'I know my Nan and I wouldn't have to ask. I just know she'd agree. So, that's one thing settled. But as for telling Duggie, that's your decision. But you don't have to tell him yet. Take your time and think about it, make plans for both reactions, get used to the idea and then you'll be strong enough to tell him.'

'Rosie, you're wonderful.'

Rosie looked thoughtful for a moment then she smiled. 'I suppose I must be if both you and my Nan think so.'

When Duggie heard that Ethel was being transferred he was immediately filled with panic. Like many pilots he was superstitious although he denied it vehemently. Ethel was his talisman; his survival depended on her being there to see him home.

He had gone to the canteen one morning and on seeing other girls there, had asked where he could find Ethel. He was told she was in the guard house awaiting transfer and he ran around the field afraid she would be gone.

It was July 1941 and the day was perfect. The sun was strong, the trees were in full leaf, a myriad shades of green, wild flowers were filling the fields with colour. Birds sang joyfully from the hedges, meadowsweet, around the edges of the field where wheat was growing, filled the air with its heady scent. In his panic, Duggie was aware of none of it.

The three girls were standing near the guard room with their suitcases, great coats over their arms, basking in the sun. Ethel and Rosie searched the field with their eyes, hoping for a last glimpse of Duggie. Kate was smiling at one of the men in the guard room who was staring back with obvious admiration. 'Such a pity we're leaving,' she whispered to Ethel with one of her famous winks. 'That one has the most dreamy smile.'

Rosie recognized Duggie first and nudged Ethel, who ran to greet him.

'Why were you leaving without telling me?' he demanded.

'I left a note for you,' she told him. 'We didn't know ourselves until six thirty this morning, less than two hours ago.' She moved away from Rosie and Kate and they talked.

'I don't want to lose touch with you, Ethel. Please let me have your home address so I can find you even if we're moved without being able to tell each other.'

'I don't have a home address,' she replied, looking away from him.

'Then the address of a friend. Please, Ethel. I don't want you walking out of my life.'

'Wait a moment.' She went to where Rosie and Kate stood and after a hurried conversation, she came back and wrote down both girls' addresses. 'I'm sure Kate, Rosie and I will stay in touch. You'll be able to reach me through them. Now, can I have your home address?' she asked, hiding her fear that he wouldn't comply.

'I'm being stood down in a few more days, being transferred to where I can help train the new lads.'

'Thank heavens for that! Where will you be?'

'I can't tell you but I'll find you somehow.' He handed her a piece of paper. 'This is my home address. Don't lose it, Ethel. I need you in my life, however short it is.'

'Don't talk like that, Duggie. I need you too,' she said softly. She meant it, but at that moment it was more important for him to believe it. She was well aware that she was his good luck charm. Besides, if she had a child, he would want to know, even if his declaration of love was a temporary thing. She could never deprive him of a child.

She loved Duggie but there was still her family looming and threatening to spoil that love. Their moments of closeness eased away the terror for him, she knew that. For herself too there had been comfort in the promises, the pretence that everything would be fine, that the future was theirs to plan.

Yet if her parents found her, something would crumple inside her. She would be afraid to give him her love, her father would consider her wicked. Even now, thinking about it made her want to run away from the implications. Sometimes when she and Duggie were loving and close, the fear was there between the brief moments of passion that blanked out everything but desire and the pleasure of giving him her love.

Kissing was something she enjoyed but which, when imminent, sometimes still terrified her as she imagined her father watching, his temper rising, enjoying the feeling of terror he induced, before storming over to make his fists begin their warning. She looked away from Duggie and wondered whether she would ever be free of Dai Twomey, her father and her worst enemy.

One of the guards came out and spoke to Kate, who turned and beckoned to Ethel.

'Seems we have to go,' Ethel said, turning her face to offer her cheek. He pulled her around and held her lips with his own, and embarrassed at having such a large and entertained audience, she froze, then relaxed into the joy of it.

'Come on, you can do all that later,' Kate said coming towards them, carrying Ethel's case as well as her own. 'Seems it's another false alarm. They can't do without us just yet.'

'Thank God,' Duggie sighed.

Kate put down the cases and turned to wave at the handsome young airman in the guard room, before trudging back to their hut.

When Duggie took off later that day, Ethel stood with the rest and watched the flight leave. Her heart was racing as she imagined the way he was feeling, believing his luck was running out, convinced that with the hours he had spent flying and the number of flights undertaken and air battles fought growing, his chances of surviving were diminishing. In days he would be safely grounded but that knowledge only added to the stress of his last few take-offs and landings.

Through the hours that followed as she went through the routines of a normal day she wondered about him. Whenever she went outside her eyes would rake the benign blue skies for sight of the planes returning. When the first engines were heard she was afraid to go out.

'Come on misery-guts,' Kate called. 'Come out and wave. You know the boys all look for us as they come in.'

Counting, trying not to count but unable to stop. Three fewer than there should be. Then two, then one. Minutes passed and still she stood and waited. Kate and Rosie went inside to make sure they were prepar-ed for the men when they returned after debriefing. They'd be there demanding char and a wad before they knew it.

Then Ethel heard the sound of an engine. Not a normal sound, but one that told her the plane was in trouble. Spluttering, seeming to stop then cough itself into life again. Then she saw it, hanging to one side, its damaged tail plane alarmingly distorted, making its way towards them. Then it turned and made for the furthest end of the field. 'Stupid fool, come in close to the fire wagons,' she muttered. She knew he was convinced of an uncontrolled landing and a fire and he wanted to keep it away from the buildings and people. A final cough and sudden burst of speed then it was down, screaming along the ground, ground-looping, before disappearing from her sight behind the team of fire wagons and red cross ambulance that raced towards it. 'No fire. Please God, no fire,' she prayed as she watched the scene.

Frozen to the spot, unaware of Kate and Rosie's calls, she stood and waited. Others had been watching too and as the stretcher was lifted into the back of the ambulance she ran towards it. The ambulance driver waited at Duggie's request as she ran breathlessly towards them.

'Hi, Ethel, hell of a poor landing, eh?' Duggie said. 'A ground loop. I'll never live it down.'

Blood covered his face but she was assured by the team that he was 'a lucky sod and he's got hardly a scratch'.

'We thought we might as well give him a ride as we were there,' one of the men joked.

Later that day he came to find her, one side of his face wrapped in white bandage like that which had frightened Rosie many weeks before. He insisted he was fine. He was smiling, half of it hidden by the bandage, and Ethel wondered if having a crash landing had broken his average and he felt less vulnerable than before. All talk of his being stood down had been forgotten – a week later he was flying again.

After his first flight following the crash he invited her out.

She was certain about the baby now and knew Duggie had to be told, but not yet. She had to wait a while longer. He might think he had been trapped. After all, there had been no mention of their marrying. If he was worried and flying ... She would blame herself if he was hurt, convince herself that she had caused him to lose concentration by telling him. It was no good, the news would have to wait until he was grounded. Then he'd be safe.

'Yes, we could all go to the pictures.' She forced a smile.

Duggie shook his head. 'Just you, Ethel. Let's leave Kate and Rosie out of it this time, shall we?'

She looked doubtful and he said softly, 'I'm not like your father, I don't hit out at every imagined insult. I love dogs and I'm kind to my grannie.' He tried to make her smile but failed. 'I won't even kiss you if that's what you prefer, although, I must tell you that I want to kiss you, and make love to you, more than I've ever wanted anything before.'

'I don't know...'

'What's wrong, love?'

How could she tell him?

'Let's go somewhere where we can talk, a café? Although,' he said ruefully, 'that wouldn't be much of a change for a Naafi girl, would it?'

She agreed, having made up her mind that now was the time to tell him about the baby. Her heart raced as she wondered how he would react. He would probably ask her to marry him and she knew that was the sensible thing to do, but how could she? How could she meet his family and not tell them about her father? She couldn't. She would have to pretend her own family didn't exist and keep up that pretence all their lives. Not a good start to a marriage, lying to his family, living in fear of her father finding her.

They went into town in a car borrowed from one of the officers who owed Duggie a favour, but it petered to a halt before they had travelled more than a couple of hundred yards and they had to push it back inside the gate.

'Damn,' Duggie joked, 'I planned for it to give out miles from home so we had to spend the night somewhere.'

They caught the bus, which was crowded with other men and women from the camp, and found a small restaurant with pork on their menu. They were given a corner table near a blacked-out window, and they ordered a meal.

'I expect we'll need a magnifying glass to find the pork,' Ethel said.

'At least the gravy should be tasty.' He leaned over and held her hands with his. 'D'you think they'll let us mop it up with some bread?'

She didn't attempt to remove her hands from his until the elderly waitress came with their meals, which were surprisingly good.

Ignoring the bus stop with the line of uni-formed figures waiting to go back to camp, they walked. Ethel had not managed to bring up the subject of her condition, although she didn't try very hard. It was so difficult to come out with such earth-shattering news on a walk through the mild summer evening. In a brief lull she took a deep breath to tell him she had something to say, but he interrupted, unaware of the effort she was making to tell him her news. It was another reprieve and she was thankful.

'Talk to me about your father,' Duggie said.

'He's a bully, what more is there to say?'

'He didn't always frighten you like he does now,' he coaxed. 'What happened to change things?'

'I don't know! That's what's making it worse. He's always been hard on my brother, Sid. I think he was disappointed that Sid didn't argue and fight like he did. He was always trying to make him fight and hitting him when he wouldn't. Me, he more or less ignored. Just before my sister killed herself in that horrifying way, he started on me, calling me names, accusing me of being wicked. He began hitting my brother more than he usually did and my mother had horrifying bruises from his flying fists.

'Something had happened that made my sister prefer dying to being alive, and sent my foul-tempered father crazy with hatred. But I don't know what it was.'

He was watching her face in the dull light as they strolled along the quiet lane. Her expression and slight intonations in her voice made him ask, 'But you do have a suspicion?'

'I do, but it isn't a very nice one.'

'Tell me,' he coaxed. They were near an isolated cottage, abandoned since the air-field came into being, and he pulled her into the protection of its walls.

'You know that my father was in prison on several occasions? Two of them long sentences?' She felt rather than saw his nod. 'It was always for fighting or some other violent behaviour. On one occasion he was in prison for two years, found guilty of grievous bodily harm. Sid said he once narrowly missed going down for longer, charged with attempted murder. It was while he was in prison that I was born. I was more than a year old before I saw him for the first time.' She hesitated a moment before adding, 'Perhaps my father found out I am not his child.'

Duggie didn't make any comment on the rights or wrongs of her deduction but instead asked, 'And how do you feel about that?'

'Relieved, I suppose. Thankful that the hot blood that runs through his veins doesn't taint mine or any children I might have.' The mention of children churned her insides but she avoided the opportunity offered to tell him her news. Instead she went on, 'It's Mam I fear for. If it's true, then she's in danger, and I don't know what I can do to help her. We both ran away and left her, my brother and I. Since then I've heard nothing. I don't even know where Sid is and he certainly doesn't know where to find me if anything has happened to her.'

He hugged her, touched her cheek with his

lips, offering her comfort and waiting for her to continue.

'Until now I've despised her for not standing up for me, for allowing him to treat us so badly, but now, if what I think is true she's more in need of sympathy than criticism.'

'How does this connect to your sister's death?'

'She must have been the one who let it out. She was fifteen years older than me, she would have known.'

'Hardly a reason to ... do what she did.'

'Killing the messenger, isn't that what they say? His anger was in need of a target and she was it. She must have been terrified by his reaction. You've no idea how frightening my father could be. He'd block out all reason, make you unable to think. I honestly believe I'd have confessed to anything once he started on me with his accusations.'

'The thing you must remember, Ethel love, is that few men are like your father. Loving someone, being loved in return is a wonderful gift. You'll have to meet my parents. Their love is a light that fills their home. It touches everyone who enters. My sisters and I had a wonderful childhood, the warmth of it has stayed with me ever since.' He moved slightly, until his cheek pressed against hers. It was only a second, smaller movement, for him to find her lips.

Ethel began to move away but his words

had filled her eyes with tears and her heart with pictures of a perfect love untouched by hatred or anger and she wanted to experience a love like that. His kiss began to heal the fear and confusion and as they walked on she knew that he was right, that love was a gift and having found it she would be a fool to let it slip away. But she still failed to tell him that she was carrying his child.

Many hours passed each day without Wesley Daniels entering her thoughts. Even when the image of him flashed on her mind, it was brief, gone in a fraction of a second. Wesley was a part of her life already fading into a misty memory, one of those vague yesterdays that were no longer real. She knew she was in love with Duggie but still had doubts, wondering whether that love was real, or a pretence that someone needed her. That was a feeling she hadn't known since her father had sent Wesley away and had driven her from home. Now there was no contact with her family, she needed to be tied to somewhere. 'I'm like a balloon escaped from a child's hand,' she remarked once to Rosie. 'Given a freedom I didn't want and wasn't prepared for.'

The war, the precariousness of life, with new faces appearing only to fade into oblivion days later; with young men telling her about their 'Dear John' letters from girls who had sworn to love them for ever, how could she be sure about Duggie? Nothing seemed real any more.

As the three friends waited for the new posting they were regularly told was imminent, the month of July moved slowly on. Wheat, barley and oats ripened and was harvested in the fields, flowers bloomed on fallow land and gave swathes of beauty in unexpected places. Pilots died and were replaced by eager-faced young men whose training was becoming more and more brief.

Duggie met Ethel whenever they were both free and they often stopped at the abandoned cottage to talk and kiss and make plans for when war ended and they were free. The place was sealed with padlocks and wrapped around in barbed wire so they couldn't get inside. Instead they would sit on Duggie's greatcoat on the ground, leaning against the stout walls.

She still hugged the secret of the baby to herself, still pretending for much of the time that she was mistaken and it wasn't true. She and Duggie talked of a future but that future was years away, with a life to build before they could live it. This baby was a future that was as close as a few months.

One evening Ethel sensed he was worried. She coaxed him to talk about his work and he admitted that he had a strong feeling that he wouldn't come back from his next flight.

'Don't tell me you've allowed the talk and

the superstitions to get to you,' she said quietly. 'I thought we agreed that rubbish was for the new boys.'

'The trouble is, they're all "new boys". The number of my flying hours are way above everyone else's and my time is up.'

They talked about fear and how it can ruin concentration and cause crashes when there's no other reason. 'You have to put this out of your head,' Ethel pleaded.

His kisses were a comfort, and as they grew more and more urgent, she didn't hold back. She desperately wanted him to believe in their future together, he had to believe that they had years of loving ahead of them, his life depended on his believing. In a matter of moments, she found herself caught up in a passion over which she had no control. It wasn't the most romantic of places, less comfortable than the canteen with its slowly dying fire.

There was no slow awakening, not gradually rising desire, just the urgent need to give him the certainty of their love. She had to convince him that he had a future and she would share it if that was what he wanted. He had to rise in the air and take part in the protection of the airfield, confident and sure.

They lay down and held each other tightly, beginning to become aware of the cold concrete, the worn path biting into them. Afterwards, Duggie was ashamed of treating her so badly. He was close to tears. 'I'm sorry, Ethel. I shouldn't have treated you like that. I didn't plan for that to happen in a place like this. You deserve better care than I give you. I'm so sorry.'

'There were two of us involved, in case you didn't notice,' she said, kissing his stricken face and finding his lips again, teasing them, softening them into a smile. 'Now, let's get up before we're frozen to the ground – and how would we explain that to the medics?'

'Please believe that I love you for more than this.'

He tried to tell her how ashamed he was, of his lack of control, his taking advantage of her in such an unromantic place, how every time should be special, but each time she stopped his words with a kiss.

'It was wonderful. You were wonderful and this is a night we'll never forget,' she whispered.

'I love you, Ethel, and in spite of my behaviour tonight, I respect you. I want to spend my whole life with you.'

Now was the time to tell him, while he could still change his mind about how he felt, but the words wouldn't come. 'I love you too,' she whispered softly.

Rosie and Kate could see by her eyes that something good had happened. In their Nissen hut, which they now shared with eight others, they whispered and wheedled

173

the story from her until a shoe went hurtling across the beds with the addition of several voices warning them to 'Be quiet or else'.

This caused Rosie to giggle and Ethel was glad of the distraction. Lovemaking and her feelings for Duggie were not subjects for general discussion. She pretended sleep when Kate spoke again, but heard Rosie whisper to Kate, asking her not to tease, that Ethel was a bit unhappy at present. She got out of bed and called them outside where she told Kate about the baby. 'So much for the nickname ice queen, eh?' she said. She expected a lecture on her stupidity but Kate was thrilled at the prospect of being 'almost an auntie'.

'How can you be "almost an auntie"?' Ethel laughed.

'Well, you two are almost my sisters, aren't you?'

There was no arguing with Kate's particular kind of logic and they talked excitedly about the fun the baby would bring into their lives.

Over the following days, Ethel stood with the rest as the planes were counted back. She didn't register any of the anxiety of previous times when some of the planes were late. Duggie was safe, her love had made sure of that.

'What will happen to me?' she asked her friends in one of their moments of quiet. 'I'll be thrown out of the Naafi, that's certain, and I've nowhere to go. If my father finds out about this he'll kill me.'

'You don't want to lose it, do you?'

'I sort of hope it isn't true. If I'm truthful I don't want it to be true. I'm not ready to look after a child. When I have a baby I want to do it properly. This isn't the time, Kate.'

'Tell Duggie. His family sound the kind to accept you. Welcome you in fact. What parent can turn their back on a grandchild?'

'My father for one!'

Rosie gave a long sigh. 'I'd love a baby to enjoy and love and watch grow. Not having a father or mother as I grew up makes me want to give a good childhood to a daughter or son. But I don't think I'll ever marry.'

'Why ever not? Of the three of us, I'd have bet good money on me being the one remaining alone, and look what happened to me. That's what's so wonderful about life. We none of us know what the new day will bring.'

That night there was a bombing raid on the airfield and as they stood in the trench Kate whispered, 'This should shift it, if that's what you want, poor little thing. You might not have to tell Duggie after all.'

All the planes took off immediately the warning was given, not wanting to remain on the ground as convenient targets. The bombers came over, heavy and sluggish

175

compared with the fast, fierce fighter planes, but their aim was good and bombs destroyed three of the stores and one of the hangars. With hats as their only protection, they couldn't resist looking up and watching the dog-fights going on above them.

They saw a bomber coming down, clearly out of control, and they ducked into the trench as an explosion rocked the ground, the sound of it going on for ever, the shrapnel clattering on corrugated roofs near them, alarmingly large pieces of planes crashing around them.

There was a brief and eerie silence before the sound of men and machines indicated the all clear and time to start clearing up. As soon as the raid ended, Ethel led the others to where the ambulances were already gathering up the wounded. They had helped before but this time they guessed the loss of personnel was high. Bodies littered the ruined buildings and were scattered on the ground, some unrecognizable as human beings.

They were unable to deal with it at first, walking slowly towards one of the victims, hoping someone would come and relieve them of the heart-breaking duty. It was little Rosie who reminded them that the tragic victims were people they had known and had probably served only hours before. She was comforted in some way by remembering how Baba had talked her through the aftermath of that first terrible raid.

'Someone's son, nephew, cousin, father, brother – or sister,' she added as she stared sadly at the body of one of the Waafs. Many of the men and women had refused to leave their work and had stayed in the hangars.

Kate found it hardest to assist. She was tearful, trembling uncontrollably, and unable to approach the still forms of the dead or comfort the people lying horribly wounded. Rosie encouraged her but, realizing it was useless, she and Ethel sent her back to the canteen, reminding her that there was a need for hot drinks with plenty of sugar. 'Forget about rationing for once. This is an emergency.'

While Kate and some of the others went back to check that the canteen was not damaged and begin the routine tasks of providing food and hot drinks, Ethel and Rosie went to help with first aid for the wounded. They were off duty but that was irrelevant at a time like this.

Outside, once the wounded and the dead had been taken away, work went on with the important task of making the runways serviceable again. The worst damage was around the buildings, which meant more injuries, but the runways had received hits and clearing the ruined buildings, salvaging what they could and filling in craters, went on at a pace, so the Spitfires could return to their base.

Their training was not thorough, but using their basic common sense and doing exactly what the doctors, nurses and orderlies told them to do, they gave valuable help in giving first aid to the wounded during the first few hours. The saddest part was laying out bodies for identification. Rosie, shy little Rosie, coped amazingly well. She spoke calmly to the wounded, dealt respectfully with the dead and, later, Ethel and several others told of the young girl's dedication.

They returned to the canteen after three hours, exhausted but satisfied they had done all they could. The canteen building had mercifully escaped serious damage, having lost several windows, and a door, blown open by the blast, that was no longer able to be closed. But their hut was no longer habitable. They were back to sleeping in one of several hastily erected tents. Ethel gathered up the books and the cash and made sure it was handed over for safe keeping. That evening they volunteered for duty as the other shift had been working for even longer than themselves. For Ethel it was better to work than to wait for the flight to return. She heard them landing but they were too busy to go out and count them down.

When one of Duggie's flight came in for sustenance, Ethel smiled and asked where

Duggie was. 'I'd have thought they'd finished debriefing by now, doesn't he want a cup of tea?' she asked. Then her throat tightened as she saw the sorrow in the man's eyes. 'He's all right, isn't he? I didn't see him among the wounded and – *tell me*!' she shouted.

'Two Spitfires were lost and Duggie's was one of them. He crashed in the field the other side of town. Making for the woods where he was unlikely to cause any further deaths,' the stricken man said. His voice was trembly and he gestured to Rosie and Kate to go to her, then turned away. Ethel would-not want to know about the fire and he didn't have the strength to talk any more. He'd had enough tragedy for one day.

A few hours later, as Ethel lay unable to sleep, the pains began and she suffered a painful and heartbreaking miscarriage.

'It was one thing considering the incon-venience of having a baby, being all cool and calm and discussing it as though it was happening to someone else, but losing it was something very different. It's devastating. Among all the deaths, all the insanity of this stupid war, it was a new life and new hope. I want it back,' she sobbed as Rosie held her. 'I want to hold Duggie's child in my arms.'

Kate was tearfully sympathetic. Having been told so recently, the news had been exciting. She hadn't had time to consider the down side of Ethel's situation. Trying to prevent anyone from guessing that Ethel was unwell, she did more than her share of the work and allowed Ethel to rest for most of the shift the following day and the next.

After nights with practically no sleep following the exhaustion of the raid and its aftermath, the three of them were looking forward to sleeping once the lunchtime session was ended. They went into the repaired Nissen hut and collapsed on their beds with a sigh of relief, but two minutes later they heard, 'Come on, ladies, the lorry's coming in fifteen minutes and this time you really are leaving us,' the sergeant shouted. 'Off to Kent you are, you lucky people. Or was it Scotland? Or East Anglia? No, I've got it, it's Berlin. You're to get the food and char ready for when our boys arrive, OK?'

'How many sugars in your tea?' Kate asked. 'Just in case you aren't skiving as usual and actually get there!'

'I can't go,' Ethel whispered. 'I'll have to report sick.'

'Oh no you don't. We aren't going to be split up because you've got a bit of a problem. We'll help. Rosie'll carry your case and you can lean on me, right? Is my lipstick on straight? My hair not too straggly? My eyeshadow even? Off we go then to find some other poor unsuspecting lads to drive crazy with desire.'

Six

Ethel was exhausted by the long journey to their new camp. They sat sideways in the back of a lorry with several other girls and a few RAF boys. The boys at first tried to engage them in conversation, but the movement of the vehicle, which was making them all feel queasy, and their uncomfortable position, made it impossible to respond.

They learned from other conversations that they were heading for a bomber station from where Lancasters flew. A recent raid had demolished the cookhouse and until it was rebuilt they were going to provide three meals a day to all the personnel plus the usual canteen and net bar services.

Kate and Rosie looked around them as they alighted from the lorry that had brought them to an airfield much larger than the one they had left.

'Here you are, ladies, three good meals a day the lads will expect, and the canteen open as usual. You'll have to get cracking.'

'All on our own?' Kate asked with a sweet sarcastic smile as she pulled her and Ethel's cases down.

'There are other Naafi girls here and they'll tell you what's needed,' their driver told them cheerfully. 'You wait till you see the pile of 'taters waiting for you, that'll take the smile off your face, gorgeous.'

The RAF driver pointed them in the direction of the guard room where they had to report, and drove off with a backward glance through his mirror. Nice one, that Kate, always ready with a smile and a cheeky response to any hopeful approach. He wondered how the shy one would cope, and the one called Ethel looked worn out. 'I wonder what she's been up to to make her look like scrag end of mutton?' he asked his oppo with a wink. 'Up to no good, I bet yah!'

The canteen facilities from where they were expected to produce all these meals were two Nissen huts joined together. There was electric lighting fixed up temporarily with a generator, but the cooking was on a huge range with a fire in the middle and ovens at both sides. They were told they had been registered as three cooks.

'I can't cook, I signed up as a counter hand,' Kate said anxiously.

'You'd have to learn some time, so learning here would be better than trying out your skills on your husband when you get wed,' Ethel said.

'I won't be doing much cooking. I intend

to marry someone rich.'

'No one is *that* rich!'

'What are you worrying about, everyone can cook,' Rosie laughed.

'Everyone except me,' Kate groaned.

They were shown to their billet, which was a long narrow Nissen hut that they would share with nine others. The usual bedside lockers had been removed to make room for more beds. Here there was no electricity. Storm lamps and candles provided light; the heater, which the girls called a donkey, was in the centre of the room. The other occupants had pulled their beds around so their feet were towards the heat.

Ethel threw herself on her bed as soon as Kate and Rosie had made it up from the bedding provided, and, leaving her there to rest, Kate and Rosie went to explore.

The sound of singing coming from the back of the canteen led them to investigate and, to their amusement, they saw a huge container full of peeled potatoes, surrounded by seven girls, all singing as they peeled the pile each one had resting on their laps.

'You the new arrivals?' one called and they went in and introduced themselves.

'Ethel Twomey is resting, she got travel sick,' Rosie explained.

'She should have got some travel pills from the MO,' another criticized loudly. 'No time for idle excuses here.'

183

'Tomorrow she'll work, today she rests, got it?' Kate said. The smile was still present but the warning was clear.

The girls moved up and allowed Kate and Rosie to squeeze in, and in the growing silence Kate began to sing, 'Sing a song of sunbeams, let the notes fall where they may...' The others joined in, the angry-looking girl walked away, and the brief threat of a confrontation faded. As usual, Rosie mouthed the words but little sound emerged.

'That's Frances, you'll have to watch out for her,' one of the girls whispered.

'She'll have to look out for us, more like!' Kate replied firmly.

'I'm starving,' Rosie complained. 'When do we get to eat?' On being told there was more than an hour to wait, she tucked into a raw potato and others followed her lead, chomping, and singing when they could, as the choruses continued.

The task finished, Rosie and Kate stood up to leave but the pugnacious girl, Frances, heavily built with short boyishly-cut hair, and red, powerful hands, stopped them. 'Where d'you think you're going? You'd better get this lot cleared before you go back to your hut. Or are you going to leave it for your so-called sick friend to do as her share?'

'We're doing neither!' Kate snapped fiercely. 'Tomorrow we start and we'll *all* do more than our share. But there's one thing we've learnt already and that's never to volunteer to help out when you're around!'

The girl slowly walked towards Kate and Rosie while the others looked on, but both girls stood their ground. The girl leaned towards them appearing enormous. Rosie, quaking in her shoes, said in a surprisingly firm voice, 'You heard. Now get out of our way.'

'Just watch it, that's all,' Frances warned as she turned away.

Several of the other girls silently mimed clapping and others showed a thumbs-up gesture, but none of them dared to show their approval of the newcomers aloud.

When they returned and told Ethel about their first encounter with the other girls, she whispered, 'If you can't join 'em, fight 'em, eh?'

The canteen was large, and so full of chairs and tables they knew the cleaning was going to be a problem. During their first lunchtime session the tables were full and people sat on tables, windowsills, the steps and crowded into corners squatting on the floor. The staff were falling over themselves as they served the large number of men and women. There were many hands to help clear up and as Ethel was far from well she was sent back to their hut to rest.

Their first attempts at providing a full meal

were shared with some of the other staff who were very friendly and helpful. Fortunately Frances kept well out of their way and there was no confrontation between her and Ethel.

After a week, during which they were given more and more freedom to deal with the menu, they were facing their first lunch for fifty men, and with a pile of potatoes ready to boil and some sausages to fry, they began to prepare. The amount used was stipulated firmly in their instructions, three portions from every pound of potatoes. Two sausages and, when available, onions to add to the gravy.

'What have I done?' Kate, who had always left the cooking to Rosie or Ethel, wailed loudly as the sausages began to spit angrily in the huge frying pan.

Rosie turned the heat down and Kate continued to look at them doubtfully, turning them frequently, anxious to get them cooked and start on another batch. Baked beans were emptied into a large saucepan and onions were browning in a second pan, to which Ethel planned to add the gravy being made by Rosie. With a constant glance at the clock, the food continued to cook and the minutes passed.

'How do I know when they're cooked?' wailed Kate.

'When they're brown they're done and when they're black they're buggered!' a young airman shouted.

'Oh dear,' Kate sighed, 'I think these are buggered.'

After a week of dealing with the meals as well as the refreshments on the counter and on trolleys, they all felt more relaxed. It was Ethel who sorted out their problems and guided them through the intricacies of preparing main course meals in quantity, and Rosie who did most of the clearing up. Kate and Ethel dealt with the accounts, orders and menu lists.

'I've never been much for writing and arithmetic,' Rosie explained. 'Action rather than administration, that's me.'

'You, Rosie Dreen,' Ethel told her several times, 'are wonderful!'

On this large camp there was no trolley to push. An open-sided van went around to the various workshops and hangars each morning and Kate volunteered to drive it, after being promised a few refresher driving lessons. During the period when there was no cookhouse, this service was out of action, and all the men had to collect their needs, usually sending one person to collect snacks for a group. Grubby pencilled lists were handed over, and orders shouted, and how they made sense of it all was a wonder to everyone concerned. The day went on without a break and all the staff were exhausted by the time the place closed at eleven

187

o'clock.

One of their jobs, when others dealt with the main meals, was making cakes, biscuits and sandwiches for the snacks counter. One standby were cakes called Nelsons. These consisted of any left-over cakes, mixed together and reheated in large trays and, when cooked, cut into slices. Although the ingredients varied, they turned out so similar that they were recognizable on sight. Called Nelsons, so they were told, because if a man ate more than one, he'd sink. They were popular nevertheless and every Naafi girl learned the secret of making them.

One evening when the weather was unseasonably chill and the men were coming into the canteen complaining about it, Ethel found some brandy in the depth of a cupboard, probably hidden by some secret tippler. She sprinkled a dash of it over the huge trays of Nelsons and served slices hot with custard. The normally mundane offerings had never been more welcomed. Any superstitions about eating two were quickly forgotten.

It was never certain, but Ethel and Kate suspected that the secret bottle had been the property of the obnoxious Frances.

When the damaged ship on which Wesley Daniels served had reached the south of England port and was awaiting repairs, he was sent to a shore base for a few weeks, waiting for a new posting. As always, he asked the girls in the Naafi whether they had met Ethel Twomey. He showed a battered photograph around but had no luck.

It was the only photograph he had of her, a dog-eared snapshot taken in her garden with Glenys and Sid and her mother. Ethel was in the centre of the picture sitting at the garden table, offering a bowl of apples. It was certain to be one of the times when her father was either working away or in prison for his latest demonstration of unacceptable behaviour. He knew that, because Ethel and her family were all smiling, and eating their tea in the garden, a picture of a happy family, something they could never imitate when Dai Twomey was around.

Pinning the picture on the wall beside his bunk, he stared at it every night as he drifted into sleep. What would he say to her when they did meet? Would she forgive him, or allow him a chance to explain? How could he excuse his cowardice? Should he even try? Why hadn't he made her leave with him that day? Why hadn't he gone with her before she reached the decision to go alone? The same thoughts danced around in his mind every time he sat to relax, or settled down to sleep. Questions with no answers.

Walter Phillips had not left the Naafi service,

although his attempts at stealing from the organization had meant he had lost his position. Instead of being a superintendent, he worked as a cleaner and occasional counter hand with no authority to handle money or stores. With manpower so short, he had to be used, but in such a way he could never again succumb to his dishonesty.

He was constantly moved. He was used for temporary positions when someone was sick or taking leave. No one wanted him to stay. He seethed with fury at the way he had been relegated from an important position to the most menial. Like many immature personalities he had to blame someone. He had stolen from the stores but Ethel, Kate and Rosie were responsible for him being caught. So his present situation was their fault, his illogical mind decided. His attraction to Ethel and her humiliating indifference made him place more blame on her than the others.

Convinced that his downfall was due mainly to Ethel's interference, and also aware that for some reason she was afraid of her father, he had set out to revenge himself by looking for Dai Twomey. Enquiries at the guard room, purporting to be a trusted friend of Ethel, resulted in failure. He had fortunately memorized the number plate of the motorbike the man was riding, and chanted it regularly as a sort of mantra of hope. But apart from learning that it had been issued in Hereford, it hadn't taken him any further. It could have been sold and resold half a dozen times since being issued and probably meant nothing. Unless he were fortunate enough to see it one day.

He chanted the numbers and letters again, checking them from the piece of paper in his pocket, committing them to memory and keeping them in the forefront of his mind. One day he'd see that motorbike. It was an expensive one, a Vincent, there weren't too many of those around. Although, he thought with growing irritation, having been moved to the south coast, for him to find it was extremely unlikely. For the moment, the chances of finding Dai Twomey and telling him where to find his daughter were remote. Having just learned that the three girls had been moved from the RAF airfield to another, 'Somewhere in England', just made it more improbable, but he resolved to keep the number plate in mind.

One of the Naafi assistants had left a jacket in the store room and Walter was asked to return it to its owner who was off duty for the following two days. It was as he entered the Nissen hut that he saw the photograph. Such a scruffy old photograph, he was curious.

Most of the men had either good, clear photographs of their loved ones or, in the case of the young and carefree, posters of glamour girls or film stars. Others pinned up drawings of the popular strip cartoon character Jane. None had such a poor effort as this gazing down at him.

Pulling out the pin, he turned to the occupants of the room, preparing to jeer and make fun of the tatty object. Then he stopped and stared at the girl in the centre of the picture. It was Ethel Twomey. Younger and with shorter hair but there was no doubt about it. Smiling, he replaced the photograph and asked casually, 'Who's bunk is this? I've got a coat to return to a chap called Daniels. Wesley Daniels, anyone know him?'

Ethel wrote to Duggie's family after a few weeks had passed. She described herself as Duggie's friend, avoiding mention of being more than that. There was no point creating a close attachment to his family, not any more. If the baby had survived it would have been different and she could have met them, allowed them to share the baby's life. She parcelled up some of his possessions but kept the scarf.

She was pleased to learn that they were still in the area covered by Albert Pugh. He turned up one day and stood at the back of the canteen watching as Ethel served, supported by the flirty Kate and the shy, but efficient Rosie. It had been difficult but he had managed to keep them together, knowing how close they were and guessing that they would have been unhappy to be separated.

Next time they moved they might not be so lucky, experienced staff were spread widely to help new arrivals to settle in and they were all very useful members of the service. With Naafi requirements it was more common sense than elaborate training and Ethel, Kate and Rosie were the kind to deal with whatever life threw at them with a minimum of fuss. He smiled as he decided to reward them by inviting them to go to the camp concert. The camp cookhouse was back in action and the Naafi canteen had reverted to its normal functions.

'Officially you're on duty this evening,' he told them when the doors were closed after lunch and the girls were starting to clear up. 'But, as it's a special night and there's a concert of famous performers, I'll turn a blind eye if you want to go.'

The ebullient Kate jumped up and kissed his cheek and Rosie squealed, her cheeks reddening with pleasure. Ethel looked at him, caught his gaze and said, 'Thanks, Albert, we'd love to go.' She walked with him to the door and added, 'I know it's against the rules and you're sticking your neck out for us, again. We're lucky to have you as a friend. Thanks.'

'Sorry to hear about Duggie. I understand you and he were close friends.'

'Close, loving friends.'

'If ever you want to talk about him, I'm here.'

'I'm glad you're there. Thanks.' She reached for his hand and squeezed it before returning to the counter and gathering up the last of the cups.

'You'll be back here with the counter stocked, tea and coffee ready to serve when it finishes, mind,' he said, trying to sound stern but glowing in Ethel's appreciation.

The concert was a touring company who were about to leave for North Africa, their small truck an Aladdin's cave from which they pulled out an assortment of drapes and costumes, stage sets and lighting systems that would hopefully work off a car battery. Plus a wind-up gramophone with a supply of records. The famous performed alongside talented beginners, and there was also a comedy act in which animal puppets, worked by rods, mimed to records played too fast or too slow, distorting the words and music to the audience's amusement.

True to their promise, the three girls left as the final sing-song began and hurried across the parade ground to open the canteen for their late-night customers, singing as they went. Albert was there before them and had the urn heating and the bars set out.

As they did the finishing touches to their display, Ethel asked him what had happened to Walter.

'He was given a menial job as cleaner cum odd-job hand with a promise of having the worse jobs given to him. Why, you aren't sorry for him, are you?' Albert asked.

'Me, sorry for him? The creep!'

'I don't think we'll be seeing him again. The last I heard he was—' There was no time to tell her more as, chattering cheerfully, laughing as they remembered their favourite acts in the evening's entertainment, the men charged in for their late-night hot drinks and other purchases.

In October the canteen had been returned to its normal business for a few weeks and Ethel and the others guessed that their time there would be short. There was no longer need for the extra staff. They would be sent to another emergency and the probability of being separated was worrying. The following day was their day off and the three girls had planned a walk, hoping to find somewhere to eat lunch that didn't include chips. Ethel was surprised and pleased when Albert invited her to go with him into town. At once she prepared to refuse, the arrangements to go out with Kate and Rosie had been made.

'It's mainly business I'm afraid,' he told

her. 'I have to see a farmer about getting a regular supply of potatoes and anything else I can scrounge. We'll be going in the lorry, hardly luxurious travel, but we should find a pub somewhere and get a bit of lunch. What d'you say?'

'She says yes!' Kate answered for her.

Rosie nodded enthusiastically. 'Just what she needs, a couple of hours away from this place.' There was no chance to refuse and she smiled her thanks for their willingness to change their plans for her.

Albert quickly made arrangements for deliveries of the vegetables he needed, leaving them the rest of the day to themselves. The cold snap was a reminder that winter was not far away and as there was no heating in the lorry, Ethel wished she had dressed more comfortably. So as soon as opening time came, they stopped and went into a small village pub, where a newly lit fire crackled and spat, and the brass and copper around the fireplace glowed with the reflection of the leaping flames.

Pie and mash was hardly an exciting meal, but it allowed them to warm their cold legs near the fire and to talk in private.

'Privacy is one of the things I miss since being in the Naafi,' Albert said as they exchanged anecdotes and their laughter rang out and rose to the smoke-stained rafters. 'What do you miss most?'

'I miss belonging,' she said softly, a sadness clouding her eyes. 'I've been so lucky to have Kate and Rosie as friends. In fact, I can't imagine ever losing them. I just know we'll be friends for the rest of our lives.'

'But...' he coaxed.

'I had a sister and brother, I had a mother and a father. Dad was wild and was often dangerous but they were my family and, hard perhaps for you to realize, I miss them.'

'I can understand you missing Glenys, after all she's gone for ever, and your brother, who might be anywhere. I know you must miss your mother, I miss my own. But your father? To say you miss him implies affection, even love. How can you say you miss a violent man who inflicted pain and terror on you all?'

'Because it's better to have a violent father than not have one.'

Albert shook his head, reaching over and covering her hands with his own. 'My parents and young brother were killed in an air raid, I lost my two closest friends in Norway when the Germans pushed us out. And another in Dunkirk. I know about loss, sadly most of us do, but your father, that's something I'll never understand.'

'He's my dad,' she said with a shrug. 'It's easy to remember the bad and forget the good, and there were good times.'

'Of course. There would have to have been,

or your mother wouldn't have stayed with him.'

'My childhood was carefree and as Dad was so often away, I usually felt safe and loved. There was nothing I wanted that I didn't have, probably because living in such a small village I didn't know about all the things other people had – there was nothing to pine for. I only remember being happy. Dad was always a threat and I learned to behave differently when he was around. It was better when he wasn't there, and we could all relax. But he was away for days at a time, and longer when he was arrested for fighting. I was treated as someone special, with a grown-up brother and sister as well as Mam. Dad was Mam's problem, not mine.

'I think the worst thing that happened was my sister's death, but it was in the days before that happened that Dad became worse, more violent. Something had occurred, something he couldn't cope with. He drove Wesley away and –' she swallowed and took a few breaths as she remembered – 'it was then he began hitting my mother. He'd often flipped her out of his way and sometimes pushed her roughly, but he'd never hit her as badly as he did in those last few days before Glenys died.'

'You still have no idea what caused this flare-up? Something to do with Wesley, perhaps?'

'I don't know why, but I've been over and over this since we last talked of it and I'm sure that I must have been the cause. But I can't work out how. If Mam had confessed that Dad wasn't my father, that I'd been the result of her carrying on when he was in prison, why did my sister kill herself?' She flopped back against the arm of the seat they shared, tears welling up in her eyes, and she sighed. 'I don't know, and without more information I never will know. And I'm never going home to find out.'

'I'm sorry, I've upset you again. I promise to avoid the subject in future.'

'Don't be sorry, Albert. I have to talk about it sometimes.'

Tentatively, aware of others now filling the bar room, Albert slid an arm around her shoulders and handed her a handkerchief. She leaned back against him and dried her eyes. They didn't move for a long time. Albert afraid of making the wrong move and Ethel grateful for the warmth and comfort of his nearness.

At two o'clock the landlady called time and, easing himself regretfully away, Albert paid the bill, helped her on with her khaki jacket and they left.

Walter was waiting for Wesley when he returned to camp two days later. He had Wesley's jacket over his arm. He had kept it although there had been no need. All he'd had to do was leave it in the hut in the care of one of the other men, to be given to him on his return, but Walter wanted to talk to the man, find out how well he knew Ethel and, if possible, learn the address of her father.

Turning him down in favour of that flyer Duggie, then causing him to lose his job, she had something coming to her and with luck payment would be soon. He removed the picture from the wall again and stared at it to reassure himself it was Ethel Twomey. Then he smiled as his inspection confirmed his first impression. It was Ethel all right.

When Wesley came in he was carrying a biscuit tin, which Walter guessed contained a cake from home. Most mothers saved the ingredients from their meagre rations to make a cake for their sons to take back to camp. His pulse quickened at the thought that Wesley might have seen Ethel a matter of hours ago.

'I was asked to return this,' he said, offering the jacket. 'You'll need it in the morning and might wonder where it was.'

Welsey thanked him off-handedly with a nod. 'There was no need, you could have left it with one of the others, or in the canteen – I know exactly where I left it.'

'Yes, but I thought ... well, the fact is, I did bring it back and when I came here I couldn't help noticing your picture of a friend of mine. If I'm not mistaken, that's Ethel Twomey with her family. Friend of yours too, is she?'

Startled, caught unaware, Wesley replied, 'Ethel? I used to know her but we've lost touch. This war, eh?'

'You know where she lives though?' Walter asked a little sharply.

Something about the man made Wesley stop the automatic response explaining that they were near neighbours, living but a short distance from each other. Instead he shook his head, stared at Walter and said, 'No idea. Sorry.'

'We were to keep in touch,' Walter explained, 'but I've mislaid her address.' Wesley knew that was a lame excuse. If Ethel had wanted to keep in touch, she would have written to him. 'Bad luck, mate,' was all he said, taking his jacket and putting it into his locker.

'If you could give me her home address,' Walter coaxed, 'I could write to her there.'

'Forget it, I can't help.' It was clear that he didn't know much about Ethel or he'd know that her family didn't know where to find her.

Wesley wrote a letter that evening, addressing it to his parents. He told them of the man's enquiry and asked them to be vigilant in case there was some threat to Ethel. His warning was vague but he had disliked the man and had a strong feeling that his need to find Ethel bode ill for her.

Walter had no trouble getting Wesley's home address. There was something about the man's reaction to his enquiry that suggested there had to be more than a once-upon-a-time friendship. A man doesn't keep a tatty photograph unless there was something special about it. If they were still together he'd have been given a more recent snap or a replacement. On his next leave, after checking at Ethel's last posting to find out where she had been sent, he would visit Wesley's home, where he was sure he'd find Dai Twomey close by. They could have a nice little chat.

There might even be money in it for him. If the man was so anxious to find his daughter he might be willing to pay. He'd play dumb at first, promise to find out where Ethel was and let the man know. That way he'd be more likely to be promised some cash.

Wesley sat on his bunk and wondered about the man called Walter Phillips. His reasons for enquiring about Ethel were unlikely to be good ones. He had a devious look about him. If only he could find Ethel, it might be a good idea to warn her or at least find out what Walter was up to. Taking the photograph from the wall once more, he went up to the canteen. Some new Naafi girls had arrived that weekend, it might be worth showing the picture and asking them. They moved around from camp to camp and there was a slim chance, a very slim chance, they had seen her.

'No,' one bright young girl replied with a smile. 'And what are you asking about her for when I'm standing in front of you, free, fascinating and fabulously rich?' Wesley smiled and turned away. A smile that didn't reach his eyes.

For Walter, finding Wesley's address had been simple, and on his next weekend leave he went to the area and tracked down the Twomeys, in spite of the lack of signposts and the refusal of local people to help for fear they were assisting an enemy spy. He booked into a bed-and-breakfast for two nights and promised himself that when he returned to camp, Dai Twomey would be aware of his daughter's whereabouts.

Outside the front door was the powerful Vincent, and the number matched the one in his memory. Remembering the violent behaviour of the red-haired man, he was cautious as he walked up the path and knocked on the door. It was to his great relief that the person who opened it was a small, grey-haired woman. Dressed in black and wearing no make-up even to hide the bruises on her cheek, she frowned and waited for him to explain the reason for his call.

'I wondered, is Ethel here?' he asked.

'You know her? You know where she is?'

'I think I can tell you exactly where she is,' he smiled.

'I ... I can't ask you in, my husband is sleeping and he wouldn't like being woken,' she said, glancing behind her nervously. Whispering now, she begged tearfully, 'Just give me an address so I can write, please.'

'Well, I can take a message, but it was her father I wanted to talk to. She's upset and wants to make up their quarrel. I know she'd be pleased if he went to see her. I'd hoped to plan a little surprise.'

'Sorry, but that wouldn't be a good idea.' He waited but she didn't explain. She asked again for an address but when he shook his head sadly, she pushed him with surprising force away from the door and closed it firmly. 'Stay away from here,' she hissed through the crack of the door. 'There's been enough trouble.'

Walter walked away, there was no need to knock again, no need make a scene. The man would come out some time, and he had all day.

There was a field opposite the Twomeys' house and, although it was cold and it soon began to drizzle, Walter waited, sheltering under a tree that was as useful as a sieve. He was soon very uncomfortable, with icy cold drips trickling through the trees, flattening his hair, soaking his shoulders and running down his neck. He ate the remains of the breakfast toast which he had brought with him and tried to ignore his growing discomfort.

There had been no movement from within the house all day. As darkness fell he saw the curtains being pulled across the windows and someone stepped outside to adjust the shutters that blacked out the porch.

A few minutes later he heard the front door open and in the gloom of the evening saw a shadow emerge. Then the motorbike started up and, with a roar, moved slowly down the narrow path and over the bridge. Before he could reach it, the driver had opened her up, it sped down the road rattling the air with its noise, and the shaded rear light disappeared from sight. Walter went back to the bed-and-breakfast to dry his clothes and find some food.

The following morning, with only four hours left before he had to leave, he once again stood in the field opposite the house and waited. It was quiet. There were only a few houses in the country road with wide spaces between them. An overnight mist was slow to clear and he felt confident of not being seen as he leaned against the smooth trunk of an elderly beech and watched the house for movement.

The hand over his mouth, another twisting his arms together and the knee in the small of his back came without warning, and shocked him. Sweat burst out on his forehead. His eyes opened wide. He tried to struggle but whoever was holding him knew how to render a man incapable and after a few seconds he relaxed and awaited his fate.

'Who are you?' a voice demanded, easing the hand away from his face to allow him to answer

'I don't mean any harm,' Walter panted.

'Who are you? Just answer my questions,' the man growled.

'Walter Phillips. I'm a friend of Ethel Twomey, I wanted to talk to her father.' Slowly and to his utter relief, the hands holding him relaxed and he was spun around to face a man six inches taller than himself, with red hair and bright blue, angry eyes. So like Ethel's father, but too young. 'But you aren't Dai Twomey? Who are you?' he dared to ask.

'Her brother! And I don't want you talking to my father, understand?'

'I wanted to try and settle the argument between your sister and your father. Life is so precarious these days and I wanted to help to bring them together, in case ... in case something awful happened to one of them.' He was lying but hoped he sounded pious enough to be believed.

'You're lying. And if I find you anywhere near Ethel or any of my family again, you'll live just long enough to regret it. You'd do well to remember that your war is with me. So far as you're concerned, I'm to be feared more than Hitler's bombers, believe me,' the man warned, before pushing Walter away from the house.

Pushing him in front of him, Sid guided the frightened Walter across a field and into a lane on the far side. He demanded Ethel's address and, fearfully, Walter told him what he knew, insisting that he didn't know her present whereabouts. He explained about seeing her father at the airfield, and told the man that Ethel and he had been been moved on separately. After a few minutes of being pushed around and threatened, Sid let him go.

Stumbling clumsily, his legs as useless as chewed string, Walter went back across the field and worked his way warily around the lanes to the bed-and-breakfast, collected his things and went to get the bus. As he found a seat he glanced back and was startled to see the red-haired man sitting astride a bicycle, watching, his expression a reminder of his threat.

When the bus had gone, Sid Twomey sat for a while, his heart racing with his performance of Sid Twomey, violent son of the violent Dai. He hadn't inherited his father's temper and neither did he enjoy fighting, but this was one time when he had been able to use the threat of his father's reputation to good effect. If Walter had swung a blow at him he'd have been able, by his remarkable strength, to push it aside, but he would have found it impossible to retaliate.

He went back home hoping his father was having one of his calmer days and that he wouldn't have to fend off an attack on himself or his mother. He had run away on the night of the row, after Ethel had pleaded with him to leave before their father killed one of them. But once Ethel had gone he had returned, knowing that his mother needed him.

Working in a munitions factory and spending almost every other moment at home was hardly a life, but until his father calmed down and accepted the situation, he had to stay. Thank goodness Wesley was in touch, news of him reaching them from his parents. One day they would find Ethel and then everything would be out in the open.

He sighed. If only he were a little more like his father, he would have forced Walter Phillips to tell him where Ethel was. He hadn't believed him when he'd insisted he didn't know. Another chance lost. Perhaps his father was right and the world really was run by bullies. The meek hardly inherited the earth with people like his father around.

And what was Hitler if not a bully? Destroying, taking what he wanted by force, using his power to rid the world of people whom he considered unsuitable.

He'd missed an opportunity to beat the truth out of Walter, but he still couldn't accept that violence was the right way to get what you wanted. Ethel would get in touch. Their father would one day be too weak to bully his way through life. He smiled grimly at that unlikely thought. Even when disease or age weakened him, the man would survive on his past record, creating fear in everyone who met him, until the day he died.

A call at six thirty one morning woke Ethel and Rosie; Kate slept peacefully on, her face shining with cream, hand underneath her head with fingers in between the metal curlers holding her rolled up hair, to ease the discomfort of her necessary suffering.

'Get your things together, you're moving on,' they were told. Half an hour later, Kate was still half asleep, struggling to untangle some recalcitrant 'Dinkie' curlers from her long hair. They had been given just enough time to drink a cup of tea and swallow a few biscuits then the three girls and four others were on their way to a new destination.

On arriving at the new camp a few hours later, one of the first people they met was Baba Morgan. He rushed up and gave Ethel a hug as the others were scrabbling around in the truck to find the clothes they had hastily thrown on board, not having time to pack properly.

Rosie turned and blushed alarmingly when she saw him. 'Baba! I wasn't expecting to see you.'

'I knew you were coming, Albert told me. He's over there getting the beds moved in.'

'Oh no, damp beds and cockroaches in the cupboard,' wailed Kate in mock distress, 'and nowhere to wash our hair.' She was laughing, pleased to see Baba too.

'I hope the canteen is up and running and we don't have to move out spiders and mice,' Rosie said. 'I'm starving, we didn't have breakfast before we left.'

'You? Hungry?' Baba teased. 'I can't believe that, Rosie Dreen. Come on, there's soup and fresh bread for you sent over from the cookhouse.' He took Rosie's arm and led them to where a table was set and a meal prepared.

Looking around them preparing to disapprove, they were gratified to see that the place was clean and ready for the eleven o'clock tea break. Having to complain about something, Ethel said, 'This tea's a funny colour, I bet that urn needs a good cleaning, eh, Rosie?'

'And that sweeping brush has swept its last crumb. I'll insist on a new one straight away,'

Kate added. She patted her curly blonde hair and rubbed a licked finger across an eyebrow. 'Got to keep up our standards.'

Baba was there on loan for a month or two, to help train new recruits in vehicle maintenance, and when the girls' first weekend off came around he was free too.

Rosie was going home to stay with her grandmother, Kate planned to visit her parents. Baba invited Ethel to go with him to London.

'Air raids. Bombs. What d'you want to go there for? Come home with me,' Kate said, a hint of jealousy in her protest.

Rosie smiled and said sadly, 'Lucky you. I wish he'd invited me. You wouldn't fancy swopping would you, and going to stay with my Nan?'

Being assured by Baba that it was definitely not a 'single room only' weekend, Ethel agreed. She had never been to London and, air raids apart, she thought it would be exciting.

Baba had been offered a lift in a friend's car and made sure he scrounged enough petrol to get them to the station. Sitting on the train in uniform, and with just a small suitcase, made the start of their weekend exciting. Knowing there were no emotional complications made Ethel feel relaxed, prepared to enjoy it even more, and her attitude towards Baba was affectionate and warm. This was such a treat. With nowhere to go on leave, she usually stayed in camp and often helped out others when asked, simply to make the time pass. Normally a weekend off meant long hours to fill until Kate and Rosie returned with news of their brief holiday. This time, thanks to Baba, she too would have a story to tell.

They had bought a newspaper and studied what was showing in the West End, planning a theatre and a late supper on their first night. Sunday was to be spent walking through some of the parks and just seeing the sights. Their train back to camp left at seven fifteen and whatever happened, they had to be on it or face being up on a charge.

They found their hotel and checked in and after leaving their cases and having a quick wash, they went out on to streets that were surprisingly busy. Arm in arm they went by underground and bus to the theatre and as they were nearing the front of the queue and about to buy their tickets, the air raid siren filled the air with its wailing.

With an arm around Ethel's shoulders, Baba led her back out on to the pavement. They followed the crowd to the street shelter, squashed into the damp, overcrowded building that seemed to Ethel less safe than the tin hat and slit trench she was used to.

'It's claustrophobic in here after being outside, watching the skies,' she whispered.

He pulled her closer to whisper, 'I'm not complaining, mind. Lovely this is.'

'Stop it, Baba, you promised to behave.'

'I will, but I won't pretend to like it. Here, come under my coat, it's not that warm in here. I can feel the damp seeping out of the walls, can't you?'

'You should have seen the first canteen we opened,' she laughed, squeezing closer to him, sliding an arm around his waist, welcoming his warmth. Snuggling up to Baba was no hardship, she admitted, and being in a strange place among strangers she was glad he was there. More than glad. She tried not to admit it to herself, but being so close to him was exciting.

The first bomb fell very close and dust filled the air. Her nostrils were filled with what she described as a 'dead buildings' smell. It brought back to her mind the old farm barn where she had found her sister but she quickly tried to brush away the painful memory.

She would have preferred to have been outside, where she could watch what was happening. Claustrophobia was easily encouraged while locked in a shelter with heaven knew what going on outside and facing the possibility of damage sealing her in. Other explosions were heard but they were a long way off and when the all clear sounded they sighed with relief. 'I thought for a moment we were going to be hit, didn't you?' Ethel said as she began at once to move towards the entrance.

'No,' he said scornfully. 'Nothing bad will happen to you while you're with Baba Morgan. He'll look after you.'

She patted his face playfully in the restricted space and he caught hold of her hand and kissed it slowly, the dim lights of the shelter making his eyes dark and mysterious, the eyes of a man she didn't really know. Excitement filled her and she leaned her head against his shoulder.

'Why are they taking so long to get out?' he asked a moment later when the doors hadn't opened and no one had moved on.

'Now we don't want no panicking, d'you hear me, ladies and gents?' a voice called. 'But we'll have to wait a while before we leave. There's something stuck against the door.'

Voices murmured and rose into a babble of alarm. Ethel clung even more tightly to Baba and took deep breaths, holding back her fear. The same voice called to them to be quiet. 'Be patient, and wait quietly. The wardens know we're here and they'll get things sorted as soon as they can – in the meantime, why don't we have a sing-song? That'll help the time pass.' There was a low groan of dismay from the rest.

'The British spirit is all very well, but being

a captive audience an' 'avin' to listen to that is treating us unfair,' someone muttered, as the strains of 'Keep the Home Fires Burning' began at the other end of the building. 'Why the 'ell don't they choose somethin' cheerful for once?' another complained. Their grumbles were lost as more and more joined in the well-known choruses.

'We'll miss some of the play,' Baba whispered into her hair, kissing her at the same time. Her forehead, her cheek, moving closer to her lips.

'Baba—' she warned.

'But I'm scared, Ethel,' he defended poutishly. 'I need to be comforted by a beautiful woman.'

Ethel said nothing. The desire to comfort him was too strong for her to be flippant. Her voice would give her away, her voice and the way her heart was beating, so close to his. She just hoped that by the time they returned to the hotel the feelings he was generating would have faded.

It was not for the first time that she wondered whether her father had been right and she was going the way of a wicked woman. To convince herself she was thinking stupid thoughts she pushed him away and joined in the singing with the rest.

When the doors opened it was a surprise at how much light there was. With more traffic on the road than she was used to at home,

the faint lights for each vehicle made sufficient contrast to see reasonably well. As a
country girl she was accustomed to moving
about with far less. She had no difficulty
finding the edge of the pavement, but when
Baba took her arm she didn't resist.

Seven

Albert came into the canteen one morning
when Ethel was alone and told her that
Walter was on his way.

'He's passing through on the way to a camp
outside Dover, but will be here for a night or
two because of the transport arrangements.'

'With luck we might not see him,' Ethel
replied. 'At least we're warned and can get
out of the way if we see him coming.'

'Unfortunately you won't be that lucky. He
isn't allowed to get off lightly and he'll be
coming to the canteen to do some painting.'

'Any chance of us changing our days off?
I'm sure one of us will have a grandmother's
funeral to attend.'

Albert shook his head, unamused by her
joke. 'I don't see how I can call the other
shift back from leave.'

Smiling, Ethel told him not to worry. 'I can

easily put him in his place,' she assured him.

Unfortunately for her, Walter saw her the moment he arrived. He had been given the rest of the day off, and when he saw her walking casually across the field to where the mechanics repair crews and riggers gathered for their mid-morning break, he felt a surge of excitement. Now he'd get her! He hurriedly checked a map and found that he was more than two hundred miles away from her home. A long way but it was the best chance he'd have, he'd have to get time off somehow, and fast. If he delayed she might easily have moved again and the chances of finding her a second time were remote. It was surprisingly easy to plead sickness and ask for the following day off. He left straight away and after a long train journey, then buses and walking when necessary, he reached the town nearest to Ethel's home with only a couple of setbacks.

Fortunately he had memorized the names of places in the vicinity and, with the buses having blackboards on which their destination was chalked, he managed reasonably well. He was sitting under the beech tree opposite the house by midnight, thankful that the weather was mild, and settled to wait among the beechmast under the leafless branches wrapped in his greatcoat. He munched the sandwiches he had fortunately remembered to pack, warmed himself from the two flasks he had brought, one filled with soup, the other containing coffee, and, wrapped in groundsheet and blanket, he slept.

He woke early, chilled and stiff but excited at the prospect of Ethel's unpleasant surprise. Moving through the field opposite the house and sliding down the bank into the road a bit further along, he walked past the house and glanced in. He saw the big man with his shock of red hair passing the window and shuddered. There was no way he was going to knock on that door. Dai Twomey and his son were the type to thump first and ask questions later. He had a note prepared, giving the address of the place where Ethel was to be found, and this he left on the seat of the motorbike.

He waited a while and was gratified to see the man come out dressed in the heavy clothes of a motorcyclist. The man picked up the note and read it, then shuffled his feet and looked around as though expecting its author to appear. Walter shrank behind the protection of his tree.

He was certain the man was Ethel's father. He could see him quite clearly and guessed he was about sixty years old. He was standing with shoulders bent forward and curled inward – as though he slept in a barrel, Walter smiled. He had a huge belly that the thick clothing failed to hide and a face lined by too much drink and endless cigarettes.

Yes, it was Dai Twomey holding the note, and from the grim expression on the man's face, he wouldn't be planning a loving greeting when he and Ethel met.

Thank goodness his message hadn't been found by the brother. He had visions of the young man running up the bank to where he was hiding and half murdering him. He felt the trickle of fear slither down his spine. Then he forgot thoughts of failure. He had succeeded, his ingenuity had brought Ethel her come-uppance. She'd regret the day she turned him down so publicly. She'd have time to think about how she had got him caught stealing from the store and ruined his career. Her father, her violent and angry father, now knew where to find her. With an insouciant swagger, Walter cut across the field, walked to the bus stop and by evening was back in camp.

He went into the canteen as the three girls were about to close. He carried a decorator's ladder and without a word to them stood it against the wall and went to collect tins of paint and some brushes. Then he stood and watched Ethel serving chips and spam to two young airmen, and Kate flirting as she dealt with others at the net bar. There was an amiable smile on his face.

'Hello, Ethel,' he said after a while had passed and no one had greeted him. 'Glad to see me back?'

'Aren't there some latrines needing your attention?' she replied.

'You won't be so cocky one of these days,' he said in a hissing whisper.

'Go away, Walter,' she sighed, and Kate and Rosie joined in supporting her.

'This man annoying you?' one of the airmen called.

Walter turned away, giving Ethel a wide, knowing smile, and left.

'Bothering me? That little squirt? Not a chance!' But there was something in the man's knowing smile that bothered her.

It was Friday and their weekend off. Once the lunch was over they were free until the following Monday morning. Baba, Kate, Rosie and Ethel were going to the pictures. Baba had arranged a lift in one of the lorries going into town and two mechanics were going with them.

The three girls hid in the back, covered with some clean sacks as the driver was not allowed to carry passengers on that particular journey. After the pictures, they went to buy fish and chips as they waited for the lorry to return to pick them up and Rosie found herself talking to one of the airmen from Scotland, a man called Connor. He seemed quiet and rather shy and she warmed to him at once. He wasn't as attractive as Baba, of course, but Baba was arm in arm with Ethel and had eyes for no one else.

Connor had a wonderful accent and his voice was soft and intimate. She wondered if he might ask her out. Perhaps this would be one of the times she'd say yes.

They all alighted from the lorry a short distance from, but in sight of, the gate. The guards were usually blind to such things as giving lifts, specially when it was the valued Naafi girls. It was a long walk into town and the buses were not that frequent.

The driver moved on and the six young people were walking, laughing, happily planning another such outing, when Ethel's father appeared. He grabbed Ethel, who screamed. Kate and Rosie clung on to her and tried to pull her free.

'You're coming home with me,' he shouted, throwing Kate and Rosie aside and leading Ethel away from the gate.

The three men struggled with him and Dai pushed them away with ease. Baba leapt on the man's back and, with hands clasped, pulled on his throat. Dai shook him off and with one hand hit him and knocked him to the ground with as little trouble as swatting a fly.

The guards saw the trouble and ran to help. Within moments there were seven men trying to hold the man. His strength was phenomenal and long minutes passed and more men joined in before he was handcuffed and restrained.

He was arrested and taken into town, Ethel being given the assurance that he would be kept overnight and possibly longer. She looked very thoughtful.

'With Dad safely locked up, it's my chance to go and see Mam and get an explanation,' she told Baba.

'I'll come with you, but I'm not much use, am I?' he said sadly.

'We all think you were very brave,' Kate said, and Rosie nodded vigorously in agreement, her blue eyes wide in admiration.

'I think so too, Baba, but I'd rather go on my own. Mam might not talk anyway but she's less likely to if there's anyone else there.'

Ethel was able to leave soon after breakfast the following day. By exchanging shifts with others she had until Tuesday to sort out the problems at home.

When she reached the bus stop for the first stage of her journey, Albert was waiting for her, sitting in the driving seat of an MG midget and gesturing for her to get into the passenger seat.

'Where have you been hiding this?' she asked, 'and where d'you think you're going?'

'It's mine for the day. I hope we aren't stopped though, the petrol in it is the wrong colour!'

When petrol was unavailable, some of the pilots managed to fill their cars with the high octane fuel used for their planes. Strictly illegal, spot checks were sometimes made on cars carrying RAF personnel. Ignoring the danger of heavy fines and disciplinary punishments, Ethel jumped in. She had seen the men riding in these cars and none used the low door so she imitated them by jumping in, falling in a heap half on the seat and half in Albert's lap. He didn't seem to mind, in fact it set the mood for the journey, and they were laughing as they waved to the guards and drove through the gates.

When her mother opened the door to them she burst noisily into tears. 'Ethel! At last! Why didn't you write? Tell me where you were? I've been so worried.'

'How could I tell you where I'd gone, you'd have told Dad and what happened yesterday would have happened sooner.'

'Yesterday? What happened? Your father's been arrested.'

'I know! He tried to kidnap me and bring me home!'

'Shall we go inside?' Albert suggested and Molly Twomey suddenly realized that she hadn't moved from the doorway. 'Come in, come in. Of course you can come in, it's your home, isn't it?' Although the words of welcome sounded sincere, Albert noticed that the agitated woman looked up and down the road nervously and he guessed at her fears that her husband might suddenly appear.

'My home? Not any longer, Mam, and unless you give me a few answers I won't be coming here ever again.'

Molly pressed herself against the wall in the small entrance to allow them to pass then followed them through to the living room at the back of the house.

'Now, I'll make myself scarce, shall I?' Albert suggested. 'While you and your mother sort out what you've come to sort.' He intended to stand guard outside, to be able to warn them if the dreaded Dai Twomey appeared.

'No, Albert. If you will, I'd like you to stay.'

He looked doubtful but agreed. He sat near the open door leading to the front of the house, hoping that he might at least hear the sound of someone approaching and be able to get Ethel out through the back.

'Tea. I'll make us some tea.' Molly moved towards the kitchen but Ethel held her arm and led her back to the armchair close to the fireplace.

'Later, Mam. First I want you to tell me why Dad was so angry and why Glenys ... died ... in the way she did.'

'How do I know what makes your father lose his temper? He'll never change. You know very well he's always been violent. Don't tell me you've forgotten all the months he's spent in prison?'

'I remember very well. I also know that just before Glenys died he became much worse. He knocked you practically unconscious, dislocated my arm, and drove Wesley away after giving him a beating. Sid disappeared and my sister killed herself rather than go on living in the same house as him. You have to tell me why, Mam.'

Tears flooded her mother's weary eyes but Ethel hardened her heart. She had to know the truth and this might be her last chance.

'A cup of tea first, then we'll talk,' Molly sobbed.

'Now, Mam. Just tell me what I've done to make him so wild with me.'

'He isn't wild with you, Ethel love, it's the rest of us.'

She looked around the room avoiding Ethel's eyes, her tears escaping and running down her cheeks. Ethel felt ashamed of bullying her mother but knew she had to insist. She stared, willing her mother to talk. 'Tell me, Mam.'

'Well, the truth is, I'm not your Mam at all.'

'What?'

Of all the explanations Ethel had dreamed up as the reason for the family row, this was a complete surprise. Her heart was racing, and suddenly she didn't want to hear any more answers. But she knew that if she walked out now the truth would be a question mark over her life, tormenting her for ever. 'Then who am I?' she whispered as she stared at her mother in disbelief.

'Glenys, who you thought was your sister, was really your mother. She was only fifteen, your father – your grandfather, I suppose he really is – was in prison and I wrote to tell him I was expecting another child. I was too old really, but he believed me and he's always thought of you as his own, his and mine.'

'How did he find out?'

'Glenys always insisted that she would tell you when you were eighteen. She thought it was only right that once you reached an age when you could consider marriage, you ought to know the truth. With you and Wesley talking about an engagement she had no more time.'

'She told Dad?' Ethel whispered.

'I knew he'd be angry but I thought his anger would be towards me for deceiving him. I didn't think he'd turn on you. After all, you had done nothing wrong.'

'He kept saying I'd go bad. Glenys had a child when she was unmarried and little more than a child herself, but I don't understand why he thinks I'll grow wicked because of my parents.' Her heart lurched at the reminder that it had in fact happened to her too. Could a weakness towards men really be inherited, she wondered sadly. Then as her mother sat silently with tears slowly dripping down her face and on to her twisting hands, trying to pluck up the courage to tell her more, Ethel asked the question to which she half dreaded the answer. What if her father had been someone evil? That would explain her father's worries. A criminal maybe, or someone as wild and violent as him.

'Who was he?' she asked, her voice surprisingly strong. 'Who was my father?'

Molly stared at her for a while. A frown crossed her face as though she wished for something better to impart. 'Glenys would never say. Now she's dead and we'll never know.'

'You must have had some suspicions? Tell me who she was friendly with at that time.'

'It was a boy she knew from school, I expect. Someone who's probably as ignorant as we are, unaware that he has a lovely daughter called Ethel.'

They stayed to drink a cup of tea and Ethel promised to send news via her former employer in the café so long as her father – or grandfather, she thought with renewed shock – wasn't told.

Driving back to camp in the noisy little car she talked all the way, shouting above the noise of the engine, describing her emotions. When she stopped talking, Albert said something to start her off again. He knew she needed to work it out of her system, to make

227

sense of it, ease away the shock. But their visit had resulted in more questions than those with which they had started – all without answers.

They stopped outside a small café offering tea and scones and went inside, the car parked on the wide expanse of waste ground at the side where, they guessed, a house had recently stood, the victim of a bomb. The broken walls and piles of rubble that remained were already being covered in greenery, colonized by what in summer would be a riotous glory of wild flowers.

When Albert had ordered, he encouraged her to continue talking about her mother's revelation.

'Remember that it doesn't alter anything,' he told her. 'You're nineteen and out in the world on your own. Your character is firmly set and you have no unpleasant traits that might have been inherited from your unknown father. They would have revealed themselves by now.'

Again her secret guilt lurched at her. 'Who was he? I don't know what I've inherited. It's not knowing, that's the nightmare.'

'Plenty of others have had to face that one,' he reminded her gently. 'Orphans abandoned by their parents and never knowing where they came from, sometimes not even knowing the town in which they were born.'

'Knowing there are others in the same

situation doesn't help *me* cope. How *could* it help?'

'At least you knew Glenys for the first eighteen years of your life. Can you really imagine her being attracted to someone like your father? Or any of the other personality failures you fear? I didn't get to meet her but you knew her well, you know she wouldn't have chosen to love an evil person or someone weak. And as for violence, surely she had enough of that without seeking out another man who couldn't control his fists? Remember her, Ethel. Remember that you loved her and feel safe.'

They ate the poor offerings described as 'Devonshire' scones, which fell apart before the margarine and thin jam could be spread. Licking the tip of a finger, Ethel picked up the crumbs and ate without enjoyment. Her mind was filled with a cavalcade of faces, one of which might be her father. She visualized all the men of her sister's age and wondered which one had lain with Glenys and created her. There weren't that many. The list was minimal, and as she visualized each one, hope sprang and then died as each face was abandoned.

'Invent him,' Albert smiled, as though he had guessed what was passing through her mind. 'Invent the kind of man you'd like to have for a father and he's yours to imagine.'

'Clark Gable?'

'If you wish. Didn't I hear somewhere that he stayed in your village one summer?' He smiled again, egging her on, encouraging her to laugh.

'James Cagney?'

'Definitely not.'

'James Stewart?'

'A possible.'

'Arthur Askey? Tommy Handley? Donald Duck?' She laughed, but Albert knew the laughter was on the edge of hysteria and tears were not far away.

He took both of her hands in his, raised them to his lips and said softly, 'Whoever he was he'd be very proud of the daughter he gave life to, any man would.'

Ethel stared at him as she fought to gain control, tears glistening in her eyes. 'If I could choose a man to call father it would be someone like you, Albert. You'd make a perfect father.'

He felt the shock stiffen on his face. So she saw him as a father-figure, not someone whom she could love. He released the hold on her hands and suggested they left.

Then she pulled him around to face her and added, 'Fortunately for me, you're young enough to be something more than a father. Thank you, Albert, for being such a friend. I don't know how I'd cope with any of this without having you in my life.'

He stared at her strangely and said, 'I'll be

in your life for as long as you want me there.'

'For always,' she smiled. But she wasn't looking at him in a way that gave the words any meaning.

As they waited for the bill, Ethel saw a policeman stop near the MG, dismount from his bicycle, write something in his book, then enter the café. He looked around at the empty tables and walked across to them. 'Is that vehicle outside belonging to you, sir?' he asked. Ethel reached for Albert's hand and held it.

'Spot checks on cars, sir, nothing to worry about. We have to do what we're told. I want to check on the petrol, is that all right with you, sir?'

'What car?' Ethel said before Albert could speak. 'We don't have a car, we're waiting for the bus, aren't we, Albert love?'

'What are those goggles in your hand then?'

'Oh, these? I found them on the chair as I sat down. I was going to throw them into the driver's seat as we left.'

Unable to know whether he was in the Royal Airforce or not as he was wearing a uniform he did not recognize, but making an assumption from the sports car outside, the policeman asked, 'Some sort of flyer, are you, sir? On a bit of a day out?'

Albert smiled but said nothing, half expecting Ethel to again answer for him.

231

The policeman smiled and snapped his notebook closed. 'I've got great admiration for our flyers myself. Whatever uniform you wear. Some sort of special service, are you?'

Again Albert didn't reply. He just gave what he hoped was a hesitant smile.

'Too smart for your own good, officer,' Ethel said in a low voice.

'Just get home as quick as you can, sir, there's a bit of an inspection going on today and tomorrow. I'd take the quieter roads if I were you.'

They thanked him politely and left. A quick glance at the map and they headed for the camp by the most tortuous, most little-used route. At the second corner they passed the policeman on his bicycle and he waved cheerily.

'Thank you,' Ethel said, as they jumped out of the car back in camp. She stretched over and kissed him, intending to touch his cheek with her lips, but he turned and their lips touched, embarrassing them both. He because he had gone too far too soon and she because she was afraid she had unintentionally encouraged him.

Rosie and Kate were curious to hear the result of Ethel's visit home, but apart from explaining about her true mother being her sister, she expanded on it very little.

'I'm tired,' she excused, but Kate guessed

that the brightness of her eyes and the glow on her cheeks meant Ethel had another story to tell. Kate mouthed the word 'interesting', with a wink at Rosie. She was amused at the thought of the serious Albert involved in a loving embrace. Rosie wondered whether Baba would be upset and whether he would need comforting.

The following evening Rosie had a date with the handsome Scottish flyer Connor, and she wished she could cancel it. Connor was a pilot and it was a point of honour never to let them down by not turning up for a date. Pilots needed all their wits about them when they went up to face the enemy. Girlfriend troubles had to be left on the ground. Their job was fearful enough and the girls had to do their best to make sure they were free of other worries and able to concentrate on the job of flying. It was an unwritten law that once a date was arranged, no one would let them down.

Rosie was no longer looking forward to meeting Connor for a visit to the cinema but Kate insisted on her dressing as smartly as she could, lending her a dress she had brought with her and using her make-up to 'enhance your lovely blue eyes'.

Protesting all the way, Rosie set off to meet the young pilot feeling self-conscious with eye-shadow on her lids, eyebrows pencilled to a darker shade, and a soft lipstick touched with a faint smear of vaseline to add a shine.

'If my Nan could see me now she'd disown me,' she said as Kate walked with her towards the guard post.

Kate had a date with the son of a wealthy furniture shop proprietor called Rowan Fotheringay, a man who had promised her what he called a good night out. There was a nightclub in the place where he was taking her and as the car he owned spun out along the evening street, through town after town, she began to wonder how far away this nightclub was. She had never been to one before and like Rosie was a little apprehensive. They had been on the road for more than an hour and a half before she realized she was going to London. She began to panic. Unwritten law or not, she wanted to cancel this date and go back to camp.

Walking home from a date after having to run from a man too passionate was a joke they all enjoyed and she thought that tonight with the worldly Rowan Fotheringay would be the night she lived the joke and found it not funny at all.

The nightclub was in a cellar in an isolated area where few buildings had been left standing. As the car slowed to a stop she looked around the area and saw streets of destroyed houses that had resulted from the Blitz of previous months.

'I don't think I want to go down there,' she

said, trying to sound unafraid as they approached the half-hidden doorway below the level of the pavement.

'Come on, gorgeous, you'll love it. Music and drink and friends having fun, what more can you ask of a night out, eh?'

The steps were in complete darkness and she was glad of Rowan's arm around her shoulders. Then as they approached the zig-zag blackout barriers and the heavy velvet curtains, he held her to him, pressing his body against hers in a way that frightened her. She pushed him away as much as the limited space allowed and told him angrily to behave.

'Behave?' he laughed. 'Surely you don't think I've brought you all this way to behave?'

Stumbling back through the passage and up the steps she reached the pavement as he caught up with her.

'Take me back at once!' she demanded.

'You are joking, you tart! Leading me on then playing the modest virgin isn't funny, you know. And I'm not the sort to be treated like a fool!'

'I'm the one who's a fool, thinking you were a man to be trusted. What sort of a girl d'you think I am? Now take me back or I'll call a policeman.'

The whole area was already dark and if there had been a policeman standing within six feet of them she wouldn't have been able to see him.

Turning away from him, convinced that he'd follow, she walked a few steps then was horrified to hear his footsteps receding back down the steps to the nightclub. In the strange landscape of the ruined buildings, with no light available, she felt in her handbag for a torch. She had to get to where she could find a bus stop. There had to be a railway station near. Somehow she had to get herself back to camp.

For Rosie the evening had started pleasantly enough. Connor was a quiet unassuming man, who did everything to make her feel important, ushering her into the seat on the bus, making sure she was comfortable and paying her fare. When they had queued for fifty minutes and knew they would have to miss the end of the main film, they hesitated about going in, but Connor insisted. 'We can always find a taxi,' he said airily. 'I've just had some money from my parents. They know how miserable life is if I can't go out occasionally and have fun.'

'We could have some fish and chips instead,' the ever-hungry Rosie suggested but Connor said no. He stood behind her and with an arm around her squeezed her shoulders, pressing her against him, kissing the top of her blonde head. Then he handed her

236

a small box of chocolates and she gasped in delight, wondering how soon she could open it.

As the queue slowly moved towards the ticket kiosk, Rosie muttered her usual hesitations about wasting his money on her and shouldn't they go back and try again another night, but he smiled and patted her arm and told her she was worth every penny, even if the film turned out to be rubbish.

They were just six from the head of the queue when a young airman came out with a girl on his arm. Seeing Connor he called and came over.

'Hi, Connor, how's Fiona?'

'Oh, she's fine,' Connor said. 'What's the film like, any good?'

'Not bad, we enjoyed it, didn't we?' he asked the girl beside him.

'Who's Fiona?' Rosie asked. 'Your sister?'

'Yes, my little sister, she's in the Land Army. Proud of her I am. Now,' he added taking a step forward, 'this looks like us at last.'

The friend who had spoken to Connor came back. Pulling something out of his pocket he handed him a photograph. 'Next time you write to your wife send her this, it's a photograph I took on your birthday bash. The others weren't suitable for her to see,' he laughed, before running back to his girl.

'Your wife?' Rosie asked, her face colouring in embarrassment. 'Fiona? She isn't your sister?'

'No, but that shouldn't spoil our evening out.'

'Of course it will!' Rosie was horrified.

'Why? You don't think men stay loyal when they're away for months and may be years on end, do you? No sensible woman would expect it. Now d'you want to go upstairs or down?'

'I don't want to go anywhere with you.' With a face as bright as the fire engine that was driving noisily past the cinema, she ran without stopping to the bus stop.

There was a notice pasted on the temporary bus stop sign that stood against the kerb. She read with dismay that due to an unexploded bomb being discovered on one of the roads out of town the buses on that route wouldn't be running until the following day. Did that mean she couldn't get back to camp?

She decided that in case she had to walk the seven miles back to camp, she'd fortify herself first with some fish and chips. It was just after she had been served that the air raid siren went. Grabbing her hot, newspaper-wrapped package she followed the crowd to the street shelter. They wouldn't have seen the film anyway, she consoled herself.

The raid was long lasting and quickly followed by two others, and it was dawn before she emerged from the shelter. Her first action was to phone the camp to explain what had happened. Kate and Ethel would be worried and she hoped someone would pass the message on.

A bus inspector walked up and down in the vicinity of the bus stop, looking important with his pencil and clip-board, his loud voice answering the questions with which he was bombarded by hopeful passengers. When she was able to get close enough she asked the way to the bus route that would take her to the camp. The route was a devious one and it was almost an hour before she was in sight of it.

When she eventually reached the bus stop there was a long line of patient people standing looking hopefully along the road. A murmur of voices made her turn and she saw one of the familiar red double-deckers approaching. She was surprised to see Kate waiting in the queue. Her make-up was less than perfect, her hair had lost its curls and she looked terrified.

'Where have you been?' they asked in unison. Briefly, as the queue worked itself towards the bus entrance, they described their disappointing evenings out.

'I thought I wouldn't get back. I had no idea where I was,' Kate told Rosie.

'I knew exactly where I was!' Rosie wailed. 'In the arms of a married man! My Nan would kill me!' The bus looked full and they sighed, certain they would have to wait for the next. Then an inspector appeared and the conductor made an announcement and everyone groaned as the passengers began to alight from the bus and the long queue reformed.

'Now what's happened?' Kate sighed.

'The roads are blocked by a collapsed building and the bus can't run,' the conductor told them. 'We're trying to arrange to take you to a point where someone will escort you to where another bus will be waiting.'

'Let's get back on then,' someone called, and the conductor shook his head.

'This bus is needed on another route. You'll have to wait an hour at least. Come back in an hour and your guide will be waiting. I suggest you go and find yourselves a cup of tea.'

'And a sticky bun! I'm starving,' Rosie groaned, having abandoned her meal in the shelter.

'So am I,' Kate said. 'I was expecting a meal last night so I ate nothing after lunch and that was only rissoles and chips.'

The café was crowded but they managed to stand and drink a cup of tea and eat a slice of cake before going once more to the bus stop. Two men in conductor's uniform were waiting and they led them through deserted streets in which several houses had been bombed. Piles of rubble were all that was left of some properties; other houses suffered little damage, even though they were not far apart.

When the orderly queue had re-formed and they were beginning to think the end of their troubles was in sight, the air raid siren began its wail. There were two more raids and it was four the following morning when they eventually emerged from the air raid shelter to which they had been led.

'I'm starving,' Rosie said.

'Quick, let's make a dash for the café before the others have the same idea!'

It was as they emerged from the all-night café which, at that early hour, had promised a pork sausage and mashed potatoes for one shilling and ninepence, that Kate saw Rowan Fotheringay. She pulled Rosie into a doorway and pointed to him. 'That's the delightful Rowan who left me to find my own way back from London. He took me there by car and I didn't even know where to find the nearest station.'

'Let's do the same to him,' Rosie suggested. 'He's parked his car over near that hotel and I didn't see him take out the key.'

'You don't mean ... we daren't!'

'He deserves it.'

They waited until Rowan had disappeared through the door of the hotel and ran to the car. Rosie was right, the key was in the ignition.

'Come on, Kate, you have to make use of those driving lessons.'

They jumped in and Kate tentatively pressed the pedals and fiddled with the gear stick. Then she turned on the ignition, the blast of sound convincing her that Rowan would hear, and releasing the brake shot off barely in control into the traffic, with Rosie squealing in delight.

Their progress was not unobtrusive. People stopped and laughed at them as the car jerked and stalled, was gunned into life, jerked and stalled again, and they went around the first corner in a series of jumps before settling down to head out of town.

They left the car just out of sight of the guard room at the gate and walked in still giggling at their adventure. They had to report and explain the reasons for their absence and they said that after being told of the unavailability of the bus they had managed to get a lift from a kind-hearted airman.

Eight

Over the following months Ethel, Kate and Rosie were moved several times. Army camps, and more airforce stations and once, during 1942, a camp in which prisoners were kept. The Italians worked in the kitchens sometimes, under supervision. Their attempts at learning English were encouraged and caused much laughter when the guards allowed. At another place in the north of England they were stationed at a camp where tanks training took place, the great cumbersome-looking vehicles a strange sight in the countryside. Fortunately the three girls stayed together, so starting again was always fun even when the work was not.

For the first time, Ethel had letters when the others collected their post. Baba Morgan wrote to her weekly, giving her news of the happenings on other stations on which they had worked. Gradually he added news of himself and his sisters, amusing stories intended to cheer her, anecdotes about himself as a child. He described his family and even sent a photograph of them. He referred to all they would do, the things he would show her when she visited his home and met them but she did not respond to the hints. Tempting as it was, she was not certain enough of her feelings for him and didn't want to give him hope then let him down.

Duggie was still in her thoughts. Duggie and their child. While she still grieved for them she wasn't free to love again. Desire to be loved as Duggie had loved her flared sometimes and would quickly subside as shame for her disloyal feelings overwhelmed her.

She felt the same ambivalence toward Albert Pugh. He wrote to her regularly and his letters were more serious, discussing the wider progress of the war and his relief that the United States of America had brought the force of their armies to help Britain's fight.

Ethel wrote back to them both, the mood differing with each recipient, humour more prevalent in the letters to Baba, and shorter, more factual notes to Albert. She was grateful to them both, the letters gave her greater happiness than either realized. To wait for the post with anticipation was new to her. To have someone who cared, loved her maybe, gave a purpose to her days and a hope for the future. Life could be lived without a ready-made base provided by a family, she told herself. Perhaps one day she would build one; a family of dear friends. Once the war ended she would be on her own, she would have to make a base for herself far from her home, but with the affection of friends. With Kate and Rosie, Baba and Albert, she wouldn't find it impossible. She knew she would cope.

Rosie's Nan had been told she had to have soldiers billeted on her and she wrote to her granddaughter telling her how much she was enjoying having them. On a visit home, Rosie learned that the men were there for training at a nearby beach. As one group left, another came and it had given Nan an idea.

'She gets a temporary ration book for them and some money, and best of all, she loves it,' Rosie reported. 'In fact she thinks she might open a guesthouse after the war. There'll be plenty of commercial travellers looking for a night's lodgings and they pay about three shillings and sixpence a night. The house is too big for just the two of us and we both enjoy cooking.'

'Mam and Dad seem to be involved with all kinds of unlikely schemes too,' Kate smiled. 'This war has certainly changed everyone's life. They'd never bothered to make friends, too busy I suppose, but now Mam belongs to a knitting circle making scarves and socks and things for the forces and goes out collecting National Savings contributions every week. Dad does fire-watching and belongs to the Home Guard. He's even joined their darts team. My Dad playing darts in the local. It's unheard of.'

'Will you go back to the shop?' Rosie asked Kate.

'I don't think so, I fancy something more glamorous – that is, unless I've married my rich, handsome American by then.'

'Heaven knows what I'll do,' Ethel frowned. 'When this lot's over I'll have to make a fresh start somewhere far away from my pre-war life.'

'Let's open a café!' Rosie suggested and they discussed the idea for a while in a non-serious way.

When they managed to have the same weekend off, they sometimes went to stay with Rosie's Nan. Once or twice they descended on a rather anxious Mr and Mrs Banner and stayed with Kate. They didn't do this often as they sensed that Mrs Banner found them hard to take.

'Your friends are welcome any time, dear, you know that, this is your home,' she told Kate, 'but I do admit to finding them rather ... boisterous.'

Kate smiled and reminded her mother that working hard and with such long hours they needed to let off steam.

'Let off steam? You make them sound like kettles, dear.' Kate laughed so loudly that Mrs Banner joined in, flattered to find herself so amusing. She repeated it to the others and again to her husband.

When she packed the inevitable parcel for them to take back, she added a few extra sweets and bars of chocolate – which, in the previous July, had joined the list of rationed goods – as well as food for the train journey.

It was autumn in 1942 when they stayed with the Banners again. All three of them, as Rosie's Nan's house was now full of soldiers. The talk was of the good-natured and attractive American soldiers who had arrived to great excitement earlier that year.

They met them on the streets, often surrounded by young boys, handing out sticks of chewing gum, which was rapidly becoming the international currency of friendship. Kind, friendly young men who were patient with the children who sometimes pestered them. They were amused by and sometimes tried the various street activities, looking ungainly as they rode the small-sized bicycles and bogie carts, and tried their hands at hopscotch, whip and top and skipping games.

They crowded the floor at the local dance hall, British soldiers watching in admiration and envy as the smartly dressed men demonstrated their new dances. They brought such fun to the normally staid affairs, and there were only a few who wished they had not arrived – usually the local boys, who were afraid they couldn't compete with the fascination of these newcomers.

Dressed in her newest clothes supplied by her doting parents, Kate went to try the new dances with fear and determination. Here was her chance to find herself a rich American husband, and learning to jive and boogy was clearly the first step.

Rosie hid well back in the line of admirers, away from the chance of being invited to dance, and Ethel too had doubts, seeing the way the girls were thrown about with such apparent indifference to their safety. But as she watched she realized that in the hands of these experts the danger was slight, the fun better than anything before.

'More chance of being knocked down in the blackout than being hurt by one of these fellas, Rosie,' she said in awe, and moved slowly towards the edge of the admiring crowd forming a circle around a few couples demonstrating their skill. When a tall, handsome young soldier approached she took a deep breath, determined not to refuse, but he went past her and took the hand of a disbelieving Rosie.

What happened next made Ethel and Kate stare mesmerized, trying not to blink for fear of missing a moment. Rosie tried to run away but then the wail of a trumpet in the unbelievably good band seemed to catch her up in the music, capture her in its magic and she gave herself into the care of her partner.

Stiff at first, but soon surrendering to the music, she relaxed and concentrated on her partner's moves. He was skilled but, aware of her shyness, he carefully coaxed her, determined she would have fun. They were not the star performers of the evening but, blushing furiously in the over-heated dance hall, Rosie declared herself happier than she could remember.

Ethel wriggled her way to where the kind young soldier was talking to friends and thanked him for the way he looked after Rosie.

'A pleasure, young lady,' he smiled and offered his arms to her. She tried but failed to reach the heights scaled by shy little Rosie. Awkwardly she apologized and asked her partner why.

'Your delightful friend wanted to please,' he replied. 'That's a wonderful gift, to be able to forget yourself and please another, specially a stranger like myself. You're very fortunate to have a friend like her.'

The words, spoken with such conviction and in his delightful accent, warmed Ethel's heart and she pushed her way back to where Kate and Rosie were drinking lemonade and hugged them both.

When they went back in a dreamily happy state to the Banners' home, Kate declared herself in love.

'Which one?' Ethel asked with a frown.

'All of them,' Kate sighed happily.

In a spare room they pushed the bed against the wall and with Kate's gramophone played records and danced until they were exhausted. Leaving the others to finish the final record, Kate went downstairs to prepare a hot drink before bed and was weepily surprised to see her parents dancing together, humming softly to the music, in the room behind the shop.

There were always newcomers to the camps, sometimes transfers and, more often, young men and women newly conscripted. It was these the three girls tried to befriend. The inoculations and injections, which all recruits had to undergo, were always a trial and they comforted the sufferers as they recovered. As they dealt with orders at the busy counter, serving hot snacks of beans on toast, chips, omelettes made from dried egg and smothered with sauce, sausage and mash and other favourites, they would seek out the quiet ones and encourage them to talk about home and family. Rosie and Kate often offered them some gifts from home, some of the chocolate given to them by Kate's mother, or cakes supplied by Rosie's Nan.

Ethel gave up her sweet ration so she too could contribute to the occasional gifts.

There were no parcels from her home to add to their generosity.

One morning while they were on their way to yet another posting, this time to a large army camp, they passed close to her home and, begging the driver to give them a couple of hours, she left him eating lunch in a café in the town and led her two friends first by bus then across fields to her former home.

She daren't go in, daren't even risk being seen close by, so after looking in the hope of seeing her mother, and seeing instead her father arriving and dismounting from his motorbike in the road outside, they turned away and went to the Baileys' farm where she had worked on occasion as a child, helping with the seasonal tasks.

She hadn't been there since leaving to join the Naafi. They might not even recognize her, she thought. She was certain her experiences over the past years had changed her. It was a long time since, as a child, she had helped with the harvest or taken food to the fields for the hedger and ditcher. So much had happened since those days. How could she still look the same?

She led her friends towards the entrance to the yard, listening to the sounds of someone moving churns around. They would have washed them after morning milking and were putting them ready to receive the evening's refills. At the roadside was a platform on which the churns were placed for collection – fifteen-and seventeen-gallon churns that were tilted and rolled with ease by the dairymen. A resurge of memory flooded back and it all became so familiar and dear to her, and yet tinged with the sadness of loss. A glimpse of childhood rescued from memory, together with the tainted overtones of all that had happened since.

A young woman she didn't know came into view first and asked what they wanted.

'Are Mr and Mrs Bailey here? I'm Ethel, I used to work here,' she explained, 'when I was little.' She gestured toward Kate and Rosie, who was bending down admiring some Light Sussex hens that were strutting around chortling a welcome.

'Mrs Bailey?' the girl called and headed for the kitchen door. She called again and Mrs Bailey came out, stared short-sightedly for a moment then ran towards Ethel, her arms wide, words of welcome issuing from her lips. 'William!' she called. 'Come and see who's here. It's Ethel Twomey, come to see us at last.'

'Please don't tell Dad I've been here,' Ethel warned when the ecstatic welcome eased and food was offered. 'I don't want him to find me again.'

Rita and William Bailey promised but asked, 'You do know he's given up his job?'

Ethel shook her head and Mrs Bailey

added, 'He's demented, determined to find you and bring you home. He refuses to tell your mother why, but he spends time going around the army and airforce camps looking for you.'

As they tucked into thick slices of fat bacon and eggs and home-made sausages that were strictly over and above the rationed allowance, their son Colin came in. He looked older than Ethel remembered, his tall frame stooped slightly, the dark brown hair was tinged with grey, but he still had the kindly manner she had known all her life. He beamed when he saw them, his eyes shone with undisguised pleasure and the years fell from him. She realized with shock that he was only thirty-eight. At first sight he had looked years older. Perhaps life with his ageing parents had made him forget his youth and settle into old age prematurely.

'Does this mean you're back home for good?' he asked, shaking hands with Rosie and Kate and giving Ethel a brief hug. She explained the situation and the need for secrecy and he too promised not to tell of her visit, but explained, 'I don't know how I'll manage to keep the smile off my face, mind!'

She asked about her brother who, she knew from her mother, had returned not long after she had run away. She wanted to see Glenys's grave but there wasn't time.

'Don't worry, dear,' Mrs Bailey said, patting her hand affectionately. 'I go up when I can and leave flowers for the dear girl. Sid goes regularly. Your mother too, of course.'

Having worked on a farm until she joined the Naafi, Rosie was interested in looking around and it was Mr Bailey and Colin who showed them, waiting patiently while they admired the two horses that were still used, and stood for a while looking over the stubbly fields where corn had been harvested, and at the pastures dotted with cows. They smiled with pleasure at the enthusiasm the girls all showed. Even Kate, with her uniform shoes instead of her usual lighthearted nonsense, didn't object too loudly about the unmentionable mess underfoot.

They left after an hour, loaded down with apples, sausage rolls and pies, sweets and with a package of food for the journey that they told Mrs Bailey would last ten squaddies a whole week.

'Or our Rosie for a day,' Kate added.

Before they left, Ethel gave Mrs Bailey Rosie's Nan's address in case there was an emergency, reminding her it was not to be given to her parents whatever the reason. Then they staggered off to rejoin the lorry. Rosie trailed behind, eating one of the still-warm sausage rolls.

'I'm helping,' she protested when they teased her. 'By eating some of the sausage rolls I'm helping to lighten our load!'

The Baileys walked with them through the fields and to the bus stop. Mr Bailey apologized for not having the petrol to drive them into town and stood in the road waving until the bus disappeared around the corner and the three faces staring back from the rear window were gone from sight.

Ethel was quiet and the other two left her to her thoughts, of home, Glenys and the kindly Baileys.

Their new camp was the largest they had seen. Army vehicles moved about between huge buildings and camouflaged supply dumps, soldiers marched on the parade ground to instructions barked at them by drill sergeants, and the guards marched around the perimeter fences armed with rifles. The guards at the gate were even more meticulous than usual checking the comings and goings of the hundreds of personnel. Passwords were given as they went out and insisted on when they returned.

Their canteen was large too, one of several. One was for officers only and another for PTI, the physical training instructors. 'Ours is for the real soldiers, the quantity *and* the quality,' Ethel insisted.

The camp boasted its own cinema and the girls looked forward to seeing films without a tedious journey into town. Although having to open the canteen between five and eleven meant it was only possible on their half day off.

There was more entertainment on the large camp than the others on which they had worked, and besides the organized concerts and film shows, impromptu shows happened most nights. The canteen was busy, noisy and enormous fun.

To Ethel the ebullience of the men seemed to be forced. They were going off on a journey fraught with danger to meet with an enemy who promised death or injuries and they were putting on an act. She made sure she joined in and helped them face the future in the only way they knew, by pretending that it was all a great, entertaining game.

It seemed to be a transit camp. Faces they began to recognize disappeared after a few weeks and others took their place. They daren't ask, as careless talk was considered a danger to them all. There were a few men who stayed longer than the rest; these worked on the lorries, painting them in camouflage colours, and even when the girls went to the huts where they worked with their mid-morning and afternoon trolleys, or drove out in the big van, they weren't allowed to see the work in progress. They learned that this was because the colours of the camouflage would give away their destination. Khaki, black and green were not universal.

Baba Morgan was sent abroad. His skills were needed in North Africa where Rommel's Panzer divisions pushed the Allies back over previously won ground, where they regrouped and prepared for another offensive, with Montgomery and Alexander in command since August. The desert was hard on vehicles and with other mechanics from different parts of the country Baba boarded ship for the perilous journey.

He had written to Ethel but had been unable to tell her his destination. Besides the danger of reporting such information, he hadn't known himself before setting off through the darkness for an early dawn embarkation. There was no opportunity to phone home, they were watched every moment, the fear of spies learning something to help the enemy was almost comic, until the realization of what careless words might cause came to their minds. They were sailing across seas that hid U-boats and under skies where planes were watching for the chance to destroy them.

He lay on his hammock and thought about Ethel. He had left messages and hoped that once he was settled he would be able to write to her. He wanted to keep in touch. Although he had addresses for Kate's and

Rosie's homes, not knowing where Ethel's family lived made him insecure. It was so easy to lose touch in wartime.

The ship was a large one protected by destroyers and cruisers which made up a convoy. Besides men and women, they carried vehicles, including tanks to replace those lost in battle, and Baba would go with them and help maintain them. He both feared and wanted to see some fighting. If he were to live through a war he had to have some stories to tell his children. That thought brought him back to dreams of Ethel.

The food was supplied by what was known as deck messing, with cooks providing the meals, and mess men to carry up plates of food to the recreation area where they ate. In the small recreation area there was a cubbyhole which was used by the Naafi to provide the day-to-day needs of the men. It was there that Baba and two of his friends went to look for some sickness tablets, too embarrassed to go to the sick bay and admit to feeling seasick.

The tablets were unavailable, and he was sitting there looking glum and wondering how soon he would have to run to the heads, when a voice said, 'You're supposed to go to the medics but if you like you can take one of mine.'

Baba looked up and saw a thin, pale young

man holding out a packet of white tablets. 'Thanks. Do they work?'

'They're what the army and navy recommend,' the man said. 'But please yourself.'

He spoke so abruptly that Baba was tempted to throw the packet back at him but his need was greater than his pride at that moment and he took the recommended dose and swallowed them with a cup of tea.

'Who was that miserable so-and-so?' he asked one of the other men.

'Oh, him, you don't want to bother with him. He hasn't a civil word for anyone, him.'

'I'll avoid him in future, don't worry,' Baba said. 'I'd hate to make him laugh and ruin his reputation.'

Wesley Daniels heard the comments, shrugged and walked away. He didn't see Baba take out a pad and begin to write to 'My darling Ethel'.

The attacks began on the second day, enemy planes diving down and dropping bombs on the armada of ships, the outer circle of destroyers and corvettes fighting back with guns and depth charges and torpedoes, the small protecting the larger ones. Two ships were sunk, with some of the the survivors being brought on to the ship where Wesley and Baba worked alongside each other, helping the men to climb aboard and making them comfortable in the limited spaces they found for them. Between battles they worked with the medics dealing with the injured.

In spite of his surliness, Baba couldn't help admiring the man who worked all through the night without a break. When he wasn't in the sick bay he was supplying food for those needing a reviving drink and a snack, or cleaning and tidying the area in which he worked, preparing for the next time his services were called upon.

Although they stood side by side for minutes on end and even washed down a survivor together, the man hardly spoke. Baba went on chatting and in an attempt to make the man laugh he asked a question and answered it himself then asked another question, but Wesley didn't respond.

Baba was curious. He couldn't be much more than twenty yet he had the expression of an old, bitter man who had seen much suffering. He was brave too, going out on deck to bring men to comparative safety while planes dive-bombed and fired at them.

Was he stupid, he wondered? Or was he so sickened by the carnage he had witnessed that he wanted to die? That thought as he stared at the man made Baba shiver.

Later that morning, while carpenters, blacksmiths and plumbers worked at repairing the damage, Baba went on deck. He had no business being there, but by carrying a piece of plywood and a hammer he was presumed to be part of the workforce and was ignored.

'Who's that miserable bugger in the Naafi then?' he asked one of the joiners.

'Miserable he might be, but he does more than his share,' the man replied aggressively.

'I was wondering why he does so much? Something wrong with him, is there?'

'Listen, mate, everyone on this ship does more than he has to. It's called survival!'

'Keep your hair on. I was only going to say he's a hero, even if he is a strange bloke. And *I* worked all night too, so cut the criticism, right?'

In his anger, his Welsh accent became more pronounced and the man stopped what he was doing for a moment and said with a grin, 'All right, Taffy! Where are you from?'

'Cardiff.'

The man held out a hand. 'Llanwonno,' he said.

'Where the 'ell's that?'

An argument ensued on the best part of Wales to live, a quiet friendly valley town or what he called the wild Welsh metropolis and when Baba returned to his quarters he realized he might have made a friend but still didn't know the name of the miserable hero.

The chippy's name was Lionel Clifford and over the next few days he and Baba spent some of their spare time together. When items began to disappear they shared disapproval of such a person, stealing from his mates, and joined in with others trying to think of ways of catching the thief. Neither said it aloud but both glanced at Wesley from time to time, a silent accusation of which he was aware.

Wesley was the 'odd-bod', an unknown factor at a time when people shared their thoughts, and it was easy to imagine the taciturn man having a grudge which he was repaying by petty theft.

Wesley didn't join in the discussion about the thefts. He rarely spoke and few bothered to speak to him. That was how he liked it. The little Welshman could try all he liked but Wesley had no intention of making a friend of him or anyone else. He'd let them down if it came to it, like he'd let Ethel down.

Facing bombs and bullets was easy, it was abstract violence, not like a personal attack on him by someone who had reason, real or imagined, to hate him. One man against another he couldn't face. Sometimes he saw men fighting each other, anger sparked by some accusation of cheating at dominoes or something equally unimportant, and he would feel his stomach turning to water and his heart racing with fear and he would have to go out and take deep breaths of air to calm the terror of his memories. He would relive the fist coming towards his face knocking him senseless, feel the boots kicking him, and see again the red angry face of Dai Twomey leaning towards him, large and throbbing with fury, threatening him, laughing at his puny efforts to defy him.

His legs moved as though running although his feet didn't leave the deck. He coughed up bile and stifled a sob. Without doubt when he met Ethel's father again he would run, leave her to her father's anger and fail her again.

Kate had to drive the van. It was something she had tried to avoid, but since the foolish drive from town on the night they had taken the car belonging to Rowan Fotheringay, Ethel and Rosie had tried to persuade her to take a few refresher lessons and drive the van which went around the camp taking food to the workshops and garages for the men and women who worked there. Once their supervisor understood that she had a driver's licence he insisted on her using her knowledge and, as well as driving the van herself, she was told to teach Ethel and Rosie until an instructor could find time.

The practice took place with an embarrassingly large audience in the waste ground beyond the target area, the soldiers both encouraging and jeering good-naturedly as she ground her way through the gears and jerked heavily on the brakes.

To Kate's surprise and relief, after a few minutes of instruction she managed well. The voice of her former instructor at the time of her eighteenth birthday came back to her and she drove around, turned and reversed without any serious problems.

'It's when I get into the driver's seat on my own that the panic will start,' she confessed to Rosie.

'I'll be with you,' Rosie said in surprise.

'And what will you do?'

'Well, er, I'll help you scream,' Rosie promised.

The three girls had often considered applying for overseas posting and something happened one day that made them decide that it would be a good move. They were in the town looking for somewhere that promised more than beans on toast or dried egg to ease Rosie's hunger, when they saw Ethel's father. He was sitting in a café looking out of the window. There was a cup of tea in front of him and rolled up beside it a newspaper.

'What's he doing here?' Ethel gasped as she stopped and pulled back from where he could see her.

'Didn't that farmer tell you he'd given up his job and was spending his time looking for you?'

'But how did he find me and why, for heaven's sake, does he want to find me and drag me home? What have I done?'

Ethel sobbed.

It was when they were back in camp preparing to open the canteen for the evening that Rosie said, 'Why don't we apply for overseas? We often talk about it and if your father is near and likely to cause more trouble, now is a good time.'

'Won't you be scared, Rosie?' Kate asked.

'Of course I will, I'd have to be stupid not to be. I'll be sick on the ship, Nan's parcels will be ages finding us and Hitler will be trying to kill us off. Of course I'll be scared. But we've been lucky so far and with the men and women out there facing day after day of fighting, I think I'm brave enough to do my bit. What about you two?'

They filled out their application and within weeks, at the end of November, they were told they were being sent to Scotland.

'Scotland? Why Scotland?' Kate wailed. 'It'll be perishing cold and I'm not allowed to wear my fur coat or my angora wool jumpers.'

'And your eye-shadow will get frosted and pull all your eyelashes out,' Ethel teased.

'And your pancake make-up will crack and look like wrinkles,' Rosie added with a laugh. Then she looked serious as she added, 'And I bet there won't be enough to eat.'

They set off by train with tickets in the form of travel warrants and a voucher to buy food which, Rosie sighed, 'Won't last us till we get to Crewe, wherever that is!'

They were fortunate that a parcel had arrived from Rosie's Nan two days before they were to leave and Ethel and Kate hid it in the hope that Rosie would be able to leave it until they reached their training camp. Rosie had been right, their travel pack and warrants were used up before they were halfway there and the parcel was ransacked with enthusiasm.

The cold hit them as soon as they alighted from the carriage. The platform was not crowded and they stood shivering and wishing they hadn't come, waiting for someone to approach them and tell them where the transport was waiting.

'I hope it's a lorry and well warmed for us,' Rosie shivered.

'I don't mind if it's a horse and cart as long as it gets us to our warm hut in record time,' Kate replied. 'I hate my nose being red. Don't I look a mess! My hair needs washing and curling and I long for a soak in a hot bath.'

'D'you think they'll allow us more than the regulation depth, just this once?' Ethel wondered hopefully.

Two squaddies marched up then and shouted their names, to which they answered, adding impatiently that they were cold and would they please show them to the transport.

'Transport? Don't you know there's a war on?' was the reply.

'Blimey. For a moment there I thought Walter was back!' Ethel groaned as they made their way out of the small station.

They didn't take notice of his actual remark, only the expression that had been so familiar to them when Walter had been their problem, so they were surprised to see an empty road with no sign of a vehicle of any kind.

'Where's the lorry?'

'Back at camp, girls. We're marching.'

'Marching?' Kate couldn't have been more horrified if they'd told her to take all her clothes off. 'How far?' she demanded, while Rosie and Ethel stared open-mouthed at the grinning soldiers.

It was almost three miles and the soldiers set up a fast pace. Sweating, with blisters already broken and bleeding, sticking their skin to their stockings and stockings to their shoes, they arrived and had to salute the guard post as they went through the gates. 'Longest way up and shortest way down,' they were reminded.

The hut was in darkness and once the door closed behind them they switched on a torch to see two rows of beds each with an occupant.

'Can we put the light on to unpack our things?' Rosie asked in a whisper.

'It's after lights out,' was the reply.

'Too bad!' Ethel felt for a switch and flooded the long narrow room with light. 'I can't take my coat off, I'm freezing,' Rosie said. 'Can you shut the windows, Kate?'

As Kate went to close the row of windows behind heavy blackout curtains she was told to stop. 'Windows are to stay open and the heater goes off at six o'clock,' one of the girls said in a bored voice.

Fully dressed, with their greatcoats over the thin blankets they had been given, they curled up with feet tucked inside their skirts, arms up inside their sleeves, and slept.

To their continuing surprise they were treated as army recruits, running, marching, physical training – and most of these things wearing very few clothes. They had been told what to expect but had not taken the warnings seriously, believing that as ATS EFIs they were still Naafi girls and nothing more.

The food was not plentiful and they had to queue for the platefuls that were handed out to them without a choice. They were so hungry they ate everything; once, Rosie dared to rejoin the end of the queue and go around again to receive a second small afternoon offering of a sandwich and cup of very strong tea. The assistant looked at her suspiciously and asked if she had been there before.

'No,' Rosie lied, her big blue eyes wearing

a look of innocence, 'you must be thinking of yesterday – the days go so fast when you're enjoying yourself, don't they?' Suspicion still clouding the assistant's eyes, Rosie received her extra helping, but she didn't dare try it again.

They were also trained in the use of guns, the instructor explaining that in the event of their being involved in fighting, they would stand beside the soldiers and fight alongside them.

'All this so we can serve char and a wad? What a way to run an army,' Ethel sighed.

'We'd have been better off tackling your dad, rot his socks,' Kate said gloomily.

'But imagine going abroad! No one I know has ever been abroad,' Rosie said, encouragingly. 'Once Nan's parcels reach us we'll be fine.'

Two weeks after they arrived, they were able to look with amusement at the shock on the faces of newer arrivals and consider themselves soldiers.

The ship on which both Wesley and Baba travelled was attacked again as they approached their destination. Bombers dived down at them and the guns fired back. Baba was ordered to stand close to the guns and assist with the supply of ammunition. At first he felt vulnerable on deck with bullets flying and bombs falling, as though he were in the middle of a crazy thunderstorm with explosives instead of rain and hail. As the attack intensified he soon became so involved that he no longer felt afraid, he was just there as part of a team doing what had to be done. It wasn't until it was over that the shock hit him and he felt himself shaking with delayed fright.

As the slightly damaged ship limped slowly on, he helped with the aftermath, throwing some of the tangled metal over the side or dragging it, still hot and difficult to handle, into piles on deck to be disposed of when they reached land.

It wasn't for several more hours that he was able to sit and relax and it was then that he learned that his friend, Lionel Clifford, had been killed.

At once the routine began, with Clifford's personal belongings gathered together to be returned to his family together with any money he had left. There was a small box decorated with burning, that he had made, presumably to take home to his wife. Inside was a diamond ring. The rest of the things which he had used on board, tools that had been supplied and uniform, were usually distributed between the rest of the man's watch, and it was as they began that sad task that they learned that he had been their thief.

A cigarette lighter, a couple of watches, a lot of money in small coinage, were found in his locker, hidden under some old clothes and a few magazines. The men claimed back what was theirs and nothing more was said. No point accusing him now, better it was forgotten, and they grieved for the loss of a shipmate and friend.

Wesley looked at the sad collection of the man's possessions and turned away without retrieving the decorated box. The men had been mistaken about it being made by Lionel Clifford for his wife. He had bought it in the hope of one day giving it to Ethel, together with their engagement ring which he kept inside it. The ring and the box would be better sent to the widow. He doubted whether he would ever have the need of them.

Nine

'So we are officially ATS EFI now,' Rosie sighed contentedly, pulling down the jacket and tightening the cloth belt. 'We're in the army now,' she sang in her soft sweet voice.

'Yes, but I still wonder why we had to do all that P T and misery, and marching in heavy boots and suffering blisters and stiff muscles, just to serve char and a wad!' Kate retorted, rubbing her still-painful toes. 'If I'd wanted to march I'd have joined the army sooner. A peaceful war with plenty of fun, enjoying the freedom from the suffocation of Mum and Dad, that's all I wanted.'

'Do you regret joining?' Ethel asked, as she packed the last of Rosie's Nan's parcel away in their locker.

Kate looked up, her pretty face showing none of the exhaustion of the past weeks, her blonde hair tied back in a snood, her eyes shining with health and contentment. 'Not a single minute. And you?'

Ethel allowed a frown to cross her face as she replied, 'I don't regret a moment of the time I've been with you two, but I wish I hadn't had to run away from my family like I did. I miss them. Miss belonging to a family.'

'We're your family now, Ethel, and we'll never let you down.'

Ethel smiled at them both, such dear, loyal friends, she was very fortunate to have found them and fortunate too that they had, beyond all expectations, managed to stay together.

Suddenly Rosie sat down, looking at them in surprise. 'I've just realized something,' she said. 'Do you know, it's Christmas!'

Kate wrote Happy Christmas on the mirror with a lipstick and Ethel added an unlikely-looking robin. 'Happy Christmas, everybody,' Kate shouted. Turning to her friends, she added, 'Here's hoping we'll spend many other Christmases together.'

'No doubt about it, we will. Now, where's Rosie's Nan's parcel?' Ethel said with mock impatience. 'I want my Christmas cake.'

Not having a family to write to and hear from still hurt, particularly when post arrived and Ethel had to sit and watch while others read their letters and opened small parcels with their touch of home. If only Glenys were alive. Then she could have stayed at home, coped with their father, and she would be celebrating the day with her family. She felt sadness and loneliness filling her heart and forced them away, stopped the thoughts, shaking away the regrets by reminding herself that Dai Twomey was not her father, he was her grandfather. For the first time, another implication of her situation came to her.

'Hey, I've just realized that my name isn't really Twomey at all! I wonder who I am?'

'Ethel Question Mark, spinster of this parish,' Rosie announced.

'Don't worry, you'll be changing your name soon anyway, you only have to decide whether it will be Mrs Albert Pugh or Mrs Baba Morgan,' Kate said, unaware of the sudden disappointment that crossed Rosie's face and darkened her bright blue eyes.

'Neither probably,' Ethel told her. 'We'll lose touch anyway before this lot is over.'

The letters from both men had dried to a trickle and it was weeks since she had heard from either of them. Rosie and Kate tried to convince her that they were forbidden mail during their stay at the training camp but Rosie's Nan's parcels had arrived without delay and letters from some of the other young men she and Kate had met and flirted with. Only Ethel missed out when the post came around.

She began to be more and more convinced that her father had been right to suspect her of 'going to the bad', as he had put it. She had given in to Duggie and had wanted, oh so badly, to give in to Baba Morgan. The words repeated as a warning came into her head. 'Men are only after one thing'; 'men don't respect women who are too easy'. Loving was forbidden if you wanted to be an acceptable wife, loving was wrong. Men needed love, women had to refuse them. It had once sounded so easy. Why hadn't anyone warned her that she would want it too? And want it so desperately?

She often dreamed in those half-waking moments before rising, that she would open her eyes and see Baba standing there, or Albert, his severe expression banished by love, smiling at her, wanting her, and her body would begin to respond to the vision. The loneliness that followed was almost too much to bear.

Sometimes she dreamed of Wesley, but Wesley was looking at her in a friendly way, guileless, without an urgent need for her. No desire on his young face. In her mind Wesley Daniels was still that boy who had planned to marry her, a comfortable friendship without the sensations of loving she had since learned. He was a part of her childhood, a pleasant memory of when they were too young to feel the passion which Duggie had awakened in her. Wesley was a vague figure from that other life when the world was small, bounded by how far she could see, or the distance she could walk in a day. A time of innocence when life was so wonderfully simple.

Once the training was done, they handed in their ATS EFI uniforms, which would be stored until they were posted abroad. Until then they would return to normal duties.

Before they were posted, the three girls were given leave and, as usual, Ethel tried to pretend she didn't want to go home with either of them. She mustn't expect them to take pity on her every time and besides, this might be their last leave for a long while and they needed to spend the time with their families and friends without an extra 'hanger on'.

'I'm going to spend the time in London,' she told them enthusiastically. 'I've heard that there are some really good dance halls and there's sure to be others there on their own.'

'Oh no you're not!' Rosie and Kate chorused.

'It's all decided,' Rosie went on. 'We're having a last fling and we can't do that without you being there.'

'Nonsense! I'll enjoy exploring and I'll be able to sort out all the best places for when we celebrate our last few days.'

No matter how the others pleaded, Ethel was adamant.

'Come to think of it,' Kate said, putting in her last curler before getting into bed, 'I'd rather be going with you. Imagine, all those beautiful Americans and Canadians there and me not being able to search for my gorgeous rich husband!'

They eventually decided that both Rosie and Kate would tell a small lie and stay only half of their leave at home before joining Ethel in London.

At the railway station they parted after having a snack at the Naafi counter where men and women from all the branches of the services stopped as they alighted from trains or waited to board them.

Ethel planned to go first to the RAF station where she had last seen Albert and try and get news of him. As she stood up and brushed crumbs from her skirt, gathered her luggage and walked away from the counter with a friendly wave, Wesley arrived at the far end, exhausted after a long and danger-filled journey, and asked for tea and a sandwich.

As always when there were Naafi people around he asked whether anyone had seen Ethel and showed her photograph. The girl at the counter smiled and twisted herself around to view it. She frowned. 'It's a bit crumpled, ain't it? But she does seem familiar. I can't remember whether I saw her today though. We see so many people and for such a short time that it's all a bit of a blur.' She laughed again as she topped up his tea, 'Fact is, I don't think I'd recognize me own Mum if she came in and ordered. When it's busy I only see the hand and the money. My ears take in the rest.'

'Thanks anyway. But do you think you might have seen her recently?'

The girl paused to take another order, smiling at a sailor who ordered char and a wad, handing him the cake and the steaming cup of tea before turning back to Wesley. She shrugged. 'What difference would it make if I had, eh? This is a place where half the world passes through on their way to God only knows where.'

She handed her next customer his request-ed doughnut and tea and paused, staring after the tall, thin figure of Wesley. Was that picture of one of the girls from the Naafi she had spoken to, she wondered? No, that would be too much of a coincidence. 'Now, dearies, who's next?' she asked cheerily.

Rosie's Nan told all her friends about her brave granddaughter and received many gifts of chocolates and sweets to add to her regular parcels, one of which had included the Christmas cake. She feared for her, aware that the Naafi girls weren't immune to injuries and death. They were never far from the fighting and many had died already. In her rare moods of melancholy she knew that if Rosie died she would regret not showing her the letters.

She opened the drawer and began to count them. Dozens and dozens, all opened and read before being added to the rest in chronological order. There were almost two hundred. She wondered whether her decision to keep them from Rosie had been the right one. She started to write to Rosie, tell her about the letters, but tore it up. She couldn't do it after all this time. How could she confess to her cruelty? It was too late and the lie would have to remain hidden in her drawer.

The girls' last few days in London were enjoyable, with dance halls filled with the wildly exciting music, and dancing as they had never seen dancing before. Rosie hadn't outgrown her shyness completely but the atmosphere of live for today as there might not be a tomorrow, plus the comforting realization that no one would know her, gave her a freedom to enjoy that she hadn't ever imagined knowing.

'It's like a clown wearing make-up with a painted-on smile and crying behind it, only in reverse,' she explained

'Pagliacci,' Ethel said.

'What are you two talking about?' Kate laughed. 'We're here to have fun not talk rubbish!'

Vincent, a dashingly handsome, dark-haired American with undoubted Italian ancestry, danced with Kate three times on their first night and most of the evening that followed. Ethel and Rosie wanted to go somewhere different every night but Kate was smitten and they couldn't allow her to go out alone in the strange city.

On their last day Kate and Vincent exchanged addresses and promised to stay in touch. On their last night Rosie and Ethel sat up and in whispers shared Kate's joy as she told them how wonderful Vincent was. They sat and listened, their eyes occasionally dropping into sleep and forcing themselves awake with an alarming jerk, to listen some more. At nine o'clock the following morning they gathered their belongings and reported to the place where they would be told their destination.

They were given a room which they shared with three other girls in what had once been a suite of offices. Told not to unpack as they would be leaving for Dover early the following morning, they ate their supper and lay on their beds trying to sleep. Excitment and apprehension prevented them, those emotions plus the sound of Kate's scribbling as she wrote a long loving letter to Vincent, which the following morning was immediately confiscated.

They travelled to Dover by train after being warned about careless talk.

'Spies are everywhere,' the officer reminded them. 'A careless word and the ship you're on could be torpedoed, so, don't forget—'

'Be like Dad, keep Mum!' the girls quoted, from the posters warning against careless talk that were to be seen on every street corner.

'It isn't a joke, even if the poster is,' was the stern response.

They went on board the camouflaged ship with a number of previously unseen ATS EFI, and the male equivalent the RASC EFI, as well as members of other services. The accommodation seemed generous but they soon learned that they were to pick up other personnel en route.

The recreation area, where the Naafi had a small store from which they could buy what they needed, had very little in the way of amusements and as they were laying off about half a mile from the port for seven days they soon began to make their own entertainment. Ethel organized darts matches, and dominoes and draughts came into their own. One man was an expert chess player and he taught a few of the more serious passengers to play.

Ethel read some of the books on board, Kate dreamed about Vincent and bemoaned her luck at finding him too late, Rosie found her way to the galley, learning new recipes and ideas from the seamen who provided their three meals each day, and helping out in the Naafi bar between times.

The throbbing of the powerful engines was the first intimation of their departure and they went on deck and stared across at the receding coast in the cold gloom of the winter evening, with smiles on their faces and fear in their hearts. Now they were really going to war. They each secretly wondered whether they would be up to it.

Apart from going into port and taking on several hundred soldiers who had been stranded after leave and were being taken back to join their unit, the journey was mercifully uneventful. The men recently arrived on board were kept separate from them, using their own canteen and not being allowed to mix. Ethel and the others heard them but their presence was limited to sounds only, the low murmurings of invisible men who were predestinate ghosts, many of whom would soon be dead, Ethel thought with a shiver.

Under cover of darkness, they dropped anchor and the men disembarked, leaving the ship strangely quiet. Wesley went with the first landing party and with five assistants began to prepare food for the men before they found the transport waiting for them and headed for the front line.

Clearing up after the meal they had provided, packing the van in which they would travel from then on, Wesley and his small team got into the vehicle, which was loaded with precious supplies, and set off in pursuit.

Below decks, Ethel was thinking about Albert and Baba, unaware that Wesley, about whom she thought so rarely, had been within yards of her for several days.

Dai Twomey had never before been short of money. His parents had owned several houses and, his father being a builder, they sold and bought making a reasonable profit each time. When they died, he and Molly had purchased the smallholding and instead of building work, which he had never enjoyed, he grew crops to sell door-to-door on a cart or small van and worked as a lorry driver to cover the extra money they needed.

His one extravagance besides the drinking which occupied most evenings was his motorbike. A powerful Vincent, it was one that few men in his situation could afford to own and it was his pride and joy. Since petrol had been added to the list of rationed goods, fuel for the bike had become a problem.

He often solved this by syphoning petrol from a car during the hours of darkness, placing one end of a tube in the tank of the car, sucking until he tasted the petrol then putting the other end of the tube into his own tank and listening to the satisfying gurgle as it filled.

Since he had given up driving lorries, their lack of money was an increasing worry. Their savings had dwindled to almost nothing, they would soon be living on a daily basis, spending each day money received from what they had managed to sell. Molly worked on their land, struggling to keep up with the work that Dai was neglecting, with occasional help from their son Sid. But unless Dai stopped driving around the country searching for Ethel, they would soon be unable to meet their bills.

Dai knew all this but he couldn't stop. He had to find Ethel and make sure she didn't give in to a man. Having a child before a wedding ring was increasingly common as the war dragged on. For her it would be far,

far worse.

He kept away from camps after twice being arrested. The fear of spies was growing and he knew that he faced imprisonment without the need for evidence if he were caught near one again, specially if he was struggling with his daughter – granddaughter, he amended with a burst of rage.

Instead, he concentrated on the public houses and dance halls in the towns close to army camps and airforce stations. With controlled and polite behaviour he would engage some of the servicemen in conversation, buy drinks and ask whether they had met his daughter, Ethel. On most occasions the men would clam up, afraid of discussing anything to do with their position in case it helped the enemy. Only once in a while would he find a young man who wanted to talk, and he would show photographs of his 'daughter' and describe how much he missed her, but he had no luck in finding her. She seemed to have vanished from the earth.

'There are thousands of places where she could work,' one RAF man told him. 'Wherever you find the serviceman you'll find the Naafi. She could even be abroad.'

At that point Dai almost gave up. He went outside and stood looking up at the sliver of moon that seemed to be wrapped in white gauze against a navy blue sky, and wondered whether he would ever see her again. Better that he didn't. He could wash his hands of her, forget she ever existed. He didn't want to know how she ended up. He had tried to stop her and had failed.

He went outside to where he had parked the Vincent. Beside it was a baker's van. With half an eye watching the pub doorway, he took out the narrow rubber pipe he used to steal petrol, then hurriedly replaced it as footsteps approached. It was the same RAF man, who said, 'You might try the CAB, the Citizens' Advice Bureau. It was set up in 1939 to help missing people to get in touch, or help families who'd been separated or bombed out. They could be a bit cagey as it's someone serving in the forces like your daughter, but worth a try.'

Thanking him, Dai shuffled off, his heavy boots scuffing through the gravel on the fore-court until he saw the man disappear once again into the pub. He syphoned enough petrol to fill his tank, replaced the petrol tank cover and drove off. Hope was revived. It was time to go home again and find out more about the CAB.

At home, Molly was sitting at the table sur-rounded by papers. Bills mainly and most of those unpaid. She had managed to keep from her son the seriousness of the situation but unless she had payment for the vege-tables she had supplied, and within the next few days, which would enable her to deal with some of the most urgent debts, there was a chance of court proceedings.

Where was Dai? He hadn't been home for two weeks. He had cleared the ground and planted the last of the winter cabbages and weeded around the leeks and sprout plants and then had gone off again on his motorbike without collecting the money they were owed.

She had tried to collect some of the debts and had managed to retrieve a few pounds, but the work on the land plus managing the house was all she could find time for. Besides, asking for money was something she didn't find easy to do. That had always been Dai's job – and few argued when he asked for settlement, she thought grimly.

The sound of his motorbike reached her ears. There was no mistaking its powerful four-stroke engine. Throwing down the pencil she went to open the door.

As usual he didn't bother to explain where he had been, only that he hadn't found Ethel. She didn't waste time arguing or asking questions, she had given up asking for explanations for his frantic search, she just asked him to collect some debts before the situation became worse.

'I'll do it first thing in the morning,' he told her as he poured himself some tea from the teapot in the hearth. 'I need some cash for work that needs doing on the bike.'

He had been drinking and went to bed almost at once, where he lay on his back, smelling less than sweet, flat out, fully dressed and snoring fit to rattle the roof tiles.

She stared down at him and thought back over their marriage, remembering the early years when everything seemed perfect. She had known about his temper before they married, but believed his promises, sure she would help him to keep them. His rages were kept under control by living out in the country, where he saw few people, and working alone, driving lorries from town to town. He was very strong and worked hard developing the market garden. All day and half the night when needed. It was only rarely that he got drunk.

The increase in his drinking was hardly noticed at first, but there was an arrest and a fine, then another and another, until the first jail sentence made her aware of how serious the problem had become. They had been happy at first, building their life together, the children bringing their joy, and although she tried to work out why it had all gone wrong, she failed to understand what it was that drove him into this wild fury that was destroying them all. Now she had gone past attempting to understand. What she wanted now was revenge.

After waiting for several hours, her eyes

gleaming with determination, she put on a dark coat and went out to where the bike was parked. Opening the petrol cap she managed to push the vehicle over on to its side. Petrol leaked out and with a piece of a metal shovel, keeping her hands and clothes well clear of the dangerous fluid, she scooped some over the shining machine. Then she dropped a lighted match at the end of the river of liquid.

Startled by the fierce violence of the gush of flames she ran back to the house, heart racing, scrubbed her hands clean, stripped off all the clothes she was wearing for fear of them being contaminated by the powerful smell, and carefully slid into bed without waking him. She didn't sleep.

Luckily they were too far out of town for a warden to come and complain about the light from the burning bike. No one was likely to see the fire and report it. She got out of bed after a while and through a gap in the curtains looked out, watching the conflagration until the metal glowed and flames died and the dark night and the silence crept back.

The girls' destination was Egypt and as they disembarked the heat was a surprise. The ship had seemed cool by comparison to the blazing sun and the heat rising from the ground. Mersa Matruh they found enchanting, with its blue lagoon and small neat bungalows. The picturesque scene was ruined by the makeshift stores and buildings all around but their first sight showed them only the beauty of the place. The beauty and the welcome from the men.

When they stepped ashore the men waiting to greet them cheered and ran towards them. To the soldiers they were a reminder of home: pretty girls in their familiar blue overalls, offering char and a wad, would be a scene to warm their hearts.

There was no time to daydream. They were put to work straight away.

Several supply ships had been sunk by enemy action but others were on the way and the stores had to be ready and made secure. Ethel was given a job in the Bulk Issue Stores from where the goods were ordered by the various canteens, the goods made up to be collected and paid for. The canteen was already active but the men had been given leave, so they would take over from the following evening. While Ethel dealt with the orders and managed the money, the Bulk Issue Stores always dealing in cash, Rosie and Kate were kept busy unpacking and stacking the heavy boxes, with a sergeant helping between ticking everything off on a list.

Exhausted, they were then taken to the newly opened canteen and told to prepare food for opening time. 'If this is how we have to carry on, I don't think I'll last the year,' Kate sighed, referring to their contract for the posting. 'A year! We'll be worse off than we were with Walter the Creep!'

'I don't mind how hard I work as long as we can stay together,' Rosie sighed as they washed and changed into their overalls for their first evening session. They began early, and their first tasks as always were sandwiches and teas and coffee, plus the famous Naafi rock cakes.

Four and a half pounds of flour, two pints of water, margarine, tinned milk, baking powder, sugar and dried eggs and twelve ounces of currants went into the mix, plus all the other ingredients that gave the cakes their special flavour. They could have chanted the list in their sleep.

The uncooked cakes had to be exactly one and a quarter ounces each, but after a few weighed for accuracy the girls had quickly learned to use their eye and rarely made a mistake. They managed to achieve the instructed seventy cakes per mix every time. The cakes were washed over with milk before baking to give them a bit of a shine.

'I wonder how many of these I've made since joining up?' Rosie sighed as they put the last batch into the huge ovens.

'I wonder how many *more* we'll have to make before we finish,' Kate sighed.

'I'm getting tired of it all too,' Ethel confessed. 'Although I've no idea what I'll do after the war ends. What jobs will be open to someone who can make Naafi rock cakes and has travelled a bit?'

'Plenty,' Rosie said firmly. 'I'd be prepared to cook anything anywhere and that must be useful. In fact, I think I might train properly, become a proper cook before we open our café. What d'you think?'

'I think it would be fine as long as I don't have to see another rock cake,' Kate laughed.

'Another batch, please, ladies,' a voice called, and with a sigh, Rosie reached towards the flour bin.

Wesley was close to the front line. His van went back and forward between base and the men, with food and hot drinks. He went as close as he dared to where the men were dug in, in a holding position just behind the line of guns. The noise at times was almost deafening, the planes overhead, the guns of both sides booming and the squeals and thuds as shells and bombs landed close, sending gouts of fire and earth skyward. Debris of destroyed vehicles and ominously still bodies were all around him as he made his way through the medics as they searched for the wounded among the dead.

He was told to go back but, pointing to his ears, he feigned deafness and carried on handing out tea and a wad to anyone who needed them. They thought he was brave but he knew different. They didn't know the truth, that when pain was involved he was a coward. The bullets and bomb splinters flying around didn't represent pain, not like having a man in front of you flexing muscles and folding his fists. The danger around him was more abstract and easier for him to cope with, but he was not the stuff heroes were made of, you only had to talk to Ethel to know that.

When the sleepless night had passed, Molly Twomey rose to make a start on her busy day. Closing the curtains, she struck a match and lit the candle that would light her way down the stairs. She moved about as she dressed, trying to wake Dai so he'd be aware of her rising at the usual time of the morning. As she was leaving the room he woke and asked the time.

'Six o'clock,' she told him, afraid to look at him in case he saw the guilt in her eyes.

'Wake me at eight,' he instructed. 'I want to go into town and find the Citizens' Advice Bureau.'

'What d'you want advice on?' she asked. Then, as there was no reply, she went downstairs and began cleaning out the grate to light the fire. Her hands shook every time she thought of what she had done. Well, he would never think of her being responsible; she was too much the cowed and submissive wife.

A knock at the door heralded the arrival of the postman. She wondered why he had knocked, then realized he must have seen the motorbike. Thank goodness she wouldn't be alone when Dai was told.

Dai thundered down the stairs still wearing the clothes of the day before, boots unlaced, his red face unwashed, smeared with yesterday's dirt that had been thrown up from the roads.

He stared disbelievingly at the remains of his beautiful Vincent, then his malevolent eyes stared at Molly. Instinctively the postman moved to stand beside her, although what he could have done to help her against the rage-filled giant of a man he couldn't guess.

'Where's Sid?' Dai demanded. 'He's done this!'

'He's at work. He finishes at six but might have worked an extra shift, you know they have to when there's a big rush on. He's been nowhere near home since last night.' She trembled at Dai's accusation. That was something she hadn't thought of.

'He wasn't at work,' he said, 'he was here, doing this!'

'Of course he wasn't!' She was on the point of confessing. She couldn't allow him to blame their son for this. 'I did it,' she said defiantly. 'I went down, pushed it over and set fire to it.'

Dai turned to her and, holding her by her thin shoulders, shook her angrily. 'D'you think I'm stupid or something? I know who did this and your attempts at covering up for him won't work.'

The postman was alarmed at the way he was hurting his wife and tried to intervene. Temper exploded and Dai shouted abuse and hit out at them both. Then, pushing Molly and the postman aside, he lumbered down the path, over the footbridge to where the postman's red pushbike stood propped against a tree, and rode off.

'Sid was at work!' Molly shouted.

'I'll give him work! I'm going to show you what a liar he is, my wonderful son! If he hasn't been there, I'll find him. I'll kill him for this,' Dai called back.

Around the next corner he felt a strange sensation in his head and his heart raced wildly. A car approached and in an attempt to avoid hitting it, Dai pulled on the brakes but nothing happened; he had no strength, his arms felt like paper, his fingers refused to do what he asked of them and his legs were unable to propel him. His eyes seemed unable to see where he was going – with the sound of the angry car-driver's horn filling his head with pain and confusion, he fell off.

'He's had a stroke, I'm afraid,' the hospital doctor told Molly and Sid later that day. 'We'll keep him in for a while but then you'll have to look after him at home.'

'But I can't,' Molly tried to explain. 'How can I look after him and keep the market garden running and everything else I have to do? What would we live on?' Then she whispered, half to herself, 'Where's our Ethel? She has to come home and help me, he can't harm her now, she has to come home.'

Two weeks later Dai was carried into the house, a young land girl was promised to give much-needed help with the vegetable crops and Molly stared angrily at her husband. For the first time since they had married she told him what she thought of him.

Once she began it poured out of her. She went on, hour after hour, listing all the resentments that had been suppressed over the years. Sid listened but didn't try to stop her. She deserved this moment. When she had finally exhausted herself and the words had dried up she realized that even though she was facing months, perhaps years of looking after him, she was going to enjoy it. Her revenge would be something to savour. If only Ethel would come home.

Post was unreliable although the authorities

realized the importance of the letters from home. Sometimes letters arrived that had been written several weeks before, many ended up at the bottom of the sea. Although none got through to Ethel, she never gave up hope; she continued to write to Albert and, although she thought it was useless, she wrote to Baba Morgan, wondering if she would ever see him again.

Albert wrote to her often and his letters were becoming more affectionate. As her letters to him dwindled and finally ceased altogether, he wrote more often, presuming that she was not receiving his and was perhaps believing he had tired of the correspondence. He had to keep on writing and hoping that his letters would eventually catch up with her. He couldn't lose her now. He cursed himself for hesitating too long.

Baba wrote to Ethel and Kate and Rosie but again, due to the many changes of address, these had so far failed to arrive. Only letters from Kate's parents and Rosie's Nan got through. And letters to Kate from Vincent.

When she was handed her mail with his neat writing on the envelope, which had been opened and on which several sentences had been blue-pencilled out, she would read and reread them and would eventually surface with such a vacant and dreamy look in her eyes that she earned the nickname

Day Dream, which didn't offend her at all.

'That's what I do most of the time I'm awake, daydream about when Vincent and I meet again,' she told them. 'And at night I dream some more. If only we could wangle some leave and I could see him again...' And off she would go into another daydream.

Wesley's letters from home reached him. His mother wrote regularly and somehow, with all the comings and goings, the secrecy of the journeys and routes and destinations, the efficient organization dealing with the mail found him. It was in a letter from his mother that he heard about Dai Twomey's stroke. He wrote back telling his mother that if there was any way she could contact Ethel she should do so and tell her what had happened.

She could go home now. From the sound of it, her father could no longer threaten her. For himself, he didn't think he could ever face the man again no matter how weak and ill he had become. His humiliation wouldn't go away that easily. He would see it in the man's eyes.

If only he knew where to find Ethel. He was on a few days' leave and with others he volunteered to travel as extra guards with the goods sent out from the Bulk Issue Stores.

Less than twenty miles away from the ship in

which Wesley sat and dreamed of her, Ethel and Rosie were setting up the counters ready for the evening opening of the canteen. They had been moved twice. Now the battle for North Africa was won, the bases were constantly moving and they moved with them. They were situated in a small garrison from where men and tanks still went out to mop up small pockets of resistance and gather in the prisoners.

Tonight there was to be a concert. The band, which was made up mostly from men and women in the camp, was practising and the piano was played by a shy young girl who worked in the kitchens. Kate was turning the pages of her music.

They were told that a train-load of supplies was due in and when called the band players went to help with the unloading and storage. As the canteen emptied, Kate and Ethel approached the piano and with the pianist's willing accompaniment they began to sing. Others heard them and they were invited to join the rest of the amateur performers that evening.

They were unable to leave their place during the concert but they sat on the counter during a lull and leaned towards the band and sang a few choruses, with Rosie singing silently between them.

On a brief respite from his duties, Wesley and others came in, stood and watched for a while then went to bed. His tired eyes didn't wander to the kitchens where Ethel was stacking used plates ready for washing. He watched Kate and Rosie for a moment wondering whether there was any point showing them his snap of Ethel but he turned away. The chances of them having seen her here were so slight it was hardly worth thinking about. He and his men were too tired to enjoy the entertainment and tomorrow they had to leave before first light. Rest was more important than entertainment or false hopes. He left as Ethel came out of the kitchen area and went among the tables to gather more dishes.

When months passed and he still had no news of Ethel, Albert began to worry. It was impossible to find out where she was stationed. With the war continuing almost world wide, she could be anywhere or she could be dead. With all the talk of spies, and notices being painted on walls all over Britain demanding a 'Second Front Now', the veil of secrecy had become even thicker and impossible to break.

He remembered then that he'd been given the addresses of Kate's and Rosie's families and, finding the addresses neatly written in his diary, he wrote to them both asking if they could tell him her present address. It was obvious – he hoped – that the loss of contact between them was because he was writing to the wrong place or had mis-remembered the numbers and letters that made up the forces' postal information. A mistake in the number could mean that the letter ended up in lost letters and was eventually destroyed. The addresses were deliberately obscure to prevent the enemy from learning the distribution of the fighting men and women.

He received a reply within days from Rosie's Nan, who told him she couldn't help. She sent him a cake as an apology, but said she had promised Ethel not to disclose any information about her to anyone. He then wrote again, including an unsealed letter to Ethel, asking Mrs Dreen to readdress the letter to her. The letter was brief, asking only whether she was well and asking her for her address if she wanted to hear from him.

The ship containing the mail bag in which the letter was carried was sunk just outside the docks. But when Rosie heard from her Nan, she was told about the letter from Albert and with Rosie's Nan having an address where she could reach him, Ethel wrote to him at once. She was still feeling dreadfully homesick and not hearing from either Albert or Baba was making it worse.

The Baileys, aware that Ethel would not know about her father's stroke, wondered whether they should write to her via her friend. Once again it was Rosie's Nan who passed on the information. Because of moving around, weeks passed before they were in contact again and Ethel learned about her father's serious stroke. It was almost the end of 1943 when she received the news and was told they were again being posted.

Her first thought was to apply for leave but as they were down for transfer there was no chance of being allowed home. Besides, she knew that once she went home she and Kate and Rosie would be separated and might never get the same posting again. Her need to see her mother was strong, but the close friendship between the girls and the responsibility they all felt for their involvement in the Service To Those Who Serve, was stronger.

'Don't you know there's a war on?' she joked as she explained her feelings to the others. 'Remember miserable Walter Phillips? That was his mantra.'

'What's a mantra?' asked Kate.

'A thing Spanish women wear on their heads.'

'No, silly,' Kate laughed. 'That's a mantilla.'

'No it isn't. That's what they put in icecream.'

Laughing at their nonsense, then sobering, Ethel asked, 'I wonder where the war has taken the old misery?'

'I don't care as long as he keeps away from us,' Kate said. 'It's my Vincent I want to see.'

'You do? Why didn't you tell us?' Rosie teased.

'Vincent. I've just remembered, my father's motorbike was a Vincent.' For some reason this was funny too.

Remembering the motorbike and its powerful engine that seemed to reflect the strength of her father, Ethel thought about home. She had been away a very long time, so much had happened, and she was overwhelmed with homesickness. It surprised her and she tried to hide what she considered her weakness from her friends.

It wasn't her family she missed, she tried to convince herself, it was just a place to call home, now she no longer had The Dell to return to. Once she had left the service and set herself up in a place of her own, she would soon build a life for herself. It would be filled only with people she loved. Rosie and Kate for a start. And Rosie's Nan, and Mr and Mrs Banner. They were the nucleus from which she would start again. She tried not to think about Baba and Albert.

The Allies had landed in Sicily earlier in the year and once a base had been achieved and the communications ship had landed its cargo of radios and telephones and all the essentials for allowing contact between the commanders of the battle fronts, the Naafi was there providing hot food and drinks for the thousands of men piling on to the beaches, establishing a base and spreading out to drive out the enemy.

It was to Italy that Ethel, Kate and Rosie were told they were to go. But it was not to be.

Ten

The three friends had been expecting to be told of their transfer to Italy but before this happened a message reached Kate, telling her that her parents' shop had been bombed and both were in hospital. Kate was given compassionate leave and, when the authorities were told that Kate had no one else to assist her, and that a grocery shop was involved, Rosie was given permission to go with her.

Afraid of being separated for the rest of the war, Ethel also applied to go but she was refused. In the present circumstances, with the push in Italy, and transport so badly needed for troops, stores and equipment, one friend was a generous gesture, they were told severely, and giving leave for two was not possible.

The next day, Ethel showed them a letter from Mrs Bailey, telling her about her father's illness and the difficulties suffered by her mother as she tried to deal with him and the market garden. Like the distribution of food, the growing of it was a priority and her leave was granted too.

Ethel sometimes wanted to see her parents very much, at others she couldn't bear the thought of walking into her house and facing them. At that moment she had no desire to revive the miseries of the past. Facing her father was a particularly joyless thought. And why should she feel the need to dash to act the dutiful daughter to help her mother? She wasn't sure she even wanted to go back to England. It was the disappointment of being separated from Kate and Rosie rather than concern for her mother that made her apply.

In her heart she still blamed her mother for the death of her sister. Mam must have known what was going on and she should have intervened. How could she be expected to stay in the same house? As for the market garden, she doubted whether her father's illness would make much difference. He was hardly ever there, from what she understood from the brief note from Mrs Bailey.

'You should go and see your mother,' Rosie coaxed. 'It doesn't seem fair to blame her for your father's foul temper.'

'It's Glenys's death I blame her for. Mam made us all suffer because she wasn't brave enough to leave. If she wanted to be a martyr and stay with him, she could have done so. But she should have sent us away.'

'That wouldn't have been easy.'

'She should have seen how unhappy Glenys was. She should have taken us away, somewhere Dad couldn't find us. If she had we would still be together, me, Sid and Glenys,' she told Kate and Rosie.

'She stuck to her marriage vows,' Kate reminded her, thinking that nothing would make her want to leave Vincent.

'Then she shouldn't have!'

'You ought to see her,' Rosie advised. 'Think of me with a mother who left me and has never once tried to find me. I'd at least listen to her if we ever met.'

'More fool you!' Ethel retorted, anger and doubts making her less reasonable. 'Best to depend on no one, that way you're safe from disappointments.'

'Family is family,' Kate said inanely, still dreaming of Vincent.

'Family,' Ethel argued loudly, 'is a pain in the arse.'

Rosie covered her face and giggled.

To their regret, the three girls were unable to travel together but decided to meet in London. They docked separately in places on the east coast and for a while regretted

305

their departure from the delightful climate of North Africa.

'At least it will be more peaceful than the front line,' Kate said, 'and I'll be seeing Vincent again.'

'Vincent? Who's Vincent?' Rosie frowned. 'You've never mentioned him.'

They were wrong about London being more peaceful than the front line. Daylight and night-time raids sent people wearily to underground shelters, the dark, cold evenings were fraught with danger from bombs and collapsing buildings and the likelihood of being knocked down by traffic that at times was invisible even inches away due to the blackout and the London winter fog.

If the weather was bleak, the dance halls made up for it. They were still oases of colour and laughter and music and pleasure, with the Americans bringing their jive and jitterbugging to the height of popularity, driving out inhibitions and hesitation from the most wary and unworldly of individuals.

Kate had to go home to begin sorting out the repairs to the shop and the restocking with rationed goods, and it was Ethel who went with her. Rosie went first to visit her Nan.

Seeing the shop boarded up was a shock for Kate, and visiting her parents in hospital recovering from broken bones and head injuries, was worse. Leaving a willing Ethel in charge of cleaning up the shop and arranging for the necessary repairs, Kate spent the first few days dashing between visiting time at the hospital, talking to the doctors about her parents' recovery prospects and sorting out the technicalities at the local Ministry of Food offices. She discovered that the customers who normally bought their rations from the shop had been transferred temporarily to another close by.

'As soon as the shop is secure and clean we'll have you up and running again,' the young woman told Kate cheerfully.

'I think it will be a few weeks before my parents can cope,' Kate said. 'They were badly hurt and are still very shocked.' She was wrong. When she had been home just five days her parents left the hospital, and with assistance from kindly neighbours they had the shop reopened and fully stocked in a week.

'So glad to have you home, dear,' Mrs Banner smiled. 'We'll be glad of your help for a while. Then you can probably find work locally, do your bit here, near your father and me.'

'Sorry, Mam, but I can't stay. I was given leave, I haven't resigned. I'm needed back out there.'

'Surely not,' her father said. 'You've been lucky so far but now you can come home honourably, having done your bit. You don't have to put your mother and me through all the worries of you being so far from home any longer.'

For a moment their soft loving voices took her back to the rather spoilt child she had once been. It would be so easy to sink back into that life, to be treated like someone special, lose herself in the cushioning comfort of their protection. Then she looked at Ethel, who winked and mimed sympathy in a teasing manner, and she laughed.

'Mam, Dad, don't you know there's a war on?'

Before she and Ethel left, Kate told her mother about Vincent. Ethel felt a twinge of envy at the glow on Kate's face as she described him and told her parents about their plans for after the war.

'Don't tell us you'll be going to America!' Mrs Banner gasped. 'I couldn't bear it, I want you home.'

'If Vincent wants to live in America I'll go, Mummy. You'll be able to visit and we'll come home to see you. We'll have to bring your grandchildren to meet you, won't we?' she added, blushing slightly.

Again Ethel wondered how Kate would cope if Vincent failed to return from one of his bombing missions. She was so much in love and the war wasn't over yet. She felt fear for her friend in her vulnerability. Please let us stay together, she prayed silently, her fingers tightly crossed. If the worst happens, Kate will need Rosie and me.

Kate left her parents once an assistant had been found to help in the shop, a young woman who promised to stay until they had fully recovered. With only a moment's regret for the security and ease she was leaving behind, counting the days before she saw Vincent again, she set off for the station with Ethel. They were carrying a few extras in the way of food, gleaned during the abandoning of old stock and the replenishment with new. They agreed not to unpack their treats until they met up again with the ever-hungry Rosie.

'She'd never forgive us if we started without her,' Kate smiled. 'For someone so small, she takes an awful lot of filling!'

Rosie's homecoming had been filled with surprises. To her relief her darling Nan seemed to be coping well, but several of her neighbours were calling daily to check on her. This was puzzling, this extra caring, until Nan admitted that she'd had a suspected heart attack.

'Nan! Why didn't you tell me?' Rosie gasped.

'I didn't want to worry you, there's enough for you to think of out there facing bombs and guns and fighting off randy soldiers,' Nan grinned wickedly.

'Don't you see, I'll worry more if I think there are things happening that you don't tell me about?'

'They aren't even sure it was a heart attack,' she told her granddaughter cheerfully. 'A bit of pleurisy and a nasty bout of indigestion from these awful fatless sponges they make us eat, if you ask me.'

Rosie checked with the doctor and was reassured. 'It might have been a slight heart attack,' she was told, 'but we can't be certain. She appears to be well at the moment and as long as she doesn't try to do too much she should be fine.'

They settled down to enjoy a few days catching up on the weeks since they had last met, until one evening there was a knock at the door. Nan looked at the clock and frowned. 'Almost ten o'clock, who can it be?'

'The warden!' Rosie gasped in mock alarm. 'He saw the light of my torch when I went to get the wood in to dry for tomorrow's fire.'

Rosie opened the door and asked the person standing there what she wanted. It was impossible to see her. Apart from guessing she was a woman from the silhouette, nothing more could be gleaned from the barely visible caller in the almost complete darkness.

'I want to see Mrs Dreen and Rosemary too, if she's home.'

Rosie hesitated, but as no further explanation was forthcoming, she invited the woman in. She asked her to wait in the hall while the blackout curtains were positioned, then, without inviting the woman any further into the house, called her grandmother.

'Who is it, love?'

'It's me, mother-in-law. Brenda Dreen.'

The woman followed Rosie into the living room, seeming not to hear Nan ask, 'What are you doing here?'

She just stared at Rosie, a strange expression on her face like someone who had just been presented with a specially longed-for gift. 'And you must be my daughter.'

She smiled and offered her hand and instinctively, bemused with shock, Rosie took it, then pulled her hand away as though she had burned it.

'Rosemary, I'm your mother. I can't tell you how I've longed for this day. May I sit down? Stay and talk to you?'

'No, you can't,' Nan said, so politely the woman might have been asking for something completely innocuous, like permission to take off her coat. 'I want you to leave my house, now this minute, and if you want to communicate with us you'll have to write.'

'I've already tried that, as you know, mother-in-law. At first all my letters were returned, marked "not known at this address",' the woman said, just as softly and politely as Nan. She was looking at Nan but talking to Rosie. 'Since then I have written to you every month but haven't received a single acknowledgement. Now I'm here and I want a few words with my daughter.'

'I said you must leave,' Nan said, still speaking calmly.

'Please go,' Rosie said, in support of Nan, but her heart was racing. She knew her cheeks were bright pink and she was filled with an almost irresistibly strong desire to drag this person who was her mother back into the living room. She had a hundred questions tormenting her, questions that had lain dormant since Nan had stopped answering her when she was a child. They bubbled to the surface in those few seconds insisting to be heard.

The woman who was her mother turned to leave but before she did, she opened her handbag and took out a small envelope with its stamp placed ready for posting stuck in the corner.

'If you want to write to me, Rosemary dear, this is where you'll find me.'

In the darkness of the hallway, Rosie peered at the envelope. She was still Mrs Dreen, so she hadn't married the man who had taken her mother away from her, the man who had wanted her mother but hadn't wanted her. There was comfort in that. Then as Nan ushered her mother to the door, Rosie said harshly, 'And I'm called Rosie. Not Rosemary. Didn't you even know that?'

The door closing seemed to touch her body with actual pain. The click of the latch startled her, shocking with its finality.

'Put it on the back of the fire,' Nan said, gesturing towards the envelope in Rosie's hands, as the door closed behind her dead son's wife.

'Was she speaking the truth, Nan? Did you send her letters back?'

'Sorry, love. I should have told you she's been trying to get in touch. I just didn't want her coming here and upsetting you. We've been happy together, haven't we? Without the likes of her coming and stirring up trouble.'

'Yes, Nan. I couldn't have been happier,' Rosie said automatically, as she had so often told Nan before, only this time, she didn't quite mean it.

She didn't sleep that night. Whenever she began to drift off, pictures filled her mind of the imaginary mother she did not remember, fanciful scenes with a beautiful lady looking at her with love in her eyes, standing watching her play with her dolls, or reading to her from one of her favourite books, or running towards her with arms outstretched. Or, best of all, standing behind a table filled with party fare, a cake with candles and a pile of gaily wrapped parcels to celebrate her birthday. Her friends were sitting around the table, faces glowing and telling her how lucky she was to have such a kind and beautiful mother. Dreams such as these had once filled her nights but it was a long time since she had seen them so vividly.

Nan did not refer to her mother's visit the following morning and Rosie made no attempt to discuss it, although she badly wanted to know why Nan had never told her about her mother's attempts to contact her.

It was the day Rosie was due to leave, to go to London and meet up with Ethel and Kate, that they returned to the subject that had kept them silent for several days. Nan opened the drawer. 'I know I should have told you, Rosie dear. But at first you were too young and needed to settle. Then time passed and it was too late.' She went out and closed the door leaving Rosie staring down at the open drawer.

The letters were all brief, just asking how she was, sending her love and telling her a little about her life. Her work, where she lived, and later, her life without Geoff who had died but whom she had never married.

Rosie learned that she taught needlework in a girls' school, and enjoyed cycling with a club. There was so much Rosie had missed. There was no time then to read them all and she left them with Nan, who promised to keep them safe.

She couldn't wait to tell Ethel and Kate about her mother and she knew that once out of the inhibiting atmosphere of the house she had shared with Nan for so long, she would write to her mother and begin asking her questions.

When Ethel and Kate reached London, they had a few days before re-embarking to return to their unit, and when they met Rosie and reported to the office for papers, travel warrants and details of their route, they were told that they were not going back. Kate and Rosie were to report to an army camp somewhere in the south of England, to which they would be taken in an army lorry.

Ethel had to wait to be told her destination. It was devastating to realize that the amazing luck that had kept them together since 1940 had finally failed them. They might be miles apart, they could even be in different countries – North Africa, Italy, Europe or wherever the long discussed Second Front finally happened. It was heartbreaking. They might not meet again until war ended and even then, when they returned to their normal, everyday lives, circumstances and destiny would need a serious nudge before they did.

On their last evening together, they didn't go out for one last fling but instead sat in the lounge of the small shabby hotel where they were staying, and talked. It was then that Kate and Ethel learned about Rosie's brief and disappointing meeting with her mother.

'I didn't even know what she looked like,' Rosie told them. 'It's so long ago, without even a faded snapshot to keep my memories alive. My imagination has built a picture that was nothing like the reality. I was disappointed at how ordinary she looked. She wasn't beautiful and glamorous like Vivien Leigh or Alice Faye or...' She frowned as she tried to explain. 'She was just an ordinary mum. I expected her to be beautiful. Because Geoff stole her away from me, I imagined her so gorgeous and dazzling that he had to have her. In my foolish imagination he'd found her so irresistible he couldn't bear to share her with anyone, not even me. But she was ... I don't know, just ordinary.'

'How can you say she was ordinary, Rosie?' Kate, ever the romantic, said. 'That was so dreamy, like a story in a magazine. She must have been lovely. You could hardly judge, with her standing for a few minutes in Nan's gas-lit living room.'

'And scared half out of her wits having to face your Nan!' Ethel added.

'Scared?' I hadn't thought of her being scared.'

'Think about it, facing the woman who thought you were unrepentantly hard, even

316

cruel, having given up a child to follow a man you loved more. And preparing to meet that child and try to explain the years of absence. What's that if it isn't scary?'

'I wonder how soon after she left that your Nan started hiding away her letters?' Ethel asked curiously. 'Perhaps she hasn't ever stopped writing to you.'

'In all these years. We moved about from place to place when I was small, she wouldn't always have known where to find us,' Rosie explained. 'Yet she always did find us, at least it seems so from the number of letters Nan has, tucked away in that drawer.'

'If it was me I'd have to write and ask her what has happened over the years, even if I didn't tell Nan,' Ethel said. 'You did keep the address, didn't you?'

'Yes, and her name is still Dreen.' Somehow that seemed important. A different name and it would have been more difficult to accept that she was her mother.

Seeing Rosie begin a letter to her estranged mother made Ethel face the fact that her own mother, or the woman she called mother, needed to hear from her. She had to put aside her own feelings, go and show her mother that she cared, even if it was more duty than love. Then she shivered as she thought that her father might have recovered. She didn't know anything about strokes. Could he have returned to full health? Could he be well again? Standing there with his red angry face, those bright blue eyes glaring at her and telling her she had to come home and not talk to Wesley or any other man? And worse, what if the story about him having a stroke was nothing more than a ruse to persuade her to go home?

When she discussed it with Rosie and Kate, they tried to persuade her to go home during the few days she had left.

'Nan has been ill and I didn't know. At least you found out. If he dies before you see him, talk to him and make your peace, you'll regret it. I know you will. Life's so precarious.'

'The bomb that damaged the shop might have killed Mam and Dad,' Kate said earnestly. 'I might never have seen them again.'

Rosie nodded frantically in agreement. 'And now there's a chance to see my mother after all these years and perhaps get to know her and learn about myself, I'm so glad. I feel you should go, now, while you can.'

'I don't want to see my father ever again, if he dies I won't feel a thing,' Ethel insisted, although the words she uttered made her feel a ripple of superstitious fear. 'And nothing anyone tells me will persuade me to walk back into that house. Right?'

'Not even the chance to find out who your father is?'

'And what about your brother Sid?'

'I know where he is. He's at home trying to help Mam keep the market garden going. As for Wesley,' she added, thinking about him with poignant regret, 'I've no idea what happened to him except that he clearly doesn't want to see me.'

'But you do know where to find your mother and father.'

Ethel stubbornly shook her head. 'Grandparents,' she corrected with a harsh laugh. 'I don't know my father, and my mother's dead.'

After tearful goodbyes and promises to write, Kate and Rosie left Ethel on the station platform watching them boarding their train. As the guard put the whistle between his lips and raised his flag, she turned sharply and walked away.

Watching them leave her had made Ethel decide that they were right and for a first step she would write to Mr and Mrs Bailey at the farm to ask about Sid – who was her uncle, she supposed sadly.

'I can't believe we won't be together,' Rosie sobbed as the train picked up speed. 'Why does everything have to be so bloody!'

Kate understood Rosie's distress, realizing it was not all because of their parting from Ethel. Seeing her mother and wanting to meet again and talk to her had left her very tearful.

'It isn't for ever, Rosie,' she coaxed. 'You

know how frequently we're posted from one place to another, and we're at least in the same country! We'll meet during leave, that's a certainty, and we can write. Cheer up, it isn't for ever.'

They were delayed for two weeks, as no one seemed very clear about their destination. They moved around covering vacancies due to leave breaks and sickness. Plans were announced then changed almost daily.

Something was going on. There was an air of expectancy around the camps and a tightening up of security, but no one seemed willing to discuss the reason. Kate and Rosie guessed it had something to do with the Second Front which the British people were demanding and that the Russians needed, to take the burden of battle from them or at least ease it a little.

Everyone was edgy, and around the camp fields had been confiscated from the local farmers and fenced off by the engineers. Buildings sprang up and large quantities of stores were delivered. The numbers of men and women were slowly increasing. They were allowed to leave camp, but were restricted in where they went, and passes and passwords were strictly adhered to.

Fortunately their mail came through with remarkable speed. Vincent was still in the same area and there was a chance of he and Kate meeting up, which excited her and had her changing hair styles and choosing clothes in every spare moment, of which there were very few.

New canteens were being opened and the girls were moved with very little notice to attend to the preliminary arrangements before being moved once again. The post followed them and Rosie heard from her mother, a cautious note suggesting that they could meet when she was next free. Nan's parcels found them and they were sad that Ethel was not able to share them. Rosie constantly wondered about Baba, her love for him a gentle ache, but no news of him came through. The last she had heard was that he had been in North Africa and she wished she had stayed where they might have met. In her more melancholy moods she thought he was probably dead.

Their permanent posting finally came and they learned that the airfield was a new one and the canteen very large. They eventually arrived at night in the middle of an air raid after a long uncomfortable ride in a heavy RAF lorry.

They were taken to the shelter and it was there they spent their first night, hungry, tired and longing for a wash and a change of clothes. They woke to the sound of heavy planes taking off. 'Lancaster bombers,' they were told as they dragged their bags from the shelter and headed in the direction of their canteen. A voice behind them made them turn.

'Come on, you two slackers. This is your manageress speaking and I want you to march like soldiers, not slouch like girl guides in a thunderstorm.'

'Ethel!' Kate shouted in delight. Rose squealed.

'I've been promoted to manageress of this delightful holiday camp. What about that, eh?'

They exchanged news as they began getting everything ready for the first teabreak, laughing in their delight at being together again.

'Better conditions all around now I'm a manageress,' Ethel whispered. 'I've had to shout a lot, and the poor kitchen hands are scared stiff of me. I'll soften up in a day or so, but it was very slack around here. No one had any idea what they were doing. New camp, new staff, chaos! Thank goodness you two are here, we'll soon have them sorted out.'

The kitchen had four cooks, seven kitchen hands and a few dogsbodies, who did the work no one else wanted to do, plus the occasional assistance of men on 'jankers' for some misbehaviour. To the kitchen hands' delight and to everyone else's dismay, in the few days before the canteen was fully operational, Ethel had made them change jobs

322

occasionally to learn respect for people doing more lowly jobs: 'Jobs which are,' she reminded them, 'as essential to the servicemen and women as the rest.'

They had to wait for their accommodation to be made ready. They weren't too surprised to discover they would be sleeping in a tent. 'Our accommodation needing to be made ready? That sounds ominous,' Rosie shivered. 'Remember that first place? A cold tent occupied by Mrs Pompous and the canteen full of spiders as big as mice and mice that looked like rats!'

'And Walter, the creep!'

Ethel showed them around the kitchens and the preparation room where a group of girls similar to ones they remembered from years back were sitting around a pile of potatoes, peeling and cutting them up, singing as they worked. 'This place needs a good sorting,' she said, looking at the careless preparation. 'Peeled and with the shoots dug out, and the potatoes cut to a uniform size,' she said, in a tone that suggested it wasn't the first time.

Rosie and Kate pushed into the circle and began to help, starting off the singing with the Evelyn Laye number, 'It's a Lovely Day Tomorrow, Tomorrow is a Lovely Day'. The frowns on the faces as they showed resentment at Ethel's criticism faded, and the voices rang out as Ethel smiled and left them.

Once everything was as clean and orderly as they liked it, and still having to wait to be told where to find the tent in which they would sleep, Kate sat in the canteen and wrote to Vincent and dreamed verbally about their reunion until even the placid Rosie told her to 'Put a sock in it!'

'I wonder if we'll see Albert,' Ethel mused.

'Don't you start,' Rosie sighed.

'Or Baba Morgan?' Rosie's heart gave a painful leap. She could never tell them how she felt.

'Or the dreaded Walter,' Ethel added with a groan.

'I can't decide whether or not to meet my mother,' Rosie told them. 'She wants us to get together on my next leave.' They listened while she explained again how she felt about her need to support Nan, and to avoid the woman who had abandoned her in favour of the new man in her life. There was strong loyalty for Nan, who had cared for her as far back as she remembered, together with the confusion of wanting to talk to her mother, get to know her and to find out who she, Rosie Dreen, really was.

'I'm only half a person,' she told them.

'You eat enough for two!' Ethel retorted with a laugh.

'I know a lot about my father even though I don't remember him,' Rosie went on. 'Nan filled in the gaps for me to know my father, so many photographs and dozens of stories, but my mother is a stranger. All Nan said about her was that she had abandoned me for this man, Geoff, who didn't like children. I want to know my mother, understand the half of me that's her.'

'Forget her,' Ethel said firmly. 'You're expecting too much. A "Pandora's box", meeting her could be. You never know where it will lead.'

'I think you *should* meet,' Kate said. She looked at the canteen ceiling, starry-eyed. 'It's real romantic, your mother giving up her first-born for the man she loved.'

'First born? D'you mean I might have stepsisters or stepbrothers?' Rosie squealed.

'Oh, Kate, did you have to start her off again?' Ethel laughed.

'Even if they didn't marry she might have...' Kate stopped, remembering the situation Ethel had found herself in, and the baby she had lost.

Ethel appeared not to have noticed as she said, 'Seriously, Rosie, you shouldn't build up your hopes like this. Too great an expectation of what your mother could bring into your life will only lead to greater disappointment. Expect the worst, it's safer.'

Kate agreed, guessing that Ethel was trying to avoid unhappiness for their friend. It was an indication of their closeness that she didn't need explanations.

'Come on, you lot, let's get us bedded down for the night,' a young corporal called.

'You should be so lucky!' they chorused.

Their accommodation was a bell tent which they shared with three others and a minuscule heater. Coming from North Africa, even with the weeks at home in which to acclimatize, this was still a shock. But after only three nights sleeping in the cold, uncomfortable place that smelled of dampness and old socks, they moved to a Nissen hut where they at least had a 'donkey' to heat the room and were able to scrounge extra blankets.

The canteen had been recently decorated and smelled of paint and disinfectant. It was a large one, offering the usual snacks plus hot meals of sausage, rissoles or pasty with chips and the already disparaged spam, plus huge quantities of baked beans. There was also a bar selling alcohol and rationed cigarettes and chocolate, as well as the usual net bar in which the men and women could shop for their necessities. There was a stage complete with a piano on which impromptu concerts were sure to be held.

On their first day there, to Kate's delight, they received a quota of make-up. Kate had made arrangements to meet Vincent later in the week and was counting the hours in great excitement. Meanwhile she happily practised with the new colours as she prepared for their date.

On a rota system with other members of the staff, Ethel, Kate and Rosie were on call during their rest hours. When the bombers were due to set off on a mission they were there to prepare boxes of rations for the crews of the bombers to take, one for each man, containing sandwiches, cakes and also fruit and chocolate, which were not available to members of the public. These flyers were special and they were treated so.

As on other airfields, Ethel and Rosie and Kate used to count the heavy bombers out and wait for them to come back, afraid to count, afraid not to. It was hard not to be aware that some of the men they had been talking to, laughing with, just hours before, would never return.

Kate watched them leave, thinking of one of the bomb-aimers on one of the huge B17s, the Flying Fortresses. She listened to the engines as the planes took off and wondered if Vincent was safe.

Letters came through easily now they were back in Blighty, and after a few weeks, at the end of March, they were given a weekend off, with extra warnings about the seriousness of careless talk. Ethel had arranged to meet Albert, Kate had spent all her money illegally buying clothing coupons and purchasing smart new clothes ready for the long awaited reunion with Vincent, and Rosie told a lie and said she was going home to see Nan.

As she saw Ethel and Kate off on the bus taking them into the town, Rosie held the most recent letter from her mother in which she had arranged to meet her. She put on her greatcoat then took it off and repeated the movements at least five times, unable to decide whether or not she wanted to go.

When the last bus to pass the camp that morning was in sight coming through the lanes, rumbling slowly towards her, she almost ran back through the heavily guarded gates, but instead she jumped on, found a seat far from the other excited passengers who had waited with her, and sat staring at nothing at all until they reached the busy town. She could always change her mind before she reached the café where they were to meet, she told herself. The indecision lasted throughout the journey and continued as her feet took her towards her destination. I won't go. I need to go. I can manage without her. I owe her the chance to explain. She doesn't deserve that chance. So it went on.

She was relieved when the decision she was unable to make was taken out of her hands. As she reached the corner of the road, with only yards separating her from the mother she was about to face properly for the first time, she almost squealed with relief as the wail of the air raid warning filled her ears.

All around her people began to change direction. It was a strange town, but she only had to follow the crowd to find the shelter and step inside, thanking the fates for the excuse to miss the appointment and go back to camp on the next bus.

The raid was short-lived, the opinion of the people around her suggesting the enemy aircraft were crossing their air-space on their way to bomb some other unfortunates. Stepping out with relief into the cold afternoon, she walked again to the corner and looked down the road towards the café her mother had named. She wouldn't be there after all this time. She swivelled on her toes and set out with the intention of returning to the bus stop. As she did she bumped into a woman dressed in a rather ancient fur coat, wide-brimmed felt hat and carrying a small suitcase.

'I'm sorry, I—'

'Hello, Rosie, shall we find ourselves a cup of tea?'

Kate's heart was racing with anxiety. A shyness overcame her and she slowed her feet as she reached the corner where she and Vincent were to meet. What if they looked at each other and the spark had gone? What if the love they both believed in was no longer there? She stopped and looked in her hand-bag mirror, believing she looked a mess, and wondered how she could expect anyone to love her. Then she looked up and saw him, he called and waved, they ran into each other's arms and she knew everything would be all right.

After hours of drinking tea and coffee and declaring their love over and over again, they decided to visit her parents. Although their friendship had been short, they were both convinced it would never end. From the first time they had danced together, they had both known. A moment of friendly attraction had quickly deepened into a tender and passionate love.

'I can't wait to introduce you to my family,' Vincent said as they stood on the over-crowded station platform waiting for their train. 'I just know they'll adore you like I do.'

Kate's parents had been warned to expect them and when they stepped into the side entrance of the shop premises, she saw with amusement that they had filled the place with decorations.

'Mum, what's this? It isn't Christmas!'

'No, but Easter wasn't long ago and the house is so drab, with so many of our nice things lost when that bomb came down, Daddy and I thought we'd start a new tradition and decorate for Easter. It's a bit late, that's all. After all, you did miss

Christmas, dear.'

Kate laughed, hugging Vincent's arm.

The short holiday was a great success, with Vincent marvelling at the meals provided, and the cheerful spirits of everyone he met.

'I don't know how you've all managed with the shortages for so long,' he said as Kate cut a sad sponge cake sparsely decorated with a few Easter chicks stuck on with melted chocolate.

'It's easy because we're all in the same boat,' Mr Banner told him, not quite truthfully. 'No one has more than anyone else, we're having to put up with the same difficulties and it's brought us closer.'

'We share what we do have, and of course swop things, barter like in the olden days. I don't use much sugar so I swop sometimes for some extra tea, or take some soap in exchange for something else.' Mrs Banner added to the lie.

'Soap is rationed too?' Vincent frowned.

'Difficult keeping the shop clean, I'll tell you.'

From his suitcase, Vincent produced a bottle of wine and some chocolates. 'If I'd taken the trouble to find out, I could have brought you something more useful,' he said sadly. 'I guess I expected you to have plenty. I thought, as you run a grocery store, you wouldn't be as troubled by rationing as some, that you'd be able to wangle all you need. I should have known you wouldn't do that.'

Mr Banner looked away to hide the guilt in his eyes and winked at his daughter, a wink so like hers. 'That's not allowed, son,' he said.

'These,' Mrs Banner said, hugging him, 'are just perfect.'

'We'll keep them for next Easter,' her father joked.

When Kate returned to camp she knew that wherever the war took her, or Vincent, they would find each other again and one day, when peace finally allowed them to return to their own lives, they would marry.

'He isn't rich and I know now that insisting on finding a man who was handsome and rich was just the bit of me that was still a child,' she told Ethel and Rosie. 'The child in me has gone now, and I know that it's happiness that's important. Whatever happens in the future, with Vincent alongside me I know I'll be happy.'

Ethel smiled but she was worried. To be as happy as Kate clearly was could be a challenge to the fates. Vincent was a bomb-aimer in one of the heavy B17s and someone somewhere would be watching his plane take off with the rest, then scouring the skies, counting the planes as they came back. Her fear was that Kate loved Vincent too much in these dangerous times, and his death, which was a strong possibility, would devastate her.

Ethel and Albert were unexpectedly shy when they renewed their friendship. Albert because of the growing love for her he had revealed in his letters, and Ethel because she had thoughts of Baba Morgan in her heart that outweighed her affection for Albert. Lively, happy Baba whom she had neither seen nor heard from for months and who might be dead.

To confuse her emotionally even further, there was still the unresolved situation with Wesley Daniels. As she was now in contact with Mr and Mrs Bailey on the farm, she had news of him. She was surprised to learn that he had been in North Africa at the same time as herself. Knowing how near they had come to meeting didn't thrill her as it might once have done. She had outgrown Wesley, she thought sadly. And he would almost certainly have changed in the way he felt about her.

Thinking of Wesley as she sat on a bus beside Albert on their way to the pictures during her half day, she felt a sudden sharp longing to go home and see her mother and brother. She leaned towards Albert and put her head on his shoulder, glad of his warmth, needing the closeness to soothe away the sudden sensation of loneliness.

It was April 1944 and still very cold. So she was surprised when Albert suggested going for a walk instead of the cinema.

'A walk? It's freezing!'

'I'll keep you warm,' he said, taking her hand and coaxing her to leave the bus before their intended stop.

Some of the once-discarded street signs had been replaced and one directed them to Ring Park. They followed the sign and entered the park from which all the railings and gates had been long removed for scrap metal. Voices reached them through the failing light. Other couples had searched for some privacy to kiss and cuddle and promise undying love. They found an empty seat near a small lake. Albert shared his greatcoat with her and they sat huddled in its warmth.

'I want you,' Albert whispered throatily after a few kisses. 'I want you so much.'

A stab of desire shot through Ethel's body, starved so long of love, and she moved, just slightly to press herself closer to him. She thought of Baba Morgan and briefly of Wesley, and of Duggie whom she had loved and had hoped to marry. Albert made a clumsy attempt to kiss her and she moved away.

'Sorry,' Albert mumbled. 'I shouldn't have tried to ... I'm sorry. I know you aren't that sort of girl.'

'It's all right, Albert. Let's forget it happened, shall we?'

'I'm sorry,' he whispered again. 'I've insulted you, I know that.'

She tried to reassure him, tell him she wasn't upset.

'It's just ... Ethel, will you marry me? As soon as this lot's over and we can get back to ordinary jobs, we could find a place, just the two of us. I'll do everything I can to make you happy.'

'Albert! Dear Albert, I'm flattered, but I don't know how I'll feel when this lot is over and neither do you. Let's leave it, shall we? Remain as good friends, and see how it goes?'

They were walking in through the camp gates, arms around each other, when Walter passed them. Ethel was talking to one of the men in the guard room, some banter about the cause of Albert's smile, so she didn't see him.

'Had a bit of a fling, have you?' Walter said to Albert, adding, 'You don't mind about not being the first then? I've been there before you, mate, and so have a few others.' Albert stopped, pulled away from Ethel.

'Ignore him, Albert. He's off his head,' Ethel said flippantly. Then someone called to Albert and with hardly a word he hurried off.

'Albert?' she called, but when he didn't respond, she shrugged and went on, presum-

335

ing he had been called away to something important. If she had seen Walter's smile, she might have worried, but she did not.

'What happened?' Kate asked after she had told Ethel the exciting outcome of her visit to her parents with Vincent. She found it difficult to listen to her friend talk about her afternoon and evening away from camp, she was so full of memories of Vincent's delight at meeting her family and friends and his oh so romantic proposal.

Ethel said nothing to her of her own marriage proposal. She was beginning to wonder if, as Albert hadn't stopped long enough for explanations, he had believed whatever rubbish Walter had told him. But it wasn't really important apart from the natural anger at being described so unkindly. It was Baba who pulled at her heart-strings in a way Albert never did. If only Baba would get in touch. She needed to know whether or not he was still alive.

Rosie was the last to return that day. She was subdued when she met Ethel and Kate on her return. She had spent her weekend in camp apart from two afternoons when she had met her mother.

At first Rosie had snapped out her questions, determined to dislike this woman who was her mother but had done no mothering. Gradually, the quiet, calm voice soothed her

336

and she found herself listening to stories about herself when she was young. That these stories ended before she began school seemed unimportant. They were lovingly told and the death of her father and her mother's loneliness and grief became real. In spite of efforts to be angry at the way she had been left by her mother, she began to understand.

'Nan is a bit possessive,' she admitted at one point.

'Not possessive, dear, I'd be unkind to think that. She had lost a son and there's no replacing a child, specially an only child. She expected me to live the rest of my life as a grieving widow and I couldn't. I was very young when you were born. I'm not yet forty, remember. For Nan the grief will never end, for me it had to.'

Later, listening to both Kate and Rosie tell their stories, Ethel made up her mind.

'On my next leave I'm going home.'

'I'll come with you,' Rosie offered at once. 'You might have to make a run for it if your old man is still as barmy as ever.'

Ethel laughed. 'And what would you do against a huge man like my father?'

Rosie squealed. 'Probably run a lot faster than you!'

Ethel hadn't spoken to Albert since he had proposed. She didn't realize it at first but now faced the fact that he was deliberately avoiding her. She decided with very little hurt that he had regretted the words and wished they could be unsaid. His was not much of a love if he could be so easily put off by a man like Walter. When they did meet she treated him exactly like the others, with no attempt to show affection and certainly with no sign of being in love.

Eleven

'Marry the man,' Rosie said, when Ethel had told them of Albert's proposal.

'I don't love him, in fact I wonder whether I'm capable of love.'

'Rot!' Kate said, hands on hips in an accusing posture. 'You love your family for a start and don't deny it, you want to go back and make things right, even with that tyrant of a father of yours.' Her voice softened and she added, 'There can't be any doubt that you loved Duggie.'

'I'm not sure I know the difference between love and sex. If I hadn't come to my senses, Albert and I would have "made love", but was that loving him? Or just a need for a moment of belonging?'

'Walking away from your family like that, it

must have made a difference to how you feel about a lot of things,' Rosie said. 'I often wondered how my mother was feeling, knowing I was there, changing, growing up, and never seeing me. It's different for you. Like my mother, you did the walking and only you can walk back.'

Ethel was silent for a while, then she said firmly, 'What I feel for Albert isn't enough to last a lifetime. Of that I am sure.'

'Good!' Kate said. 'Now that's sorted can we talk about my wedding? I want you to be my bridesmaids and—' She was silenced by a pillow thrown by Ethel and another, accompanied by a squeal, from Rosie. In spite of groans and teasing, they couldn't silence Kate on the subject of Vincent for long.

A few days later all three received letters. Kate excitedly read a long letter from Vincent's mother which included photographs of all his family.

'They like me! They really like me and welcome me into their family. I'm going to marry Vincent and become an American!'

It was on the same day that Ethel received news that Baba Morgan was safe. He had been taken prisoner and was now on his way home. In a second she knew why she couldn't commit herself to Albert. She had been waiting for news of Baba. She still wasn't sure about love, but the excitement the news had created in her convinced her that it was Baba who held the key to her heart.

Rosie's letter was from her newly discovered mother, inviting her to stay with her on Rosie's next leave.

'Will you go?' a jubilant Ethel asked her.

'If we finally persuaded you into going home to talk to your family,' Rosie said, 'I'd decided to go with you. But now, with Baba on his way, I doubt if anything we say will convince you that your family are priority.'

'Baba won't be back for days, even weeks. I think you're right. I have to go home and find out what my father knows that makes him fear for me. I have to find out before I meet Baba. You see,' she hesitated nervously before going on, 'you see I think I must have inherited some dread disease and he's afraid I'll pass it on to my children.'

Rosie and Kate stared at her.

'Is that what you've been worrying about all this time?' Kate asked. 'You were having nightmares about something as awful as that and you didn't tell us?'

'Oh, Ethel. I thought we were your trusted friends. I'd have dragged you to the MO myself, you idiot,' Rosie said, tears filling her large blue eyes.

'At least it's answered one question,' Kate said thoughtfully. 'You didn't want to face the truth for Albert's sake, did you? Only when Baba got in touch. You want the truth now, in case you marry Baba. Love, I'd say, wouldn't you, Rosie?'

Hiding her still painful disappointment over the destroyed dream of Baba returning and wanting her, Rosie nodded with her usual silent enthusiasm.

Over the following days Kate and Rosie made their plans to go with Ethel to visit her parents. They both agreed they should stay with her while she got to the truth behind her father's obsessive behaviour. There wasn't time to dwell too long on possible explanations or what Ethel should say as they were kept very busy. Temporary buildings increased in number and these were filled with stores and other undisclosed items which were strictly guarded by armed soldiers who had permission to shoot.

More men began to arrive and were accommodated in dozens of bell tents and fed by the cookhouse and the canteen. Serving so many extra mouths became a nightmare, and judging the amount of food a constant worry. The girls secretly gave thanks they were in an army camp, as generally the soldiers were inclined to be more helpful than the airmen, helping to clear tables, stack dishes and carry them to the kitchen to be washed by the hard worked kitchen 'slaves'. China and cutlery were washed and dried as fast as possible and returned to the counter for reuse.

Although there were more people, the entertainment fell flat. Apart from a few who tried to force others to enjoy themselves, most were withdrawn, and the atmosphere was tense. A man called Gerald continued playing the piano whenever he was free of duties but few leaned on the instrument beside him and sang the regular favourites.

After the canteen closed, the routine work went on as usual, endless cleaning, filling in the books, balancing the money. And always baking cakes and pastries, making sandwiches. The ubiquitous chip appeared in unbelievable quantities, involving soldiers – usually those on 'jankers' – to do the boring task of peeling and cutting them. Like the girls, they sang as they worked too, but the words were parodies of favourite songs and unsuitable for the Naafi girls' tender ears.

Sometimes they were so tired they didn't wash properly, just gave themselves what Rosie called a cat's lick and a promise, before flopping into bed exhausted. No matter how late and however tired she was, Kate still always rolled up her hair in dinkie curlers so she would 'look my best for our boys' the following day.

Besides the British divisions, soldiers of many nations filed into the camp. The American soldiers both white and black, smiling, always polite and respectful of the girls, 'Treating us like their kid sisters', as one of the canteen staff said.

Kate sighed as she searched the sea of faces and wished she could see Vincent. But fully aware of where the men were heading, she thought perhaps not. She hoped he was in fact far away from the south of England and Wales at that time, somewhere safe, stood down from flying.

As she prepared more sandwiches for the counter she thought of him setting off on a mission, being handed his food pack by the girls in the American PX and hoped they were generous with what they gave him. If only she could see him, reassure herself he was safe. But letters would have to be sufficient for the moment. Busy serving teas to some of the lads, she found time to offer up a quick prayer for his safety.

This was echoed in the hearts of Ethel and Rosie. If Vincent lost his life in the chaos that was surely to come, Kate would be devastated. She was deeply and irrevocably in love with Vincent. Both friends also prayed for Baba, both loving him, only one allowed to say it aloud.

Besides the stores that had built up to feed the extra men, vehicles came and were quickly camouflaged against spying enemy aircraft with their all-seeing cameras. Lorries and amphibians, tanks and armoured cars and guns as well as boxes of ammunition were piled on to the fields around them in a widened area taken over by the war machine weeks before and fenced and heavily guarded.

From an airfield close by, bombing raids on the French coast were intensified and the crews came back for a brief rest while their planes were serviced and repaired, before being sent off again – their numbers made up from reserve crew arriving with frightening regularity, to replace the injured or the dead. Kate watched them taking off and landing and guessed the rest.

Long trailers were seen on the roads, blocking traffic and occasionally causing chaos. Rumours spread that they contained sections of bridges to be used when the Second Front opened. In fact the long vehicles, which bore the nickname 'Queen Mary's', held planes, built to replace those lost in the daily air battles, something Kate tried not to think about.

An air of tension gradually changed to one of anticipation as the day – the date of which was still unknown to the men – approached. The place was filled to capacity and still they came. Serving them all was a nightmare of organization; with so many staff working they were falling over each other. Still the girls smiled and joked and laughed at the teasing as though they hadn't heard any of it before. As May moved on, the men began to relax a little and the pianist began to attract a more interested audience around him.

It was at the end of May 1944 that the three girls planned to go and face Ethel's parents, but without warning the camp was sealed. No post or deliveries of any kind came in or went out and no one was allowed to leave. Letters to and from home were held in abeyance.

So sudden was the closing of the camp that one local girl who had called to collect a handbag left behind when she had been moved a few weeks before, came in, greeted a few friends and was not allowed back out. She couldn't even tell her parents where she was.

'Stay out all night? My father'll think the worst and he'll kill me,' she wailed, but to no avail.

One evening, fresh supplies were opened and, although they were officially off duty, having worked all that day without a break, the girls were called to help to prepare portable canteen packs for the men. Exhausted, they nevertheless worked almost throughout the night with no one uttering a word of complaint. The following day the task went on. No one said anything but they all knew that this was 'it'. Today was the day we would invade Europe.

At midnight they went to bed and lay

awake, unable to shut off their minds to what was going on just a few miles away. They heard the bombers and fighters flying over, the different engine sounds, some low and powerful, others high pitched and sounding impatient to be off, performing a kind of symphony in the night air. In the darkness Kate crossed her fingers and wished Vincent luck. With so many men on the move he was certain to be one of them – bombarding the enemy to make it safer for those on the ground, the vehicles moving forward and the men who were clearing the way.

The planes had all gone and the sound of low-geared engines filled the night air; they listened for what seemed hours, as the lorries and the rest moved out. The hands of the clock in the dim light seemed to crawl as line after line of vehicles left the fields around. There were few voices heard. Everyone knew exactly what was needed of them and the exodus was carried out steadily, effortlessly without a delay.

The girls tried to sleep, but long before they needed to, they got out of bed where they had lain fully dressed in case they were needed, and looked out of the window. The camp and all the fields around it were completely, eerily empty.

At midnight in a place near Caen, the gliders

had landed the first of the Allied forces on French soil, their task to secure important bridges. Overhead, bombers rained down their destruction on to the German defences.

At home, as soon as the ships at the southern and eastern docks were filled with men and equipment they set out for France, the Americans going to the beach they called Utah, Canadians landing on Juno and the British on sections of the coast they called Sword and Gold.

On board ship on his way towards the coast of France, Wesley was getting food to the men on the heavily laden ship, ignoring the guns and the bombs that threatened them. More and more bombers and fighters flew towards the coast of Normandy. It was overcast, the planes droned unseen above him. Vincent was just one of hundreds aiming his bombs at his targets, battering the German lines. The powerful plane had been hit several times but the crew remained determined to do what was asked of them and help the infantry and ground troops below.

Some days later, Wesley's ship was outward bound on its seventh voyage. When the ship was hit he seemed oblivious of the danger, he just followed the men to the first aid room, usually the mess room but used by the medics when needed, and stood ready to help the dedicated men with their heartbreaking work. When the call came to abandon ship, he stood back and allowed others to go before him, uncaring of his own safety, not from a heroic stance but because he really did not care what became of him.

They were not very far from the beach where the Mulberry Harbour was already in place, having been towed out in sections and fixed so that lorries and tanks could roll off the ships and up to the beach. He swam lazily towards it, rested for a while then went on to the beach.

Bombs falling, guns firing and the bodies of the dead and wounded made the beach into a hellish scene. He stopped to help the wounded when he could and directed the busy first aid men to where the more serious cases were, before heading to where the Naafi were already set up and offering char and a wad to those near enough to reach them. Wesley offered his services and was soon making sandwiches, unpacking chocolate and biscuits, carrying food and hot drinks and offering comfort to the men.

The noise was so great, between the loud crunch of bombs falling and the heavy artillery pounding close by, that he became deaf for a while, but presumed that it must be the same for everyone, so he carried on.

Explosions fell close to him at times and once or twice knocked him off his feet. Others were doing the same as himself, offering sustenance to the fighting men, and he went to uncover one Naafi assistant who had been hidden by the huge amount of sand that had rained down on him. The man, who had so narrowly cheated death, went back to the Naafi area and complained that the cups had been filled with sand and could he have replacement teas, and quick.

So it went on, the slow continuous crawl from the beach and on through villages and towns, in the days that followed. There was little sleep for anyone; once or twice Wesley began to feel delirious and, like many others, took a tablet to help him go on. His last thought, when he finally slept, was of Ethel, wondering vaguely whether she would perhaps be proud of him at last.

Once a beach head was established the security at the army camp began to ease. The guards were still cautious about who came and went, passwords were used and passes inspected with the usual thoroughness but, to everyone's delight, letters came, plus a parcel from Rosie's Nan.

They were all tired after the extra hours they had worked but hearing the news from across the Channel cheered them and the three girls began to replan their next leave.

Kate wrote page after page to her beloved Vincent, shutting her mind off from the possibility that he was one of hundreds who hadn't returned after the D Day invasions on the Normandy coast.

Rosie wrote to her mother and to Nan, telling them both that she wanted them all to meet. 'I don't think Nan will agree,' she told the others. 'After losing her son, my father, she expected my mother to stay with her to offer comfort and share the grief, but instead she ran off and left me and Nan, to live with this other man. How can I expect Nan to accept her after all these years?'

'Reassure your Nan that you love her best and she will always come first,' Kate said. 'Love is the answer to most things, you know.'

Ethel laughed. 'Since you met Vincent the world is filled with love!'

'Better than dragging hatred on and on and prolonging the misery.'

Rosie sucked the end of her pencil thoughtfully. 'I think I'll use that, it sound's good. Prolonging the misery, eh?'

Ethel wrote to Baba, long letters telling him about Rosie's mother's unexpected return and about Kate and her love for Vincent. She said little about herself, it had been too long for catching up with how she felt, and besides, she didn't know what he wanted to hear. No point making a fool of herself by telling him how much she had missed him if he hadn't felt more than casual friendship. 'The trouble with war,' she said to Kate and Rosie, 'is that everything gets too intense.'

'What are you talking about now?' Kate asked, but Ethel didn't try to explain.

As the battle for the liberation of France continued, their weekend passes finally came through. Ethel was still undecided about whether she would go home. Hoping Kate and Rosie would agree, she suggested delaying it, insisting she wanted to stay in camp in case Baba arrived, but the others wouldn't hear of it.

'I can't see Vincent, he isn't free,' Kate said. 'So, I'm coming home with you. You have to sort this thing out with your father some time and better you do it before you see Baba, don't you agree?'

'I'll come too,' Rosie said. She sighed. 'I can't decide whether to go to Nan's or meet my mother again. So, I'll do neither.' She sighed again. 'If only Nan would agree to Mam coming there, we might have a chance of getting somewhere but Nan refuses to open the door to Mam, and Mam won't go there without an invitation from Nan. So where does that get me?'

'Come to stay with me,' Kate said. 'Invite your Nan and your mother and let them meet on neutral ground. Mam and Dad wouldn't mind. It'll be a bit of a crush though. I'll ask them, shall I?'

'Thanks, Kate. I might try that. But Nan's

house is big enough for Mam to stay there and keep out of Nan's way if she wanted to.' She smiled and said, 'I can just imagine it, every five minutes one or the other would flounce off and shut herself away like an aged primadonna.'

'Right. Next time we're all off together, that's what we'll do, get them together somewhere and make them talk. Agreed?' Kate said. 'But this weekend is for Ethel and the mad dad. All right?'

Ethel didn't tell her mother she was coming. Instead the three girls found inexpensive lodgings in the town and the following day, a Saturday, they went by bus and on foot to her home. Ethel didn't walk straight in, too much had happened for her to feel able to do that. Besides, there was also the atavistic need to be outside, in the open, where she could run and make her escape! 'If he starts,' she warned her friends, 'then I'm off and it's every man for himself.' She knocked and stood back with her friends and waited until the door opened.

'Ethel!' her brother Sid shouted, running forward to hug her. 'Ethel, thank goodness you've come. Are you all right? Have you heard about Dad? Are you home for good?' The questions shot from him, then he calmed down and invited them in.

The introductions were lost in the confusion of his welcome and Ethel left them and

352

went into the small, overfilled living room. There, standing near the fire, shaking with emotion, stood her mother. Silently they held each other, tears flowing, while Sid beckoned to Kate and Rosie to follow him into the kitchen, where he began to prepare a tray of tea and toast with illegally obtained, delicious farm butter.

'Sorry, Mam, but I couldn't come before now. Today was hard enough. I couldn't have managed without Kate and Rosie.' Ethel struggled to hold back sobs as her mother held her at arm's length to examine her and see how well she looked. 'Sorry I ran away and left you to deal with it,' she added as she slipped again into her mother's arms.

'Don't apologize, love. The fault is with me. I should have done something to stop your father years before.'

'Is he ... is he here?'

'Up in his bed and there he'll stay until he dies.' There was harshness in Molly's voice for the first time, and the tears left unshed glistened in her eyes.

Sid came in followed by Kate and Rosie, and as the tea was poured and toast handed around, Ethel said, 'I think I want to see Dad before I eat this.'

Sid followed her and she went up the familiar stairs and into the bedroom where her parents had slept all their married life. The big bed was empty, the room neat and orderly.

'He's in the box room,' Sid said, and there was a hint of sadness in his blue eyes.

She peered around the door of the mean little room and stared at her father. She dreaded seeing those eyes glaring at her, so like Sid's, but which frightened her as no others could.

His red hair had faded to grey, the skin had lost its angry redness. He looked smaller and his face had collapsed into softness, paler and thinner than she remembered. 'Hello, Dad,' she said, gripping her forearms to stop their shaking.

Sounds came from the man who no longer looked like her father. He didn't look at her, presuming perhaps that the other figure standing beside his son was that of his wife. He pointed to a cup on the side table, tea that had gone cold. Sid went over to hand it to his father and help him to drink.

'Mam does that,' Sid told her sadly. 'She's still getting her own back on him for the years he misused her. Putting things just out of reach, deliberately misunderstanding him when he wants something.'

'She shouldn't,' Ethel said in a shocked whisper.

Her voice suddenly penetrated the man's confused brain and he turned his head slowly and stared at her. The eyes were the same bright, angry blue. But behind them the man whom she had feared to face was no longer there. A stranger sat there, propped up by pillows and helplessly accepting the drink Sid was holding for him.

He moved his face away from the cup and stared, then realization showed in his expression. The one arm capable of movement waved in the air and his voice called out, unintelligable babble which Sid seemed to understand.

'He's telling you to go, to keep away from me.'

'Why? Surely he doesn't include you in his warnings about men?' She laughed nervously.

Dai gestured pitifully towards a photograph of the family and painstakingly pointed to her sister. When she tried to make sympathetic remarks he silenced her with more wild sounds and pointed to Sid. Even Ethel recognized the word 'evil'.

'What does he mean?' she asked, moving closer to her brother. This seemed to anger the sick man further, and again he pointed to the picture of Glenys then at Sid. Then, with a roar of rage, at her. Tears weakened the anger in his eyes and with an effort he pointed to them again. Glenys, Sid and then herself.

'My God. He thinks you and Glenys ... that you're—'

'He knows Glenys was your mother and

believes I am your father,' Sid said sadly. 'Please believe me when I swear to you that it isn't true.'

'But why would he think such a thing?'

'Let's go downstairs, shall we?'

Leaving the distressed man alone in his comfortless and sparely furnished room they went down to join the others. Kate and Rosie were quickly included in the latest twist to Ethel's story but they remained silent, not adding a word that would distract from the situation between Ethel and Sid and Molly Twomey.

'You know about this?' Ethel asked her mother. 'That Dad blamed Sid?'

'I do now. Sid and I discussed it and we decided that it was because, at the time of Glenys's death, Sid said he was to blame for her having a child when she was so young. He meant he should have taken more care of her. Your father misunderstood. He was always one to think the worst of anyone, specially his family,' she added bitterly.

'Nothing any of us said made any difference. He wouldn't listen to explanations or be persuaded to change his mind about what he believed was the truth. He preferred to blame me, you see,' Sid explained. 'He loved Glenys and coped better by convincing himself that I was the one responsible, that she was the innocent and unfortunate victim.'

'I meant I used to see her kissing the boy

and did nothing to warn her. I should have made sure she kept away from him.'

A feeling of dread enveloped Ethel and she was convinced she was going to be sick.

'The boy', the mysterious 'him' – Sid had said, 'I should have made sure she kept away from him.' She had to ask just one more question and she would know the true identity of her father, but dare she do it? Dare she say the words that could ruin her happiness? A fraction of a second and she would know whether he was a fool or a genius, a strong man or a weakling. Whether she carried some dread disease that would make marriage to Baba impossible and make her glad Duggie's child had died. Did she have a father to be proud of, or someone whose name would make her keep the secret until she died?

'Who was he, who is my true father?' To her surprise the words came out strong and confident. She looked from Sid to the woman she had always called Mam. 'Tell me!'

'I don't know, Glenys wouldn't tell me,' Mrs Twomey said.

'You must have an idea,' Ethel pleaded. 'Please, I have to know.' She looked at her brother.

'It was Colin Bailey from the farm,' Sid told her softly.

Ethel felt the shock of it invade every part

of her; then she allowed her mind to wander over the thoughts and fears she had suffered since Glenys's tragic death. Colin Bailey was a kind, gentle man who had always been a friend but had never interfered in her life. The truth was far kinder than any of her imaginings. 'I wish Glenys had told me,' she said at last, 'then she needn't have died.' With Kate and Rosie holding her and soothing her, Sid comforting her mother, she cried, while upstairs the man she had always called Dad cried too.

They didn't stay long but before they went for their bus Kate and Rosie went for a walk while Ethel went to see Colin.

'I'm glad you know,' he said smiling. 'My only regret is that I didn't know in time or we'd have married, young as we were. Your mother had taken the child, given you her name before I knew and Glenys begged me to keep it a secret. I've watched you grow and taken pleasure in the way you have developed into a lovely, capable young woman. I was on hand if you needed me but content to watch from a distance and marvel at the wonderful person your sister and I gave life to. I'm still here and always will be. But nothing will change unless you want it to.'

The three girls turned back and waved from the bus as Colin, Sid and the woman she still called mother stood watching them leave. Ethel wasn't able to discuss what had happened and Kate and Rosie understood. Rosie asked just one question. 'Are you glad we made you go?'

A still tearful Ethel simply nodded. As Rosie well knew, sometimes a nod was sufficient.

The war continued to rage in Italy, Russia and the Far East as well as nearer to home, in Europe. Caen had been taken by the Allies and London was again being attacked from the air, this time with pilotless planes, V1s that quickly earned the nickname doodlebugs or buzz bombs.

City dwellers became aware and quickly learned to recognize the sound of this new terror. They would watch nervously, knowing that when the engine stopped, the flying bomb would fall to the ground at terrific speed bringing death and terror. After the engine fell silent, they would count to seven and wait for the devastating blast that followed. Life or death was decided in those seven seconds.

When Ethel, Kate and Rosie returned to camp it was to learn to their horror that gunners on the ground were told to fire at these planes and try to shoot them down.

'Shoot them down? But we're underneath them!' Kate gasped. 'And with stores filled with petrol and ammunition all around us? Are you mad? You mean we're standing here while you lot are trying to bring the bombs down on ourselves?'

'You'll be safe enough in the slit trenches,' they were told laconically by one of the gunners.

'You make sure you aim to miss till I've got my hat on!' Kate warned.

'You should have let me keep my best hat instead of throwing it under that train,' Rosie grinned. 'That would have stopped them!'

One day when several raids had disrupted the whole day, preventing Ethel from completing her tasks; when the cakes were overcooked and the potatoes ran out before they had finished serving lunch and a dozen other small incidents had annoyed her, Albert came in and looked around as though hoping to see someone else he could approach. He eventually asked if the books and money had been made up for him to check.

'No they haven't, and I won't get them done until tomorrow because I'm going out!' she snapped, irritated by his juvenile behaviour.

'You know they have to be completed each day,' he said stiffly. 'It's the only way to ensure accuracy. No one can rely on their memory being precise if there's a query.'

'And talking about queries,' she said angrily, 'what upset you last time we went out? Was it because I said a few swears? Or offended your inhibited, pompous heart by some other such dreadful misdemeanour?' Her day had been so frustrating she spoke more fiercely than she normally would, her patience had all been used up. 'Or was it your stupidity in proposing, so you could seduce me into bed?'

'I wouldn't have been the first to do that, would I?'

'What d'you mean?' she demanded. 'Who's been lying to you?'

'Lying? Walter was very convincing when he told me that you and he ... that I wouldn't be the first.'

Anger left her like air out of a burst balloon and laughter took its place. 'Walter? You believed him? Walter Phillips? He'd be so lucky!'

'He told me that—'

'Forget it, Albert. I'm laughing at *you*, not pathetic Walter who has to lie, to pretend, because no one will give him a moment of their time. Me and Walter? What a laugh, wait till I tell Rosie and Kate!'

'I'm sorry. I—'

'Don't be sorry. I'm not. It's shown me just what a fool I've been to think you could even be a friend, let alone something more. Friends trust each other. Walter! You amaze me! You believed that of me? And without even allowing me to answer? Goodbye, Albert.' She was still laughing when she went to find the others.

Predictably, Kate was writing to Vincent. Beside her was a notepad covered with surprisingly good sketches of wedding gowns, together with small bridesmaids' dresses coloured faintly in pink crayon.

'Mum thinks it's my favourite colour and I'd hate to disappoint her,' she explained.

They were in and out of bed that night with constant air raid warnings and Hitler's latest weapon causing havoc in the cities. The gunners were improving their technique and some were being shot from the skies before reaching their intended target. Others went off course and fell harmlessly into the sea or the fields around south-east England.

Besides the V1 rockets, there were still a few raids in which bombs were dropped, and civilians as well as camps and airfields were strafed by lone aircraft on nuisance raids. There was a brief attack one morning, and during the lull that followed, the injured were taken to the sick bay, the mess cleared, then everything continued as before.

A solitary plane turned back and came in low over the camp and fired into the groups of fitters working around the planes. The medics ran to the scene but no one was hurt. Rosie, who unlike Ethel had failed to become a proficient driver, was on her way back from taking food and hot drinks to the ground crews. It was very warm and as she was pushing the trolley towards the nearest line of lorries she was singing cheerfully, puffing her hair from her face between notes. Around the fields guns began to fire. Above, the plane was turning and coming in for another attack.

Kate watched her friend and smiled. Rosie was stretched out, leaning forward, head down, struggling over the uneven ground towards the men, some of whom were walking towards her to help push the ungainly trolley.

Kate saw, then heard the plane, realized that it was coming towards them, dropping down, increasing speed and heading for the field, and she ran, calling to Rosie to get down. The noise of the plane's engines deafened her, and her voice was unheard by Rosie. The sound of the plane filled her head as it came closer, large and deadly, the unbelievably loud roar stopping all thought.

The line of bullets crossed Kate's back, the blood spurting up like roses blooming on the khaki cloth. Ethel and Rosie saw what had happened and the world seemed to stop and everything fell silent. The drone of the aircraft faded away. The sun still shone. The sky was still a clear, summer blue.

Then voices and people running and Rosie bending down staring in utter disbelief at the still form of her friend. Someone gently turned Kate over and Rosie straightened her hair, folded it neatly around the face that was so lovely in repose.

When they put Kate's body on to a stretcher, covered her beautiful face and took her away, Rosie screamed and clung to the men, trying to stop them, and it was Ethel who helped her and soothed her until the screams died away.

'We were so afraid she would lose Vincent,' Rosie sobbed. 'We didn't once imagine it would be Kate who left us.'

After Kate's body had been taken to her stricken parents for burial, Ethel and Rosie were given permission to attend the funeral.

The funeral was a large one as Kate's parents were business people and well known in the town. Ethel and Rosie stood beside other friends of Kate and representatives of the Navy, Army and Air Force. Others too, those serving the war effort in munition factories and on the land, or in the manufacture of the hundreds of items needed by men and women in every branch of the services. Vincent stood beside Mr and Mrs Banner, sharing their grief, helping them with his love and strength.

There were many there who had lost members of their own families, and others who had been bombed out of their homes, but today their thoughts were for the newly bereaved parents of Kate Banner and their quiet sympathy was touching. Crying could be heard, muffled by handkerchiefs, and the flowing of tears was part of the healing that would surely come one day.

They were both staying with Rosie's Nan and she went to church with them to listen to the vicar trying to explain why and how a caring God could allow such a cruel thing to happen. As they left the church, leaving the men to go with the cortege to the burial, they saw that Rosie's mother had come too.

It was all so unreal, unbelievable. Ethel and Rosie stared at each other at times as though begging for the joke to end and for Kate, their lovely, happy friend, to walk in and laugh and hug them. They watched Vincent sitting with Kate's parents and wondered how he was coping, after seeing so much death and now sitting beside the coffin of his darling Kate – the one death he did not expect.

'When we get back, how d'you feel about applying for overseas again?' Ethel asked as they walked away from the grieving house. 'I don't think I can cope with staying on and expecting Kate to be there.'

'The news is good. If we're to go we might as well go now before we miss all the excitement. Wouldn't it be wonderful to be in Germany when the war ends?'

The Allied advance was steadily progressing towards Germany, the Naafi was present, serving the armies as they freed village after village, town after town. Bulk stores had been set up along the route, leapfrogging ahead beyond the front line. Rest centres were set up for the men to move back and relax for a while and recover before going once again in to the fighting. These were sometimes a hall, a large house, or a café, and sometimes a hotel that had been commandeered and made comfortable for the army's use. At times the situation was very confused, the front line moving sometimes within hours, and the men and women were determined that the comforts and necessities should always be there when needed.

'We'll go,' Ethel said. 'But first we'll go and sort out your Nan and your mother. We don't have to be back for two more days.'

Rosie had previously written to her Nan, telling her to invite her mother to call. With the funeral taking all of her thoughts she hadn't mentioned this, but seeing her mother in church that day had given her hope.

To her relief, Nan had offered no argument. She too had been upset by the death of Kate and perhaps it was that which made her decide to start putting things right between her daughter-in-law and Rosie.

Having saved her meagre bacon ration for a few weeks and receiving it in a small and rather fat joint, she cooked mashed potatoes and a hard cabbage that she called 'cannon-ball cabbage', usually grown to feed animals. Served with a cheese sauce, the result was an insipid plateful. 'No one can afford to be fussy any more,' she said as an apology. 'Edible means practically the same as eatable these days.'

There were many meatless meals served in every household and they ate the meal appreciatively, aware of her generosity with her precious ration. So many meals consisted only of vegetables and gravy, that many declared that throughout those years of shortages, it was Bisto and Oxo which fed the nation.

When the three members of the Dreen family sat down to talk, Ethel excused herself and went to the pictures. On her return, the atmosphere was relaxed and she thought that, against all the odds, Rosie had found a mother she could care for and maybe, one day, would learn to love. Lucky Rosie, she thought with a sigh.

There would never be a loving reunion for her. How could she ever return to her family and be greeted with such affection? How could she forgive her father for the years of misery? Or her mother for allowing the dangerous situation to continue when she should have taken them away? She might visit but would never again call The Dell her home.

Perhaps the kind of loyalty which made my mother stay is something special, she thought with a stab of guilt, something of which I am not capable. But from the viewpoint of the child that was me, it was not loyalty but cowardice. That oft-repeated blame placed at her mother's feet had been comforting, a reason for her to perpetuate her refusal to consider her mother's side, blame for her mother was a garment that sat too comfortably upon her, and it was now beginning to worry her. Growing doubts about the easy excuse for her resentment and hatred were keeping her awake.

On their return to camp, heavy-eyed with crying, Baba was there to greet them.

Rosie smiled at him, hoping her face didn't show either her pleasure or her regrets. She politely welcomed him back then left Ethel and him to talk. Once out of sight of the guard room, Baba opened his arms to Ethel and they hugged. Their joyful reunion made Ethel think again about love and sex and she knew that her feelings for Baba were more than a need to belong. She did belong. To him.

'I have a father now, if I want him,' she explained to Baba later. 'And Mr and Mrs Bailey are my grandparents. And their daughter is my aunt. What d'you think of that?' She was laughing with happiness and

crying for Kate at the same time and Baba
held her and soothed her when tears overcame her, understanding how she grieved.

'I hope you'll still have room in your full
life for my three sisters,' Baba laughed.
'They'll want a share of you too, mind.'

'And I have a brother who's my uncle and
a mother who's my grandmother and besides all that, I know I have an extended
family in Rosie and Rosie's Nan, plus her
mother, who will always be there when I
need them. Oh Baba, I miss Kate dreadfully,
and I always will, but another part of me has
never been happier. Is that thoughtless and
hard, d'you think? To be so happy at such a
time?'

'Can you imagine Kate begrudging you a
moment of it?' Baba asked and Ethel cried
some more.

Loneliness need never be a fear, ever again.
Her feelings for Baba were nothing to do
with loneliness or an artificial pretence of
belonging. Whatever happened to them, she
wanted to be with him. 'Perhaps this really
is love,' she whispered to a photograph of
Kate. 'You'd understand what I mean,
wouldn't you? You who loved everyone so
much that you made people happier just by
meeting you.'

Twelve

Baba and Ethel returned to a loving closeness that soothed some of her distress at the death of Kate and the confusion of her feelings toward her family. In his arms she could forget everything except his need of her and her willing response. He never brought up the subject of her family, but was always willing to listen when she felt the need to talk. His comments were few, he was non-judgemental about Dai and Molly, but his support of her unwillingness to return home in the full sense, and become a part of her family once more, was balm.

She dreamed of a future far away from The Dell and all its tragedies, with Baba and, one day, their children. She would have his sisters and parents and the many cousins and aunts and uncles he had told her about who would become her family, and life would be perfect.

Rosie's attitude was different. She was grateful for the growing respect and understanding between Nan and her mother and deliriously happy to have her mother back in her life. She wanted that same happiness for Ethel. Ethel wouldn't be complete until she accepted her family for what they were. To accept them she would first have to understand.

'And you'll never understand until you go back home, stay for a while and talk about it all, including the death of Glenys,' she told her friend often, but Ethel refused to give up on hating her father and despising her mother. Even the image of Dai sitting alone, uncared for, in that silent cell of a room failed to move her sufficiently to make her relent her decision. She tried not to think of Wesley at all.

Wesley, having lost contact with his ship, had attached himself to the canteen service close to the front line in France. Messages had been sent to inform the authorities of his present whereabouts but no word had yet come through to tell him where to report. He worked alongside the other canteen personnel but made no friends. He volunteered for anything others didn't want to do and had become a bit of a joke. 'Wesley'll do it,' became a sort of catch-phrase. If he was aware of this he did not react.

Apart from the goods which came from the Bulk Issue Stores, Naafi staff were adept at finding additions to their supplies. Orchards long abandoned and forgotten lofts in barns

371

were raided for fresh fruit. Gardens no longer tended by the owners, who had died or fled, were useful for the fresh vegetables they occasionally still held. There were even a few chickens roaming around and these were a popular addition to the rather boring contents of a stewpot. Having been brought up in the country, Wesley was talented in hunting skills and on occasions took a gun and returned with something edible, his shots causing concern to sentries of both sides.

He was reasonably content. He concentrated on each day, each task, to the exclusion of everything else. His thoughts rarely wandered homewards. Home meant shame, guilt and the loss of Ethel's love.

Sid wrote to Ethel regularly now contact had been made and he was unhappy about her decision to apply for overseas again. 'What if it isn't France?' he asked, 'although that would be bad enough. What if they send you to the Far East? Japan is still fighting and will be after Germany's defeat. Think about it, please, Ethel,' he ended. As a postscript, her mother had added her pleas for her not to go.

'That does it, I'm going to see about it right away,' she said, showing the letter to Rosie.

'I'll come too. I just hope we'll stay

together. Although it's unlikely we'll be lucky once again.'

They were told that they would be going to France and, as they knew their destination and date of travel, they knew also that there would be no further leave and they would be confined to camp.

Baba was told and he was shocked to think that Ethel had chosen to leave him.

'I thought after just finding each other again you'd never leave me,' he said, and there was unaccustomed anger in his eyes. 'I feel you've let me down, Ethel.'

'I'm sorry, Baba, but I thought you'd understand.'

'Understand? Or accept that you always want to please yourself without discussion?'

'It isn't like that. Losing Kate like that, it was so unbelievable. Rosie and I were worried that she would have to face life without Vincent and then it was she who was killed. I have to continue helping with the fight. I'd feel I was letting her down if I left now. There's still a job to do. You must understand how I feel?'

'I know all about the job we have to do, but, be honest, that isn't your reason. You have a letter from your mother, whom you profess to despise, she tells you not to leave and straight away you forget all about us, about me and what I want, and arrange to go. It shows me clearly how low I come on your list of priorities.'

Trying to explain her reaction to her mother failed. As she put into words her instinctive need to disobey the woman who she felt had let her down so badly, the excuse sounded utterly stupid – even to herself it made no sense.

'I was going to tell you,' she added lamely.

'Tell me. That says it all, Ethel. Not discuss it, you were going to tell me. What sort of future is there for us if this is what you call sharing?'

She pleaded, apologized and coaxed and they finally made love and settled for a kind of peace, but as she went back to her billet Ethel knew she had damaged their relationship severely. The worst thing was there was no time to spend putting it right.

She was shocked by his reaction and wished she could change her mind, but there was no possibility of that. She explained to Rosie about his disappointment at her leaving but not the extent of his anger and hurt. 'I have to go and I don't think I'd cancel even if I could,' she admitted. 'I want to finish what we started. Doesn't he know there's a war on?' she asked with a wan smile.

Sid received Ethel's letter telling them of her decision to go. She was unable at that point to tell them where she was being posted. He guessed that she was going abroad to avoid coming home. He knew where Rosie's nan lived and went there to see whether she had more news, but both families were unable to do more than hope that the girls would be safe. He bought his ration of sweets and took them back to Mrs Dreen to add to her next parcel.

Without reverting to their previous closeness, Ethel said goodbye to Baba and she and Rosie left a week later with a group of twenty girls and boarded a ship bound for France.

Having seen the devastation of their own cities and towns, and expecting to see something similar, the sight of the French countryside was a heart-rending shock. Besides being bombed, the ground had been fought over more than once and for day after dreadful day. The result was large areas that were flattened and completely devoid of buildings or habitation, except in a few places where they saw people living in the cellars of what had once been their homes. Rubble had been pressed into the ground. The earth had been churned up by tanks and hundreds of other vehicles, gunfire had battered the few walls that were still standing and it seemed impossible as they travelled across northern France to imagine that it could ever be returned to a place where people would choose to live.

The situation was confusing, as the front

line varied from day to day. The soft-topped Naafi vans went around the troops handing out tea and a wad, makeshift kitchens managing to churn out the usual fare. Ethel and Rosie were told to help in a canteen that had been set up as a rest centre for men back from the front to relax and unwind from the horrors of the fighting. It was fully equipped with a bar selling teas and coffee and snacks as well as a bar selling beer and cigarettes.

The premises had been a hotel, but the once-elegant walls had been ravaged by gunfire, the contents ransacked by the armies who had passed through and used its protection for temporary relief. Chairs had been found from somewhere, an odd collection of rugs was spread on the wooden floors. There were heavy curtains at the windows, and even some billowing nets, found in a chest in the cellar, wrapped in tissue waiting for the summer that hadn't come.

They weren't there long. Following the progress of the Allied forces, they were sent to open a canteen in a town close by, with a few Naafi staff and some local women and men to help with the heavy work. They were given bicycles for transport to and from the rooms they had in the hotel.

While the others moved rubble and cleaned outhouses ready for the stores to arrive, Ethel and Rosie spent the first two days scrubbing the kitchen and painting its walls.

They were warned that china was scarce and, searching for more cups and plates, asking in the almost empty shops without success, they eventually found a supply of jam jars – something they had resorted to once or twice before – and deciding to use these, they washed them and stacked them ready to satisfy the needs of the large number of troops who would soon pile in looking for a bit of home. They knew the unusual receptacles would cause much needed laughter.

This canteen was on two floors, the first was the snacks and tea bar, above, the drinks bar. The top, where the roof leaked into buckets and bowls and baths, was left to the mice who had been treating the place like their own grand hotel. There was also a cellar which promised useful storage, and with a couple of torches Ethel and Rosie went to explore.

It had once been used as a wine cellar but there were no bottles now apart from a few empty ones. Boxes and baskets and a few broken chairs were all it contained, and when a creature which they guessed was a rat ran across their path, they swore they would never venture there again.

They told some of the local girls about the unwelcome lodgers. In monosyllabic English, which they incorrectly thought might be better understood, they asked the girls not to report the rats. In the insanity of the killings all around them, destroying the rats was something they couldn't cope with.

The following day they were told they had been dealt with. Fortunately, the ratcatcher had come on their day off and they saw nothing of what went on. Rats were also seen by others and, aware of the dangers of infection through contaminated food, the staff knew that something more had to be done.

One day a chicken came in and at once Rosie stood guard over it and dared anyone to kill it. Named Veronica, which Rosie insisted was what it said, it became a mascot and survived the war.

Rosie had never mastered the art of driving but Ethel felt confident to drive practically anything. 'As long as it starts when I turn the handle, I'll be fine,' she told anyone who asked. 'What goes on under the bonnet I know nothing about and I'm happy for that to remain a mystery.' So when the man who normally drove the van around to the men nearer to the front line was ill, she volunteered to take his place, as long as Rosie could go with her.

They did this for several days, but the fighting became confused as areas were taken, lost and retaken, with pockets of resistance holding up one group while others advanced. Sometimes when they reached the place where they had been told to set up, there was no one there. They would stop, open the flap which was their counter and wait, but when no one came they would drive on until the men saw them and approached. They would stay and serve for as long as they were wanted, then return to base, fill up and prepare to go out again.

They rarely went out at night – the men refused to allow it insisting that they, battle-hardened soldiers, were better able to cope should they meet the enemy. Ethel and Rosie had both learned to shoot during their initial training in Scotland, but Rosie was thankful not to have to carry a weapon with instructions to use it. She didn't think she could ever pull a trigger and watch those blooms of red roses appear on the jacket of a human being. Ethel insisted she could and would, but whether she would act swiftly enough, or gather the courage to do so, was something she secretly doubted.

The news was coming through of further attacks on London and other cities. This time with another flying bomb, Hitler's V2 Rocket which carried a ton of explosives and fell to earth at a phenomenal speed. Now there was the worry of not being near home while their families faced this new terror.

'There's nothing I could do even if I was stationed in the same town,' Rosie said, 'but knowing Nan's there on her own makes me afraid for her. There's no logic in that but it's how I feel.'

'Perhaps she isn't alone. Maybe your mother is with her.'

'That's a nice thought. I'll tell myself they're together, shall I?' She looked at Ethel and added, 'Like your family, all close together.' Ethel didn't reply.

The rats continued to be troublesome and some squaddies were instructed to blow up an unused drainage system, which succeeded in removing the rats but unfortunately made the water undrinkable. Until the engineers could put things right, the staff had to carry water from a nearby house in galvanized baths and buckets and any other container they could find, for everything they needed.

As the battles, the intermittent resistance and the inexorable push towards Germany continued, the two girls faced the day-to-day wearisome routine with fortitude. When they were tired, thoughts of Kate urged them to greater effort, each in her own way using the memory of their friend to help them through. Rosie still dreamed of Baba and Ethel's thoughts were with him too, worried by the argument they'd had before she left and had failed to settle. With preparations for their posting, there had been no time to spend talking through their disagreement, reaffirm their love. They had parted after a final meeting and had passionately made love but without returning to their previous certainty that all was well.

Letters got through but there were none for either of the girls, and they were usually too tired to consider the disappointment or think about writing. Finding clean water and heating it to make hot drinks, cook food, wash dishes, and cleaning places to keep their stores safe from infestation took most of the time when they weren't serving in the canteen or on the road with the van.

When they set out with the heavily loaded van, they were given clear instructions on where to go and were kept well clear of the front line. They were warned to stay well back from the gunfire. 'You'll be no use to anyone if you get in the way,' came the chill warning. 'Remember, both sides have guns that can kill, there's no priority when a shell lands, no matter which side fired it. If you're in the wrong place, you're dead!'

One morning in October 1944, they set off as usual. It had been raining most of the previous day and through the night. Mud covered the ground and formed a slippery carpet on the roads and they wondered whether their rather smooth tyres would cope. As they drove, the sounds of dull thuds were heard, warning them that they were in a war zone, as if they needed reminding; the devastation could be clearly seen all around them. Their route had been changed due to bombing and now led them through what had once been orchards and the remains of a village. Swerving past destroyed buildings, around huge craters and across once peaceful meadows was saddening. The rain continued, reducing visibility, but following the written instructions and knowing that the point for which they were heading was not far away, they were confident, until they found that the route they should have taken was blocked.

Explosions had destroyed a bridge over a small river that had worn its way down into the earth and now flowed several feet below ground level. They stopped and studied their instructions but soon gave up trying to work out a way through from what little information they had. They turned away to find another way through. Within a short time they were lost.

They drove on, following tracks which they hoped would take them to a place from where they could be redirected. Then a heavy bombardment began and the shells were coming from behind them. They had overtaken the front line and were almost certainly in enemy-held territory.

With a swear from Ethel, they stopped and considered what to do. Rosie gave an excited squeal. 'Ethel, we might be in Berlin before the army!'

'We can't stay here, but I don't think I can

turn,' Ethel frowned, looking back at the uneven surface and the narrow track. The track was pitted with water-filled holes that Ethel had managed to avoid driving forward but would surely hit if she tried to reverse.

'There's a farm just ahead.' Rosie pointed to the right where a huddle of ruined buildings stood, with a track that seemed fairly sound leading towards the main house. Ethel hesitated, wondering whether she could manage to reverse to a place where the van could be turned around. Then she saw that parked beside one of the buildings was an army lorry. A British army lorry. There was no sign of a driver and, as she brought the vehicle to a stop, no soldiers appeared to demand they identify themselves.

The rain was unceasing, drumming on to the mud, and the sound of gunfire and explosions were muted to a dull distant rumbling. Restarting the engine, she took the corner carefully and headed for the main buildings. The track was narrower than the one they had left, and she was watching the road and trying to keep an eye on the buildings, half expecting to see the nose of a rifle appear at the corner of one of the walls.

'What's German for do you want tea and a wad?' she whispered nervously. When she saw a water-filled crater ahead she was unable to avoid it and the van lurched and stopped with one back wheel in the depression.

They got out and tried to place stones under the tyres to give purchase, but apart from getting covered in mud and soaking wet, they achieved nothing. They stood there, the rain a pattering, monotonous murmur. They were so wet and miserable it was tempting to climb aboard the van and sit there until someone arrived, friend or foe, at that moment they didn't really care.

'I'll go and see if there's anyone about,' Ethel said. Rosie tried to dissuade her.

'Perhaps we could walk back the way we came and see if we can get back to base.'

'I think we'll be wiser to stay with the van. At least it's shelter.'

'And food,' Rosie said with an attempt at a grin.

'I'll just walk to the corner of the building by that lorry and look around,' Ethel said, trying to sound casual.

'What if it's a trap, or a mine field?' Rosie pleaded. 'Stay here, we ought to stay together.'

Ethel told her to wait and, promising not to go further than the corner, she squelched her way around to the side of the van. She was no hero, she was plain terrified. The alternative, to sit and wait until someone found them was worse. Still she hesitated. She looked at the farm buildings that seemed threatening in the dull light of the gloomy day. They could hide Germans or British soldiers. Or she could find lifeless bodies of either, or both.

Thankfully the rain had finally stopped. Taking a couple of cakes and leaving Rosie to open up in case there were troops in the vicinity needing their services, a vain hope intending to cheer her friend, Ethel walked nervously towards the lorry along the narrow track.

It was empty. A copy of the tuppenny magazine *Everybody's*, was on the seat, an empty Woodbine packet beside it. Taking a deep breath to calm her racing heart, she went cautiously around the corner. It wasn't until she had walked to the furthest side of the farm that she saw another lorry, this time with two men in the cab.

The gunfire was continuing, sounding close at times then fading. The men hadn't heard the van approach. There were no guards set and she walked closer. The men were talking and to her relief the voices were British. A Geordie lad and a Welshman, discussing their recent darts tournament. The man on the passenger side had a cigarette between his fingers and he flicked away the end of it and held out his hand, waving it about, gesturing to make some point, and Ethel slapped a cake into his palm.

The man yelled and ducked down, mutter-

385

ing a long list of swears.

'Char and a wad?' she asked cheerfully. The cake fell to the ground as the man jerked and shouted again in shock.

'Tut tut, what a waste,' Ethel complained, looking down at the cake. 'Don't you know there's a war on?'

'Where the bloody 'ell did you spring from?'

'His language was what you might call flowery,' she told Rosie a few minutes later as they finished preparing the counter ready to serve, 'and not something I'd like to repeat into your innocent ears.'

The guns still sounded, but spasmodically and some distance away. Rosie and Ethel set up the counter having been told that the rest of the men who had become separated from their group had gone on a 'reccy' and would be back soon. The others came back about twenty minutes later having been back to find their lines and receive orders on how they should proceed. The officers had been killed and only sixteen men remained of the forty who had set out. The two men in the lorry had been left behind to observe and wait.

'Some observation!' Ethel teased.

'All right, I won't tell anyone how you got the van stuck in a crater that could be seen half a mile away, if you don't tell Winston Churchill I'm a slacker. Right?' the Welshman laughed.

As the clouds lifted and drifted away, the bombardment started up again in the distance and the air was filled with the screaming of shells and explosions and in some places fires started and added to the terrifying display. Sights, sounds and the choking smell of the fierce battles continuing around them filled their heads with fear and imaginings, and both Rosie and Ethel wondered whether they would ever be free of the nightmares that already disturbed their sleep.

For a while shells fell closer, screaming and seeming to be heading straight for them and the puny soft-top van. They left the van and hurried for the only slightly less doubtful protection of the farm buildings. They saw shrapnel hit the van and the sides were peppered with small holes but fortunately the damage was well away from the petrol tank and it survived in a road-worthy state.

An hour later, when the guns ahead of them had fallen silent, a large contingent of men came to push further on. The girls disposed of all their stock between the grateful men, the khaki-clad figures laughing and joking as though their situation was nothing to be concerned about, just a bit of a game, the pretence for a few brief moments bringing a touch of sanity into their lives. Ethel promised, somewhat foolishly, that the van would be back later that day.

They were both shaking with the shock of what they had done as they stood and watched the men freeing, then turning, the van, while others described the route back to their base. Ethel started the engine and headed back wondering how the men could stand the tensions of the fighting day after day, without going crazy. She wished they could all follow them and take advantage of the rest centres, but knew that the war was not over yet. Not by a long way.

Back at base, with the van showing honourable evidence of their closeness to danger, they stepped out to be greeted by several figures coming forward to check on their safety. The first person Ethel saw was Wesley Daniels.

He started when he recognized the dirt-streaked face with the hat at its usual rakish angle and said her name in a whisper. His arms raised up as though to embrace her and hers too jerked a little as though to do the same, but something stopped him and he stepped back to allow her to enter the canteen.

Ethel was shocked both by the suddenness of his appearance and how much he had changed. She looked away after her first glance, convinced it was not Wesley, only someone with a passing likeness. Then another look and another, until she saw in the sad eyes the man she had once known.

Wesley had never been anything but slim but the flesh seemed to have fallen from him. His features had sharpened and age had come upon him, there was deep sadness in his eyes and he looked away from her steady gaze as though afraid to face her.

'Wesley?' she murmured hesitantly and he turned his gaze towards her, half smiled then looked away again. There was no sense of a happy reunion, no joyous relief at Wesley's survival. It was as though he were someone from a former fantasy life, a stranger who had no part in the present reality. She wondered if they would have anything to say to each other after the years of absence.

A voice that insisted on being obeyed called them and they began to move towards its irritable insistence. Ethel pointed to Wesley and to Rosie and after brief and oddly strained introductions, the two girls went straight away to report their adventures and receive the reprimand that they knew they didn't really deserve.

Ethel was shaking and Rosie knew that it was not because of their recent perilous journey, but the sight of a ghost from her past. She held her friend's hand to reassure her and they went to stand in front of the man who had summoned them.

Their explanation about the bridge being down and their attempts to find another route were listened to but discarded. There was no other reason but stupidity for them wandering on to the front line. They listened wearily as they were reminded that they were a liability. 'Men would have had to help you instead of thinking about what they were doing or their own safety. Your stupidity could have cost lives. What would you have done if the men on that farm had been Germans?'

'Offered them char and a wad?' Rosie whispered.

'I'll pretend I didn't hear that!'

Ethel quickly handed her friend a handkerchief to hide her giggles, hoping the officer would presume them to be sobs.

Wesley was waiting for Ethel when she had showered and finished making an official report.

'Ethel, how are you?' he asked. 'Everyone here has been talking about the missing Naafi van. I can't tell you my surprise that the driver was you.'

'Well, here I am, safe and sound. I thought you were with the NCS serving on ships?'

She was still strangely ill at ease with this man whom she had once loved and who had vanished from her life so suddenly. They went to the canteen and after insisting that Rosie stayed they slowly caught up with their last four years; but there was to be no great loving reunion. He was unable to tell her how ashamed he felt about leaving her to her father's anger and she waited, expecting not an apology for his cowardice but an explanation of the hasty departure that had led to more than four years of silence, when her whereabouts had been unknown to him. They sat far apart, like strangers. The conversation faltered and stumbled, both wanting to say how they felt but unable to do so. Rosie tried to wriggle her hand out of Ethel's and escape but Ethel looked at her and with her eyes pleaded with her to stay.

Mostly in silence, and through a few inadequate sentences, Ethel was looking at him. He had aged so much, and was so thin and subdued and without a spark of joy. Her mind drifted and she thought of Baba and how exciting their reunions had always been. She tried not to dwell on their last meeting, and Baba's disappointment and anger when, at her own instigation, they had parted once more.

Unable to bear the stilted conversation any longer she made an excuse and left him. As soon as she reached her bed she lay on it and wrote to Baba, telling him how much she loved him and was longing to see him again. If she had had any doubts or guilt reguarding Wesley, a few minutes of his company had dispelled them.

She knew Rosie was keeping out of her way, meeting other girls during her time off, sensing Ethel's need to talk to Wesley, and she was grateful for her friend's understanding. Although he had no part in her life any more she felt some obligation to meet him and talk to him but it was far from easy and each time they met she would return to her room with relief and write a loving letter to Baba.

There weren't many places for them to go but with Rosie's help she smuggled Wesley into their room one cold, wet afternoon and tried to break down the invisible barriers and talk. The words wouldn't come and they sat at separate ends of the room, speaking in bursts of conversation that quickly died, unable to break down the floodgates and return to their previous ease.

She saw Wesley drive off two days later and was left with a strong feeling of disappointment. When she told Rosie, her friend again insisted it was because of the rift in the family.

'You can't rebuild the bits you want and discard the rest. Go home, move in and get back to how things used to be, just for a while. Your father has mellowed and accepts his mistakes. Your mam wants you to be her daughter again. And there's Sid who loves you like the sister you will always be. Get that lot sorted and your feelings for Wesley will slot into place.'

In her heart, Rosie had hoped that after rediscovering her childhood sweetheart,

Ethel might have revived her love for him and forgotten Baba. She wrote to Baba, just a friendly letter, in case there was the slightest hope he might turn to her if Ethel finally rejected him.

'Are you homesick? Do you wish we could go home?' Rosie asked Ethel a few weeks after their alarming experience, when they were decorating the canteen with a bit of Christmas cheer.

'I want to see it all again. The lights were switched back on in November. That must have been a great moment. No more falling over each other in the blackout.'

'And the Home Guard, Dad's Army, is no more.'

'There's still food rationing though and it might last for a long time yet.'

They stayed in France, following the advancing troops and, later, working for a time in a rest centre in Paris, a beautiful place where men and women could spend their leave before returning to their units. There were dances held and Rosie was more confident after the years away from home and all her experiences, and was a frequently sought partner.

News of the surrender came rather casually via a man who walked past them as they were setting up the bar, announcing, 'It's over. Hitler's lot have been beaten.'

'What did he say?' Rosie frowned.

'I thought he said it's over. D'you think he means the war?'

Then a group of squaddies ran in, kissed them, pulled them on to the floor and began dancing.

'What's happened?' Ethel asked, afraid to presume the words they'd heard was true.

'It's only over! It's bloody well over! Unconditional surrender, that's what's happened.'

'Mother, put the kettle on, your boy's comin' 'ome,' shouted another. Others ran in shouting, back-slapping, singing. The place filled until there seemed no room to fit in another body. Officers came and shouted orders which went unheard.

'Where are they all coming from?' gasped Rosie as she and Ethel tried to serve the excited men. 'I think the whole of the front line is in here.'

Ethel shouted, 'Oi, you lot! You'd better be careful. With all the allied forces in our canteen, who's back there watching Hitler's lot?'

The celebration went on all night, then everything calmed down and the men went back to duties with the happy feeling that they would soon be counting the days before they returned to Blighty.

The war in Europe had ended but there was still the fighting in the Far East. The celebrations of victory in Europe were muted by the fact that there were still men and women on the front lines a very long way from home. Although everyone believed that the end was truly in sight.

In July 1945 Ethel and Rosie were given home leave.

'We've missed most of the celebrations,' Rosie said excitedly. 'The street parties, and the crowds gathering in London. But I dare say we'll have a few of our own.'

The first thing Rosie did was to go to Nan's house where, to her surprise and delight, she found her mother and her Nan living together, taking in boarders and earning a reasonable living. She went back to the farm where she had worked and looked around, praising the land girls who had done a remarkable job keeping everything going throughout the war years.

'Want your job back do you, Rosie?' the farmer asked, but she shook her head.

'The Naafi hasn't finished with me yet and when the war's finally over, I don't know what I'll do. Stay on maybe. While there's an army there'll be need for a Naafi.'

Ethel tried to find Baba but he was away and couldn't be contacted. So she went to Wesley's house. Wesley was there and they talked for a while, then he offered to go with her to see her father. He had his own demons to put to rest. Walking over the footbridge and up the front path still brought fear to her heart and she reached for Wesley's hand, smiling reassurance at him, hiding her own terrors.

The house was neater and better furnished than on her previous visits. The windows shone and the house was pervaded with a smell of polish and a sense of comfortable wealth. There were two girls working on the land, which had been extended into two extra fields. A large greenhouse had been built along a wall and there were areas where soft fruits were grown inside protective netting. Things had certainly improved. As she went upstairs to visit her father, still holding tightly to Wesley's hand, she expected to see similar changes there.

Her father looked the same, no extra comforts in the bare little room and still a cup of cold tea standing just out of reach on the bedside table. She guessed it would not be until Sid came home from work that he had any attention. She fed him with some chocolate she had brought, which he seemed to enjoy, then offered him the cold drink. He watched her as he drank and she saw the pain in those round blue eyes which had once frightened her so much, and wanted to weep.

They didn't stay long: 'No longer than a man collecting weekly insurance payments,' she joked to Wesley. She joked a lot as they went back to his house and later on the way to the bus to start her journey back to her hotel. She felt such shame for the way her father was being treated but couldn't stay long enough to do anything about it. It wasn't until Wesley promised to talk to Sid and get something done that she was able to cry.

Thirteen

An official letter reached Ethel via Rosie's Nan, telling her she was not to return to France but report to a camp in Bedfordshire which was closing down. She was bitterly disappointed that she and Rosie wouldn't end the war together but a few days later she learned that Rosie's letter had given the same news. They were going on what might be their last posting, against all the odds, still together.

Another letter arrived for Ethel, this time from Baba, and he named a time and place for them to meet. Rosie squealed in delight at Ethel's good news and no one guessed the heartbreak she felt. If only Baba had fallen for me, she whispered into her pillow at night, daring to imagine how perfect life would have been. When Wesley had re-appeared in Ethel's life so unexpectedly, she had prayed for their abandoned love to be revived but it was not to be. Baba was the one promising Ethel a happy future and she, Rosie, was promised nothing but emptiness. She silently reprimanded herself for wishing her friend anything but joy and forced her expression into one of delight.

'Don't forget that when you and Baba marry, I'm to be chief bridesmaid,' she reminded Ethel.

Ethel smiled but said nothing. That Baba loved her she didn't doubt and her love for him was a certainty but it was not wise to be too confident, that was tempting the fates to torment and play games with you.

Ethel was still upset about Dai, the man she continued to think of as her father, when she went to see Baba. They met for an hour only between his visits to a suppliers to order and later to collect paint and turps and sundry other requirements. They found a café where they were offered a sandwich of bloater paste with a leaf of lettuce, which neither was able to eat.

'I saw Wesley,' she told him.

'Any reason for me to be jealous?' he teased.

She went on to explain the circumstances that had led to their first unlikely meeting in

France and the recent occasion when he had gone with her to visit her father. Baba was upset when he learned of the danger she had faced. 'Darling girl, I've been such a fool. I quarrelled with you as you were leaving, and tried to stop you doing your duty. I let you face danger without the peace of mind that would have helped you to cope. My last words to you should have been words of love and reassurance, not petty anger at not having my own way. I'm sorry.'

'Meet me tonight and show me how sorry,' she said as his lips met hers in a long-awaited kiss.

For Ethel, that leave was spent either with Baba or in waiting for him, hoping he could wangle a few hours off to spend with her. She had savings, having spent very little of her money while in the service, and she found a small place to stay where Baba could join her whenever he was free. She went to see Rosie's Nan and stayed for two nights but refused all Rosie's entreaties to return to see Wesley or her family again. She was still in touch with Sid, but she refused to write to her mother directly and tried not to think about her father in his cold, lonely room.

'Baba is my family and I don't need anyone else,' she told Rosie, unaware of how much this still hurt her friend.

There was one thing stopping Ethel from

being truly happy. Although Baba had often talked about his sisters, he had never issued a firm invitation for Ethel to go home with him and meet them. Unlike poor Kate, whose American prospective in-laws had welcomed her lovingly, with long letters and many photographs, she had never had any contact with Baba's family. So when he announced that he was going home for the weekend, she suggested going with him.

'Not yet, lovely girl,' he replied. 'There's a few things that need sorting before I take you to meet my family.'

'What things? We don't have secrets, do we?'

'Not between you and me, love, no. But these are other people's secrets, personal things, not my story to tell. But once everything's sorted, then I'll take you and introduce you to all the Morgan family and the neighbours and friends and we'll have a fabulous celebration.'

Ethel smiled and swallowed her doubts. How secrets belonging to other people could affect her being introduced to his family she couldn't imagine, but if she loved Baba then she had to trust him. He would explain one day, there couldn't be anything in the world he couldn't tell her.

Her leave ended and she called to see Rosie to discuss their travel arrangements. Unintentionally she told her friend about

Baba's apparent reluctance to invite her to meet the Morgan family and Rosie hastily reassured her.

'Perhaps his home isn't as grand as he would like, people can be very silly about such things. Or maybe he has a few girl-friends around who might tell you things he'd rather you didn't know! Or perhaps he still sleeps with a teddy bear or has Mickey Mouse pictures on his bedroom wall, or keeps spiders as pets, or sucks his thumb when he sleeps or—'

'All right, I'm convinced!' Ethel laughed at her friend's ridiculous suggestions. 'I'll give him time to say goodbye to childhood and ex-girlfriends.'

They reported to their new posting and found that their job consisted mostly of packing unwanted stores for return to the Bulk Issue Stores for redirecting. There was still a canteen, and cooking meals and snacks, and making tea and coffee for the men who were dismantling the prefabricated buildings took a lot of their time.

There were also lists. Dozens of lists stating the number and description of what went into each packing case. The noise of the work of demolition was deafening at times, and as a contrast there was the peaceful scene of sheep once more allowed to graze in the fields, where tents had blossomed like mushrooms and vehicles had rent the silence with their roaring engines.

Sometimes they thought they heard the sound of laughter and distant singing, the ghosts of all those young men and women who hadn't returned, still there but fading with every blow of the hammers.

Baba came and was instructed to sort out the transport, repairing to sell where possible, the rest to be discarded and sold as scrap. To the girls' surprise Walter turned up, having been given the unpleasant job of knocking down the brick buildings as the site was cleared.

He had put on weight and his face was puffy with excess drinking. Rosie saw him first and came running to tell Ethel: 'His face looks like a jelly taken too soon out of its mould.'

They shared memories and he explained that although he could leave the Naafi at any time, he had nowhere to go. His family were no longer where he had left them, having moved away with the evacuees and not returned. 'I didn't bother to keep in touch,' he admitted sadly. 'I was away from home and I wanted to shrug off my boring past and start again. But now I'm left with nowhere to go.'

Rosie felt sympathy for him. 'Find them,' she told him. 'It can't be that difficult. Talk to someone and get things started. The Citizens' Advice Bureau and the Salvation Army are experts at putting people in touch.'

'You won't be the only one looking for your family,' Ethel added. 'And they are probably searching for you. I'm sure they'll welcome you back with relief.'

'And you'll be a war hero, Walter, think of that!' Rosie said. 'Poor man,' she sighed as Walter ambled slowly back to the office to do what she had suggested. 'I hope he finds them.'

'So do I.' Being so utterly happy herself, Ethel found it easy to wish the same for others.

Baba was full of loving talk and plans for their future whenever they met. Their lovemaking was as exciting as before they had parted so miserably when Ethel had left for France. There seemed to be no problems, they behaved naturally with each other without the slightest inhibition. Ethel knew that one day soon he would make their position official by proposing to her. Then he went home for a week, and again Ethel was not invited.

She turned to Rosie for reassurance and pretended to find comfort in the kindly meant lies and fanciful excuses. 'I don't understand it. Why is he so unwilling for me to meet his family? We're as close as two people can be and he knows I'm longing to meet them, to be accepted, yet he makes excuses and vague promises about next time. But next time, like tomorrow, never comes. He must be either ashamed of me or ashamed of them.'

'That's rubbish, Ethel. He can't be ashamed of you. He hasn't kept you a secret here. Everyone knows you and he are ... well ... seeing each other.'

'Then he must have some guilt about his relations. They might be criminals. Or so poor he can't cope with my seeing just how they have to live.'

'On a more cheerful note, perhaps he's planning a big surprise for you,' Rosie suggested. 'You know how full of fun he is. I bet he's making plans for a huge party to welcome you, getting everyone making cakes and raiding their store cupboards. Getting out all the decorations. Now this minute they'll be beavering away getting everything perfect for when you arrive. Imagine it, Ethel, just imagine the big welcome you'll get.'

For a while Ethel believed her.

When Baba returned after his week's leave he looked serious. Ethel had never seen him so serious. His was a face meant for smiling and to see the frowns creasing his brow didn't augur well for his explanation. She wondered if there had been a tragedy in his family but he only shrugged when she asked what was wrong. After a couple of days she knew he was avoiding her. She and Rosie had planned to go to a dance in the nearby village on the following Saturday and, as they left the canteen on their way to the lorry that was to take them, she saw him walking into a store room. She stopped and looked at the door through which he had disappeared. It was no good, she couldn't go to the dance, it was time to find out what had gone wrong. Something had happened and she would insist on being told.

Waving the lorry to go on without her, and giving a hasty apology to Rosie, she went to the store room and called to him. The place was empty. She looked around and saw him heading for one of the partly demolished hangars, where the sound of metal being hammered into submission echoed around them.

'Baba, please tell me why you're avoiding me. What's wrong?'

'I'm getting married, Ethel.'

She stared at him, a half smile on her face, waiting for the joke to continue. Was this his hesitant way of broaching the subject of their engagement?

'I'm getting married, to the girl I left behind. There. So now you know.' He stared at her as she watched his face, waiting for the joke to be explained, the half smile still masking her fears, until it slowly changed into a look of such grief that he almost denied his words and turned them into the joke she wanted them to be. But he did not.

'The wedding is all planned, see, been planned for ages. The whole village is involved, everyone doing something towards the big day. It's that sort of place, see, everyone sharing and helping one another. Wonderful place. I just can't let them all down.'

'But you can let me down without a thought?'

He seemed not to hear her or perhaps simply refused to reply. 'The families on both sides have come together to buy us a cottage on the edge of the town. Cheap, mind, but sound and with a good garden. All this was a surprise, see, planned by them all for ages.'

'You must have led them on. Lying to them and not telling them about us.'

'No, lovely girl, it's you I've been lying to.'

'What?'

'I honestly thought you were what I wanted, but going home this time and seeing Janice so happy and everyone presuming we'll marry, and everything arranged—'

'Go!'

'But, Ethel, love, we could still see each other and—'

'Just go!'

She watched as he walked away from her into a future in which she had no part. Was this really happening? Was she going to end this war alone, and return to emptiness? After Duggie, and Baba, and even the dull Albert offering an end to her loneliness, was she to end the war more lonely than when it had begun?

Rosie hadn't joined the others on their way to the dance and she stood in the shadows watching. From the movements and the way Baba had walked, almost run away from Ethel she knew something was wrong. She called softly and walked over to her friend.

In their room she sat with Ethel and encouraged her to talk until the whole sorry mess was out in the open. When Ethel finished explaining with great bitterness how she felt, Rosie said, 'Ethel, love, go home.'

'Why? There's nothing there for me except a violent man who stopped his violent behaviour not from choice but because his body won't let him continue. How can I go? If I walk into that house it will be interpreted as forgiveness and how can I ever forgive him? If he'd made the effort and learned to control his temper I might have been at least able to talk to him, feel some sympathy, but not now, not ever.'

Rosie looked thoughtful for a while then asked, 'Are you a hero if you walk into danger without fear? Aren't you more of a hero if you're scared silly and still go? Then what about a man who has a bad temper and struggles not to lose it? Isn't he more to be admired than someone like you and me who keep our anger under control not through real effort but because we were lucky enough to have been born even-tempered?'

'Nice try, Rosie. Fine words. But Dad never tried.'

'How d'you know that? His whole life might have been a constant battle to keep his anger in check. The times he succeeded you wouldn't have known about, would you?'

Ethel's shoulders drooped and she said, 'Rosie, you're very wise.'

'Me? Wise? No, I just want everyone to get on, like each other. It can't be that difficult.'

Ethel attempted a smile. 'Pity Adolf Hitler hadn't had a daughter like you.'

'There you are! There's someone worse than your dad!'

'Will you come with me?'

Rosie shook her fair head. 'No, Ethel. I think this is one thing you have to do on your own.'

Now they were in touch again, Wesley wrote to Ethel more and more frequently. At first the letters were short, with vague reports on some of the places he had been during his war. It was a surprise to realize that on more than one occasion they had served close enough to meet although they never had until that most unlikely of meetings in France.

As he gradually opened up and told her of his thoughts, he talked about people and places they had known as children, and these made her homesick for those innocent days when problems were for other people to solve and their days had been filled with simple pleasures. Those days were gone for ever and there was no going back.

Although Ethel couldn't understand how, those letters slowly dissolved the barriers built on the day Dai had attacked Wesley and he, as that young and foolish man, had run away in shame. Much more slowly, from Wesley's letters and Rosie's words, an understanding of Dai's behaviour dawned. She would never understand or forgive his cruel treatment of her mother, or the incessant need for violence that had sent him to prison so many times; but his worries for her became just slightly more clear. For the first time she could see that, although misdirected and badly handled, his concern was based on love. He was a man who dealt with things in the only way he could: with fists and heavily clad feet rather than debate. Words would never have come easily to him. She was aware of the beginnings of pity.

Ethel and Baba continued to work on the same airfield but their excessive politeness made it clear that there would be no grand reunion. The affair had ended and sorrow weighed heavily on both of them. Rosie supported Ethel by being as casual about Baba as she could, allowing Ethel to talk out her disappointment and humiliation. Discussing Baba's betrayal helped Rosie to accept the end of her love for him as well as her friend's. When they heard that Baba had moved on to another disused airfield Ethel only shrugged. There was nothing more to say.

The celebrations on the final end of hostilities when Japan surrendered were an excuse for more parties, but for Ethel and Rosie the end of the war was connected with the end of much more and neither seemed able to get into the spirit of joy and relief felt by so many. It was over, no more men and women would have to die, loved ones would be coming home, all these things were a huge relief tinged with happiness, and they cheered with the rest, but for themselves there was no wonderful future beckoning.

They were going home to the mundane existence they thought they had left behind them. Ethel couldn't imagine living with Wesley, not after the excitement of loving Baba. Rosie knew that if she went back she couldn't expect anything more than a return to a life in which Nan treated her like a little girl and expected her to wear knitted hats. Even the arrival of her mother after so many years of hoping brought little comfort. They both tried to make plans to escape their miserable destinies, discussing endlessly the grand schemes they thought up and soon abandoned.

Wesley's letters began to hint at love and early in September, as thoughts that there might be a future for them one day began to grow, Ethel realized she was again expecting a child. A confidential visit to a doctor told her the child would be born in March. After the initial shock, dismay and downright panic, trying to decide on the best thing to do, hope sprang into life and she wrote to Baba. Now he would have to marry her.

As she waited for his reply, unable to sleep or forget for a moment her predicament which might turn out to be such good fortune, her thoughts were like a switchback ride. She wavered from the thought of a reluctant Baba Morgan as her husband, to the quiet uneventful peace of returning home and becoming Mrs Wesley Daniels. Days passed as the letter worked its way through the system to find him at his new posting. When it came, Baba's letter was brief.

'I'll always love you, but I am marrying Janice.' There wasn't even a signature.

Wesley became ill. Since his war experiences he had lost so much weight that he was prone to every ailment, and influenza, a painful cough and suspected TB kept him in hospital for two weeks, after which he was sent home to convalesce. He wrote to Ethel, begging her to come home. 'What shall I do?' Ethel asked Rosie.

'You don't need me to tell you.'

'I'll stay with his mother, I'm not going back to The Dell.'

Wesley was waiting at the railway station and this time the embrace didn't falter and fade. She held him close, frightened by his thinness, feeling his heart beating against her own, drinking in the familiar clean smell of his hair and the unique scent of his soapy perfumed skin, and felt the comfort of a homecoming: peaceful, unexciting, but pleasant.

Arm in arm they walked along familiar lanes, visiting everyone they knew, including the Baileys at the farm, where they reminisced about past summers and dreamed of those to come. Apart from visits to Rosie's Nan, every moment of every leave was spent with Wesley. In October, when Wesley was strong again, he proposed and she accepted, and with their long delayed engagement revived, their marriage was planned for the following spring.

'There's only one hurdle still to clear,' she told Rosie when she returned to camp. 'I'm going to have a baby and I can't keep it.'

'A baby? But that's wonderful.' Rosie

presumed, wrongly, that the child was Wesley's, a result of their long talks in the room above the canteen in France, and she wondered if those private moments and the news of the baby had been the real reason Baba had left her. 'Wesley will accept it, won't he? He wouldn't turn away his child.'

'I don't think so,' was all she said. How could she tell Rosie the child was Baba's?

They discussed the problem over the next few days, during which time Rosie wanted to confess her love for Baba and her belief that she would never hold a child of her own in her arms. Ethel was so wrapped in her own misery she either ignored Rosie's attempts or didn't hear them. When Rosie pleaded with her to tell Wesley she shook her head and insisted that adoption was the only way.

'I have no desire for a child. It's the wrong time. I'm not ready for the responsibility.'

'And Wesley? Won't you give him the chance to decide?'

'This is my problem and the decision on how I deal with it is mine too.'

Rosie pleaded and argued with Ethel, telling her she should keep the child or she would carry the guilt all her life. 'I was fond of Baba and now I doubt whether I'll ever marry.' Realizing that Ethel was at last listening to her, she went on, 'I mean really fond of him. I seem to fall for men who don't fall for me. Duggie, then Baba, who both

413

wanted someone like you and had no interest in me. I know I'll never marry. I'd be so thrilled to have a child of my own and now I never will.'

Ethel was unmoved. There was so much to sort out in her life. This child had the wrong father, she thought bitterly, but she didn't express that thought to her friend. When she told Rosie she had an appointment to see an adoption society, Rosie surprised her by saying, 'If you really can't keep this baby then I will! I'll write to Nan and tell her I've got myself in the family way and I know she'll help me. My mother will too.'

'But, Rosie, a child is such a commitment and you'll want a husband and children of your own one day. You'll forget Baba Morgan. I know it sounds impossible but you will, believe me.' She almost added that Baba wasn't worthy of her love but she didn't want to spoil her friend's dream.

'I want a child and I know I'll never marry. We don't live that far apart and you can see him as often as you want. Ethel, it's the perfect solution.'

The only other person Ethel told was Sid, who promised to help and to keep her secret. With a burst of honesty heavily laden with guilt, Rosie told her Nan and mother the truth. They took a lot of convincing, but when Rosie threatened to leave and find a way to cope alone they gave in. They tried at first to persuade Ethel and Rosie to make it a legal adoption but that was something neither girl wanted. It was extremely unlikely that as a single woman Rosie would be allowed to adopt, and besides, Rosie didn't want to be the legal parent in case Ethel should change her mind. Ethel wanted to avoid the long drawn-out legalities with the accompanying risk of Wesley and their families finding out.

Ethel and Rosie excitedly made their preparations. If Ethel was less enthusiastic she hid it well. She pretended to share Rosie's joy but all the time she harboured the secret hope that Baba would relent and come to find her and tell her he had changed his mind. She was ashamed of her thoughts, aware that, for her, Wesley was a poor second.

Sid promised financial assistance and with their combined savings and generous help from Rosie's Nan and her now thoroughly involved mother, Ethel left the Naafi. Rosie gave notice that she too was leaving the service.

During the weeks before her condition was apparent, Ethel and Wesley spent a lot of time together. Every opportunity for a few days' leave and occasionally during a few hours off, they met and walked and talked, restoring their damaged relationship. Wesley tried again to explain the reason for his disappearance, even though Ethel with slight irritation begged him not to.

'I was so ashamed at the way I let you down,' he told her one autumn day when they walked across the field on their way back from the Baileys' farm. 'I ran away and left you at the mercy of your father in one of his worst rages. How could I face you after that?'

'If you hadn't run off and called the police, it's possible my mother would have died.'

'I should have stayed to protect you. That scene haunted me throughout the war. It seemed far worse than the bombs, torpedoes and guns, leaving you to face your father.'

'Thank goodness you did. It might have meant another funeral, and losing Glenys was bad enough.' She looked at him, at the way his head was bent low in shame, hiding his face from her. She pulled on his arm, waited until he looked at her and then kissed him. Not in the rather formal way they had kissed since their reunion, but deeply, and holding nothing back.

They continued on their way saying very little, just smiling at each other from time to time as though sharing a wonderful secret. Ethel was aware of a feeling of perfect peace. It was like the end of a trying and difficult journey, back in the safety of her true love. From that day she could even remember

Duggie without being engulfed in the terrible pain of grief. Duggie and Baba were the dream, a part of the experience of war. Wesley was the reality.

She looked at him; older, wiser but so comfortable and familiar, and she realized that after all that had happened they belonged together. It wouldn't be the wild passionate love she had known with Duggie and Baba, where their emotions were heightened by danger, but a more gentle, trusting and long-lasting love.

It was a discovery that was as surprising as it was exciting. Her happiness made her more and more tearful as her revived love for Wesley grew. She was more weepy these days and wondered whether it was the baby making her so, or whether that was one of Rosie's Nan's fanciful stories. Perhaps she was crying for the loss of the friends she had briefly found through the years of the war. There would never be enough tears for the young men she had known, liked and lost.

With Rosie's help she found a job in a shop with accommodation above. Helped by an understanding boss, she stayed on even when she was no longer able to work the usual hours, and it was there that the child was born.

The story she told Wesley was that she was away on Naafi business, travelling a great deal and could be contacted only through

Rosie. With their letters passed on by Rosie, Ethel and Wesley made their plans. For a while, until they had both decided what they wanted to do with their lives, they would work alongside Molly and Sid Twomey, helping to run the now thriving market garden. Ethel could also make sure the man she still called father was not treated too unkindly.

'Will you tell Wesley about his child, one day?' Rosie asked as she admired Ethel's newly born son.

'No. Confession might be good for the soul, but in this case, as in many others, it's nothing more than self-indulgence,' she said emphatically. 'It might make you feel better, but it's simply burdening someone else with your troubles.'

'There's only one thing I would change to make life perfect,' Rosie said as she held the child in her arms three weeks later and prepared to board the train that would take them home. She blushed as she said, 'I wish the baby were Baba's child.'

'He is,' Ethel told her softly.

Rosie squealed in delight.

Going home after giving birth, Ethel was again tearful. She felt bereft. Her arms ached to hold the child she had given up and there were moments when she wanted to rush to Rosie and tell her it had been a terrible mistake. But determination to set her feet on the future path she had chosen overcame the momentary regrets, and she went back to The Dell and Wesley.

In the nearby town men were returning after years of absence. For some the home-comings were blissfully happy, others found their loved ones had become strangers. There were a few who returned to find wives with children they knew they couldn't have fathered. Ethel thought it ironic that she was one of the returning ones who, instead of coming back to find problems, had brought the trouble with her.

She watched Wesley and wondered how he would have reacted to her news and she wondered, even then, whether he should be told. But she settled back into the routine of her mother's house and said nothing. She visited Rosie often and sometimes Wesley went with her. Showing affection for the baby was understandable and nothing was said to arouse Wesley's suspicions. That the baby was loved and cared for was clear. He was surrounded with love and would want for nothing. If Ethel grieved for the loss of him and the life with Baba she had once expected, she hid it well.

Sid was regularly meeting a woman who had helped the Twomeys in the house and on the market garden. Wendy was a war widow and she and Sid were planning to marry. He and

Wendy visited Rosie and admired the baby, whom they had called Colin, after Ethel's true father. It was Rosie who was the first to hear about their plans to marry.

'The trouble is,' Sid told her, 'if Wendy and I stay at home and run the market garden, there would be enough to keep us occupied, but with Ethel and Wesley working there too, there wouldn't be enough to support us. We'd have to leave, find something else to do, somewhere else to live, and the garden is what we both want to do.'

'If gardening is what Ethel and Wesley really want, we'll go,' Wendy explained. 'But if they're only doing it because they think they should, then it will be a pity for us to leave when we really want to stay.'

'You wouldn't mind helping to look after Sid's father?' Rosie asked.

'I'm prepared to take on his family and do whatever is necessary. That's what marriage is, accepting the whole package.' She touched Sid's arm and smiled at him.

'Both Wesley and Ethel worked in catering before the war; perhaps they would prefer to go back but can't admit it,' Sid added. 'They haven't had much experience of growing things. It can be very tedious at times.'

Wendy groaned. 'Pricking out a couple of hundred lettuce plants for example.'

When Sid and Wendy had left, Rosie gave a big sigh and said, 'Oh, Nan, why don't people talk to each other? Half the world's problems could be forgotten if only people would talk.'

She was unaware that that was what Ethel was trying to do at that moment.

Wesley and she were hoeing between rows of winter cabbages, newly emerged broad beans and leeks. They stopped frequently and looked back along the cleared ground then ahead at the weed-covered area still to be done.

'Are you enjoying this, Wesley?' Ethel asked, throwing down the hoe and leaning on the wheelbarrow.

'I can cope,' he replied.

'That wasn't the question. Can you see yourself doing this sort of thing, year after year?'

'What are you saying, Ethel?'

'What do you really want to do with your life? I don't really know what I want but I know it isn't this.'

'I always dreamed of being the owner of a grand restaurant, but those dreams have gone. Now I'm not sure. So for the present this will do.'

'I think we should talk to Sid. I think it's time for some honesty, don't you?' She was thinking only of the work they had agreed to do and had no intention of making any confessions about Duggie and Baba or baby Colin.

They used a horse and cart to collect and deliver their requirements and when they had finished the weeding, they piled the tools on to the flat cart and began to ride home.

'Talking about honesty...' Wesley began and Ethel stared at him in surprise. Surely he didn't have terrible secrets too?

'Did you ever wonder what happened to the engagement ring I bought for you?'

'You still have it?'

They heard a car approaching and from the sound of the engine it was travelling fast. Wesley pulled the horse to the side of the lane and glanced back. 'I gave it to another woman,' he said, but before he could say anything more, a low sports car came around the corner, touched the cart and careered off. The driver managed to regain control and the car came to a stop in a gateway further down the lane.

The horse panicked and pulled them further along the lane but without Wesley's guiding hands on the reins the cart caught against a tree and spilt them both out.

The driver of the car got out and looked at them: Ethel holding her face which was bleeding from cuts from branches, and the utterly still figure of Wesley.

'I'll go for help,' he said and reversing the car out of the field he sped away.

Wesley stirred and assured Ethel that he

was unharmed. 'For a moment there I was imagining myself back on active service,' he said. 'Come on, let's make sure Dolly is all right.' They released Dolly from the cart and walked back home, one each side of the horse, which seemed unaffected by the incident.

Ethel was thinking, not of the narrow escape they'd had, but of the woman to whom Wesley had given her engagement ring. Nothing more was said and throughout the night, between uneasy dozing, Ethel thought about the mysterious woman and wondered how much Wesley had been about to confess. Had he made this woman promises he hadn't kept? Baba was certainly not the only man to do that. Had they fallen in love? Had they slept together? Had he succumbed to loneliness as desperately as she had? If so, could she tell him about the baby?

The following day they worked together in the field and he didn't add to what he had begun to tell her. 'Perhaps I should help him?' she said to Rosie that evening, when she went to the house where she felt so much at home. 'If his war was similar to mine, perhaps I would make him feel less unhappy if I told him about Duggie and even Baba. Then whatever it is he's trying to tell me won't seem as terrible.'

Rosie said nothing.

'I must have been crazy to imagine he

didn't meet women and share moments of comfort. Most men did when they thought death was waiting for them. I didn't think about it for a moment, but now, I think his guilty memories have been bothering him ever since we met in France. He's so sensitive and it would explain why he's so subdued.'

Rosie didn't agree or disagree. This was beyond her. All she hoped was that if the truth about the baby emerged, it wouldn't mean she would lose him. Baby Colin was her life. How would she cope without him?

Her mind made up, Ethel went back and called to see Wesley. It was a cold November night but she insisted they went for a walk. Wrapping up warmly, they went through the fields towards where the lights of the town glittered on the frosty air.

'Tell me about this woman you gave my ring to, Wesley. I'll understand. Loneliness and fear had to be dealt with, we all learned that. We all have secrets, specially after being away for years. I know you want to tell me, but you're afraid I'll be upset. Well, my secrets are likely to be worse, so tell me. Please.'

Wesley stopped and in the darkness she couldn't read his expression. There was no clue in his voice as he said, 'You first. Nothing held back, mind.'

'All right, I had an affair with a man called

Duggie. He ... he was killed. His was one of the planes which didn't return.'

'Serious was it, you and this Duggie?'

'Yes, I thought so. You were gone from my life and I had no family; danger was a constant companion and I needed someone. Then, some time later, there was George Morgan, everyone called him Baba.'

'Baba Morgan? I heard about him. He was carrying on with a woman, and left her with a baby and went home ... to ... Ethel, please don't tell me that was you?'

She hadn't intended to mention the baby, but now it seemed pointless to deny it. She had forgotten how much gossip was passed between stations, and Wesley had worked on the demolition of obsolete airfields too.

He took her arm and walked at a fast pace back to her home where he left her without a word. The following day there was a note through the door, explaining about finding the ring in the box of a man who had stolen it while on board a ship. Not bothering to claim it, he had allowed it to be sent to the man's widow. Such a trivial confession compared with her own.

Wesley's mother told her he had gone away and she had no idea where. Ethel was imbued with a calmness that surprised her. Although disappointed at the outcome, she had no regrets about the truth being exposed. If they were to have a future it was better there were no secrets. Rosie would have agreed with that. Secrets never remained hidden for ever. They had a habit of popping up unexpectedly, long after the event, like a time bomb quietly waiting until it could do the most damage.

As always she went to talk to Rosie.

'What will you do?' Rosie asked.

'Give him a month, then I'll go away too. Somewhere I'm not known where I can make a fresh start.'

'Sid will be pleased, I think.'

'Pleased if I go away?'

'Pleased if you don't want to live at home and work on the gardens. He and Wendy can get married if the place doesn't have to support you and Wesley.' She looked at Ethel's surprised expression and burst out laughing. 'Why don't families talk to each other, eh?'

'Because too much talking can destroy them.'

A month passed, and Ethel made sure that Dai was being looked after properly. Molly's attitude towards Dai had softened, and the sick man had better care. Ethel felt able to leave. She began to look at advertisements for live-in jobs at hotels. In January, when baby Colin was ten months old she called to see him.

He was pulling himself up and standing strongly, banging anything he might use as a drum and exploring his world in ever widening circles, to his delight, and to the anxiety of Rosie, her mother and her Nan.

'He's so strong and busy,' Rosie told her proudly. 'And we're enjoying every moment.' Ethel was happy to know he was in safe hands. She was leaving but would always stay in touch.

She was packing when Wesley came to see her. She looked at him coldly, about to say the words she had rehearsed: 'Running away is your way of dealing with things, isn't it?' But the words didn't come, she was relieved to see him.

She turned away and said instead, 'I was just going to tuck Dad up for the night.'

'I'll come with you,' he replied.

He helped her tidy the bedcovers and watched as she gave Dai a drink. Then he sat on a chair and gestured for her to sit opposite him.

'I needed to get away to make a few decisions, Ethel. I'm sorry I walked out on you again, but since I came home my mind has been a constant jangle. Now I have everything clear.'

'Good,' she said, sarcastically. 'How nice for you.'

'I'm going to train to become a nurse.' His words surprised her and she stared at him. 'Working in the sick bay on board ship made me aware of how much more I could have done with proper training.'

'You've never mentioned it,' she said accusingly.

'I wasn't sure I could do it, but now I know I can, and should. I have a place in a hospital near London and, if you're interested, there's a job in the canteen which could probably be yours. You have to go next week for an interview.'

'You disappear for years, then again vanish for weeks without a word, then casually arrange for me to go to London with you and work in a hospital canteen?'

'We can marry before you go if you wish, or come back later.'

'I think I want to see Rosie.'

'I'll come with you. It's time I was properly introduced to your son,' he said.

Two weeks later, Sid and Wendy had arranged their wedding and Ethel, still bemused by the strength of Wesley's decision-making, agreed to make it a double ceremony.

'Rosie, what if I'm making a mistake?' Ethel said to her friend a few days after the announcement. 'What if I meet someone like Baba and fall for them? What if life with Wesley isn't enough for me?'

'This isn't wartime. Everything was topsy-turvy then. Would you have fallen for anyone else if you and Wesley had been married and living around here?'

Shamefaced, Ethel looked away and said

428

softly, 'I might have. How do I know?'

'The war threw everything in the air and it landed in a muddle that will take years to sort out. If you love Wesley, marry him, but you have to be sure.'

'That's the problem, I'm not.'

She went to see Wesley that evening and sat looking at him, aware of love for him, but it was a love that was tinged with pity. Rosie had been right when she said they would have been happy if they had married and there hadn't been a war, but too much had happened for them to return to how they were then.

Over the days that followed she evaded the plans for the double wedding, telling Sid and Wendy she hadn't made up her mind whenever they asked for a decision or an opinion. Her thoughts wavered between 'I'll take a chance' and 'This isn't for me', until she was exhausted. While she continued to work on the land, Wesley left to begin his training and she was offered the job in the hospital canteen. The work was what she knew best, but something held her back from accepting.

On impulse she wrote to the Naafi asking to return. She couldn't settle for marriage to Wesley. A loving affection just wasn't enough, either for herself or Wesley. When everything was arranged and she told Wesley her decision, to her relief and with some disappointment, Wesley didn't argue or try very hard to dissuade her.

'I've never felt confident that we'd go back to how we were,' he told her. 'When we met in France I saw a stranger. You had changed but I hadn't.'

She thought that was fair. Duggie, Baba, baby Colin, there was no way he could compete with all that had happened to her.

As she stood on the railway station to go to her new posting, she looked around her at the neatly dressed passengers. All civilians, several with a morning paper which they were trying to read. No lively girls with which to share the journey, no parcel of food from Rosie's Nan to enjoy. She would miss Rosie, and Rosie's Nan's parcels, she thought, and smiled a sad smile.

Then a voice called and she turned to see Rosie, with a struggling Colin in her arms and a carrier bag in her other hand.

'Ethel, wait, Nan sent this.' Puffing with the exertion of her hasty arrival, Rosie handed her the bag. 'Cake, biscuits, a bar of Cadbury's and a pot of Nan's home-made jam. Nan says a parcel of luxuries is a good way to start making friends.'

'But she's using her rations,' Ethel protested.

'Loves you she does and wishes you nothing but happiness.'

Tearfully, Ethel hugged them both and

when the train came she leaned out of the window and waved until the station was out of sight.